Cit

Sizzling passion in the heat of the city…

Three romantic novels!

In June 2007 Mills & Boon bring back
two of their classic collections, each
featuring three favourite romances
by our bestselling authors…

CITY HEAT

The Parisian Playboy by Helen Brooks
City Cinderella by Catherine George
Manhattan Merger
by Rebecca Winters

BLIND-DATE GROOMS

The Blind-Date Bride by Emma Darcy
Marriage by Deception by Sara Craven
The Blind-Date Proposal
by Jessica Hart

City Heat

THE PARISIAN PLAYBOY
by
Helen Brooks

CITY CINDERELLA
by
Catherine George

MANHATTAN MERGER
by
Rebecca Winters

MILLS & BOON®

MILLS & BOON and MILLS & BOON with the Rose Device
are registered trademarks of the publisher.
Harlequin Mills & Boon Limited,
Eton House, 18-24 Paradise Road, Richmond, Surrey, TW9 1SR

CITY HEAT © by Harlequin Enterprises II B.V./S.à.r.l 2007

The Parisian Playboy, City Cinderella and Manhattan Merger
were first published in Great Britain by Harlequin Mills & Boon
Limited in separate, single volumes.

The Parisian Playboy © Helen Brooks 2002
City Cinderella © Catherine George 2003
Manhattan Merger © Rebecca Winters 2003

ISBN: 978 0 263 85518 0

05-0607

Printed and bound in Spain
by Litografia Rosés S.A., Barcelona

THE PARISIAN PLAYBOY

by

Helen Brooks

Helen Brooks lives in Northamptonshire and is married with three children. As she is a committed Christian, busy housewife and mother, her spare time is at a premium, but her hobbies include reading, swimming, gardening and walking her old, faithful dog. Her long-cherished aspiration to write became a reality when she put pen to paper on reaching the age of forty, and sent the result off to Mills & Boon.

CHAPTER ONE

'AND how is the lovely Holly this morning? Had fun over the weekend, darling? You look like a girl who knows how to have a good time.'

As Holly raised her eyes from her word processor she steeled herself to show no reaction at all when she saw Jeff Roberts's podgy face leering at her from the doorway. 'Good morning, Mr Roberts,' she said flatly, her voice dismissive. And then she felt her stomach muscles contract as he sauntered over to her desk.

He was close enough now for his eye-wateringly pungent aftershave to invade her air space, but Holly continued typing without glancing at him again, hoping he would take the hint and leave.

There were basically three ways to deal with the problem of a serial groper in the office, Holly had decided some weeks before, when she had first started work at Querruel International.

One—ignore and avoid the sad individual in question, whilst letting him know by as icy a manner as possible that his advances were not appreciated.

Two—yell sexual harassment and take it as high as it needed.

Three—go for ultimate satisfaction and sock the scumbag a strong right hook on the jaw.

Holly had been trying the rational approach for eight weeks on the scumbag concerned with no visible result, and reporting him was a no-go unless she was prepared

5

to lose her job because Jeff Roberts was the son of the managing director and the apple of his doting father's eye.

The third option would definitely mean she sacrificed all possibility of a future reference as well as the job—a job which had promised bright prospects and an interesting and rosy future at her initial interview. But—and the but had become increasingly attractive over the last couple of months—it would certainly teach the little wimp a lesson he wouldn't forget in a hurry.

He leant over her, reading the report she was copying from the draft on her desk, and his voice was low when he said, 'I've told you before, call me Jeff when there's just the two of us.'

There was always a faintly musty, almost unwashed odour emanating from his clothes, or maybe his skin, and Holly had to suppress a shudder of distaste. It didn't help that her tiny office was little more than a cubby-hole off Jeff's father's secretary's office, with one small window and wall-to-wall filing cabinets. There was one other door apart from that opening into the secretary's domain, and this would have led into the corridor outside but for the fact that two filing cabinets had been placed in front of it. Now necessity dictated one entered and left through the one door; something Jeff hadn't been slow to take advantage of from her first week.

'If you are looking for Margaret she should be back from the canteen in just a moment,' Holly said pointedly.

'Is that so?' As she continued with her work he adjusted his position, bending down and reaching across her for a pen and managing to brush the side of her breast as he did so. 'I'll just borrow this for a moment, if I may?'

Holly stopped typing, forcing herself to stare up into his sallow, moist face as she said steadily, 'I've told you before, Mr. Roberts, I don't want you to do that.'

'Do what?' He didn't even bother to try to sound indignant, and when his gaze moved over her breasts and then down to her legs before returning to her face his tongue wet his lower lip.

'I don't want you to touch me,' she spelt out tightly.

'Did I touch you?' He smiled, bending closer again and giving her the full benefit of his bad breath as he murmured, 'Why don't we go for a nice little drink after work, eh? I know just the place. You'd like that, wouldn't you?'

When hell froze over! 'I'm afraid I've got other plans,' Holly said stiffly.

'Tomorrow, then?' Speckled hazel eyes of a muddy hue slithered over her greedily. 'I'll buy you dinner too if you're a good girl. Can't say fairer than that.'

Where *was* this man coming from? What did it take to puncture this inflated ego that thought because of his standing in the firm he could behave however he liked? Holly knew from talk she'd heard in the canteen during her coffee breaks that Jeff Roberts pawed whomsoever he could, but most of the other girls worked in conditions where there was safety in numbers.

She stared him straight in the eye as she said coldly, 'I'm sorry but I can't go for a drink with you tomorrow or any other time, Mr. Roberts.'

His face changed. 'I can do you some good here, Holly, if you play your cards right,' he said very softly, 'but the opposite also applies. Do you understand what I'm saying?'

'I understand you very well,' Holly returned icily.

'And?'

'And my answer remains the same. Now, I need to get this report finished.'

He looked at her for a moment more before straightening up, and Holly was fooled into thinking he was going to leave as her eyes returned to her word processor. And then, for a shocking second, two meaty hands appeared over her shoulders and grabbed her breasts, squeezing them painfully hard before he went to walk away.

She didn't have to think about what to do. She was up out of her chair in the blink of an eye and all her strength was behind the ringing slap she delivered across his face.

He clearly hadn't expected anything like such a fiery reaction. He staggered backwards for a good few steps, thudding against a filing cabinet before letting forth with a string of obscenities which turned the air blue. As he straightened Holly knew he was going to come at her again and she prepared herself, her blue eyes flashing and her slim, petite body held stiff and tense.

'What the hell is happening here?'

The voice from the doorway brought Jeff swinging round and Holly's startled eyes focusing on the tall, dark figure standing in the aperture. She knew instantly who he was, even if the heavy French accent hadn't proclaimed it. She had heard so much from the other girls about the unique owner of Querruel International she could have described him down to the last eyelash, even though she'd never seen the ruggedly handsome Frenchman in person.

Jacques Querruel. Thirty-two years of age; unattached but with a string of mistresses and affairs that made him the favourite of society magazines and the tabloids, alike; the ultimate playboy except in Jacques Querruel's case he worked hard as well as playing hard. A self-made millionaire who had risen from the depths of squalor in a Paris slum to become a wealthy and successful industrialist, his original furniture company in Paris now having a string of subsidiaries in France as well as the United States and England.

And he played life by his own rules, as his present

ensemble proclaimed. According to office gossip he owned several flashy cars, as one would expect of a young French millionaire, but his favourite transport when he visited England was his Harley-Davidson.

'Mind-blowing piece of equipment,' one of the young lads in the accounts department had told Holly dreamily a couple of weeks ago. 'A Road King in monochrome black ice. You could really reel in the big miles on that beauty.'

'You ought to see Mr Querruel in his black leathers.' This had been from one of the females at the lunch table who clearly didn't want to waste time talking about a machine when it could be used discussing the rider. 'Everything stops when he walks in, I tell you. There's not a woman here who doesn't go weak at the knees. We're talking pure dynamite, Holly.'

And now she was seeing the pure dynamite for herself, Holly thought a trifle hysterically. And it was dangerous stuff all right. But then her attention was snapped away from the big black figure in the doorway and back to Jeff, when he said quickly, 'Mr Querruel, I'm sorry you had to be a party to this, sir. It's inexcusable, I know. I was reprimanding Miss Stanton on the inferior quality of some work she did for me and she reacted badly. I'm afraid I lost my temper when she hit me.'

'You liar!' Holly was amazed at his duplicity. 'How dare you—?'

'That's enough.' As her voice rose Jacques Querruel cut into her protest, his voice quiet but razor-sharp. 'We will discuss this in Mr Roberts's office, please. You will both accompany me there now.'

'Now, just hang on a minute!' Holly had thrown caution to the wind, she was so mad. She knew what would happen when Mr Roberts Senior got involved in this—

she'd be out on her ear quicker than you could say Harley-Davidson. 'He's lying. There was no work—'

'Have I not made myself clear?' The French accent was stronger than ever. 'We will discuss this matter in the privacy of Mr Roberts's office, Miss Stanton. I have already been informed that Mr Roberts is not expected back from a prior appointment for another hour, so we will not be interrupted.'

Had he guessed the reason for her objection? Holly stared into narrowed amber eyes that had all the softness of that solid fossilised resin, and found she couldn't drag herself away from the translucent gaze. They were unnerving, those eyes. Mesmerising and beautiful but cold, like the predatory surveillance of a wolf or one of the big cats.

And then she mentally shook herself, angry with the fanciful description. What on earth was the matter with her? she asked herself silently as she followed the two men through into Margaret's office, and then beyond into Mr Roberts Senior's large and opulent domain.

She just had time to notice Margaret standing against her desk, looking aghast, which implied the managing director's secretary had heard something of the events which had transpired in her coffee break, but then the door was firmly shut and she was alone with Jacques Querruel and a blustering Jeff Roberts. 'Really, Mr Querruel, there is no need for you to concern yourself with this unfortunate matter,' he was saying with ingratiating and sickening servility. 'You've obviously got more important things to do and—'

'On the contrary, Jeff.' It was cool, very cool, and as Jacques Querruel indicated for them both to be seated with an authoritative wave of his hand Jeff said nothing more.

Holly had expected the Frenchman to seat himself behind the massive oak desk which dominated the room, but instead he perched easily on the edge of it, the piercing eyes surveying her critically.

She forced herself not to fiddle with her hair or make any other nervous movement, but it was hard. Especially in the circumstances and with Jeff sitting a foot or so away. But there was absolutely no way she was going to give any ground over this. She raised her small chin at the thought, her eyes stormy.

'So...' Jacques's compelling gaze moved from her flushed face to Jeff's sulky one, and the amber eyes took full note of the unmistakable handprint etched on the other man's plump cheek. 'I think there is a problem, yes?'

'Nothing I can't handle, Mr Querruel—'

'Yes, there darn well is!' It was Holly's turn to cut across Jeff's voice and she did it vehemently. 'I have asked Mr Roberts to keep his hands to himself on several occasions and today was the last straw. The man's a pervert and I refuse to be mauled by him one more time.'

Dark eyebrows lifted and the carved lips twitched a little before Jacques said, 'Do not beat about the bush, Miss Stanton. Say what you feel.'

So he thought this was funny, did he? The flare of furious resentment in Holly's eyes turned the blue purple as she glared at the illustrious head of Querruel International, and in that moment she didn't care a jot who he was. She stood to her feet, her voice shaking with rage as she said, 'Thank you, Mr Querruel. That's exactly what I intend to do. Your managing director's son is a liar as well as a lech. There is nothing wrong with my work and far from reprimanding me he had taken his molesting of recent weeks to a new high. That was why I slapped his face and he was lucky to get off so lightly.'

'This I can see.' It was a quiet murmur.

It wasn't the moment to think that he had the sexiest voice she had ever heard, richly seductive in spite of the disparagement, Holly thought with a strong burst of self-disgust.

'That's all utter rubbish.' Jeff decided he'd been out of the conversation long enough and he glared up at her, spite prevalent in his voice as he said, 'The actual fact of the matter is that Miss Stanton is not up to the job for which she was employed but I felt sorry for her. I've given her endless chances over the last weeks and realised too late she had misconstrued my kindness as personal interest in her. When I had to make it clear I did not appreciate her flirting with me she suddenly went crazy. A woman scorned and all that.'

Jacques Querruel's steady gaze moved over the fat, greasy-haired individual sitting in front of him before returning to the lovely young woman standing in front of the desk. She had hair the colour of dark, rich chocolate, smoothly groomed into a shoulder-length bob, eyes as blue as cornflowers and the sort of cheekbones many a model would have killed for. And she was mad. Boy, was she mad. It was as likely she'd made up to the slug in the chair as the pope marrying. He smiled. 'Do I take it you refute Mr Roberts's explanation?' he asked silkily.

Her nostrils flared. 'Darn right I do.' He was aggressively good-looking, hard and chiselled with no sign of softness about him at all. Funny, but from the other woman's gossip she'd pictured him as more pretty-boy handsome than anything, especially when they'd gone on about the tan and the jet-black hair and wickedly thick eyelashes. He *had* got all those things, and the eyelashes were gorgeous enough to be utterly wasted on a man, but there was nothing remotely boyish about Jacques

Querruel. In fact she wouldn't have been surprised to learn he had been born six feet two and radiating power and authority. He couldn't ever have been a helpless baby or vulnerable little boy.

'It would appear we have something of a stalemate.' The piercing amber eyes looked from one face to the other. 'Have either of you proof of what you claim? I take it Miss Stanton's work bears evidence of her ineptitude?' he asked Jeff smoothly.

'She—er—I mean, by the time it's been corrected…it's eventually brought up to scratch,' the other man finished lamely.

'And you, Miss Stanton? You have witnesses to Mr Roberts's over-familiarity?' The dark eyebrows rose again.

'It's not over-familiarity,' Holly said tightly. 'It's downright groping of the most intimate kind, and he thinks he can get away with it because he's the managing director's son. All the girls avoid him when they can. And, no, I haven't got any witnesses—Mr Roberts has always made sure of that. Stuck in that little box out there I haven't exactly got a way of escape or a camera whirring to record his goings-on, have I? And if you are going to ask me if any of the others would come forward to back up what I say, I don't know. Possibly, if they want to continue working here, the answer would be no.'

'A somewhat jaundiced view, Miss Stanton,' he drawled, his accent making her name sound very different.

'No, merely realistic,' she snapped back quickly. She was not going to bow and scrape to this arrogant individual like everyone else; neither was she going to be intimidated into saying anything less than the truth. No doubt Mr Roberts Senior would produce half a dozen female staff to swear that Jeff was approaching sainthood, along with suggesting to Margaret that her new assistant wasn't *quite* on the ball, but she couldn't do anything about that. Whatever, her days at Querruel International were numbered, which was a shame. She had fought off some stiff competition to secure the job and for it to end like this…

'So you have no faith in company procedure for this kind of incident?' Jacques Querruel asked softly.

Holly raised her head, her glossy curtain of hair shimmering with the movement. His keen appraisal was making her feel isolated and insignificant but those feelings weren't new to her and she was adept at hiding them. She swallowed, aware of tension tightening her jaw, but her voice was firm and steady when she replied, 'I have only been in this company's employ for eight weeks so I cannot answer that in a general sense.' She paused. 'However, with regard to this particular incident, and taking into account the person involved—' she shot Jeff a glance of pure loathing '—I would say it would be very naïve of me to think justice would be done.'

'I see.' Twice in the last few minutes Jeff Roberts had gone to speak and twice a commanding hand had motioned him to silence. Now Jacques Querruel turned his gaze on the other man as he said even more softly, his voice cold behind the velvet tone, 'And you, Jeff. Do you think justice will be done?'

'I have every faith in company procedure,' Jeff said pompously.

How could a man like Michael Roberts, a man he had every respect for and who was damn good at his job, have a son like this? And moreover think the world of him too? Jacques stood up, hiding his irritation at the situation and himself as he did so. He had known some time ago that he didn't want Michael's son to be a permanent fixture in the company, but the man had seemed efficient enough and there had been no reason to suggest getting rid of him.

Jacques walked over to the massive plate-glass window, staring down into the busy London street below for a moment. He should have followed through on his gut instinct, had Jeff Roberts transferred over to the French office for a few months so he could see how Michael's son functioned away from his father's protective hand. Of course, he hadn't known about this other side of the man... His mouth twisted sardonically. And now he was paying for his procrastination.

He turned, his mind made up. 'Suspension on full pay for the time being, Jeff, while this matter is fully investigated.'

'But—'

'No buts.' The words were crisp and without expression. 'This is the policy, as you know.'

'But I thought...' Jeff's voice trailed away. And then he made the mistake of continuing, 'You can't think there's any truth in this girl's story? She's a typist, and I'm...' He stopped abruptly as Jacques looked straight at him, the Frenchman's eyes amber flares of light. 'I mean, my father—'

'Will appreciate the need for absolute integrity in a matter of this kind,' Jacques finished smoothly.

Holly knew her mouth was slightly agape just a second after the devastating gaze swung her way, and although she brought her lips quickly together she saw the acknowledgement of her amazement touch the hard mouth in a slight smile.

'Have you anything further to say for the moment, Miss Stanton?'

Had she? Lots, probably, but right now her brain was as scrambled as an omelette. She shook her head dumbly.

'Then perhaps you would like to go into your…little box and write out a full statement of exactly what you allege occurred today, along with any other incidents which are relevant. Dates and times as far as possible, please. Mr Roberts will be doing the same in here with me.' He reached over and pressed the buzzer on the desk as he finished speaking, and Margaret appeared immediately like a genie out of a bottle, indicating the managing director's secretary had been burning with curiosity.

'Coffee, please, Margaret,' Jacques said pleasantly as Holly began to walk out of the room. 'And a cup for Miss Stanton too, if you would be so kind? She will take hers in the little box.'

'I'm sorry, Mr Querruel?'

Holly left them to it, shutting the door behind her before she dived across Margaret's office and into hers. She sat down at her word processor, glancing about the small space and aware her heart was beating like a drum and tears born of reaction weren't too far away. She took several deep breaths, willing herself to keep calm. It *was* a little box. He might not have liked the terminology, but, nevertheless, that was what it was, she told herself militantly as she forced her mind away from the main trouble of the day and on to Jacques Querruel's last words.

Margaret appeared in the doorway a moment later and her homely, middle-aged face was a picture. 'So what's *happened*?' she whispered urgently, adding inconsequentially, 'I've ordered the coffee.'

Holly told her as quickly and concisely as she could whilst they both kept an ear cocked for any movement from Mr Roberts's office, and when she had finished the older woman amazed her by putting a comforting arm round her shoulders as she said, 'He's a nauseating little bug, Holly, and he's needed squashing for a long time.

I've never had any trouble with him, of course—'
Margaret had been happily married for three decades and
had two grown-up children '—but I know at least one girl
who's left rather than cause a fuss when he kept bothering
her. I've tried to speak to his father about it on a couple
of occasions but I met with a blank wall. Mr and Mrs
Roberts lost two children in a road accident before Jeff
was born the following year, so he's always been able to
do nothing wrong in their eyes.'

'Whatever happens, I'm not going to be the flavour of
the month with him, then, am I?' Holly commented
miserably.

'Oh, don't worry, it'll be all right,' Margaret said brac-
ingly, and then as one of the canteen staff entered her
own office with the coffee she gave Holly another reassuring pat on the shoulder before bustling away.

She had better start looking for another job right now,
tonight. Holly sat staring at the dingy grey filing cabinets
for a moment or two, and then, as Margaret came in with
her cup of coffee, began typing out her statement. Just her
luck to end up in a place where the company lech was
the son of the managing director!

She found she had to concentrate very hard on what
she was doing over the next hour or so. Not that she
couldn't remember all the details of the incidents over the
last weeks—she could. Even though some of the dates
escaped her. But it was more the fact that the image of
an aggressively masculine face kept getting between her
and the keys.

She checked everything twice before she printed the
pages out, and then once the report was in her hand she
checked it again. She hadn't elaborated or exaggerated
anything, she decided at last. She hadn't had to. The bare
facts were bad enough. Seeing it all in black and white

like this made her wonder why she'd waited so long to give Jeff his come-uppance! She loathed bullies, and he was one of the sickest kind.

'It is that bad, yes?'

Her head jerked up from the papers in her hand to see Jacques Querruel standing watching her. One dark eyebrow was quirked mockingly and there was a disturbing gleam in the amber eyes. He had taken off his leather biking jacket, she noticed dazedly, and the plain charcoal T-shirt he was wearing sat on broad, muscled shoulders. He must work out every day to have a physique like that.

She felt her heart thudding against her ribcage and it annoyed her, along with his air of relaxed authority. He'd be fully aware of the effect he had on women, she thought hotly, expecting every female from Margaret's age down to fall at his feet in worship. For a moment she just sat there, dry-mouthed and silent, but then his arrogance sent the adrenalin flowing fiercely. He might be the sacred head of Querruel International, and drop-dead gorgeous to boot, but he had absolutely no effect on her at all, she told herself vehemently. Added to which she had the distinct feeling she wouldn't be working here much longer anyway.

She straightened, aware of the hectic colour staining her cheeks but unable to do anything about it. 'Judge for yourself,' she said curtly, knowing it wasn't at all the way to speak to the ultimate kingpin but unable to help herself.

The smile had been wiped off his handsome face, Holly noted with some satisfaction as he walked over to her and took the papers she was holding out. And she didn't know why but she made very sure their fingers didn't touch.

She had hoped he would take the report back to his office and read it there, but instead he idly brushed some papers out of the way and perched on the side of her desk.

Her little cubby-hole had never been big by any standards, as she'd already made abundantly plain to him, but now it seemed to shrink away to nothing. He was so close she could smell the exclusive, subtle odour of his aftershave, and that, together with the leather trousers stretched tight over lean male thighs, was making her face burn in the most peculiar way.

She forced her eyes upwards a little, where they fell on to his hands. They were powerful, with long, strong fingers and short, clean fingernails. An artist's hands, or maybe a musician's... And then she caught the thoughts angrily. He was neither of those things, for goodness' sake, she told herself irritably. She knew from office gossip that he was a ruthless, hard and inexorable business-man, who gave no favours and asked for none. He liked fast cars and motorbikes, and even faster women—so she had heard—and was a millionaire many times over. Not exactly the type of man to sit painting watercolours!

The chiselled profile was frowning when she looked at his face, and he raked back his hair—as black as a raven's wing—a couple of times as he read. Even sitting quite still as he was now vitality radiated from him; she had never come across such a disturbing man before. It was probably quite unreasonable, because to date she had to admit he had been pretty fair in the circumstances, but she didn't think she liked Jacques Querruel one little bit.

He was on the last page of the statement; he'd obviously got to the bit she'd written about the incident that morning, and to her surprise she heard him swear softly under his breath. She didn't speak French but there was no doubting the content of the muttered expletives. He turned his head, his amber eyes meeting her blue, and his tone was almost an accusation when he said, 'Why the hell did you not do something about this before? You are not the type who cannot say boo to the goose.'

The fact that his perfect English had let him down just a fraction gave Holly a disproportionate amount of satisfaction as she said coldly, 'I was hoping to deal with it myself with the minimum of unpleasantness.'

'Then you have not succeeded.'

'That's hardly my fault, is it?' she snapped back angrily. Hateful man! He'd be blaming her for everything in a moment. 'I wanted to keep my job; that's not a crime.'

'Indeed it is not, Miss Stanton,' he agreed smoothly. 'I understand you have only been with Querruel International a few weeks?'

'Eight,' she clarified militantly. 'And if you say Mr Roberts has been with the company for a lot longer without anyone complaining before that's not because there haven't been grounds, I assure you.'

'I see.' He stared at her consideringly and she made herself stare back without flinching. 'I was not going to say that, Miss Stanton.' He lifted the hand holding her statement. 'I may keep this?' he enquired softly.

She nodded. 'Yes, it's finished.' Just as she was finished at Querruel International. It might take a week or a month or six months, but sooner or later Jeff's father would find an excuse to get rid of her, however this thing turned out. And she wouldn't want to continue working so close to him as his secretary's assistant now anyway. The job had gone sour.

Jacques Querruel stood up, and once more she found herself pinned by his gaze. 'For what it is worth, I despise the type of man who threatens a woman in this way,' he said quietly. 'I can assure you I will investigate this matter very thoroughly, Miss Stanton, and rest assured Jeff's position in this company will not affect the outcome.'

Oh, come on, who was he kidding? He flitted here, there and everywhere, but Jeff's father ran this place for Jacques Querruel, and people were hardly going to slate his son knowing once the big boss left they would have no protection against any comeback from daring to speak the truth.

Holly wasn't aware her face was speaking volumes, not until the big, dark man in front of her said softly, 'You do not believe this?'

'No,' she said, because there was no point in lying. 'At least, I believe you'll do your best to get to the truth, but you won't. You see, everyone likes Mr Roberts Senior as much as they dislike his son, and they know how much he and his wife think of him. Also...' She paused, wondering if she should go on.

'Yes, Miss Stanton?'

'You are not here most of the time,' she said baldly.

'Ah, this I see.' The beautiful eyes narrowed thoughtfully. 'Then my enquiries will have to be in confidence and no names mentioned to Jeff's father, apart from yours, of course.'

Oh, great, wonderful. The sacrificial lamb. Still, it was only what she had expected after all; it just grated doubly that he seemed so unconcerned.

'That's all right, then.' She tried, she really tried to keep the sarcasm to a minimum but she was so angry she could spit.

Like before, he read her mind perfectly. The firm, slightly stern mouth suddenly twisted with the nearest thing to genuine amusement she had seen in the last caustic hour or so.

'You are not in awe of me, Miss Stanton,' he said softly.

It was a statement, not a question, which was just as well because Holly was beyond speaking at that moment. He had leant forward as he'd spoken, both hands resting on the desk and his body close enough for the warmth and smell of him to surround her. She felt her senses quivering and was furious with herself for being so weak and trembly.

'And that is unusual,' he continued thoughtfully, almost as though he was speaking to himself now. 'I am surrounded by a whole host of sycophantic beings, Miss Stanton. It comes, as they say, with the territory. The people who really speak their mind to me I can count on one hand and I would not use all my fingers.'

She didn't know what to say and so she said nothing.

'This was a…novelty at first. Perhaps even satisfying, I am ashamed to admit, in the early days.'

He didn't look ashamed, Holly thought, and she had no doubt he loved every moment of the power he was able to command so effortlessly, especially where the fairer sex was concerned. She had seen men like him before, men who considered themselves nothing less than demi-gods with the ability to direct and control other people's lives. Admittedly none of the others had looked as good as Jacques Querruel, but that would have to have made him more puffed up in anything.

She became aware he was waiting for her to speak. She pulled herself together and said evenly, 'So it isn't satisfying now, Mr Querruel?'

He looked at her for a moment without speaking and she wondered if she had gone too far, even though her tone hadn't been openly acidic. And then he grinned. 'Occasionally,' he admitted softly. 'Yes, occasionally it serves a purpose.'

Oh, wow! Oh, wow, oh, wow, oh, *wow*. Where had all the natural arrogance gone? If the other girls thought he was dynamite normally he had just moved up to nuclear-missile potential.

Holly cleared her throat, thinking that if she had known this morning she was going to have such an amazing, one-in-a-million day she would have worn her new suit and given more attention to her hair and make-up. And then she suddenly realised where her thoughts were going and checked herself firmly. It wouldn't make any difference if she was covered from head to foot in Dior and diamonds. Jacques Querruel was as far removed from her orbit as the man in the moon! Not only that, he was a heartless so-and-so.

'Margaret tells me your work is more than acceptable,' Jacques continued after a moment. 'In fact, "excellent" is the word she used.'

Good old Margaret!

'How old are you, Miss Stanton?' he asked with a directness that took her by surprise.

'Twenty-five.' She frowned. 'Why?'

He liked that in this young woman, the candidness, but she was something of a paradox and he did not like that. He did not trust what he did not understand, and one of his strengths was that he could sum people up very swiftly. She appeared to be strong and determined, one could almost say aggressively so, and yet several times now he had seen something else behind those great blue eyes. She intrigued him, and it had been a long time since that had happened.

'Why?' He repeated the word and then didn't answer her question, saying instead, 'Have you ever considered working abroad, Miss Stanton, or are you bound to home shores by family or maybe a boyfriend?'

Holly blinked. What had that got to do with anything? She stared at him, wondering how they had arrived at this from his initial reading of her statement. He was watching her coolly and she envied his detachment as her nerve-ends began to prickle. Her wary expression seemed to amuse him. His amber eyes glinted and a faint cynical smile twisted his lips. 'Well?' he prompted lazily.

'I...I wouldn't be averse to travelling in the future,' she said carefully, hating the little stutter at the beginning of her words and warning herself to show no weakness before this man.

'And family commitment? Love commitments?'

His French accent gave the last two words a sexy intonation an English voice couldn't hope to compete with. Holly hoped the heat which had surged in her blood wasn't reflected in her face, but she had the nasty feeling she was a definite shade of pink. 'I live alone in rented accommodation, Mr Querruel,' she answered primly, 'and I have some good friends but not a special man-friend if that's what you mean.'

He surveyed her for a second more as he straightened and then he said quietly, 'Mr Roberts has already left the premises so you can relax. I have some business to deal with but I would like to see you again before you leave tonight, Miss Stanton. You will not forget this?'

She wanted to ask why. He had her statement, and there was nothing she was prepared to add or delete from it. But, in view of the way he had successfully deflected any unwanted questions to date, she didn't bother, inclining her head as she said, 'Of course not, Mr Querruel. In Mr Roberts's office?'

'Just so.'

And with that he was gone.

CHAPTER TWO

THE rest of the day was an anticlimax. Holly went to lunch as usual with Margaret, in the excellent canteen the firm boasted, but the other woman didn't mention the events of the morning at all and fielded any attempt Holly made to discuss them. Holly was left with the distinct impression Margaret had been warned not to talk about the matter by a higher source: perhaps by Jeff's father, who was now ensconced in his office with Jacques Querruel, or the tycoon himself.

The afternoon was spent typing a long and involved but boring report with one ear cocked towards the outer office. Although Holly was aware of Jeff's father leaving at some point after she and Margaret had returned from lunch, Mr Roberts Senior did not look in on her, for which she was grateful. Another confrontation was beyond her for the present.

There was the usual coming and going in Margaret's office, and once or twice Holly heard a female speaking in a hushed but excited tone—no doubt due to the occupant of the room beyond, Holly thought cynically—but she worked on undisturbed. Once the report was finished she printed three copies, as Margaret had requested, and clipped each of them together before placing them in three prepared folders.

And then she stretched tiredly, shutting her eyes for a moment as she raised her hands high above her head with a big sigh. She had tried not to think about the impending meeting with Jacques Querruel but now it was imminent. She didn't want to see him again. Not ever.

'Tired?'

Her eyes shot open and there he was, standing in the open doorway, but now dressed in a light grey suit that must have cost a mint of money. The jacket was unbuttoned, revealing an ivory shirt tucked into the flat waistband of his immaculate trousers. He was the epitome of the successful tycoon, from the top of his sleek, dark head to the tips of his handmade shoes. He looked even more sexy than he had done in the leathers.

Holly was horrified the last thought had slipped in and straightened hastily in her seat, flushing hotly.

'It is nearly five-thirty.' He didn't wait for her to speak. 'And I think our little chat could be conducted more comfortably over dinner, yes? Are you free tonight, Miss Stanton?'

'*What?*' She was hallucinating now, she had to be, because he couldn't possibly have said what she thought he'd just said.

'Dinner?' he said with a patience which bordered on the insulting. 'I take it you do eat dinner? I asked you if you were able to accompany me tonight.'

Holly's flush deepened. Either he was stark staring mad or she was.

'There is a job proposition I would like to put to you,' he continued smoothly, 'which will obviously need some discussion. I am hungry and I am thirsty, and a good bottle of cabernet sauvignon is calling. If you are free tonight I will run you home and you can change. I have a table booked for seven.'

She stared at him, utterly taken aback. And then the thought surfaced—who would he be taking to dinner if she refused? The table was already booked and Jacques

Querruel didn't look the type to eat alone. No doubt he had a little black book to deal with such an eventuality. She forced herself to say, and calmly, 'I don't understand, Mr Querruel. You said a job proposition?'

'Don't tell me that you were not thinking of looking for another position forthwith?' he said quietly.

Holly's jaw set. This was a catch-22 question and however she answered it she couldn't win. If she denied it he would assume she was lying. That much was clear. If she confirmed his suspicions she might well find herself leaving Querruel International sooner than she had expected. Jacques Querruel was the type of employer who demanded absolute loyalty.

'What gave you that idea?' Holly chose her words carefully.

'Nicely fielded, Miss Stanton,' he said gravely.

Impossible man! She glared at him and he smiled back, a cynical twist of his cleanly sculpted mouth. 'So...I will give you another ten minutes to finish off here and then we will call by your apartment, yes?' he asked, his black eyebrows rising with derisive amusement at her confusion.

Holly thought of all the reasons that made it imperative she say no to this ridiculous invitation. The man was dangerous—*lethal*, in fact, as an adversary. She'd heard stories about his ruthlessness that would make the straightest hair curl. And she had made a formal complaint against the son of Jacques Querruel's managing director here in England. At the very least her accusations were going to cost the company time and effort, and she just might have stirred up something of a hornets' nest. This man was wealthy and powerful, cold and arrogant. He was also devastatingly attractive and used to having any woman he wanted with a click of his well-manicured fingers. She hated to admit it to herself but he scared her half to death.

And—and here she inwardly berated herself for the shallowness of her thoughts—she had nothing suitable to wear for dinner with a multimillionaire, and her little bed-sit was not exactly the type of home Jacques Querruel would be used to.

So, in view of all that, why could she hear herself saying 'Thank you, Mr Querruel. I would be pleased to hear what you have to say over dinner?'

'Excellent.' His gaze ran over her for one more second and then he turned without another word and she was alone again.

For as long as it took for the door to Michael Roberts's office to close, anyway. Then Margaret was standing where Jacques had just stood, her eyebrows disappearing into her hair. 'I don't believe what I just heard,' she whispered, coming right into the room and standing by Holly's desk. 'I've worked for Mr Roberts for five years and I've seen females galore throw themselves at Mr Querruel, and he's never even *noticed*. He's a man who keeps work and play totally separate.'

'This *is* work.' Holly was embarrassed and hot. 'He said something about a job proposition. I think he suspected that I couldn't stay on after what happened this morning.'

'Did you feel that?' Margaret asked unhappily.

Holly nodded. 'I guess so,' she admitted. 'It would be too awkward with me working for you and you being Mr Roberts's secretary. You see that, don't you, Margaret?'

Margaret stared at the lovely young face in front of her, and now her motherly instincts came to the fore as she said softly, 'Holly, be careful, won't you? Jacques Querruel is renowned as a love-'em-and-leave-'em type, and normally his partners are selected from women who think like him, if you know what I mean. They're all beautiful and so-phisticated and often holding high-powered jobs—real ca-reer women. They don't want the ties of hearth and home any more than he does.'

Now it was Holly's turn to stare at the other woman. 'Margaret, he's only asked me out to discuss some sort of work proposal,' she said in astonishment. 'I think he believed me about Jeff Roberts, although he never said so, and he's probably feeling he owes me some sort of alternative job, that's all.' She could hardly believe Margaret was suggesting anything else. Jacques Querruel and a typist? It was laughable.

Margaret sniffed a very worldly-wise and maternal sniff. 'Be that as it may,' she said grimly. 'You just re-member what I've said, that's all.'

'He asked me in your hearing,' Holly pointed out rea-sonably. 'He wouldn't do that if he wasn't serious about a job, would he?'

Margaret just looked at her, her plump chin settled in her ample neck and her eyebrows raised in a way she didn't mean to be comical but which struck Holly so.

'I promise I'll be careful,' Holly said at last, biting back a smile. 'OK? And I'll tell you everything that transpires in the morning, although I'm sure you're worrying un-necessarily. But thanks anyway,' she added, reaching out a hand and patting the other woman's arm.

She received a warm smile in return. 'I know you think I'm a fussy old woman but, in spite of the fact we've only known each other a little while, I think of you as a friend,' Margaret said earnestly. 'And with you not having any family as such, I feel you're a bit...'

'Vulnerable?' Holly proffered.

Margaret nodded unhappily.

'Believe me, Margaret, vulnerable I'm not,' Holly said firmly. 'I learnt to look after myself from when I could toddle; I had to—no one else was going to. And, if nothing else, being pushed around by the establishment and having six foster homes before I was eighteen makes one resilient.'

'You're telling me you're tough?'

The tone was so disbelieving Holly laughed out loud. 'I'm not a push-over,' she qualified. 'And I haven't met a man yet who could soft-soap me into doing something I didn't want to do.'

'Ah, but you hadn't met Jacques Querruel before.' Margaret gave a wise-owl nod of her head just as the telephone in her office began to ring, causing her to bustle back into the other room.

Dear Margaret. Holly sat for a moment, nipping at her lower lip with small white teeth. It was true, they had hit it off right away at the interview for the job, which Margaret herself had conducted, and she had enjoyed working with the other woman the last weeks. She'd thought she was really set up here; with Margaret backing her there had been no reason why she couldn't have worked herself up to a prime position in a few years with a nice fat salary to boot. She wasn't afraid of hard work— in fact, she thrived on it—and with no home commitments she could work as late as she liked when necessity commanded.

Margaret's warning continued to whirl round in Holly's head as she tidied her desk and turned off the word processor. She locked the filing cabinets—her last job of the day—with the spare set of keys Margaret had given her in her first week at Querruel International, before walking through into the other room.

This office was spacious, as befitted the managing director's secretary, holding two easy chairs and a small coffee-table along with Margaret's huge L-shaped desk. In one corner a bookcase held a selection of Querruel International brochures and magazines where their furniture had been advertised, and in another stood two filing cabinets holding material of a confidential nature. It was as different from Holly's little cubby-hole as chalk from cheese.

Margaret was still talking on the telephone as Holly emerged, and in the same moment Jacques Querruel strode through the open doorway of the other office. 'Ready?' he asked abruptly, and as Holly nodded he took her arm, calling goodnight to Margaret as he whisked Holly out into the corridor, whereupon the lift doors opened immediately he touched the button.

They had never done that for her, Holly thought bemusedly. She normally had to wait for at least a minute or two before the lift graciously consented to answer her call.

Once inside the lift Holly found herself tongue-tied. She searched her mind feverishly for some light comment to relieve the tension but it was a blank. She blessed the years of harsh training when she had learnt to disguise her feelings and appear calm and collected, however she was feeling inside, as she glanced at her reflection in the mirrored wall of the lift.

It showed an averagely tall, slim young woman with cool blue eyes and a composed face; an image she had carefully cultivated and took pleasure in. It was her wall of safety, her security, and part of her distress this morning had been because first Jeff Roberts, and then Jacques Querruel—in quite a different way from the former—had broken through the deliberately constructed barrier.

'The taxi is waiting for us.' She had been aware of his overt inspection as the lift swiftly took them downwards, but it wasn't until the doors opened in Reception that he spoke. She turned her head and looked at him then as he added, 'Your apartment is in Battersea, yes?'

'Yes.' How did he know that? Had he asked Margaret where she lived or had he checked out her personal file? The latter; she'd bet her boots on it.

'And our restaurant, Lemaires, is in Chelsea, so that is most convenient, is it not?'

She didn't know about that. The thought of Jacques Querruel sitting in the tiny bedsit which was her 'apartment' was an absolute no-go—there wasn't room to swing a cat—and the thought of him waiting outside with a taxi clocking up every minute she took to get ready wasn't an option either. As they stepped out of the smart, air-conditioned building into a pleasantly warm May evening Holly took a deep hidden breath and said steadily, 'If you would like to go on ahead to the restaurant after you've dropped me off that would be fine, Mr Querruel. I'll join you as soon as I can.'

'This is the polite English way of stating what you would prefer, I think.' The hand which was gripping her elbow felt as cool and hard through her thin cloth jacket as his voice, but as they crossed the pavement and he opened the taxi door for her he continued, 'I will send the taxi back for you, Miss Stanton. Is that acceptable? And, please, take time to refresh yourself.'

Refresh herself! As Holly slid into the taxi she had to bite back the desire to laugh out loud. She would be rushing around like a whirling dervish!

She barely noticed the taxi pull away as she began a mental list of all her clothes, desperately trying to pull an outfit worthy of Lemaires from her limited wardrobe. She'd heard of Lemaires before, of course—it was one of the very 'in' places and frequented by clientele who never had to look at the prices on the menu—but never in her wildest dreams had she imagined she'd set foot on such hallowed ground, and certainly not without at least a few hours' grace to rush out and buy something fabulous.

'...and take it from there?'

'I'm sorry?' Too late she had become aware Jacques Querruel had been speaking and she'd been miles away.

She turned to him quickly and saw he was frowning. 'I am sorry to interrupt your thoughts, Miss Stanton,' he said icily, 'but I was just outlining the way I saw the evening progressing. I suggested we could enjoy a cocktail or two as I explain my proposal, which you could think over whilst we eat, and then we will take it from there.'

Touchy, touchy. Holly got the impression it wasn't often Jacques Querruel didn't have a woman's full and undivided attention. 'Yes, of course,' she said quickly, becoming acutely aware of the close confines of the taxi for the first time as her anxiety about the clothes was put to one side for a few minutes.

He wasn't touching her—in fact there was at least six inches of space between them—but never had she been so fiercely conscious of another human being's body. She could feel the heat which had begun in the core of her spread to her throat and face as she met the amber eyes, and then, as his gaze became curiously intent, she forced herself to break the piercing hold and turned her head to look out of the window.

'It's a beautiful evening, isn't it?' she murmured quietly, managing a tone which was just offhand enough to appear genuine.

He didn't reply for a moment, but now her senses were open the subtle and delicious smell of him teased her nerves before he said softly, 'Indeed it is. Too beautiful to waste in the city streets. It is a night for breathing in the aroma of a thousand flowers as the sky slowly turns to silver. A night for watching the moonlight shimmering on a mother-of-pearl lake, and hearing the call of the wild swans as they marshal their newly fledged little ones to sleep.'

She was surprised into looking at him again, and he answered her quizzical gaze with a slow smile. 'My château.' He replied to the unspoken question very quietly. 'It is very lovely on a night like this.'

There were enough panic buttons going off in Holly's head to deafen the whole of London. 'Is it?' She smiled brightly. 'Lucky you.'

'You have been to France, Miss Stanton?'

She shook her head. She hadn't been anywhere but she wasn't about to tell him that. No doubt he was used to being in company where the merits of Switzerland or Monaco or the Caribbean were discussed with a wealth of experience.

'It is a very diverse country,' he said quietly. 'I have an apartment in Paris, close to my offices, but my real home is my château, thirty miles south of the city. It is a place of peace, a place for recharging the batteries.'

Funny, but she couldn't quite equate Jacques Querruel with peace and quiet. She kept her voice from betraying anything of what she was thinking as she said, 'You spend a lot of time there?'

'Not as much as I would like,' he said a touch ruefully. 'Part of this is my own fault, of course. I do not find it easy to delegate, Miss Stanton.'

Now, that she could believe without any trouble at all! Her face must have spoken for itself because he smiled drily. 'I think we will change the subject.'

During the rest of the twenty-minute ride to her bedsit

Holly was on tenterhooks. Not that Jacques was anything but coolly polite and amusing, and seemingly at ease. He sat one leg crossed casually over the other, his whole body suggesting a relaxed composure that Holly envied with all her heart. He didn't seem to be aware of the atmosphere within the car, which was strange, she thought, when she wouldn't have been surprised if the air had started to crackle with electricity. But then she obviously registered on him with as much force as a bowl of cold rice pudding.

The street in which her bedsit was located was not the best in the world, and as they drew up outside the terraced three-storey house that was identical to a hundred others she saw Mrs Gibson's cats had been having a field-day with the dustbins again and most of their contents were scattered all over the minute paved front garden and the pavement.

Holly liked Mrs Gibson, who occupied the basement bedsit and had bright orange hair despite being eighty years old if a day, and she didn't even mind the three cats, who had a disconcerting habit of vomiting up their trophies from the dustbins at the most inopportune moments, but she could have done without them today. Of course, they had gathered *en masse* on the crumbling steps to the front door. It was that sort of day.

The big ginger tom had just begun to lead the way in a Mexican wave of retching as Holly leapt out of the taxi, and she positioned herself straight in front of the car window as she said briskly, 'You really needn't send the taxi back, Mr. Querruel. I can ring for one myself once I'm ready.'

'I wouldn't hear of it.' He had leant forward slightly as he spoke, his attention directed somewhere behind Holly's left shoulder, and now he said a little bemusedly, 'There is an elderly lady with a tea cosy on her head waving to you.'

It figured. Holly glanced behind her, waving back to Mrs Gibson before she said, 'That's Mrs Gibson. She is a friend of mine,' her tone defiant. 'I'll see you in a little while, then.'

'I will look forward to it.' The answer was polite but distracted. One of the cats had just gone for a gold medal in the realm of projectile vomiting, breaking all previous records, and Mrs Gibson was doing a kind of soft-shoe shuffle as she tried to prevent all three felines diving into the hall. Jacques looked fascinated.

As the taxi drew away Holly turned round, her tone resigned as she said, 'I'll get a bucket of water and some disinfectant and clear all this up, Mrs Gibson.'

'Would you, Holly? There's a dear. Mr Bateman, the silly old fool, has gone and put kippers in the dustbins again. I told him Tigger would have the lids off before you could blink, but would he listen? The man's an idiot.'

'Mrs Gibson, why are you wearing a tea cosy on your head?' Holly asked matter-of-factly.

'Am I, dear? Well, there's a thing!' Mrs Gibson blinked at her as she removed the offending article from her sparse bright hair and then giggled like a schoolgirl. 'I've been wondering where this was for a few days. I must have put it on the coat stand instead of my woolly hat when I washed them both. I wonder what I've done with the hat, because it isn't on the teapot.'

'Don't worry about it,' Holly said, smiling into the pert little face which was as wrinkled and lined as a pink prune. 'It'll turn up.'

By the time Holly had cleared up after the cats and weighed down the dustbins with two bricks apiece, kept specially for the purpose but rarely used by anyone but herself, she'd lost ten minutes of valuable time.

She dashed up to her bedsit on the first floor, stripping off her clothes and flinging on her robe before hurtling along to the bathroom at the end of her landing. A quick two-minute shower in cold water—the water heater was playing up again—ensured a bracing if teeth-chattering pick-me-up, and then she was back to the bedsit, pulling off her shower cap and standing in front of her wardrobe as she surveyed her sum total of clothes.

She had one or two really nice things, she thought despairingly, but were they suitable for somewhere like Lemaires? She doubted it, but nevertheless the black and blue ruched and printed bandeau dress and vertiginous high heels she had bought to celebrate securing the job at Querruel International would have to do. If nothing else the shoes would give her an extra few inches, which wouldn't go amiss considering Jacques Querruel had seemed to tower over her in the lift, and her black wrap—the bargain of the year twelve months before, when she'd spied the beautiful Versace wrap in a charity shop for a fraction of its original price—would dress up the whole outfit.

She peeped out of the window before she went to work with her make-up and the taxi was already back and waiting. No time to put her hair up, then. She contented herself with eyeshadow and mascara, along with a careful application of her lipstick pencil, finishing her toilette with a dab of perfume on her wrists. Silver studs in her ears and a silver bangle on one wrist and she was ready. She stood in front of the mirror, breathing deeply in and out for a moment or two. She had never felt so scared in all her life.

'Look at it this way,' she said to the wide-eyed, dark-haired girl staring back at her from out of the mirror. 'You have got nothing to lose and everything to gain from hearing what he has to say. You'd already decided you wouldn't be able to stay at Querruel International, not working for Margaret anyway. He might, he just *might* make you an offer you can't refuse.'

No, she hadn't phrased that quite right, Holly thought agitatedly as the mental image of a tall, dark and extremely handsome Frenchman sent the juices flowing. What she'd meant was, she might find she didn't have to start the dismal rounds of searching out the right kind of job again.

She would hear him out, weigh up the pros and cons of what he said and then make an informed decision. Simple. No big deal, not really, not unless she made it one. OK, so he was taking her to dinner, but he'd been pretty nonchalant about it. He clearly hadn't been over-bothered one way or the other. And that was fine. Great. Perfect. The last thing she needed was for him to get any sort of ideas.

She gathered up her small black purse and the wrap, and squared her slim shoulders as though she was going into battle instead of to dinner. But that was what it felt like…

Jacques saw her the moment she walked through the doors of Lemaires; he had been watching the entrance intently ever since he had sat down at the secluded little table for two. He rose immediately and raised his hand, and as the waiter guided her over to him he said quietly, 'Thank you, Claude. And perhaps you would bring one of your delicious champagne cocktails for Miss Stanton?'

Once she was seated, Holly said a little breathlessly, 'I hope I haven't kept you waiting too long, Mr Querruel.'

'Not at all,' Jacques said pleasantly. He had settled back in his seat once she was comfortable, his eyes unreadable and his big body relaxed.

Holly envied him. She felt as taut as piano wire. Whether her tenseness communicated itself to him she didn't know, but he took the wind out of her sails completely in the next moment when he leant forward and said quietly, 'In view of the surroundings I think we could be less formal, don't you? Loosen up a little—is that the phrase? My name is Jacques and yours is Holly, I understand? An unusual name, even for someone born at the end of December.'

So he *had* looked up her file. Holly felt horribly flustered even as she told herself she'd known it all along. Jacques Querruel was the type of man who would want every fact at his fingertips before he talked about a job offer. But there were a hundred and one things one could never learn from the anonymous black print of a personnel file.

And this was borne out when Jacques continued, 'Your mother's choice of name or your father's?'

'Neither.' She purposely didn't elaborate, hoping he would take the hint and accept a change of subject when she continued, 'It's very kind of you to buy me dinner, Mr Querruel, but it really wasn't necessary.'

The amber eyes moved over her face very slowly before he said, 'Yes, it was. And the name's Jacques.' His gaze intensified, the thick black lashes adding to the piercing quality. 'And if it was not your parents who gave you your name, then who did?' he persisted softly.

'The sister in charge of the maternity unit where I was taken after being abandoned.' She didn't try to soften the statement. '"The Holly and the Ivy" was playing on the radio when they brought me in.'

He didn't come back with any of the comments she might have expected and had experienced in the past on the rare occasions the circumstances of her birth had become known, but then she should have known he wouldn't. He was not a flock animal. He merely expelled a silent breath before saying, 'Tough start. Very tough.'

She nodded tightly. 'Yes, it was.'

'Did they find the woman who had given birth to you?'

She was glad he hadn't called Angela Stanton her mother, because for a long time now she had understood the biological ability to produce did not make a mother. She nodded again. 'At the point she gave birth to me she'd already got three children, all by different fathers; she didn't want a fourth,' she said evenly. 'After she was traced she visited me once or twice, I understand, but that's all. I contacted her when I was twenty-one and we met briefly; she was happy to tell me anything I wanted to know. My father was a married man she'd had a short affair with. She didn't tell me his name and I didn't ask. All her other children were put in care at some point and are in various parts of the country. There were two more after me.'

Her mouth was unyielding and set in a controlled line. Ridiculously he wanted to kiss the warm fullness back. The strength of his feeling shocked him and his mouth was dry when he said, 'I am truly sorry, Holly.'

She shrugged, and he realised the gesture went hand in hand with the closed expression on her face. Both were too old for a young woman of twenty-five. 'It happens,' she said dismissively. 'And lots of people suffer worse every day.'

The waiter arrived with two long fluted glasses filled to the brim with sparkling, effervescent liquid, and Jacques watched her face change as she looked up at the balding, middle-aged man, smiling her thanks. She hadn't liked talking about herself. She hadn't liked it at all. And she didn't like him. He felt his pulse quicken and didn't know if the feeling coursing through him was desire, pique, excitement or curiosity, or maybe a mixture of them all.

He took control of himself and the situation, raising his glass and touching hers in a toast as he said lightly, 'To an excellent meal and a good bottle of wine when it comes.'

Holly laughed; she couldn't help it. 'That's a little self-indulgent, isn't it?' she commented just as lightly.

'Perhaps.' He smiled at her, a social, easy smile. 'But it's to your benefit too.'

'True.' She considered, her head slightly tilted to one side. 'All right, then. To the meal and the wine.'

The cocktail was delicious but she could feel the bubbles going straight to her head, and too late Holly told herself she should have eaten something earlier. She hadn't had a bite since lunch and even then she had only nibbled at a sandwich, the events of the morning ruining her appetite. She took a firm hold on herself, putting the glass down and fixing the dark, handsome face opposite with what she hoped was an efficient, matter-of-fact expression as she said, 'You mentioned a job proposition?' She would have liked to add 'Mr Querruel' but he had insisted she call him Jacques earlier, and she couldn't, she just *couldn't* bring herself to do that. Consequently the question just trailed to a finish.

'Later. You need to unwind.'

Did she? She didn't think she did. In fact she thought it imperative she didn't 'unwind', as he put it. She needed to have all her wits about her tonight. But he was the big boss and she couldn't very well argue. She wriggled her bottom nervously; she was out of her depth here. Margaret was right; she shouldn't have accepted this ridiculous invitation to dinner.

'And stop looking at me as though you are little Red Riding Hood and I am the big bad wolf,' Jacques said softly, his accent lending a resonance to the words that sent a little shiver right down her spine. 'Tell me about Mrs Gibson instead, and your apartment. Are any of your other neighbours so colourful?'

'It's not an apartment, it's a bedsit,' said Holly after a fortifying sip of champagne. 'There's a big difference there, you know. And Mrs Gibson is just a dear old lady who's marvellous for her age and a trifle eccentric. Perhaps more than a trifle.'

She slipped the wrap from her shoulders as she spoke and saw his eyes follow the movement, their light resting on the creamy skin before moving downwards to where the soft swell of her breasts were just visible above the bodice of the dress. And then he raised his eyes back to her hot face, not even trying to pretend he wasn't looking as he said, 'You look very beautiful, Holly.'

Perhaps it was his French accent, or the incredible lush surroundings and glittering occupants of the restaurant, or just the fact she was trying to hide how overwhelmed she felt, but Holly felt a nervous giggle escape before she could bite it back. This was so utterly, *completely* silver-screen material!

'I have amused you?' It was frosty and his expression had changed to one of chilled hauteur.

Oh, help. Holly took a deep breath. 'Of course not.'

'But something has.'

She stared at him across the small table covered in thick cream linen, a single white rose in a silver vase perfuming the air, and for no reason at all that she could name Holly suddenly rebelled against his autocracy. 'It's all this,' she said before she had a chance to think too hard about what she was going to say. 'It's not real life, is it? Of course, it's very nice…' Her voice trailed away.

'Oh, thank you.' His voice dripped with sarcasm.

'No, really, it *is* very lovely as a treat.' She was making this worse, she realised helplessly. Much worse. And when all was said and done he *had* brought her out to this fabulous restaurant where everything was so gorgeous and special. It was just that everyone seemed to take themselves so seriously, she supposed. And she'd been fighting taking herself seriously—or anyone else for that matter—all her life. She didn't like this last thought and so she filed it away to look at again later.

Silence had fallen. Jacques was sitting with his glass held loosely between his fingers as it rested on the table, his eyes on her flushed face.

Holly nerved herself to meet the amber gaze, which she was sure would be as coldly sarcastic as his voice, but as their eyes caught and held she felt the weird electrical current she'd sensed in the taxi. Her heartbeat went haywire, and suddenly the whole world was narrowed down to one small table and two pairs of eyes.

'So you are not a woman who expects to be wined and dined and spoilt?' he asked very, very softly. 'In spite of being so beautiful. What is the matter with your English men, *ma chérie*?'

Holly's eyes widened and for a full ten seconds she found herself speechless. He was flirting with her—Jacques Querruel? *Jacques Querruel.* And nothing in her past had prepared her for how to handle this. It had always been one of her rigid rules to keep her distance—literally—from men. To avoid their touch, their invasion into her air space. Which was why Jeff Roberts had annoyed her so much. She loathed men like him who thought they had some preordained right to make advances to any female they liked, to touch and maul and manhandle. And so it had been easier to keep the whole pack of them at arm's length; that way no one had any excuse for getting the wrong idea.

She grabbed her glass and tossed back the last of the champagne cocktail. Its fortifying effects enabled her to say, fairly evenly, 'Nothing is the matter with English men as far as I know,' before following up with a bright, artificial smile.

'But you do not have a boyfriend, a partner?'

'The same could be said for thousands of women, surely?'

She pushed back her sleek veil of hair as she spoke and he saw her eyes were violet with defiance and something else he didn't recognise. He had touched a nerve here. Careful not to appear anything but relaxed and casual, Jacques said easily, 'Maybe, but not often ones with eyes the colour of your English cornflowers and hair of warm, silky chocolate. When was your last love affair, Holly?'

She moved back in her seat, an instinctive but very revealing gesture. He waited, without saying a word.

The waiter returned with two terrifyingly chic and elegant menus, placing them in their hands with almost reverent decorum before taking an order from Jacques for two more cocktails. Holly wanted to protest but she didn't. Somehow she felt she would need the boost the alcohol gave her to survive this evening intact.

The waiter having glided off to get the drinks, Jacques peered at her over the top of his open menu. 'The Chinese black bean and green pepper chicken is good to start with,' he suggested smoothly, pretending not to notice as her eyes ran anxiously over the pages, which were all in

French. Double Dutch to Holly. 'And it complements the coriander salmon with mango perfectly. Trust me?'

She met his gaze. Trusting Jacques Querruel was not an option! 'That sounds very nice,' she said primly.

'Oh, it is nice,' he assured her gravely as the waiter returned with the cocktails. After he had given their order for the food and wine and they were alone again, Jacques relaxed back in his seat once more. 'So, the last boyfriend,' he said silkily. 'The love of your life or just another young hopeful?'

The question hammered at her aplomb and there was a moment of silence so charged she knew he'd sensed it. She had lowered her eyes and she took a long, hidden breath before staring straight at him. 'There hasn't been much time for boyfriends,' she said coolly.

His pulse quickened. What the hell did that mean? 'No?'

'No.'

He was damned if he was going to leave it at that. 'Why not, Holly?' he asked quietly.

She had been sipping at her cocktail and now plonked her glass down with an air of Oh, for goodness' sake! Which Jacques ignored.

He wasn't going to leave this alone until she'd spelt it out for him, was he? Holly thought tensely. She wished she could just walk out of here and go home, but that would be way, way over the top. He hadn't insulted her or been difficult in any way; most people would class this as perfectly acceptable social intercourse.

Bright patches of colour staining the creamy skin of her cheeks, Holly said, 'I stayed on at school until eighteen to finish my A levels and then left to get a job and somewhere to live. I worked for two years so I could put myself through university without entering into a whole load of debt with loans and such. I worked long hours; there was no time for a social life.'

'Why did you leave home as well as school?'

'I didn't have a home!' It was a snap, and Holly warned herself to take control of her voice before she said more calmly, 'What I mean is I lived in a foster home and I didn't get on with the rest of the family particularly well. It was better for everyone I left and, besides, I was too old to continue with them. I finished university when I was twenty-three and have had one other job besides my present one. I made up my mind to be a career girl and concentrate on my work rather than a love life.'

He didn't buy this. He did not buy this at all. 'Very sensible,' he said understandingly. 'But you enjoyed yourself at university no doubt?'

She ignored the meaning behind the words. 'I had a great time,' she agreed stiffly.

Jacques wanted to push some more but now was not the time. 'Everyone does,' he remarked drily. 'Raging hormones and hundreds of young people let loose for the first time in their lives makes for some interesting diary reading.' And then he completely backtracked on his earlier decision as he said, 'Did you keep a diary, Holly?' making sure his voice suggested amusement and nothing of the burning curiosity he was feeling.

He was watching her closely, seriously, despite the smile on his lips, and Holly had the feeling they were fencing like two duellists, one of which was hopelessly ill-equipped. She made an enormous effort and said lightly, 'I prefer reading to writing.'

'Yes?' His voice was smoky. 'But this is such a solitary pursuit, is it not? Two cannot play at this.' He shifted in his seat, shrugging off his suit jacket just as the waiter appeared with their first course. Once the food was in front of them Jacques leant forward slightly, forcing her to acknowledge her own awareness of him as he said, his hand gesturing at his tie, 'Do you mind? I always feel as if these things are strangling me.'

'No, not at all,' she gulped hastily, still reeling from the way her senses had tingled at his nearness. He pulled the tie loose, undoing the first couple of buttons of his shirt, and she could see the beginnings of the dark body hair which must cover his chest. She finished the champagne cocktail and reached for the glass of wine the waiter had poured after serving their first course. And then she put it down again. She had to eat something, she warned herself feverishly. She was going to be tipsy at this rate and that would never do.

It wasn't hard to continue eating once she had tasted the chicken, in spite of her jangling nerves. The food was absolutely delicious, and the TV dinner she had been going to pull out of the freezer compartment of her little fridge couldn't begin to compete.

It helped that with the arrival of the food Jacques had metamorphosed into Mr Congeniality, his conversation humorous and diverting and his manner amiable.

After the main course, which was even more delicious than the one before, the waiter brought the dessert menus. Jacques quietly talked her through the delectable list in such a way she didn't feel in the least embarrassed at her lack of knowledge.

'Chocolate terrine ribboned in caramel sounds lovely,' Holly said wistfully, 'but the orange and strawberry granita with liqueur muscat chantilly sounds pretty good too.'

'We'll have one of each and share.'

She stared at him, frankly horrified, her stomach clenching. Ridiculously, it seemed far too intimate to share puddings. 'No, it's all right,' Holly said hastily. 'I'll choose one.'

'No need.' He said it as casually as if he hadn't noticed the look on her face, and as the ever-attentive waiter materialised at their sides like a genie out of a bottle Holly realised it was a *fait accompli*. As most things seemed to be around Jacques Querruel.

It was in that moment she understood the last hour or so had lulled her into a state of false security. She still didn't have a clue what this evening was all about, or what the job offer comprised, and she'd been with him for—she surreptitiously glanced at her wrist-watch—over two hours. She had to get things back to a more…official footing. She took a sip of wine, wiped her mouth carefully with her napkin and opened her mouth to speak. She was a moment too late.

'So, Holly.' The air of charming companion had fallen away from him like a cloak; Jacques was suddenly very much the millionaire tycoon. 'To business. You took your degree in textiles, yes? What are you doing sitting behind a desk typing reports?'

Holly stiffened, recognising all over again that he was dangerous. She stared at him for a moment before she said, 'There were no openings in the areas I was interested in, besides which I also took business studies. I thought it would be good to get an all-round knowledge of Querruel International and—'

'I need a textile technologist responsive to design, and enthusiasm is more important to me than experience,' Jacques stated impatiently, cutting into her words with all the ruthlessness she'd sensed in him. 'You would work hand in hand with my designers and the rest of the team to produce high-quality, sophisticated products that will sell in the UK and overseas. Querruel International is efficient and competitive but we need more flexibility, more innovation. Do you understand what I am saying?'

She nodded, breathless.

'I would offer a three-month contract to begin with, to see how you fit into the team. Most of them have been with me since I started and it's imperative to maintain a good working relationship,' Jacques went on evenly. 'They are all well-qualified people of the right calibre and all fiercely loyal to Querruel International. I will accept nothing less. Remuneration is accordingly high.' He mentioned a starting salary that made Holly grateful she was sitting down. It was four times more than she was presently earning. 'For this I demand working round the clock when it is necessary, which is not often,' he added with the ghost of a smile. 'You will not be expected to be perfect but you will be expected to give Querruel International one hundred per cent commitment.'

Holly couldn't believe her ears. This was the once-in-a-lifetime chance, the crock of gold at the end of the rainbow. She could work for years and years and years and not be given an opportunity like this one again.

'So, Holly, are you interested in hearing more?' he asked quietly, his eyes intent on her flushed, excited face. 'What are you thinking?'

'Mainly how soon can I start?' she answered breathlessly.

'As soon as you can organise a passport and your affairs in England.'

Holly floundered. He wasn't saying...

'The job would require you moving to Paris,' Jacques stated expressionlessly, seeing the sudden dawning of understanding in her face. 'I thought you understood this?'

No. She hadn't understood that at all.

CHAPTER THREE

WHEN Holly awoke the next morning it was to the sound of pouring rain outside her window, and the knowledge that she had tossed and turned half the night.

The grey sky and greasy streets were as different from the previous lovely, warm day as could be, and they reflected rather aptly how twenty-four hours could bring about mind-boggling change, she thought, standing in the crush of a rush-hour underground train.

Yesterday she had been content. She had had the security of a good job with long-term prospects and the bolt-hole of her little home. OK, the bedsit might not be everyone's idea of Utopia, but in the months she had been living there since leaving university she had made it her own. For the first time in her life she'd been able to relax knowing *she* decided who walked through the door. Her autonomy had been hard-won and precious.

Holly turned her head, staring at her murky reflection in the dirty train window. Now she was in utter confusion. On the one hand she faced the uncertainty and trauma of trying to secure another job with the same scope for bettering herself in the future the present one had promised, and on the other…

She moved carefully—sandwiched as she was between an enormous lady with a very large briefcase and a young teenager with pink hair and black lipstick—and brushed her hair away from her face.

On the other hand there was the enormity of a move to Paris and everything—and everyone—that entailed. And

the everyone narrowed down to one very strong and charismatic Frenchman if she was being truthful.

Jacques Querruel had been more than fair last night,
though; she had to admit that. He had guaranteed to provide an excellent reference should she decide to stay in
England and look for another position here, whilst assuring her there was no need for her to leave her current job
at Querruel International unless she wished to do so. He
would make sure she was not—he'd hesitated there for a
moment, she remembered—pressurised for her decision to
make a complaint against Jeff Roberts. Which sounded
fine in theory.

The train pulled in to a station and the girl with candy-
floss hair and black lips got off. Everyone shuffled about
a bit as new passengers boarded, and they were off again,
even more tightly packed than before. She hated this, the
Underground. At least in the rush hour. The press of bodies and the warmth and the smells. Like today. Damp,
fusty clothes and the odour of rain on hair that had ab-
sorbed the smell of cooking the night before. As with the
lady next to her with the briefcase.

Holly brought her mind back resolutely to the problem
in hand. Jacques Querruel had also said that, until the
three-month trial period was over and all parties concerned had declared themselves happy with the status quo,
he would arrange for payment for her bedsit to continue
as normal, with no deduction from her salary. Which was
amazingly generous and reasonable and… She sighed irritably. If she told any of her friends about this they would
think she was crazy not to give the job in Paris a go. And
she would, she would like a shot, except for *him*.

She sighed again, and then, as she caught the eye of
the lady with the briefcase, realised the woman had mis-
interpreted her huffing and puffing as a complaint against

the current sardines-in-a-tin situation. Holly smiled weakly into the stony face and exited smartly at the next station, which thankfully was her own.

The offices of Querruel International were just a short two-minute walk from the subway, but it was time enough for Holly's stomach to tie itself into knots.

He hadn't made a move on her last night—not that she'd expected the illustrious head of Querruel International to do that with a mere minion anyway—and had been friendly and amusing, so why was she so—she refused to accept the word 'frightened' in her mind and substituted—nervous about the possibility of working in close proximity to this man? She was just an employee to him, one of hundreds, and but for the fact he had overheard her confrontation with Jeff yesterday he wouldn't know her from Adam.

OK, so he was clearly a sensual man, dynamic, dangerous, a man to be avoided where possible, but she avoided anything of a personal nature with all men.

Perhaps it was because he made her feel edgy and jittery around him? Or because, unlike with other men, she couldn't weigh Jacques Querruel up and give him a label in her mind? Even the creeps like Jeff Roberts were easy to identify, and once that had been accomplished they became no threat where it mattered—in her head.

She came to the steps of Querruel International and stood on the pavement for a moment, despite the pouring rain. She didn't want to see him again, she really didn't, so why were there little *frissons* of something she couldn't put a name to shivering down her spine?

Once inside the building she walked over to the lift and pressed the button, and after the doors had slid open and then shut again she found she was alone in the mirrored box. She turned and inspected herself, tidying her hair and checking her mascara hadn't smudged, and as she stared at her reflection something in her eyes brought her heart thudding into her throat.

No. The answer to the Paris job had to be no. She knew it did. He was too disturbing, too threatening to be around. The aggressive sexuality that was part of his persona might send some women weak at the knees but she didn't like it. She became aware her hands were shaking slightly and made a sound of quiet self-disgust low in her throat. What on earth was the matter with her? This man wasn't omnipotent, for goodness' sake, although he'd just love it if he knew she'd got herself into a bit of a state over him!

As the lift glided to a halt and the doors began to open Holly did what she had been doing all her life. She straightened her drooping shoulders, lifted her chin and narrowed her eyes, clothing herself with an invisible armour of cool detachment. Jacques Querruel had not, and would not, get under her skin. She wouldn't let him.

Last night had admittedly been a little…overwhelming, but she was back on turf she understood now and it was broad daylight. She would thank him politely for the opportunity to work in Paris when she saw him today, decline gracefully and that would be that. And she *would* leave Querruel International as soon as she could, even if she had to take a drop in salary. In fact she could temp for a time; she'd temped through all the university holidays and the agency she had used then would be glad to have her back. She'd go and see them this weekend, or even tonight.

She stepped out of the lift determinedly, turned a smart left and found herself in Jacques Querruel's arms, the file he had been holding spreading its papers all over the floor as he dropped it in an endeavour to steady them both.

Too late Holly realised she had been miles away in a

world of her own instead of concentrating on what was in front of her nose. Strong arms were holding her firmly, and as she looked up into clear amber eyes she was alarmingly conscious of a whiff of subtle lemony aftershave.

'Good morning.' It was an amused, throaty murmur and brought even more hot colour flooding into her cheeks, which were already a bright shade of pink.

'Oh, I'm sorry, Mr Querruel.' But for his quick thinking she would have ended up in an ungainly heap on the floor with the force of their impact and the high heels she was wearing. She had power-dressed that morning: her new salmon suit with its pencil-slim skirt ending just above her knees and court shoes that were just high enough to make her ankles fragile.

Jacques was wearing the suit of the night before but with a different shirt and tie in pale charcoal. He looked devastating. Her brain made no apology for the word. Even following up with, utterly drop-dead gorgeous.

'I thought we decided last night it was "Jacques"?'

He was still holding her and she was so mesmerised that she made no move to free herself. 'But that was away from the office,' Holly said weakly.

'And this is *in* the office and I still wish you to call me by my first name, *mademoiselle*.'

He smiled, and panic warred with enchantment. But only for a moment. Panic won. Holly pulled away, breaking the contact between them and taking hold of her fluttering heart as she did so. 'I don't think that is wise,' she said quickly. 'People might get the wrong idea.'

'Why?' He knelt down to pick up the papers as he spoke and her eyes were drawn as if by a magnet to muscled, lean thighs. 'And what the hell is it to do with anyone else anyway? I am the boss, am I not? I can do whatever I want.'

It was so charmingly boyish she was fascinated. She stared at him for a full ten seconds before she remembered to speak. 'That's not really the point, is it?' she said, but not as firmly as she would have liked.

'Oh, but it is exactly the point.' He stood up again, and any impression of boyishness was gone as she stared up into the hard masculine face that was a good six inches above hers despite the heels. 'I do not allow anyone to dictate to me, Holly. I never have done. My father always used to say that I would either be locked away in prison by the time I was twenty-one or on the way to making my first million. Fortunately it was the latter.'

He grinned, and she smiled weakly back. The wearing of her suit, her careful make-up and discreet dab of perfume that morning had been in the form of a silent declaration that she was perfectly in control of her feelings and her life, she realised now. A statement that nothing had changed in the last twenty-four hours. She had been kidding herself.

'I'm sure your father is relieved about that,' she managed fairly normally.

'I think this is so,' he agreed softly, 'and for my mother too. I have two younger sisters who are very beautiful and she worries about them constantly as they are both still—how do you say—playing the field, yes? So it is a relief that one of her ducklings is a pillar of the establishment.'

Pillar of the establishment? Jacques Querruel? Never! Holly smiled politely before she said, 'I had better let Margaret know I've arrived.'

'Of course.' The amber eyes held hers for a second, and then he nodded before moving swiftly down the corridor towards the managing director's secretary's domain.

Holly found herself staring after him. His voice worried her—it was so deep and smoky, and the accent gave it a kick of pure sensuality. His manner worried her—it was one of autocratic authority, however reasonable he gave the impression of being. *He* worried her—there was a sort of dark power about him that made it seem utterly feasible that he had risen from obscurity to dizzy heights in a decade. Vitality and strength radiated from him and it gave her the crazy desire to run and keep running.

Fanciful! She gave a half-smile and shook her head at her whimsical thoughts. And it wasn't like her. She was the last person in the world to indulge in capricious flights of fancy.

She would simply tell him later in the day before he left for France that she had considered his kind offer but it was no, thanks. Simple.

'So?' Margaret's head shot up as Holly entered the office. 'How did you get on last night?'

'Let me get my coat off,' Holly said, laughing a little at the very un-Margaret-like urgency. If anyone in the world was calm and unflappable it was Mr. Roberts's capable and organised secretary.

'Mr Querruel's left some papers for your attention on your desk,' Margaret volunteered as Holly walked across the room. It was clear the other woman was burning with curiosity. 'Said they related to your discussions last night?'

'He offered me a job on his team in France.' Holly walked through and slipped off her jacket, hanging it on the back of her chair as Margaret appeared in the doorway to the cubby-hole. 'I said I'd think about it. Textile technologist. It's what I've always hoped to get involved in eventually, but…'

'There's a but? Holly, are you mad?' Margaret breathed quietly, coming right up to the desk where Holly was now sitting and bending forward as she whispered, 'Accept quickly before he changes his mind or something. I know people who would give their eye-teeth to be part of his élite team in France. I'm not kidding. Why are you even thinking about it for more than one second?'

Holly stared into the plump, homely face. 'Margaret, you were the one who warned me off him yesterday,' she reminded her soberly.

'That was when I thought he was…well, you know,' Margaret returned quickly. 'But this is different. If he's offered you a job it means he's not interested in anything more; he's renowned for never mixing business and pleasure.'

Holly nodded. That was good news, wasn't it? Of course it was. So why the flat feeling in the pit of her stomach?

They heard the buzzer on Margaret's desk sound, long and hard, and Margaret grimaced as she murmured, 'Mr Roberts is in a filthy fit; I'd better go. And keep your head down whilst he's about. He's out all afternoon so we can relax a bit then.'

Great. This wet Tuesday morning was just getting better and better.

Once Holly was alone she took a deep breath as she looked at the large manila envelope lying on her desk. It was bulging and sealed, with her name written across it in a bold black script she just knew was Jacques's handwriting. Well, she could look at what it contained, couldn't she? That didn't mean she was going to change her mind.

Fifteen minutes later her mind was changed. The work sounded exciting and interesting, the salary was phenomenal with added bonuses Jacques hadn't mentioned last night, and the package included Querruel International finding a place for her to rent until the three-month trial period was over, at which point they were prepared to pay full relocation expenses. She had nothing to lose and everything to gain. And he wasn't interested in her. Margaret had said so. Not that she had imagined for one minute he was, of course.

Jacques had said the night before that he was leaving England about mid-afternoon, so when—at just gone eleven—he appeared in the doorway of her room dressed for the road and his Harley-Davidson, Holly stared at him in surprise.

'Change of plan.' He answered the unspoken question abruptly. 'I need to leave early.'

'Oh.' She nodded, the colour rushing into her face. 'I...I've looked at all the data you left this morning and I would like to accept your offer, Mr Querruel.'

'Good.' His eyes narrowed, the amber light brilliant against his black lashes. 'But all my immediate team in Paris are on Christian-name terms, OK? Does this make ''Jacques'' any safer?'

There was sufficient innuendo for Holly to feel she had been put in her place by an expert. 'I don't know what you mean,' she lied quickly.

'No?' He alarmed her by walking into the room, pushing aside some papers as he perched easily on her desk, his eyes skimming over her face. 'This is not true, I think. You like the idea of the job but you do not like the idea of working too closely with me. Or is it any man, I wonder?' The tone was mocking. 'No, I think it is me, n'est-ce pas?'

'That's ridiculous,' Holly said stiffly.

'Maybe.' He smiled, one hand reaching out and tilting her face up to meet the full scrutiny of the cool eyes. 'Maybe not. It does not matter. I need a new textile technologist. You seem to fit the bill. I will advise my secretary, Chantal, to make all the necessary arrangements; please do not concern yourself with anything but being ready to leave in two weeks' time. She will contact you tomorrow. *Au revoir*, Holly.'

'But where will I live in France? And what about the hearing concerning Mr Roberts?' Everything was happening much too fast.

'Chantal will take care of these things.' He let go of her, standing to his feet. His face was remote now, cold, and she had the feeling he had already left the building and was mentally in Paris, dealing with whatever the problem was. For a second she had the absurd urge to do something to get his attention, but she curbed it instantly.

Instead she said calmly and politely, 'Goodbye, then. I hope you have a pleasant journey.'

'Oh, I shall, Holly.' He glanced towards her tiny window. 'See, the sun is already making an appearance.'

So even the weather was under his control!

Holly wasn't aware her thoughts had shown on her face but when Jacques gave a small laugh, low in his throat, she said quickly, 'What's the matter?'

'Nothing,' he said softly. 'Not a thing. I shall not return to England before you join us in Paris, but if you wish to speak to me at any time before this you can ring the office. If I am not there my secretary will advise you where I am. If you find it is necessary to speak to me out of working hours my home numbers are on this card. The top one is my apartment in Paris, but I am rarely there unless there is some emergency or other which keeps me in the office most of the time. The other is my château. Monique will probably answer the call. She is my housekeeper, you understand?'

Understand? She didn't understand a thing where this man was concerned. She had never felt so disturbed in her life. Holly smiled coolly. 'I'm sure it won't be necessary to bother you, Mr...'

The amber eyes dared her to continue.

'Jacques,' she substituted stiffly.

He nodded. 'I too am sure. You will make certain of this, I think.'

There was a definite edge to the smooth voice, like silk draped over finely honed steel, but before Holly could respond in any way he walked over to the door. He turned in the doorway and his tone was quite different when he said, 'It is the right decision to spread your wings, Holly. Be assured of this. In Paris you will find out who the real Holly is.'

She stared at him in amazement. 'I know who I am,' she said at last. 'I told you, I found out all the details of my birth.'

'I was not thinking of your beginnings,' he said softly. Did she realise how beautiful she was? It was strange but he rather thought not, and that was unusual. Certainly among the women he knew. But then, maybe he knew the wrong sort of women? He didn't like this thought any more than the fact that he had found himself unable to sleep the night before. Images of her had raced through his head and kept him awake until dawn, and this was not acceptable. He had not experienced this before. Jacques collected his thoughts, filed them away in a box in his head and slammed the lid down hard.

'*Au revoir,*' he said again, giving her a curt nod, and then he turned and walked away. Holly heard the door to Margaret's office open and close and then silence.

She sat for some moments more, staring at the space where he had been, her head whirling. And then she stood up and walked over to the small, narrow window. She had always considered the view uninspiring, considering it consisted of the entrance and exit to the company car park situated in the bowels of the building, but now she found her heart thudding.

She stood quietly peering out, willing Margaret to remain ensconced in Michael Roberts's office, where she had been for the past half an hour, and after a few minutes her patience was rewarded. The motorbike was a beauty, a magnificent black and silver monster which paused briefly before roaring off, but it was the black figure controlling the beautiful colossus which drew her gaze. Jacques was crouched over the beast, helmet in place, but she could almost see the narrowed amber eyes intent on the road ahead, the single-minded concentration pulling his mouth into a stern line and tensing the muscles of the big masculine body.

She watched the bike and rider until they disappeared round a corner in a blaze of silver and black, and then gave a deep, shuddering sigh. She'd been mad to accept the job. She had known it but she'd still done it. Which meant, whatever happened, she'd walked into this with her eyes wide open. Not exactly a comforting thought…

Reseated at her desk, Holly made no attempt to continue with the pile of work awaiting her attention. He had accused her of wanting the job but disliking the idea of working with him, and he had been right in a way. She worried at her bottom lip with small white teeth. Yes, he had been right. He was too male, too vigorous, too strong. She had nothing against dynamic, energetic men in the workplace, she had worked with a few in her previous job, but not one of them had been remotely like Jacques Querruel. There was something about him which panicked her and she didn't understand it.

She shut her eyes tightly, the memories which she always kept buried surfacing in spite of herself. Suddenly she was eight years old again, upset and unhappy at being moved from the foster parents who had cared for her since she was a few months old.

She had loved Kate and Angus West dearly, and had looked on their other two foster children, who were younger than her, and their two natural children, who were much older, as her brothers and sisters. But within weeks of Angus being diagnosed with a rare form of bone cancer his wife had had a severe stroke, brought about by shock and stress, according to the doctors, and the little family Holly had looked upon as hers had been fragmented.

David and Cassie Kirby had been very different from the middle-aged and homely Kate and Angus, and everyone—social workers, teachers and so on—had assumed she was just finding the change of home and lifestyle strange and unsettling. David and Cassie had lived in a massive six-bedroomed house with four bathrooms and a swimming pool; Holly had her own bedroom, a wardrobe full of new clothes, riding lessons—she would adapt and love it. Of course she would. What child wouldn't? And the other two children who lived with David and Cassie adored their foster parents.

Holly had heard this accolade repeated over and over again in the next six months, but then, just before her ninth birthday, she'd understood why she felt uneasy and frightened around the charismatic, handsome and wealthy David. Understood why she didn't like his kisses and hugs, his encouragement for her to sit on his knee, to be his 'little princess'.

She hadn't understood what he was trying to do when he'd come to her bedroom that night. He had come before, ostensibly to check her homework or have what he called his 'daddy talks', but this time he hadn't stopped at hugging her close and touching her in the scary way, and kissing her with his mouth wide open. But she hadn't been like his other foster children, probably because they had been with David and Cassie since they were babies and they were completely under his control.

She had resisted what he'd wanted her to do to him, and he to her, refusing to be swayed by first his pleas and then his threats, and even though his superior strength had overcome her struggles in the end she had still managed to thwart his intention, which was nothing short of rape.

He had locked her in her room after he left, and when she had cried and banged on the door and Cassie had come she'd heard him telling his wife some story about her cheeking him.

She had tried to tell Cassie what had happened the next morning, before she'd left for school, but David's wife had been furious with her for 'telling such wicked, wicked lies', whisking her upstairs and locking her in her bedroom again. And then she had learnt how powerful David was. He had forced the other two children—a boy and a girl—to say Holly had regularly attacked them, that she had destroyed their homework, wrecked their toys and so on. That she was unruly and out of hand. She had stolen small trinkets from the house and probably from local shops, he had stated to the social worker he'd called in. She was running amok and although they had tried everything, bending over backwards to keep her, they sadly had to admit defeat. For the sake of the other children. And neither Cassie or the other children had lifted a finger to help her.

She had been labelled a problem and had been too scared to continue to press her accusations, too hurt and confused. The next home had been a disaster from day one. A sense of bitter, impotent injustice compounded by a paralysing fear at any overture of friendship by a member of the opposite sex—especially one in authority over her—had set the tone for the next few years. Years of being moved from one place to another; of always being the odd one out; of being lonely and alone.

Looking back from an adult viewpoint, she now saw that many of the grown-ups she had come into contact with through that time had tried to help her, but her treatment at the hands of David and Cassie Kirby had made her hostile and suspicious. But she had survived...

Holly opened her eyes, breathing deeply to control her racing heartbeat. She had made a life for herself on her own terms and without asking help from anyone, and she had collected a few friends along the way. Of course, they were mostly female, apart from dear old Mr Bateman at the top of the house, who was seventy-five years old and pining from unrequited love for Mrs Gibson, and James Holden, one of her university professors. It had been James who had found her crying uncontrollably and for no reason that she knew of in a corner of the university library late one evening. She had wanted to die and she had told him so.

He had shepherded her to his apartment, where his wife, Lucy, had diagnosed complete exhaustion due to overwork and stress. Lucy was a sister at the local hospital. They had covered for her with the powers that be, labelling her condition a severe attack of the flu, and she had stayed in their spare bedroom for three weeks, doing nothing and seeing no one. Lucy had fed her hot meals, which she'd forced the patient to eat, brought her magazines and light books to read and refused to let her get out of bed. James had just been a friend, watching TV with her and cracking silly jokes.

It had been her first experience of real, genuine friendship from the male of the species, and she knew now it had saved her reason if not her life. She had been verging on a breakdown, and although she hadn't confided in James and Lucy about the Kirbys she had realised it was the years of frustration and pain on account of them that had brought her so close to a serious illness.

She had told herself, through the quiet afternoons in the peace and tranquillity of the Holdens' apartment, that she would rise above her past. She was not a victim unless she thought of herself as one, she'd determined resolutely.

After three weeks she'd returned to her studies and eventually obtained her degree, leaving the university but not her friendship with James and Lucy. That had continued, albeit from afar, with the three of them meeting up every few months or so. The last occasion had been at the christening of their daughter, Melanie Anne, when Holly had been one of the godparents.

Why was she thinking of all this now? Holly asked herself irritably, glaring at the stack of work in front of her as though it were the culprit. She knew David Kirby had died a few months after her brief stay with James and Lucy, and after that it had been easier to fight dredging up the past.

Christina, the Kirbys' foster daughter, had written informing Holly of David's death at the time, having traced her through the social services. It appeared David had tried his tricks with some young girls at the local youth club where he helped out, and when the police had started investigating the complaints Christina had come forward at last to speak of her own abuse at the hands of her foster father. The police had taken the young woman seriously, in view of the other complaints, and within a day or two—knowing his sordid secret was about to be revealed—David Kirby had taken an overdose.

David Kirby couldn't hurt anyone any more. His power over the weak and innocent was finished. And she was autonomous now, completely independent. Holly stared down at her hands, which were trembling. She could look after herself and she would never willingly give that precious and hard-won sovereignty up.

And Jacques Querruel? A separate section of her mind asked probingly. What about Jacques Querruel? This ruthless and quite extraordinary Frenchman who rode a Harley-Davidson with panache and didn't give a damn what anyone thought of him?

Jacques Querruel was everything she didn't like in the male of the species. Handsome, wealthy, hard and answerable to no one. A law unto himself. Intimidating everyone around him with his influence and authority. But he didn't intimidate her and she was not frightened of him either. He might be her employer, and of course she would be only too pleased to give a hundred per cent effort to this new venture, but if he imagined he had bought her soul along with the job he was in for a nasty shock. She would not be bullied or ridden roughshod over. Not ever again.

And if Paris didn't work out? She contemplated the thought before reaching for the papers on the top of the pile at the side of her word processor.

She'd cut her losses and move on. Simple. In fact she didn't know why she had ever got into a state about Jacques Querruel...

CHAPTER FOUR

THE short journey had been a pleasant one, but then with Jacques Querruel's secretary booking her in business class it could hardly have been anything else, Holly reflected as she stood waiting to be collected in the airport terminal. There had been a taxi to the airport too, all paid for and a handsome tip included, the cheerful taxi driver had informed her when she had tried to press money on him. It seemed Jacques Querruel thought of everything.

She would be met at the airport and taken to her rented apartment, where she could offload her luggage and freshen up a little, before her escort would bring her to the offices of Querruel International. There she would meet Jacques again and he would introduce her to the rest of the team.

All this had been explained by Jacques's secretary by telephone a few days ago and confirmed in a letter Holly had received twenty-four hours later. Efficient, clinical and unemotional. Unlike Holly's oscillating feelings.

The last two weeks she had fluctuated from being absolutely sure she was doing the right thing in moving to Paris to being equally sure she wasn't, her emotions seesawing violently, sometimes within the space of a few minutes. Her nights had been a mixture of disturbed, strange dreams—the sort she'd only had before when she was ill and feverish—and thick, heavy sleep that left her feeling more tired in the mornings than before she had got into bed.

But she was here now. She glanced down at the two

large cases and one small one which contained all of her clothes and shoes and a few personal possessions. And, with Michael Roberts refusing to even acknowledge her existence and his son taking legal advice, she wasn't actually sorry to leave England.

Margaret had told her on the quiet that Jacques had advised Michael Roberts that quite a few other women were prepared to stand up in court and testify that Jeff had sexually harassed them if it came to it, and that she doubted if Jeff would pursue any defence once he realised Jacques was absolutely serious in seeing the thing through. 'He'll go for keeping it all quiet and sneaking away to another job which his father will set up for him,' Margaret had said confidingly. 'But this time he'll have to keep his nose clean and actually work for his living. It'll do him the world of good.'

Holly didn't care whether it did or not. The whole episode had left a nasty taste in her mouth and she just wanted to forget Jeff Roberts and concentrate on the new job, which at the moment was causing the butterflies in her stomach to go berserk. She couldn't speak French; all the rest of the team had been together for years and years; she didn't know a soul in France and she had no idea if she was up to the sort of work which would be expected of her. And there was Jacques Querruel. Which was the biggest obstacle of all.

And then, as though her frantic thoughts had conjured him up, she saw him. Tall, long-legged and broad-shouldered, he was head and shoulders above the rest of the milling throng, and, as before in England, the energy and drive which was an integral part of his persona surrounded him like a dark aura.

She stood perfectly still as he made his way over to her, her heart in her mouth. He was wearing black jeans and a silky midnight-blue shirt, his arms brown and strong and his chiselled features appearing as if they were cut in granite. And Holly noticed that more than one female in the vicinity was giving him second and third glances, one young blonde girl, who couldn't have been more than eighteen, even going so far as to stop dead and follow him unashamedly with her wide eyes.

'*Bonjour, mademoiselle.*' It was faintly mocking and amused as he took in her rigid posture. 'I trust you had a comfortable journey?'

She nodded tightly, horrified at how seeing him again had affected her. 'Fine, thank you,' she responded stiffly. 'I thought—'

'Yes?' The black eyebrows rose enquiringly.

'I thought your secretary said a car and driver would meet me?' She stared at him steadily, holding the piercing gaze.

'The car is waiting, Holly, and I can drive,' he said with silky smoothness. He signalled imperiously and a porter appeared as if by magic at their sides as Jacques continued, 'Let us leave the airport with haste; these places are not conducive to conversation.'

Airports *and* Jacques Querruel, Holly thought with a trace of dark amusement, but then, as he took her arm and whisked her out of the terminal building, she ceased to think at all with the myriad impressions bombarding her mind.

Bright May sunshine, a crystal-clear blue sky, people buzzing about everywhere and the feel and faint delicious smell of the man at her side. These and a host of other things hit her senses with blinding impact.

She watched the porter depositing her cases into a sleek silver Jaguar before Jacques tipped him—handsomely, if the effusive quality of the man's thanks was anything to

go by—and then she was in the passenger seat and
Jacques was shutting the door behind her. As he slid into
the driving seat a moment later she felt her whole body
react to his, although she didn't betray this by so much
as the flicker of an eyelash. And then they were off,
sweeping out of the airport confines before she could
catch her breath.

'I was not sure if you would come.'

For a moment Holly thought she had misheard the soft
voice, but as her eyes flashed to the handsome profile he
glanced at her once. 'I had said I would,' she managed
quietly.

'Of course.' He nodded, and she had no way of knowing what he was thinking as she glanced away. 'And it is
a beautiful day to see the city of love, is it not?'

'A city is just buildings; one is very like another,' Holly
said from her vast experience of travelling nowhere at all.

'*Mon Dieu!* You are aware that such a comment is sac-
rilege to any red-blooded Frenchman?' Jacques asked
with cool mockery. 'Paris has a special magic, an *esprit*
that fascinates all who visit her, and passion is very much
part of this. It was passion that built the great boulevards,
the churches, the art collections and the reputation for
gourmet food. The French proverb, *''Pour être Parisien,
il n'est pas necessaire d'être ne a Paris, il suffit d'y re-
naitre''* is just as true today as ever it was.'

'Which means?' Holly asked warily.

'To be a Parisian one need not be born there, only reborn there,' Jacques supplied silkily. 'But to fully understand this one must walk the streets and sense the life that
inhabits them, a life not only of the present but also of
the past. Almost every street has its trophies: a tree
planted by Victor Hugo on the Avenue Raspail, a doorway
in Belleville where the singer Edith Piaf was born, or a

mark on the Rue Bellechasse which records the height of the great flood. Paris lives and breathes, you understand? It has always been that way.'

Holly glanced at him, not sure if he was serious or not. And then she said, determined to not be overawed, 'If you feel like that about it, why is your château miles away from the city?'

'Ah, but not too far, you know. And I have my apartment here, so in truth I have not really left at all,' he said easily. 'Added to which my parents and sisters live south of the Latin quarter so the Querruel name is well-represented.'

'Is that where you were born?' she asked quietly, remembering the gossip that he had risen from squalor to riches.

'Not exactly.' He negotiated a sharp turn around a car which had suddenly decided to pull up without any warning at all, its occupant waving and shouting to someone who was obviously a friend on the pavement. Holly noticed Jacques was neither fazed nor surprised, and assumed such occurrences weren't uncommon. She decided she wouldn't try to drive in Paris.

'I was born a few miles from where my parents now live, but in Paris a mile can take you into another world,' he said expressionlessly. 'I wanted to buy them a château out of town when I was able to do so but they would not have it. They wanted to stay where they knew everyone, where things were familiar, I think. My father enjoys his game of boules with his old cronies every afternoon, and they meet friends for breakfast in the sidewalk cafés, that sort of thing. But they let me move them to a small house in a quiet cobbled street with a pretty garden for my mother to grow flowers. She was never able to have more than a small window box when I was little. They are content and that is the main thing.'

He obviously loved his family very much. Holly didn't know why that should give her such an ache in her heart region and she changed the subject as she said, 'I don't have to see the apartment now if you would rather go to the office. I'd like to start work straight away.'

'I think this would not be good.' He glanced briefly her way. 'We will take your things as planned and then we will have lunch. There will be time enough for work later. I am not quite the slave-driver you seem to imagine.'

Oh, dear, he sounded affronted. This was a great start to the new job—offending the boss. 'Lunch with the others, you mean?' she asked innocently.

There was a long pause. 'No, that is not what I mean.'

'Oh.'

She was about to say more when he pointed to her left. 'There on the pavement. You see? A gypsy circus.'

They had passed too soon but Holly saw the performing goat and two brightly dressed clowns, along with an organ grinder with an enormous hat for collecting money. She was enchanted, turning round in her seat to see more.

'The clowns keep a watch-out for the police,' Jacques said drily. 'They are all adept at melting away at a moment's notice, even the goat.'

Holly smiled; she couldn't help it.

'That is better,' he murmured softly. 'You smile so rarely.'

She stared at him in surprise. 'How do you know?' she asked boldly. 'You hardly know me at all.'

'Something which will be rectified in the coming days, I hope.' It was polite but there was an edge she couldn't place.

She nodded briskly. 'Of course. I'm looking forward to meeting all the others on the team too.'

He murmured something under his breath that she almost thought sounded like 'Damn the team', but of course she must have misheard. She stared at him uncertainly for a moment. She knew the company was situated on the Right Bank, which was the very essence of bourgeois respectability, and now she asked tentatively, 'Where exactly is my apartment?'

'A ten-minute walk from the office.' He smiled easily. 'And the Restaurant de l'Etoile is in the next street, so this means you will be at work once we have eaten, my eager little beaver.'

It was mocking and she was immediately on the defensive. She was here to work, wasn't she? He needn't sound so patronising about her enthusiasm. She frowned, deciding to say nothing more until they reached their destination.

It appeared Jacques was of like mind. As the powerful car nosed its way through the crazy traffic Holly became more and more aware of the big, dark man at her side as the silence held and electrified. His jeans were tight across the hips and his legs were long; he exuded a flagrant masculinity that was impossible to ignore.

She wished she'd worn a longer skirt. The one she'd decided on was a modest knee-length when she was standing, beautifully cut and close-fitting, but, seated in the low-slung car as she was, she noticed it seemed to insist on riding halfway up her thighs. Every time she tried to pull it down it slipped out of her fingers and rode higher. She wriggled a little, attempting another manoeuvre that would reduce the area of exposed flesh.

'For crying out loud, woman, will you relax?'

Holly bristled as her cheeks flamed. 'I beg your pardon?'

'You are like the cat on the hot tin roof,' he grated. '*Mon Dieu!* What do you think I am about to do to you in the middle of the day, surrounded by traffic in a busy thoroughfare, anyway? What stories have you heard that make you so nervous around me?'

Holly glared at him in a most unemployee-like way. 'I haven't the faintest idea what you are talking about,' she stated tightly, brushing her hair away from her hot cheeks. Horrible, *horrible* man!

'You mean you were not expecting me to try to put my hand on your knee?' he snapped irritably.

'Of course not.' She was truly shocked and it showed.

'I see.' His scowl smoothed to a quizzical ruffle. 'But you are nervous, yes?'

'Of course I'm nervous,' she shot back testily. 'Anyone would be, wouldn't they? I've just arrived in a strange country to meet people I don't know and work at a place I've never seen.' *And my boss, who has decided to meet me, is easily the most sexy and charismatic man I've ever seen.*

There was a brief silence whilst the formidably intelligent computer brain dissected the information it had been fed. 'Yes, I can understand this, but you are of the indomitable spirit, *n'est-ce pas*?'

'I am also a normal human being,' she stated sharply. 'Or do you only employ the Rambo types who know no fear?'

For a moment she thought she had gone too far. He *was* her boss after all, and her tone had been distinctly shrewish.

There was a longer silence and then he smiled, and humour was back in his voice as he said, 'The Rambo types I do not like, Holly. Of this I assure you.' He turned to look at her for a moment, the amber eyes warm and the smile still on his lips, and then he was facing the front again.

Which was just as well because she was incapable of doing anything but breathe, and even that was coming in gulps. Did he look at his women like that before he made love to them? The thought hammered into her consciousness. Because if so they must fall into his arms like ripe plums. Of course, it was all charm, and probably cold-blooded at that, but boy, was it good!

Jacques had just turned into a wide, winding road off the main thoroughfare, and they had only gone a few yards more when the car drew to a halt. A large modern apartment building with a pretty fountain set in the middle of a small square was in front of them.

'Come along.' He had left the car, was walking round the bonnet and opening the passenger door, but still Holly had to order her legs to obey the message to get moving. The car ride had done nothing to convince her that she had made the right decision in coming to Paris, but it was too late now. Far, far too late.

The elderly concierge sprang to attention as Jacques walked into the foyer of the building with Holly's cases, and it was clear from the tenor of the exchange between the two men that Jacques was known to him, but as the conversation was all in French Holly didn't understand a word.

'And this is Mademoiselle Stanton, Pierre.' Jacques turned and drew her forward. 'Pierre speaks very good English and he will be only too pleased to help you in any way he can,' he added to Holly.

'*Bonjour, Monsieur.*' They were about the only French

words she knew. She smiled and held out her hand to the
little man.

The wrinkled and aged Pierre smiled back, his gnome-
like face cheery and bright black button eyes warm. '*Bonjour, mademoiselle.* I am pleased to meet the friend of
Monsieur Querruel and I 'ope you will be 'appy 'ere. I
am at your service, *mademoiselle.*'

'Thank you.'

A lift took them up to the third floor and—Jacques
having refused help from Pierre with the cases—the two
of them stepped out into a thickly carpeted corridor which
carried a faint, pleasant, flowery smell in the air. Jacques
strode to the last door on their right whereupon he put the
cases down and fished out some keys from his jeans
pocket. 'Your new home, *mademoiselle.*' He offered her
the keys smilingly. 'This one opens the front door and, as
this is now your apartment, I think you should do the
honours.'

As the door swung open Holly found herself stepping
into a small passageway which opened almost immediately into one of the most charming sitting rooms she had
ever seen. It wasn't large, but by making the most of
proportion and unifying with shades of lemon and cream
an elegance had been achieved which belied the flat's di-
minutive size.

The sitting room featured two floor-to-ceiling windows
and a large alcove which provided space for a desk and
bookcase, and the pale, muted colours emphasised the
light and maximised the space as well as contributing to
the overall sense of simplicity.

There was no door to divide the sitting room from the
tiny dining area and kitchen, but with careful arrangement
of the furniture each area felt remarkably self-contained.

Floor-length voile curtains waved gently in the breeze

from the partly open windows, and their colour was reflected in the two-seater sofa and two chairs covered in calico. A small balcony off the sitting room held a table and two chairs, besides pots of busy lizzies and camellias, and a tiny fountain in one corner which was making a gentle 'plink-plink' sound. This overlooked half of Paris, or so it seemed to Holly's enchanted gaze.

A bedroom led off the sitting room through one door and a bathroom through another, and these rooms were very much extensions of the rest of the flat with similar colour schemes. A buttery-blond carpet covered the floor in all three rooms, and the pale theme was lifted here and there by the clever use of shot-silk cushions in golden yellow and burnt orange, a bowl of fruit on the dining table, a tall, intricately patterned Japanese vase in one corner and other such stylish touches.

Jacques had positioned himself leaning against the wall of the sitting room as Holly had explored her small but exquisitely designed and furnished new home, his muscled arms folded over his chest and his amber eyes intent on her face.

'Well?' His gaze had been waiting for her. 'Do you like it?' he asked lazily.

'How could anyone not like this?' Holly said bemusedly. 'But when you said Querruel International would provide temporary quarters for three months I didn't expect anything like this. This must be costing the company a small fortune.'

He looked down at his Italian-made shoes, considering his reply. He had wanted her to work for him here in Paris and therefore he had deliberately offered her a package it would have been almost impossible to refuse. That was acceptable. He had done the same sort of thing before when necessary. He knew she didn't know anyone here or speak French, and therefore he had wanted her to be in accommodation which was safe and secure as well as pleasant. Again, this was acceptable, and nothing more than the duty of a responsible employer. However, apartments in this area were like gold dust and, as she so rightly suspected, extremely expensive. He should know. He owned the penthouse at the top of this building…

He really did have unfairly thick lashes, thought Holly as she took the opportunity to study him. His open-necked shirt revealed the soft black body hair which must cover his chest, and his arms were dusted with the same. He was easily the most intimidatingly masculine male she had ever come across, his wide shoulders and strong, sinewy body offering no shred of weakness.

He looked up and caught her watching him, and it took some effort of will for Holly not to drop her eyes.

'A small fortune?' He repeated her words thoughtfully. 'Money is relative, I think. An inexpensive place may provide all sorts of problems and then it becomes very expensive in essence, does it not? I know the security system here to be exceptionally sound. The inhabitants have their own key to the front lobby, of course, but Pierre monitors all visitors by an announced entry programme so they do not have immediate access into the building. An unfortunate requirement but in this day and age sometimes necessary.'

For her? Hardly. For a politician maybe, or some other high-profile personality. Holly stared at him, and then she said, 'But you walked straight in downstairs.'

'Pierre saw me approaching the doors and opened them automatically,' Jacques said smoothly. 'Therefore I did not have to use your keys. Or mine.'

For a moment the last two words didn't register and then she saw her eyes open wide as comprehension hit. He pre-empted any protest by saying coolly and matter-of-factly, 'I have an apartment at the top of the building, which is why I knew about this one when it became available just about the time you agreed to work in Paris. My secretary was saved the trouble of securing a suitable property, which was most convenient, and of course being so close to the company this place is very time-efficient.'

Her voice higher-pitched than usual, Holly said, 'I'm sorry, but have you considered how this might look to other people?'

'Other people?' The look on his face and the tone of his voice suggested she could have been talking in double Dutch.

'Yes, other people,' Holly reiterated tightly. Darn it, he knew full well what she was getting at. 'Folk are very good at putting two and two together and making ten at the best of times. You bring me over from England and then provide accommodation in the same building in which you live. They might get the wrong idea.'

Amber eyes surveyed her steadily. 'You have your own front-door key and so do I,' he said calmly. 'How could anyone misconstrue this?'

If he had got to thirty-two years of age without knowing the answer to that, she was Minnie Mouse! 'People talk,' she said stonily. 'They like nothing better than a good gossip.'

'Not about me, Holly.' In the space of a moment he had changed from charming, genial associate-cum-employer into someone who was positively chilling. 'Not if they value their well-being.'

'Maybe not in front of you,' she persisted doggedly, 'but I can assure you they *will* talk.'

'And this would bother you? That these nameless and

rather sad individuals might waste their breath in idle gossip?'

He was being deliberately obtuse here. She found herself glaring at him. 'That really is not the point.'

'That's exactly the point,' he said drily. 'And frankly the girl who stood up to Jeff Roberts and was prepared to confront me too is quite capable of squashing any prattle with one look from her beautiful blue eyes.' He smiled slowly. 'Look at you now,' he drawled softly, dark eyebrows lifting slightly. 'You are fearsome.'

No, she was not going to be charmed or sweet-talked over this, Holly told herself resolutely, even as she bit back a secret smile. 'I just don't think—'

'Good. Let me do the thinking.' As her eyes opened wide at his audacity he gave her no chance to reply, taking her arm and adding, 'We will talk over lunch, yes? I am starving. Would you like to freshen up a little before we leave?'

He was like a human bulldozer, this man! Holly stared at him, her eyes turning from sapphire-blue to deep violet. And arrogant in the extreme. No doubt he was used to everyone falling in with his plans—whatever they happened to be—for fear of offending him. Well, surprise, surprise, Mr Querruel; this little cog in the great Querruel International machine might just throw a spark or two.

And then he took the wind right out of her sails when he said quietly, 'Please, Holly?'

Now, why did he have to do that? she asked herself crossly. Speak in that smoky, warm voice which was more wistful than aggressive? She shrugged warily, determined not to let him see how he affected her. 'I won't be a minute,' she said coolly, reaching for her handbag, 'and we will definitely discuss this further over lunch.'

'Of course.' It was too meek and there was laughter in

his eyes. 'A good meal always makes one more reasonable, yes?'

She retreated into the bathroom with as much dignity as she could muster and shut the door very firmly behind her.

Lunch was in a delightful little restaurant built in a semicircle around an open courtyard. Large glass panels slid to one side when the weather was fine, ensuring the restaurant was open to the sunshine, and the alfresco feel seemed very foreign to Holly. Unlike in England the menu was written in both English and French, and the choice was enormous.

Holly chose *salade de tomates et d'ouefs* to begin with—egg and tomato salad—followed by *poulet à l'estragon*—chicken with tarragon—and both dishes were delicious, as was the dessert, pineapples in kirsch liqueur. However, in spite of the beautifully cooked and served food, Holly found herself eating mechanically, every nerve and fibre of her being painfully aware of Jacques Querruel.

She didn't know how French employers treated their employees but she suspected it couldn't be *that* different from English protocol. And Jacques was not staying in the frame. Not that he was flirting with her—not exactly, she reasoned silently. It was more that he was acting as though she was an equal, a friend, rather than someone who worked for him. He was full of humour—something which hadn't come across so forcefully in England—and supremely interesting—something which had.

She was intrigued, she admitted reluctantly, which was a warning in itself, along with the unexpected quivers and the sensual stirring of her blood. And that was dangerous. She didn't want to feel any sort of attraction for him—or any other male if it came to that. Autonomy and control were the important things. And she had managed to live by their safe guidelines quite happily until Jacques had come on to the scene.

'It will be all right.' They were sitting at their table drinking coffee when Jacques spoke after a minute or two of silence. They had both been watching two little girls playing with their dolls in a corner of the courtyard for a few moments, the children's curls turned bronze by the bright sunlight. Holly found she rather liked the way the French seemed to eat out in families rather than just couples; there were quite a few children scattered about the place and they were all very well-behaved.

She turned to Jacques now, her voice enquiring as she said, 'I'm sorry?' even as she prayed he hadn't guessed how she was feeling about him.

'You are anxious,' Jacques said quietly. 'Which is understandable. But you will find the other members of the team are very easy to get on with.'

Holly finished her coffee in one gulp and put the cup down on the saucer, wiping her mouth with the linen napkin before she said lightly, 'I'm sure they are.'

'As am I.' It was faintly challenging.

Now, that she wasn't at all sure of. She nodded. 'Of course,' she said evenly, careful to keep her face expressionless.

'Of course.' He repeated her words in a soft drawl, his voice holding the edge of irony. 'Tell me, Holly, what does one have to do to break through the barrier you have in place?'

He rose without waiting for an answer, and she could do little more than follow him out of the restaurant after he had paid the bill. Once he had opened the car door for her and she had slid inside, she watched him as he walked round the bonnet. His black hair was so dark it had blue lights in the sunshine, and the black jeans and midnight-blue shirt sat wonderfully well on the big masculine body. He looked the epitome of the successful man about town—a film star maybe, or a devil-may-care playboy. Larger than life in every respect anyway.

'So, we now begin the ordeal by introduction.'

He glanced at her and she saw the amber eyes were smiling tolerantly. She wondered for a moment what his reaction would be if she spoke the truth and said meeting his colleagues was absolutely nothing compared to the last hour or two on her overheated nerves. Instead she merely smiled back.

'Let me run through a few names with you so that they will be familiar when you meet the people concerned. There is Gerard Bousquet; he is my production manager and you will have quite a lot to do with him. And Jean-Pierre Delbouis, Gerard's assistant. Chantal you have already spoken to on the telephone, and Auguste and Christian are two of the best designers in the business. They left very well-paid jobs to come and work for me in the beginning and I owe them much.'

As he continued to speak, going through the immediate team and then other relevant personnel on the fringe, Holly struggled to keep her mind on what he was saying.

They had barely discussed the matter of her flat at lunch. When she had raised the subject Jacques had coolly declared that there was no problem as far as he could see. He was rarely in residence at his apartment anyway— most of the time he preferred to commute to his château, some thirty miles clear of Paris, unless there was a work crisis or he was having dinner with his parents or friends in the city, or attending some function or other. Everyone was quite aware of this.

He had stated this clearly and firmly, and as the waiter had chosen that particular moment to bring their hors d'oeuvres to the table she had been able to say nothing, and once the waiter had departed Jacques had talked of something else and the moment to protest further had been lost.

Which might have been exactly what he intended. Holly frowned to herself thoughtfully. She didn't know. In fact she was feeling she didn't know anything about anything! But that could only get better...couldn't it?

CHAPTER FIVE

SURPRISINGLY, in view of all her doubts and misgivings, Holly found she took to the new job, her associates and the French way of life like a duck to water.

Her work colleagues were a great bunch on the whole, and Holly's only complaint—if she had voiced it—was that they to a man or woman openly revered Jacques Querruel. Only with the women there was an extra element to their hero-worship that set Holly's teeth on edge. But she could understand why. Oh, yes. Having worked with the human dynamo which was Jacques Querruel for eight weeks, she could certainly understand why, Holly admitted to herself one warm July evening as she strolled home through bustling Paris streets.

He was an inspiration, although she hated to admit it, and he never asked for more commitment or hard work from his employees than he was prepared to give himself. First in the office in the mornings and the last to leave, he set a pace which was as exhausting as it was exciting. Fascinating, mesmerising, hypnotic and wildly seductive—she had heard all those descriptions of the compelling magnet which was Jacques Querruel and she had to agree with every one. He was a one-off. A unique, inimitable being, a *sui generis* who was impossible to define and label.

Which made it all the more humiliating that she had ever imagined—for a *second*—that he had any designs on her as a woman. He had obviously been absolutely truthful when he had declared the reasons for taking her flat;

they had been ones of convenience and efficiency and that was all.

In all the weeks she had worked for him he hadn't put a foot—or a hand, or any other part of his anatomy—wrong, and, not only that, she had been forced to listen to the others talking about his extensive—and very active—love life.

Beautiful women were Jacques's forte it would appear—glossy, sleek, expensive consorts who openly adored him and worshipped the ground he walked on.

And why not? she asked herself honestly. He was magnificent. Jacques had been in the States for the last five days and yet his presence still brooded over the offices, impelling people to work just that little bit harder, stretch themselves just that little bit further.

She was just about to pass one of the numerous delightful squares which were dotted about the Paris streets, and now she stopped for a moment, her eyes idly following a group of elderly men who were occupied in playing a game of boules. Jacques had said his father was passionate about the game, and from the spirit of camaraderie in front of her she could understand why.

The scents and smells of a city summer evening were heavy in the air as she watched the gnarled veterans playing the old and popular sport, each player intent on getting as close to the small *cushonet*—or marker—with their own three steel boules as they could. There was a great deal of good-natured banter from what Holly could determine, the spirit of *joie de vivre* belying the men's ages, which must average around eighty if a day. She couldn't understand a word of what they were saying to each other but she found herself smiling just the same.

Music was playing on the street corner opposite the square—a group of outlandishly dressed students playing a selection of instruments to amuse themselves and anyone else who wanted to stop and listen.

Holly stood, the smile still touching her lips, and just drank the moment in. The sun was still hot enough to caress her skin with a languid heat and she brushed back her hair from her face, shutting her eyes for a moment as she exulted in just being alive.

When she opened them again Jacques was standing in front of her, his amazing eyes intent on her face and his lips curved with amusement. 'You see,' he said softly. 'The *esprit* of Paris is already working.'

'*Jacques.*' She knew she was blushing, which was so stupid, so gauche. 'I thought… You're in America.'

'Then perhaps it is only my ghost who is here with you now?' His smile widened.

She pulled herself together fast. 'I'm sorry, that was silly,' she said quickly. 'I meant—'

'I know what you meant.' His gaze ran over her face and the sheen of dark, rich, silky hair. 'And you could never be silly.'

She stared at him, terribly uncertain now. He seemed different somehow, she thought confusedly. This was not the dynamic tycoon or brilliantly intelligent and somewhat formidable business associate she had come to thoroughly respect over the last weeks. Neither was it the slightly distant occupier of the penthouse at the top of the building where she lived, or the darkly powerful, legendary socialite and womaniser who was reported to have a different lady on his arm every night of the week. But just who it was she couldn't quite pin down.

'I…I'm just on my way back to the flat,' she managed shakily after a long moment or two. 'Are you going to the office?'

Jacques's thick black lashes hid the expression in his

eyes for a second. She *hoped* he was going to the office, the tone of her voice had told him so, and now he cursed himself inwardly for revealing too much. And then he remembered the decision he had made over the last few days when he had found thoughts of her intruding at the oddest moments.

It was a ridiculous situation, he'd told himself grimly. He had walked on eggshells the last weeks over this woman and it was not going to continue. He had hoped she would loosen up a little and she had—with everyone but him. He heard her talking and laughing with the others sometimes, even Gerard, who was not known for his sense of humour, but as soon as he, Jacques, appeared on the scene she closed up like a clam. And it grated on him. More and more as the weeks had gone by. *Zut!* He was going to break through that reserve of hers if it was the last thing he did.

'No, I am not going to the office,' he said very quietly. 'I have just flown in from the States and needed to stretch my legs, unwind a little. You know?'

Jacques Querruel unwind? Holly thought of several polite and nonchalant replies which would fit the occasion, and then said, 'But you're not like that.'

'Like what?'

'You're not the sort of man who needs to try and chill out. You thrive on work.'

His eyes were clear, unblinking, his hard, firm mouth curved cynically. 'You think I am a robot?' he asked silkily. 'A machine? But this is not so. You cut me and I bleed like any other man, Holly.'

The mild, gentle tone didn't fool her. He was annoyed, and in retrospect she couldn't blame him. 'I didn't mean it like that,' she said uncomfortably, just as a great whoop and holler from the group playing boules indicated there had been a winner.

'For a woman you lie incredibly badly.'

Maybe, but then she didn't look on that as a failing. She had seen what accomplished lying by an expert could do when she was eight years old. 'I'll let you get on with your walk,' she said evenly.

'I walked this way because I knew it was the route you took from the office,' Jacques said quietly. 'I have an invitation for you.'

'An invitation?' It was wary.

He bit down on the sudden flare of anger and said smoothly, 'From my mother. I have spoken of the little mouse of an English girl who has come all alone to the big, bad city to work for me, and she feels sorry for you. She wants to feed you dinner.'

Little mouse? Holly opened her mouth to fire a machine-gun round, but then she caught the glint in his eyes. 'You're joking,' she said weakly.

'Partly.' A warm, strong hand tilted her chin and she was too surprised to jerk away. 'The invitation to dinner stands, though. She is hospitable, my dear mama, and she was horrified to learn that a stranger to our city eats alone in her solitary apartment.'

'By choice, I hope you told her,' Holly said stiffly. 'The others have invited me to their homes for a meal but at the moment there is still so much to learn that I study at night. And I like to get to bed early so I'm fresh for the morning.'

'Commendable.' He said it as though it wasn't. 'Very commendable.'

You bet your sweet life it was, and it was his darn company which benefited from her diligence, Holly thought aggressively. She intended to make a go of this job if it killed her; failing in front of this man was not an option. 'Please thank your mother for me and tell her—'

'You can tell her yourself tonight when you come to dinner.'

Had he listened to a word she'd said? Holly thought helplessly, the sense of *déjà vu* strong. Yet again she was in danger of being manipulated by this charismatic and extremely annoying individual and if he thought she didn't recognise it…

'Your mother can't be expecting me tonight.' She decided calm reason was the best policy. 'You've only just got back from the States.'

'I rang her *en route* and told her to expect us about eight,' he said firmly. 'She was very pleased.'

'But I might have been going out tonight.'

'Are you?' he asked directly.

She considered lying as she studied him through angry blue eyes but it was quite true what he'd said—she did lie incredibly badly. Nevertheless, just to assume she was ready and waiting to leap at his invitation was the height of arrogance. 'That's not the point.'

'You're right, of course.' He did one of the mercurial changes of attitude that had caught her out once or twice before, his voice meek. 'I ask your forgiveness, *mademoiselle*.'

Holly eyed him with dark suspicion before clearing her throat. 'I can't go tonight, not empty-handed,' she said firmly.

'You could, but if you want to take something my mother adores a particular kind of handmade chocolate truffle from a little shop in the Latin quarter, OK?' Jacques offered helpfully. 'We could stop *en route* if you like?'

She wanted to ask him if he was in the habit of taking

work colleagues or friends to his parents' home for dinner, but she didn't. He had made it clear his mother had taken pity on a stranger who hardly knew anyone in Paris, and, much as she didn't appreciate being cast in the role of little orphan Annie, she didn't want Jacques to think she'd made the mistake of regarding his mother's invitation as anything other than what it was. She knew this wasn't a date or anything personal. She suddenly decided she had been distinctly chary in causing such a fuss.

Jacques had been watching the play of emotions over her face with covert interest, and like the master strategist he was he knew exactly when to strike. 'So I can confirm she can expect us at eight?' he asked humbly.

Holly felt awful now. She nodded quickly, blushing as she said, 'It's very kind of her and I do appreciate the gesture.'

He could afford to be generous now he'd got exactly what he wanted. Jacques smiled gently, his voice soothing as he said, 'I know that, Holly. It was just that I surprised you, *n'est-ce pas*? But this will give my mother pleasure; she will enjoy having another duckling to fuss over. She is longing for the day she is presented with her first grandchild, but to date my sisters seem to be in no hurry to oblige.'

And he clearly hadn't even considered the notion of settling down. Obviously he was having too good a time playing the field. The thought grated although she knew it shouldn't have.

'So we will go home and dress up, yes?' To her dismay Holly found her arm tucked through his in the next moment and then they were walking together along the dusty pavements.

Ridiculously she found she had forgotten how to put one foot in front of the other, the strange, prickly sensa-

tions running up and down her spine causing her almost
to stumble. She was overwhelmingly aware of the bulk of
him at her side, the feel of a hard male thigh and his
considerable height taking her breath away.

Momentary panic gave way to shaky pleasure as
Jacques continued to walk along without making any effort to pull her closer or touch her more intimately. Holly
wondered—with a faint touch of hysteria—what he would
say if she told him this was the first time she had strolled
with a man on a sunny summer's evening. Laugh his head
off, most likely. Or pin her with one of those lethal, laser-
type glances that he used so effectively in the business
world. She had seen him cut an adversary to pieces without saying a word.

David Kirby had been able to do that. Most of the time
he had been winsome and charming, using his clean-cut
good looks and warm, pleasant manner to maximum advantage, but she had seen him reduce Cassie to tears on
more than one occasion and without saying a word. He
had specialised in cold silences too, when one of them
had annoyed him in some way, demanding that the of-
fender grovel before he would communicate with them
again.

'Holly?'

As she lifted her eyes to Jacques's face she saw he was
staring down at her with a strangely tight expression, and
she realised he must have said something and she hadn't
heard a word.

'What is it? What's the matter?' He stopped, turning
her to face him with his hands on her shoulders, and she
wasn't to know the look on her face had appalled him.
'Is it meeting everyone tonight—?'

'No, no.' She interrupted him quickly, her face scarlet.

'Then what? You looked...' He couldn't find a word to describe what he had seen.

Holly continued to stare up at him, angry with herself that she had let her guard down and allowed thoughts of David Kirby to intrude even for a moment. She felt a strange warmth at his concern but at the same time she wanted to run a mile. 'I...I was just thinking of someone,' she said at last. 'Someone in the past.' She moved restlessly but he didn't take the hint and let go of her.

'A man?'

His voice was different somehow and she suddenly felt trapped. He had moved her against the wall of a building as they had stopped, and she was expecting to feel the distaste and panicky fright she always felt if a male got a little too close but it didn't come. Instead her agitation was more in response to the way her body was reacting to the smell and feel of his. She had never felt the powerful enchantment of desire before but she was feeling it now.

Mainly because she was so tied up with how she was feeling, she answered without considering her words, her voice shaky as she whispered, 'Yes, a man.'

'He hurt you.'

'Yes.'

'Is it over?'

'What?' Too late she realised where the conversation had led. He thought she'd been speaking about a romance she'd had; a lover.

'I said, is it over?' he repeated quietly. 'In your heart as well as every other way?'

'Yes, it's over.' Her stomach was doing cartwheels but she lifted her chin in the familiar gesture of defiance he had come to recognise as she added, 'And I really don't want to talk about it.'

Jacques expelled a silent breath. Mystery sat on this woman in illusive veils that appeared as soft and gentle as silk but in reality were cold, hard sheet metal. He stepped back a pace from her, his voice casual as he said, 'That is fine, Holly, but the offer of a shoulder is always available. I will not say that talking about a difficulty or a heartache always makes it better because I do not concede to the "trouble shared is a trouble halved" kind of thinking, but sometimes it helps to clear one's mind of dross. Now, when you meet my sisters you will find, unfortunately, that within ten minutes you will receive their life stories, which are singularly unremarkable...'

He continued talking along this line as she fell into step beside him again, his voice easy and relaxed and his manner reassuringly nonchalant, and by the time they reached the apartment block Holly was telling herself she had overreacted to what had been nothing more than friendly observation on Jacques's part. He wasn't interested in her past life one way or the other; he'd just been making conversation on a warm summer's night, that was all.

Holly showered the stickiness of a working day away before washing her hair and quickly blow-drying it into a smooth bob once she was alone in the sanctuary of her little apartment.

Jacques had spoken about dressing up so she assumed this was not a casual jeans and top evening, but she didn't want to look overdressed either. She decided on a pretty khaki-flowered wrap-over top and cream pencil skirt she'd bought the week before in a wonderful little shop near the Rue Mouffetard, one of the oldest street markets in Paris, teaming it with strappy cream sandals and a short-sleeved cashmere cardigan. She was back down in the lobby within twenty minutes but Jacques was already waiting for her, chatting idly to Pierre as he did so.

She was relieved to see from his attire of charcoal trousers and open-necked pale-blue silk shirt that she'd got the mix of smart-casual about right, and his eyes complimented her even before he said softly, 'Prompt as well as spectacularly lovely. You are quite a find, Mademoiselle Stanton.'

'Thank you,' she said lightly, before turning to Pierre and smiling warmly at the old man. 'It's a beautiful evening, Pierre.'

They left the building amid further pleasantries but on the drive to his parents' home Jacques said very little, which made Holly even more nervous, all her senses tuned in with unbearable sensitivity to the big, dark man at her side. She pretended an interest in the changing scene outside the Jaguar's windows as she mentally rehearsed several opening lines of conversation with Jacques's family, and when they stopped to buy the chocolate for his mother she was annoyed to find her hands were shaking slightly as she passed the money to the shop's proprietor.

When they arrived at the small stone house in a quiet cobbled street south of the Latin quarter there were children playing outside open doors, old couples sitting in wicker chairs on their doorsteps, enjoying the warmth of the dying sun, and a general air of tranquil benevolence in the heavy air.

Holly liked Jacques's parents immediately. Marc Querruel was tall, like his son, and Jacques had inherited his father's handsome, faintly autocratic features and thick head of hair, although the older man's was now white.

Camille, Jacques's mother, was small in contrast, with dark eyes and hair that only held the odd suggestion of silver, and her two daughters, Josephine and Barbe, had followed their mother's build. They were all attractive but not beautiful, their aquiline noses being too strong on female faces to qualify them for such a title, but the two girls, like their mother, were perfectly groomed and possessed of a happy self-confidence Holly found herself envying as the evening progressed.

The house itself was a jumble of whimsical, rustic antiques and traditional country colours which filled every room with faded elegance and decorative flair, and it was clear it was very much a family home. Holly loved it. The big, exposed beams; plainly painted white walls covered with pictures and mirrors; and the splashes of bright colour among the gentle vintage fabrics and abundance of plants and baskets of fresh and dried flowers were charming as well as homely.

They ate dinner sitting at an iron and scrollwork table in the secluded garden, which was a lush haven burgeoning with heady aromas from the rich foliage, and the full-bodied, fruity, deep red wine Jacques had brought perfectly complemented the delicious meal that seemed to last for ever.

Jacques was expansive and lazily amusing, and for the first time since Holly had known him she found herself daring to really relax and enjoy herself. His sisters were fun and at times a little shocking, although Holly got the impression the two girls liked to create a little consternation now and again, not least with their handsome brother. He was quite protective of them, Holly noted with a little pang in her heart region as she listened to the two young women teasing Jacques about their latest beaux. Even a little old-fashioned.

This last Barbe picked up on in answer to a comment from her brother regarding the number of young men

she'd seen recently. 'You are one to talk!' Barbe slanted
midnight-black eyes at her handsome sibling. 'Or are you
going to argue the typical male chauvinist approach? A
man can do whatever he likes and he is just a bit of a
rogue, whereas a woman who has a few partners is labelled a tart?'

'Barbe!' Camille cast a quick look at Holly as she said
drily, 'Gone are the days when I could pack them off to
bed for speaking out of turn at the dinner table.'

'It's all right.' Holly grinned at the unrepentant Barbe.
'And I agree, there's still some way to go before women
have full equality in certain areas.'

'There, you see? Holly agrees with me!' Barbe eyed
her scowling brother slyly. 'Men like you are the worst
sort of hypocrites, you know; one law for yourselves and
one for the female of the species. Don't you ever consider
the fact that all your women probably have fathers and
brothers who think about them the way you think about
me and Josephine?'

Jacques looked as if he was ready to explode but before
he could say a word they heard a voice calling from
within the house, and the next moment a couple of Marc
and Camille's age appeared at the open French windows
leading into the garden. By the time more chairs had been
found and the couple had joined them with a glass of wine
and a bowl of Camille's superb custard-cream flan, an
uneasy harmony had settled again, although from the mur-
derous glances Jacques continued to send his youngest
sister Holly suspected Barbe was not forgiven.

Just before the party came to a close at the end of the
evening, Barbe leant across to Holly and whispered in her
ear, 'Take no notice of what I said, Holly. I was only
trying to annoy Jacques earlier. You must be different. He
hasn't brought anyone else home before.'

'Oh, it's not like that, really.' Holly was horrified. 'I just work for him, that's all, and your mother heard I was a stranger in town and invited me for a meal.'

Barbe raised worldly eyebrows, her face saying volumes before she drawled, 'My mistake. Well, in that case, Josephine and I must take you out with us now and again, yes? Introduce you around.'

Holly smiled politely. Barbe and Josephine were good company and vivacious, and an evening spent with them would certainly be one to remember, but she had no intention of accepting Barbe's invitation. Before she could make this clear, however, Barbe had turned her attention to Jacques, who had just finished talking to the couple who had joined them earlier. Whatever his sister said in rapid French turned his handsome face dark and, after one clipped sentence in his mother tongue that caused Barbe to sit back in her seat with her mouth closed, Jacques rose to his feet.

'It is time for me and Holly to leave.' He drew Holly to her feet as he spoke, his mouth smiling and his voice pleasant, but Holly was aware of something simmering at the backs of the amber eyes and wondered what Barbe had said to him.

She found out shortly after the effusive goodbyes when Camille and Marc made it clear they expected to see her again soon. Jacques drove the car for a short distance without speaking before pulling off the road at the side of a small park, deserted and slumbering in the soft moonlight. 'Let's walk.'

'Walk?' It was a nervous squeak and Holly heard herself with hot mortification. 'I don't think—'

'Holly, relax.' Jacques captured her fluttering hand as he turned to her, looking deep into her eyes. Holly was suddenly taken with a peculiar notion that she was floating, that she was weightless, that the only real thing in all the world was the golden brightness of his eyes. 'I need to talk to you, to make a few things clear, that's all. OK?'

'OK.' It was a whisper but all she could manage. Something had changed in the last few minutes. The easy, lazily amusing manner had been replaced by something else, something she wasn't at all sure she could handle. But at least he hadn't asked her to come up to his apartment to see his etchings, she told herself with grim humour as she allowed Jacques to help her out of the car. Not that Jacques Querruel would have such a crass chat-up line, of course.

The park was little more than a small area of grass enclosed by mature trees, and couldn't have measured more than a few hundred yards, but there were a couple of wooden benches alongside the quietly tinkling fountain in the middle of it, and it was to one of these that Jacques drew her.

As they sat down he half turned to face her, one arm draped along the seat at the back of her and the other hand raising her chin so he could look into her eyes. Holly couldn't believe that she was here, that she had allowed him to coerce her into such a vulnerable position, and yet… She forced herself to reflect honestly. He hadn't had to use much persuasion, she admitted silently. She was twenty-five years old and she had never been kissed by a man, and since the first moment she had laid eyes on Jacques nearly three months ago she had wondered what it would be like to feel that hard, stern, sexy mouth on hers. And in a weird sort of way, despite all her fears and nervousness around him, it was a relief to know she could actually feel hotly attracted to a member of the opposite sex. Because she did. To Jacques Querruel she did.

He gave her a long, silent look. 'You might not like what I am about to say,' he said softly, surprising her.

She was trembling inside and praying it wouldn't become obvious to those devastatingly piercing eyes. 'Oh?'

'I told Barbe there is no way she and Josephine are going to introduce you to all the local young bloods,' he said very quietly. 'I told her that I like you. I like you very much.'

She was drowning in the amber light now, and as he took her face between his hands she shivered.

'Do you understand what I am saying, Holly?' he asked, still in the soft, gentle voice. 'I want you and I do not share what is mine.'

Too much was happening too fast, and yet it wasn't fast, not really. She had always known this would happen one day and now that it had she was amazed to find she was surprised he had waited so long before making a move. Oh, she was a mess, such a mess inside, she thought desperately. He had no idea...

'Do you like me, Holly?' he asked, watching the play of emotion in the large blue eyes staring up at him, eyes that were as clear and beautiful as the still blue lake back at his château, and just as unfathomable.

'It...it's not a question of liking.' She found her voice somehow but he wouldn't let go of her face when she tried to glance away.

'Yes, it is. I have been patient but this is not an attribute I embrace easily,' he admitted, his mouth twisting. 'My mother was fond of preaching *"Petit à petit l'oiseau fait son nid"* when I was growing up—little by little the bird builds his nest—but I see no merit in this.'

She tried to pull away again, forcing a harsher note into her voice as she said, 'You see, you want, you take? Is that it?' She had to break the intimacy; it was terrifying.

She had expected a denial but instead he nodded, his face moving closer, and then his lips were on hers. It was not a tentative or apologetic kiss but one of definite intent, his mouth closing over hers as though it had a perfect right to do so.

Holly's heart was thudding but there was none of the repugnance she had been frightened she might feel as imagination became reality; instead a sweet thrill of excitement and pleasure quivered down her spine, and her mouth responded like a bud opening under soft summer rain.

His arms were holding her firmly but not intimidatingly as his lips moved over hers, his experience very obvious as he encouraged her gently into more and more intimacy. Holly was enchanted, this first kiss as an adult everything she would have wished it to be. His lips were firm and warm and the delicious smell of him was all about her, his body hard and muscled as he moved her further into him.

For a few mesmerising moments Holly found herself in a strange world of sensuous delight, an alien place she had never visited before but which was full of wonder and sweet body stirrings that told her she was not an oddity, or frigid, or any of the other negative things she had been scared of. She was being kissed and it was wonderful, natural…

When finally Jacques raised his head Holly felt giddy and breathless, and his voice was low and unusually husky as he murmured, 'I knew how you would taste; I have always known. Like warm, sweet honey. You are very beautiful, *chérie,* and very kissable. Soft, tantalisingly soft; a sweet torment that could drive a man mad…'

He kissed her again, moving all over her face in burning little nuzzling caresses before his mouth moved to her throat, causing her to arch against him. 'Mmm,' he sighed softly. 'You smell good, you feel good.'

She had to stop this. She wasn't quite sure why—her brain had scrambled and was advising her that caution and inhibition were nasty words—but she knew she had to stop this. It couldn't lead anywhere; Jacques was the original wolf and he wasn't even in sheep's clothing.

'I've wanted to do this—hold you, kiss you—since we met, do you know that, *petite*? I want to undress you, to kiss you until you melt like wax in my arms, to take you to a place where no other lover has taken you before—'

His words hit her like a physical blow and she reacted in much the same way; jerking away from him with enough force to almost send herself flying off the edge of the bench if Jacques hadn't caught her first.

She shrugged off his hands, rising to her feet as she said shakily, 'I want to go now. I want to go back.'

'What is it?' He had risen with her, his handsome face intent. 'What is the matter?'

Holly couldn't move, couldn't even avert her gaze from his. She felt she was incapable of making a sound.

'Is it this man you knew before? This man who hurt you so badly? Tell me about him. What sort of man was he?'

'What?' She stared at him as though he was mad.

'You say you have forgotten him but I do not think so,' Jacques said softly. 'Do you still love him? Is that it?'

The shock and revulsion on her face told him he was on the wrong track and he mentally cursed himself, before saying quietly, 'What is it, Holly? What went wrong?'

How could she tell him? How could she tell anyone? She had tried once and it had been horrific. He might be disgusted. He would think that somehow, in some way, she had encouraged what had happened. She had thought that for years, so why wouldn't he? If she didn't tell him he couldn't despise her. 'I want to go.'

'He has damaged you? This man?' He wasn't letting up and she felt a sense of panic that was indescribable. 'Was he violent, is that it? Abusive?' he asked gently, very gently.

She swallowed hard, trying to keep a check on her emotions whilst deciding what do say. But her brain was dead. She felt stupid, numb. She forced herself to say, 'It was a long time ago and I don't want to talk about it.'

'That is a mistake.'

'How on earth would you know?' The words had come from the pit of her stomach and even to her own ears they sounded harsh and guttural.

She had seen the amber eyes widen and knew how she must have registered on his senses, but he stood before her without saying anything more, observing her in a silence that was more oppressive than any ranting and raving. 'Look, it's not what you think.'

'How do you know what I think, Holly?' he asked very softly.

She didn't. It was true, she didn't. Sudden anger leaped up inside her. She was nothing to him in the overall run of things. He was a man who was used to clicking his fingers and having a dozen women fighting over the chance to be in his bed; she'd heard enough gossip to know that at least some of it must be based on fact. She hadn't run true to form—she had been a little different from the rest of them. That was what his overtures tonight were based on. The hunting instinct. Cavemen mentality. Well, he could go and… 'I want to go back. Do I have to walk home or are you taking me in the car?' she asked with icy intent.

Jacques said nothing for a full ten seconds and the silence was so loud it hurt her eardrums. Then he drew back a fraction, his handsome face settling in rigid lines as he said quietly, 'Of course I will take you home, Holly.' He smiled thinly. 'Contrary to what you might believe, I am a civilised human being.'

She stared at him, utterly lost for words for a moment or two before she managed to say, 'I know that.' And she did, at heart. The problem here wasn't his. It was hers. And didn't she know it? All he had done was kiss her. He hadn't tried to force her, he hadn't been aggressive— quite the contrary. And she had reacted as though he'd tried to— What? Rape her?

Suddenly the past was so real she could taste it—could feel David's strong, cruel hands and his wet, hot mouth. She felt nauseous, her stomach rebelling against her thoughts. 'I'm…I'm sorry.' She forced herself to speak although in reality she wanted to scream and wail and shout. 'It's just that…I'm not ready for…'

She didn't know what she was trying to say herself, so it was all the more surprising when his whole countenance changed, and his voice was even but not harsh or unkind when he said, 'Let's forget it, yes?' His eyes held hers, very steady, very calm. 'We are friends, work colleagues. Nothing complicated, nothing heavy. This is acceptable?'

It would have been acceptable but for the fact that his very presence charged the air with painful sensitivity and a sensuality that was mind-blowing. She looked at him silently, her heart contracting. She should never have come to Paris. Never have worked for him. Never had accepted the invitation to his parents' home… 'Yes, that is acceptable,' she said tonelessly. 'That is quite acceptable.'

CHAPTER SIX

JULY departed in a blaze of hot sunshine but August was ushered in on the crest of an even stickier month. France was in the grip of a heatwave, although with air-conditioning at the offices and in her apartment Holly found she could enjoy the unusually hot weather quite comfortably.

She had been incredibly embarrassed and nervous the first morning after the visit to Jacques's parents' home when she'd gone to work, but in the event Jacques had been so impersonally friendly and concentrated on the job in hand that she had relaxed almost immediately. It had helped that he had left within hours to return to the States, the situation he had been dealing with there and which he had thought resolved having taken a sudden nosedive which necessitated his urgent attention.

That had been two weeks ago now, and—due wholly to the heartsearching the aftermath of that evening had produced—Holly had begun to make an effort to integrate herself into the lives of her colleagues. She had accepted one or two invitations to their homes for dinner, gone out to lunch twice with Chantal, Jacques's secretary, and Marianne, one of the production team, and had numerous cups of coffee and croissants or pastries in the sidewalk cafés both before and after work with this person or that.

Holly had found that, besides the enormous world of culture and entertainment in Paris, the city seemed to be preoccupied with food. Wherever one was, a sidewalk café wouldn't be far away, and every other shop appeared

105

to be filled with some kind of delicacy—pastries, cheese, pâtés, sausages and wine. The average Frenchman's reasoning was simple. Like the other senses, taste should be taken seriously. Art for the eyes, music for the ears and fine food for the palate.

However, in all of the socialising, Holly was always thinking about one particular Frenchman who wasn't at all average. She was longing to see Jacques again and absolutely dreading it, and since he had been gone on the second trip to the States she had found he haunted her dreams and occupied the daylight hours in a way that was positively galling.

She didn't *want* to think about him, or about the aggressive sexuality that was both exciting and frightening. Most of all she didn't want to think about the kisses they had shared when he had shown himself to be both hypnotisingly seductive and sensitive.

It wasn't until after she had had time to think about what had happened quietly and rationally that she'd realised just how much restraint Jacques had employed. He hadn't tried to rush her or ask for more than she'd been prepared to give, and this from a man who was vastly sexually experienced and used to full relationships in every sense of the word. And after she had rejected his advances he hadn't seemed too put out or disappointed. But then, with all his other fish to fry perhaps he hadn't cared much one way or the other?

Holly frowned to herself. She couldn't figure him out and he confused her. He had said he wanted to make love to her—she hadn't imagined that—and yet he seemed able to turn his feelings off and on at will. She had worked closely with him as well as the rest of the team since arriving in France, had actually met his family, had been kissed and caressed by him, and yet she didn't have a clue what made him tick. But he fascinated her.

She frowned harder. It was an unwelcome truth, but she was too honest with herself to deny it. And if his kisses had been the most mind-blowing experience of her life, what would it be like if he *really* started to make love to her?

She shivered in spite of the warm, pleasant air, stretching her slim legs in front of her and settling herself back in the comfortably cushioned chair on the balcony even as she told herself she must start thinking about her evening meal.

She spent more time on the balcony than she did in the rest of the flat: eating her meals out there alfresco, reading, dozing in the sunshine at the weekends, or just watching the sun set in glorious rivers of myriad reds and golds until the sky turned to soft indigo and a violet dusk replaced the blazing displays.

She had seen small birds fluttering to drink from the tiny water feature in one corner of the balcony in the mornings, and since she'd bought some seed from a pet shop on her way home one evening several bright-eyed and cheeky little sparrows were now regular visitors.

Somehow, and Holly wasn't quite sure exactly when it had happened, this tiny French apartment in the middle of Paris felt more like home than her bedsit in England. Although she still missed Mrs Gibson and Mr Bateman, of course, she qualified quickly.

Thoughts of her friends reminded Holly she had intended to phone Lucy and James earlier. It had been a couple of weeks since she'd spoken to them last and she liked to keep up to date with all the latest adventures of her god-daughter. Melanie Anne was now a mobile nine-month-old, and the fact that the child could only hotch about on her well-padded behind didn't mean she wasn't into everything, Lucy had assured her wryly.

Holly actually had her hand on the telephone when the front doorbell rang. She knew who was outside immediately. If it had been anyone other than Jacques Pierre would have informed her first from his post in the lobby, although in all the time she had been in Paris Jacques had only visited her apartment twice, not counting the first day she'd arrived in France. Both occasions had been relating to a matter of work. Even when he stayed in the penthouse at the top of the building—which wasn't often, as usually he drove home to the château he had mentioned—he had made no effort to invite her up for coffee or a meal. Not that she'd expected him to, of course, she qualified hastily. Not at all.

The doorbell rang again, an authoritative ring that demanded attention. With her heart thudding Holly walked to the front door, refusing to admit that the churning in her stomach consisted of excited anticipation more than anything else.

'Bonjour, chérie.' He had moved away from the door and was leaning against the wall of the corridor when she opened it, his stance easy and nonchalant and his arms folded across his chest. He looked wonderful, and as always the amber eyes drew hers like magnets. He wasn't smiling.

'Hello, Jacques.' She was rather pleased at how even her voice sounded. 'I didn't know you were back.' *Keep it light and easy, as though you haven't been thinking of him every minute of the night and day.*

'Just got in.'

She nodded carefully. 'Did you manage to get everything sorted in the end?'

'Eventually.' He levered himself off the wall, stretching

as he did so, and she suddenly thought how tired he looked. It caused a funny little pang which panicked her more than any sexual desire could have done. 'Till the next crisis, of course.'

He smiled then, a slow smile that warmed his face, his eyes. Holly swallowed before forcing a smile in return.

'Have dinner with me tonight?'

'Tonight?' she said, taken aback more than a little, especially after the result of their last dinner date. 'I don't think that's a good idea,' she said at last. 'I thought we'd decided we'd just be friends? I work for you…' Her voice trailed away. His eyes were holding hers captive and she couldn't remember what she was going to say next.

'Friends don't eat together?' he asked gravely.

'Of course.' The exasperation that was getting to be a familiar feeling when she was around him made itself felt. 'I didn't mean that. It's just that—'

'You've shared a meal with quite a few people now; why not me?' he said evenly.

She stared at him. 'Have you been checking up on me whilst you've been away?'

'It is a crime to enquire if my newest employee is being made to feel welcome?' he asked silkily.

Holly didn't feel she could go down that road without Jacques winning hands down. She tried another tack. 'I *have* shared a meal with you.'

'This is so.' He moved, taking a step or two until he was right in front of her, so close she could feel the warmth and delicious smell of him. 'So share another, yes? It would please me.' Dark eyebrows rose in a dry amusement that told her she was being absolutely ridiculous.

How did this man always make her feel as though she

was behaving like a child? Holly hesitated. 'Thank you,' she said primly. 'Dinner would be very nice.'

'That is better,' he said approvingly, eyes laughing.

'I'll just change.' She gestured at the thin sleeveless top and jeans she'd changed into after showering when she'd arrived home.

'No need.' He smiled winningly. 'I thought we would drive out to the château; I've been meaning to show you my home for some time now.'

Right. She gave him a long, silent look before she said, 'As a friend, yes?'

He had been watching her with a kind of amused speculation and now he bent down, swiftly depositing a warm kiss on her lips before he said, 'Labels bore me, *petite*. Now, lock your door and let us have no more of this nonsense.'

The moon, like a huge opalescent pearl, was just beginning to cast its gentle light into the soft, scented dusk as Holly and Jacques strolled down towards the lake.

The meal Jacques's housekeeper, Monique, had prepared and served had been delicious, and the château itself was magnificent, a fairy-tale castle kind of place with turrets covered with green and red ivy and balconies ablaze with pots of flowers. It wasn't huge as châteaux went, Jacques had assured her on her tour of his home. Some of the old country houses numbered thirty bedrooms and umpteen reception rooms, which made his six bedrooms and four reception rooms modest in comparison, but the grounds were second to none.

Holly wholly agreed with him. The lawns were emerald-green expanses dotted with leafy mature trees that must provide welcome shade in the heat of the day, but it was the lake that was the real taste of heaven on earth. Delicate water lilies bloomed galore, their honeyed, waxy perfume heavy in the still air, and frail and beautiful dragonflies were skimming the surface of the mother-of-pearl water in which wild swans, crested grebes and fat ducks reposed. Tufts of forget-me-nots and other wild flowers dotted the boundary, and beyond the lake and still on Jacques's property a thick wood provided sanctuary to a host of wildlife.

There was a timeless quality to the air, along with the outlines of a row of ash trees silhouetted against the shimmering water, which appeared as transparent as porcelain.

'It's beautiful…' Holly breathed the words, glancing up at Jacques as she spoke.

His eyes were waiting for her, and as he drew her down on a gnarled wooden bench positioned under one of the trees the look on his face made her shiver with anticipation. 'So are you…' It was soft, throaty. One finger touched her mouth, tracing the outline of her lips before moving down to her chin and slowly, very slowly, trailing down her throat and to the soft swell of her breasts.

Her heart thudding, Holly watched him with big eyes, aware she was beginning to tremble but unable to do anything about it. An odd sensation had taken hold of her, a mingling of fear and exhilaration and excitement, and although he wasn't holding her or restraining her in any way she felt utterly unable to move.

'Holly. Sweet, sweet Holly…' It was half-sigh, half-whisper, and as he pulled her close to his hard, lean body his mouth came down on hers with an urgent passion that should have panicked her. But it didn't.

Her arms went round him and she responded to the kiss because now he was here, now he was back, she realised just how much she had missed him. The last days had been a period of limbo, of waiting, and much as she didn't want to acknowledge it the truth was inescapable. She liked Jacques; she liked him very much. Her brain wouldn't accept more than that.

His hands were moving over her soft, rounded curves, creating a tender urgency which filled her with unfamiliar hunger. His kiss became more passionate and the sensuous pleasure Holly was feeling was so alien, so captivating that her reserve was burnt up in the heat of it. She was hotly aware of the muscled strength of his male body but amazingly—wonderfully—it didn't fill her with panic or revulsion, just an exhilarating awareness of her own femininity. *She was alive.* She felt the pounding of her blood from the top of her head to the tips of her toes, a hot, surging flow which made her conscious of every part of her body.

'Holly?' His voice was like warm velvet, his accent so seductive it made her shiver. 'Do you mind me holding you like this, touching you?'

Did she? He had raised his head, his eyes burning on her face, and after a long moment when she struggled to find words and failed she merely shook her head.

'I want you, but you know that.'

In spite of the flow of pleasure she stiffened, and he was immediately aware of it.

'I'm not going to apologise for wanting you, Holly. I want you in my arms, in my bed, but only when you want it too. In your head and your heart as well as your body. Do you understand what I am saying?'

She drew away from him just the slightest bit. 'Full co-operation in the seduction game?' she said lightly, in spite of her racing heart.

'If you want to put it like that.' He still had his arms round her and she got the feeling he wouldn't let her move away any further if she tried. Perversely she did try and she was right. Her soft mouth tightened.

'Surely you have enough female company without bothering with me?' This time the lightness didn't come off and she was mortifyingly aware of it.

'Ah, I see.'

Quite what he saw she wasn't sure, but when he twisted her round suddenly and she ended up on his knee she gave a squeak of protest before becoming very still. He was looking at her in a way she hadn't seen before, and somewhere deep inside her trepidation and cold fear had her transfixed. David Kirby had held her like this, on his knee, so many times. And even before that awful, cataclysmic night, when so many nervous feelings and awkward, half-formed fears had come together in one devastating whole, she'd known she didn't like it. David had made her feel sick and frightened, panicky without knowing why. How did she feel now?

She wasn't quite sure but she did know she didn't feel afraid. As she acknowledged the truth she felt weak with relief, the trepidation and fear melting away.

'I don't want female company plural, Holly.' She was so close she could see individual eyelashes and the beginnings of black stubble on his square chin, and she had to restrain herself from reaching out and caressing his face. 'I only want you,' he added on a low note.

He wouldn't if he knew what she was really like. All the old insecurities rose up in a flood which so engulfed her she couldn't speak for a moment or two. And then she said, her voice lower than his, 'You don't know me, Jacques. Not really. You just see what you want to see. The outside.'

He was getting closer. Jacques bit down on the frustration and spoke quietly when he said, 'The outside looks pretty good to me but you're wrong, *petite*. I have known you for months now and I am a good judge of human character. I have to be to survive. It is what has brought me all I own.'

'Maybe.' She moved quickly, slipping away from him before she gave in to the impulse to let him kiss her again. This was crazy, stupid. What on earth was she doing? She couldn't begin an affair with Jacques Querruel. He was flirting with her and whatever he said this was just a game to him. She would be one of many such brief liaisons, and he would expect her to abide by the rules, but unlike his other women she didn't even know what the rules were!

'No, not maybe. Fact.' The amber eyes were regarding her intensely. 'You know, sooner or later you will have to take the risk of trusting someone again, however badly this man behaved.'

'Why?' She faced him defiantly. 'Why should I?'

'Because if you do not he will have won.'

'You don't understand,' she said tonelessly.

'Try me.'

She could feel her heart beating in her throat and it was the oddest feeling. She tore her eyes away from him, glancing out over the tranquil water and into the shadows beyond before she lifted her eyes to the night sky, gathering her courage. 'No.'

She would never humiliate herself by trying to explain what had happened. She had tried that once and she could remember the horror and disgust on Cassie's face as though it were yesterday. And when she had tried a tentative approach to one of the social workers involved in finding her a new foster home the woman had made it clear she thought Holly was imagining things. Just thinking about it now, even after all these years, made her want to cringe.

'You are thinking about him now, aren't you?' he accused roughly. 'Did you finish it or did he?'

For an awful moment she thought she was going to laugh a laugh born of hysteria, but she caught at her spiralling emotions. He had no idea. No idea at all. But then, how could he? 'I told you, you don't understand,' she managed fairly levelly.

There was silence for some moments, the only sound coming from a sudden squawking across the water as two ducks had a brief squabble about who was sleeping where. A flapping of wings and a skid across the water from one aggrieved party settled the matter and all was quiet again.

'Come here, Holly,' he said, and there was a huskiness to his voice that brought her eyes snapping to his face.

She knew she should go back to the lights of the château, to Monique bustling about and normality, but instead she found herself moving towards him. He pulled her into his arms and took her mouth hungrily, and this time there was no restraint. And she kissed him back just as fiercely, yearning springing up with such power it frightened her. Something was happening and she didn't understand it. He only had to touch her and she forgot all the reasons a relationship between them wouldn't work. She didn't know herself any more, not when she was around this man.

He kissed her for a long time down by the tranquil silver water, fiercely, hungrily, and then just as gently and tenderly, as though she was something very fragile and delicate that might break. His body was hard and strong against hers and spoke eloquently of his need of her, but although their caresses became more intimate and their kisses more passionate he didn't follow through on their lovemaking as Holly had half expected him to.

When he at last drew away slightly his breathing was ragged and his voice wasn't quite steady as he said, with wry self-derision, 'One more kiss and I shall—how do you say—blot the copybook? I am not used to such self-restraint when making love to a woman.'

She had felt the fine tremors across his muscled back as she had clung to him and knew he was making light of it because it was the only way he could deal with it, and now she said, striving for the same dry lightness, 'You have been spoiled, no doubt. Dozens of adoring women only too willing to become your slave? Not always getting exactly what you want is good for you.'

'You are good for me,' he said softly, and there wasn't a trace of amusement in his voice.

She stared at him, the air charged with subtle, painful awareness, and felt something raw grip her. If only he hadn't been so experienced, so handsome, so wealthy, so magnetic. Why couldn't he have been an ordinary man? Jacques had had lots of women, women who would have known exactly how to please him in bed and hold his interest. How could she compete with that? She was such a mess inside, she knew it, and ironically meeting him had made her face that she still had big issues to come to terms with.

Sexually she was still as innocent as the eight-year-old girl she had been when David had tried to rape her; she knew nothing about love and life and men. Not a thing. She had cut herself off from any possibility of romantic involvement with the opposite sex to such an extent she didn't know where to start. All the normal stages that adolescent girls and boys went through had completely passed her by—boyfriends at school, kissing behind the bike sheds, fumbling caresses and petting in front of the TV when the family were out, or heated embraces in the back seat of a car.

She wasn't aware her face had been a reflection of her troubled thoughts, so when Jacques suddenly pulled her hand through the crook of his arm, planting a swift but possessive kiss on her half-open lips before saying easily, 'Let's walk a while,' she was surprised at his change of manner. 'I'll show you the swan's nest and the cygnets, although they are nearly as big as *maman* now,' he continued as she fell into step beside him, 'and the home of the owl who also had a little one to feed until quite recently, when he decided he was big enough to pack his bags and cut the apron strings.'

Holly looked at him in surprise. He was a hard, ruthless businessman, and even his friends would have had to call him cynical and obdurate. She hadn't expected an interest in something like an owl's fledgling.

'What is it?' He had noticed her expression.

'Nothing.'

He stopped, moving her against the slim trunk of an ash tree. 'What is it?' he repeated softly.

'Nothing really,' she said uncomfortably. 'I just hadn't got you down as a wildlife enthusiast, that's all.'

'No?' He smiled, taking the opportunity to kiss her again before they walked on. 'What have you got me down as, Holly?' he asked very quietly after a moment or two. 'Or perhaps it would be best—for my already battered and bruised ego, that is—if you did not answer this truthfully?'

She glanced at him warily. There had been the usual dry mockery in his dark, smoky voice but just a touch of something else that had a distinct edge to it.

He caught the look and surprised her for the umpteenth

time that night by laughing out loud, a laugh of genuine amusement. 'You are priceless. You know this?' he murmured when he had control of himself again. 'As my father often says to my mother, God must have sent you to keep me humble.'

'Keep you humble?' The comparison with his parents had caused a dart of pleasure and it was against this weakness she said primly, 'Humble is not a word I would readily use when referring to you.'

He swept her against him, kissing her until she was breathless and glowing, but when they resumed their walk Jacques began to talk and suddenly she was hearing some of the history which had made him into the man he was. Bitter memories mixed with happy ones—his disadvantaged childhood and the cruelty—intentional and unintentional—a prosperous society could inflict; his father's serious accident when Jacques was a small baby, which had financially crippled the family; his mother's fortitude and quiet bravery…

'My father worked for a furniture firm and a heavy oak dresser fell on him one day and crushed both his legs. My father trusted them when they said they would make it right, but instead they paid people to lie and my father never got a penny in compensation,' Jacques said quietly. 'He had no money to fight them in the courts and we were forced to leave our home and move to a squalid tenement. My mother worked all hours, as a cleaner, a waitress, whatever she could get.'

'But he walks all right now?'

Jacques shrugged. 'He suffers a great deal of pain all the time but he has learnt to hide it. He also has a weak heart, caused, my mother is sure, by the injuries he sustained. Each day he is with her she looks upon as a gift. He is not a well man.'

'I'm so sorry, Jacques.' She pictured the tall, aristocratic man with the shock of prematurely white hair and his small black-eyed wife who clearly adored her handsome husband, and felt heart sorry.

'The first thing I did when I made my money was to break the firm my father had worked for,' Jacques said evenly. 'They were an old family business dating back a century and were very proud. They cheated my father out of greed and selfishness and it cost them their livelihood and all they held dear, including their reputation. I was not sorry about this and have never regretted it.'

No, she could believe that. You would cross this man at great cost to your own well-being.

'I learnt very early in life that society despises the weak and helpless and only respects power and influence.' Jacques turned his head, the amber eyes sending their searching light on to her face. 'I am shocking you?' he asked quietly.

'No.' She paused. 'But I don't think it is as cut and dried as that.' And it was only as she said the words that she realised that a great, solid ball of bitterness which had been lodged in her chest for years was gone. 'There are good people in all walks of society who try to right wrongs and stand for what is true, but I agree it's a battle. And innocents do get hurt. The manipulators, the cold, conscienceless individuals have a lever the moral don't. But you can't come down to their level in the fight.'

'I agree.' They looked at each other for a second before he smiled coldly. 'I fought them fair and square without breaking the law, although at times I admit I was tempted to take a short cut. But I had the element of pride on my side, you see. Their pride. How could the son of a menial, a menial they had dispatched with less consideration they would show to a pet dog, win through? Impossible. So they thought.'

'You hate them.'

It was a statement but he replied to it nevertheless. 'I did once, deeply and passionately.' His dim, hard profile was thoughtful. 'But not now. Once the power and wealth that was holding them together was gone the family fragmented, fighting amongst themselves for mere morsels. It was not pretty. My family is still together and stronger than ever.' Jacques gave a faint little smile that held no amusement. 'To hate what you have conquered is a waste of time and energy, *n'est-ce pas*? Almost as futile as fighting against the power of love.'

Holly's throat was locked and she couldn't utter a word for a full thirty seconds. How could she have been so blind? She asked herself wretchedly as they walked on. *She loved him.* And he was right—it *was* futile to fight against the power of love, but how could she have recognised that emotion for what it was before tonight? Before fate had pointed it out so cruelly? She hadn't meant for it to happen. A man like Jacques Querruel was not for her. She couldn't be more different from the sort of woman he dallied with.

She was a novelty at present. As they walked on amidst the wild flowers and sweet-smelling wild mint, Holly forced herself to face facts. She hadn't fallen into his arms at the first glance like everyone else. She'd been reserved, distant, and it had attracted the hunter that lurked under the psyche of every red-blooded male.

'Stay the night with me?' His voice was soft, a murmur. There was a significant little silence before his voice came again, saying, 'It doesn't have to be anything you don't want it to be. I promise this.'

She took a deep breath. 'Is that the line you give every

female you bring here?' she asked with what she hoped sounded like light amusement.

Jacques said nothing, and when the silence became screaming she forced herself to look at him. His eyes were tight on her face and they were both angry and searching. 'That is not you,' he said grimly. 'Why are you pretending to be something you are not? I thought we had got past the games tonight. For weeks you have hidden behind the glib repartee and I have had enough of it.'

'I've obviously been annoying you,' she shot back tightly. 'I think it would be better if I went home now.'

'Is that your answer to everything? To run away?'

'How *dare* you?' She was so furious she could have hit him and it showed in the stormy blue of her eyes. 'I have never run away from anything in my life, I'll have you know, in spite of having plenty of reason to.'

'Prove it. Stay here tonight,' he said swiftly. 'Your own room if you insist.'

'No.' She glared at him, burning spots of colour in her cheeks.

'Why not?' His voice was low, all anger gone. 'Why not, Holly?'

'I don't want to.' She straightened her shoulders defiantly.

'Liar.' He had the audacity to smile at her before he turned, pointing to a high tree lit by moonlight as he said, 'Up there, listen. The owl. Can you hear it?'

She said something very rude about the owl which shocked them both and sent Holly scarlet with angry embarrassment.

Jacques's eyes narrowed and he gave her a long look. 'I'll make it easy for you, OK?' he said quietly. 'You are staying the night. End of story, *n'est-ce pas*? It is a thirty-mile walk back to the city and not one to be attempted in the dark.'

'I don't believe I'm hearing this!' she snapped.

'I do not believe I am saying it,' he countered wryly. 'It is the first time I have had to employ such methods to secure a lady's company.' Dark eyebrows rose in cynical self-mockery.

'I don't doubt it.' It was scathing. 'Normally they are queuing up, I suppose!'

'Lines of them.' He nodded pleasantly.

'There's a name for men like you.'

'Several,' he agreed cheerfully. 'Charming, irresistible, debonair… Shall I go on?'

He grinned at her as he studied her hot face, and in spite of herself a warmth spread through her that was nothing at all to do with anger.

'It is an old cliché and I hesitate to use it, but you are lovely when you are angry,' he said with outrageous satisfaction.

'You're right, it *is* an old cliché,' she said sarcastically, refusing to let herself be sweet-talked round. He was impossible. Absolutely impossible. 'And I can't stay here. I have nothing with me and I can hardly go to the office in what I'm wearing tonight.'

'I wouldn't mind and I *am* the boss.' And then his voice changed, the amusement dying as he said very softly, 'Can't you tell me about it, Holly? I've been around; I am no callow youth to be shocked by anything you say. And I am asking because I care about you.'

From feeling so angry she could cheerfully have throttled him Holly was now fighting back the tears. He looked tough and fiercely male and yet very tender at the same time, and she couldn't cope with what it did to her bruised emotions. She swallowed, determined not to break down.

For the first time in her life she was longing to be in a man's arms and have him take care of her, accept her for exactly what she was and love her in spite of it. It was scary.

Her legs were trembling and she knew the shakiness came across in her voice when she said, 'I would if I could but…I'm not that sort of person.' She would lose all her hard-won self-respect, her sense of self if she told him; she knew she would. He would be disgusted, he'd think about her differently; she knew it. At best he would feel sorry for her the way people did for a victim, and at worst he might wonder if she had done something to provoke David to act the way he had—encouraged him even. People did think like that sometimes. She had experienced it first-hand.

Whatever way it went, he certainly wouldn't view her the same anyway. A woman of twenty-five who had never had a lover, even a relationship? He would think she was an oddity, a freak, just as the social workers and all the people who had dealt with her in her youth had.

She could remember the first foster mother she'd had after leaving the Kirbys talking to the social worker when they'd thought she was out playing. 'I have to say we haven't seen any signs of the aggression the other family reported,' the woman had said in a low voice, 'but she's an odd child, isn't she? Uncommunicative and a little…worrying. Has she seen a psychiatrist? No? Well, it might be an idea. After everything that went on before she came to us one can't be too careful with other children in the family.'

'Holly?' Jacques tilted her chin so her eyes lifted to his dark face. 'You can't shut me out forever. I will not let you. I thought at first you did not like me, that there was no hope in us being anything other than working colleagues, but I do not think that now. I have held you in my arms, I have kissed you, felt you tremble against me. Your body tells me what you will not admit.'

'I...I don't dislike you, of course I don't,' she whispered, 'but...' Her voice had a tell-tale tremor in it and she paused, trying to gain control before she said anything more.

But then she knew he had detected the wobble in her voice when he said, very softly, 'Always a but and always this battle inside you.' He drew her against him so her face was buried in the warmth of his chest, one hand stroking the raw silk of her hair as they stood quietly there, all words spent.

She wanted to cry, more than anything she wanted to cry, but she knew if she once started she wouldn't be able to stop. From when she had first left Kate and Angus West and the family she had grown up thinking was hers in everything that mattered, Holly had felt she was on her own. She had to face and overcome her problems herself, she'd known that. No one was going to help her if she didn't help herself—the affair with David Kirby had emphasised that only too clearly. She had had to quickly become self-sufficient and independent where it mattered, in her head, or sink. But she wasn't spineless or a wimp, she'd discovered, and she didn't intend to sink. Never. She wouldn't give them—the David and Cassie Kirbys of the world—that satisfaction.

But sometimes, like now, she felt so very weary and drained of resources, so tired of appearing someone quite different from the Holly she knew lived inside her. She gave a deep, helpless sigh and then straightened, drawing away from him as she said quietly, 'Please take me home, Jacques.'

'No.' It wasn't unkind, just very definite. And as her

eyes widened he continued, 'You are staying. Separate room, but you're staying, OK? In the morning we will eat breakfast together and then I will take you to the apartment so you can change your clothes before we go in to work.'

It all sounded too cosy. She forced a resentment she didn't feel into her voice as she said, 'We are not at work right now and to be honest I resent you giving me orders. I'll do and go where I want, and tonight I want to go home.'

He smiled, but the amber eyes were curiously opaque in the patch of moonlight slanting on his face and the cat-like orbs were fixed on her in a way that dried out her mouth and made her heart beat faster. In contrast, his voice was quiet and even pleasant when he said, 'Nice try but wrong approach, Holly. I do not take orders either. Now, if you had tried the defenceless feminine approach—all forlorn vulnerability and perhaps even a tear or two…'

She stiffened, his tone instantly dispelling any lingering weakness his tenderness had produced. 'I'm not into "trying" anything,' she bit out tightly.

'No, you are not, are you?' His tone was thoughtful. 'Which makes you unusual in my experience of the female of the species. I might even say unique.'

'I don't particularly care *what* you would say.' She was angry, not least because of the entirely unacceptable feeling of loss now that his arms were not holding her close.

'I hope that is not true.' His voice held the edge of irony. 'But I rather suspect it might be. Whatever…' He took her arm in a completely impersonal grip which was more insulting than any harsh words. 'You are staying at the château tonight so at least do me the courtesy of pretending it is not a fate worse than death?'

She glared at him, refusing to be drawn.

'And, whilst we are on the subject, I do not intend that tonight should be the last time you grace my home. All right? Just so you know, *petite*.'

'Jacques—'

'No, not another word.' His voice was rough and suddenly she found she was wary of pushing him any further. 'The trial period is over, *mademoiselle*. It is decision time. I would like you to stay in Paris and continue in your position at Querruel International. What is your verdict on this?'

'Verdict?' She forced a smile. 'You make it sound like a life-or-death decision.' She was annoyed to find her voice shook slightly and hoped he hadn't noticed.

Jacques looked at her without saying a word, and eventually—after a full thirty seconds had ticked by without him responding—she said, 'I…I enjoy the work and I would like to stay, if you are offering me the job, that is?'

'Yes, Holly. I am offering you the job,' he said softly.

CHAPTER SEVEN

HOLLY catnapped the night away in the sumptuous guest bedroom, which was a vision of pale angelica and warm ochre, with walls painted the colour of summer leaves. Every creak, every groan the beautiful old house gave brought her wide awake and looking towards the heavy oak door, but the handle didn't turn and the tall dark Adonis of her troubled dreams did not materialise.

At five o'clock she gave up all thoughts of further tossing and turning and had a shower, standing for long minutes under the warm, silky flow of water in the luxurious *en suite* as she contemplated how on earth she had come to find herself in her present position.

But it was him, Jacques Querruel. She dug her fingers into her scalp as she washed her hair, massaging her skin with unnecessary vigour. He swept everything and everyone before him like some great bulldozer, she told herself aggressively. He didn't hear anything he didn't want to hear or take notice of anyone's desires but his own.

Desires... The word curled round her consciousness until she turned the shower on to icy cold to dispel the heat it had produced.

She wanted to be angry with him. She *needed* to be angry with him; it was the only way she could keep her love for him at bay. She groaned, lifting her face to the icy flow. She was mad, crazy, to fall for a man like Jacques. He would eat her up and spit her out and go on his way quite happily. Of course he would. She would disappoint him in bed; she would disappoint him in every way. She just couldn't do any of this.

She was shivering convulsively by the time she left the bathroom wrapped in a big, fluffy bathrobe which had been lying across the bed the night before. It smelt wonderful, lemony fresh and expensive. As no doubt it was. Every brick, every square inch of the place reeked of wealth and power.

It was too early to get dressed and so she lay down on the bed again, still in the robe, fanning her damp hair out behind her on the pillow to dry.

It would be all right. It would. Sooner or later he would tire of his temporary interest in her and start to consider the entrance of the next female into his life and, no doubt, his bed. A woman who would be perfectly capable of meeting him on his own terms, sexually, mentally and emotionally. Who would act as his hostess if so required, understand any business worries, talk intelligently about almost any subject under the sun and behave like a lady in public and a whore in the bedroom. Jacques's normal type—if office gossip was anything to go by. She had seen pictures of one or two of his old flames in magazines which his fan club at the office had showed her, and without exception the women had been beautiful, intelligent, accomplished and socially élite. Sickeningly so.

One, a ravishingly lovely redhead, had been the executive managing director of her own company, and the other, an equally gorgeous blonde, had been a top model. Both formidably powerful women with brains to match. Of course. *Of course.*

She twisted on the silk coverlet, putting her hands over her ears as though the action would shut out her thoughts. She had to stop this. It was self-destructive and stupid, and she had never been either of those things until she had met Jacques.

She hadn't been aware of drifting off to sleep, so when she found herself surfacing from a thick, half-remembered dream and felt the firm, warm mouth over hers it took a second or two to come awake. And then her eyes opened and she was looking into his. They were very clear and bright, the colour of sunlight, and the expression in them caused her heart to stop for a second before it rushed on like an express train.

'Good morning, *petite*.' He gave her no chance to answer before he kissed her again, a long, drugged kiss, and some time during it he had sat down beside her, gathering her into his arms and adjusting her position so she was lying across him. 'I like starting the day this way,' he said eventually with a great deal of satisfaction.

'You…you're taking advantage.' It was a weak protest but all she could manage. Freshly shaved and with his hair still damp from the shower, he was mind-blowingly gorgeous, and she suddenly found herself wondering what on earth *she* looked like. No make-up and she'd gone to sleep with her hair wet.

'I have to with you. You do not play fair.' He kept his voice soft and easy, the memory of how she had looked when he had first come into the room still making his guts twist. Young, beautiful, untouched. He wanted her so badly it was tearing him apart, but the worst thing, the very worst thing, was wondering what torment this swine she'd got mixed up with had put her through.

He kissed her again, his hands sliding under the robe, which was loosely caught with the belt, and although she tensed for a moment she didn't push him away.

Holly's heart hammered painfully but after the long, lonely night of heartsearching all she wanted was his arms round her, his kisses, feeling him close and knowing that he wanted her. Not forever, she knew it couldn't last, but for now he *did* want her. Suddenly she wanted to forget everything else—the past, the future. There was only now, this minute, this second.

His hands had stilled for a moment when they discovered her nakedness under the soft towelling, but now as they explored the silky skin of her flat stomach before moving to stroke the soft swell of her breasts she began to tremble. Her arms had wound themselves round his neck and she was kissing him fiercely, hungrily, so when he suddenly put her from him and rose, walking across to open the curtains and then the windows beyond, she sank back on the bed in confusion.

'Monique will be here in one moment with your morning tea.' His voice was thick, husky, and as he turned to face her and saw the hurt and bewilderment she couldn't hide he said grimly, 'Did you want her to find us *in flagrante delicto*? I came to see you because I could not stay away, but—'

The quiet knock on the door checked his voice and brought Holly scrambling under the light covers in a whirl of legs and hot embarrassment, but when Monique bustled into the room carrying a small tray holding a cup of tea and a plate of tiny star-shaped biscuits the housekeeper appeared to notice nothing amiss.

Did all his women bow to discretion and make a pretence of sleeping in one of the guest rooms? Holly asked herself, even as she answered Monique's polite enquiry regarding how well she had slept. Or didn't they care? Did they allow Monique to bring a double tray to the master bedroom where they were curled up at his side, replete and satisfied after a night of love?

Before she had met Jacques the thought of a man's

hands and kisses on her body had brought a mild sense of panic and a definite feeling of repugnance, but now…now she didn't know herself.

Monique left the room after informing them both that breakfast would be ready in twenty minutes, and with the housekeeper's departure Jacques walked slowly to the door, a phantom of a smile on his face as he looked at her in the bed. 'I told you, Holly, it has to be with your head and your heart as well as your body,' he said softly, 'and we are not there yet. Neither will our first time be a quick coupling with the possibility of someone walking in on us.'

She stared at him, colour flushing her cheeks. 'You seem very sure there will be a first time,' she said as coolly as she could manage considering her limbs were still fluid from his touch.

'You doubt this?'

She nodded; it seemed safer. She wasn't sure that her voice wouldn't betray her surprise and disappointment that he was leaving. Which would be the final humiliation.

'I do not.' He studied her face, his eyes serious and very intent. 'There are some things which are as inevitable as the tides of the sea, *petite*. I have come to realise this. Once in a lifetime, if one is lucky, one catches a glimpse of destiny—personal destiny. The altercation with Jeff was meant to be. It brought you to my notice, and me to you, otherwise we may have gone on wasting time.'

There was no laughter in his face or voice and the whole conversation was weighty with something Holly couldn't quite get a handle on. She felt a deep sense of uneasiness come over her and it must have shown on her countenance because he suddenly was smiling again. 'Do not fret,' he said drily. 'We have time.'

'Time?' She eyed him warily. 'Time for what exactly?'

'To get to know each other better before we become lovers.'

In the weeks that followed Holly was kept busy—at work, as more and more responsibility was given her; tidying up her affairs in England and informing friends the new job was permanent; and seeing Jacques on a personal basis. The first two situations were a piece of cake to deal with compared to the third.

It wasn't that she didn't enjoy Jacques's company—she did, too much. And away from the pressures and demands of Querruel International Jacques showed her more and more facets of his complex personality, each one drawing her closer to the real man behind the powerful and successful tycoon the rest of the world saw.

They spent time together in the evenings and at weekends, sometimes going to the theatre or a movie or one of the fascinating nightclubs Jacques knew. Other times they just had a meal together at the château or went for a spin on the Harley-Davidson, stopping for a drink at charming little out-of-the-way places which Jacques seemed to find like magic.

Holly found herself telling him things she had never told a living soul. The insecurities, fears and pain of her troubled childhood slipped out more often than she would have liked in the light and easy relationship Jacques had woven. But she never mentioned David Kirby, and if Jacques tried to quiz her on past romances he met a brick wall. To admit Jacques was the first man she'd ever dated would have opened Pandora's box, and she could not have coped with that. However, she was becoming more and more aware that Jacques wouldn't accept the status quo for ever; he wasn't that type of man. Sooner or later time would run out.

Holly had accepted Jacques was allowing their relationship to progress at what he saw as her pace because he cared about her as well as desiring her. The more she'd got to know him she had come to understand he was a highly discriminating individual, the gossip concerning his love life exaggerated. He'd had lovers, she knew that, but she also knew Jacques would have had to like and care about each woman as a person. He wouldn't take a woman to his bed just because she was beautiful and had indicated she was available.

Jacques thoroughly enjoyed playing the seduction game but he played fair, although Holly felt it would have been easier to resist the slow and subtle invasion into her psyche if he hadn't.

When they didn't leave a nightclub or party until the early hours Jacques usually slept at the penthouse, but he never pressurised her to sleep in his apartment or in his bed. On such occasions she often found herself whisked up to the top floor to share breakfast with him the next morning, and that was fun. The apartment was a bachelor pad with a colour scheme of silver and charcoal and every modern convenience known to man, a technological dream. Utterly different from the warm, homely feel of the luxury at the château, but mind-blowing nevertheless.

And so the determined and persistent seduction continued, like the relentless drip, drip, drip of water on the protective shell of her heart, and summer faded to a crystal-clear and beautiful autumn. Holly found she was enjoying life in a way she had never imagined possible, but when the urge came to analyse exactly why she repressed it, refusing to acknowledge the unease which accompanied such feelings.

Since she had met Jacques there were times when she felt like a fully grown and confident woman who was learning to be at peace with herself and the world around her, then others when the past was so real she was eight years old again.

She could recall the frantic panic as David Kirby literally ripped the clothes off her back, the concentrated horror in her mind as she had fought him, twisting and turning and scrambling about the bed until at last he had given up. But not before he had left her with deep scratches on the tops of her legs and thighs, and bruises all over.

She should have made Cassie or someone look at the marks his lust had made on her tender flesh—how often had she berated herself with that thought? But she had been a small child—bewildered, scared out of her wits and horribly ashamed.

It hadn't been her fault, none of it, but it had taken a long, long time for that fact to become an accepted reality, along with the truth that Kate and Angus West had had no choice but to give her up. They hadn't abandoned her or got rid of her, although that was what it had felt like for years. She had learnt much later, when in her teens, that the couple had died within weeks of each other just three months after she had been taken away from the family, and so there had been the best reasons in the world why they had never made contact again or tried to see her.

But sometimes—just sometimes—all the reasoned arguments and rationalisation in the world didn't help, and the sense of aloneness would sweep over her with a fierceness that was consuming. And strangely that happened more often when she had been in Jacques's arms, when he had been kissing and caressing her with a primitive possessiveness which made her head reel and her body come alive in a way she'd never dreamt of. And every time he pushed the sexual boundaries just a little bit more.

It couldn't continue, of course. But when the final confrontation came it happened in a way she had never expected and wasn't prepared for.

'I want you to—how do you say—put the glad rags on tonight, eh?'

Holly was in Jacques's office on a crisp Friday evening in October and everyone else had gone home. He had just kissed her until she was breathless and trembling on her legs, her heart pounding, and the amber eyes were surveying her with complacent satisfaction.

She put a little space between them after placing the report she had been delivering on his desk, and then was able to say fairly steadily, 'Why?'

'Some old friends of mine are having a party and we're invited. Alain and Marguerite have heard about this little slip of an English girl with hair like raw silk and eyes the colour of cornflowers and they want to meet you.'

Her cheeks grew warm. 'You've told them about me?'

'Of course I have told them about you,' he said softly, very softly. 'They have been abroad for a few months with Alain's job but now they are back and anxious to see the siren who has captured my heart.'

His eyes were full of laughter, one dark eyebrow quirked, but there was something in the tone of his voice which sent warning signals buzzing in her head. He looked perfectly calm and relaxed, and there was no need to think his words carried any significance beyond mild flirtatiousness, but suddenly Holly wasn't sure.

But all this was just a game to Jacques, she knew that, she told herself silently. He was the original love 'em and leave 'em Romeo, a confirmed bachelor and man-about-town who enjoyed women's company and treated them well but never made any commitment. In all the time they had been dating she hadn't asked him if he was seeing her exclusively because she had not felt she had the right, but she had made it clear she considered their relationship one with no strings attached. Light and easy. No ties, no obligations. That way when he left her for someone else who could be everything he wanted it wouldn't be so bad…would it? And she had been obsessional about hiding her love for him, which just would *not* die a death. But that was her problem.

Holly drew in a deep silent breath before saying brightly, 'I think a party would be a great way to start the weekend. What time do you want me ready?'

'Eight o'clock?' His eyes narrowed on her face. 'But wait a few minutes and we'll walk home together, yes?'

'I've got some shopping to do,' she said lightly. 'It's best I see you later.' She had decided, very early on in her new life, to keep work and play totally separate in spite of Jacques's presence in both. Therefore she had made it plain to him that arriving at the office together or leaving at the same time was not an option. He hadn't liked it, he still didn't like it, but he'd played ball.

For a long moment more Jacques studied her face, his eyes searching. 'Fine,' he said casually, conscious that she then relaxed at the word, which made him angry. She fought him at every turn and there were times when he had come very near to forgetting every principle he held dear and using her own need and desire of him against her. And she did want him, physically. The rest he wasn't quite sure of. And he didn't like that. In fact he was beginning to think that maybe a mental acceptance of his place in her life would only come after the physical act had been accomplished and got out of the way.

His eyes narrowed still more as a sliver of ruthless excitement curled down his spine. *Whoever this man was, whatever he had been to her, he was in the past.* Where he would remain.

Jacques's nostrils flared, his hard mouth twisting as he forced a smile. 'See you at eight.' He lowered his head to the papers on his desk, purposely dismissive in both tone and action.

He had been patient for months and where was it getting him? Nowhere. Where words and reason had failed, action would prevail. He wasn't about to let this ridiculous situation continue any longer. He heard the door to his office open and close, and it was only then he raised his head again.

Perched on the top of a hill to the west of Paris, the tiny village of Montfort L'Amaury dated from the Middle Ages. As Jacques's Jaguar approached the tranquil and beautiful setting it resembled a Christmas card, the deep, dark, velvet sky pierced with twinkling stars shining down on the sleeping village. Lights were glowing in windows here and there, squares of colour in the dark streets, and as Jacques drew up outside his friends' large house a dog barked somewhere in the distance, the sound melancholy.

Jacques leant across to her before he exited the car, his lips caressing her cheek as he murmured, 'You look beautiful, *chérie*. They will be enchanted.'

Holly watched him as he walked round the bonnet to open her door. In the months she had been with him she had learnt to accept such courtesies as part of Jacques; it came as second nature to him to open doors for her, see she was seated before he sat himself—all manner of things she had found alien at first. She wasn't used to being looked after or cherished, and it had been difficult to take in such small but gallant civilities at first. And then she had realised it wasn't an act on Jacques's part. It was natural to him, as natural as breathing, and she had understood he had probably always behaved such. It was dangerously nice.

Once out of the car she smoothed her hair and resisted the impulse to fiddle with her earrings. She had made an extra-special effort to look good tonight although she couldn't have explained why. The ice-blue tux jacket teamed perfectly with her silver top and silver sequinned mini, and she knew that cool colours brought out the violet in her eyes and emphasised the richness of her hair. Nevertheless, she was nervous and she didn't know why. She had got used to meeting Jacques's friends and colleagues in the last months and this evening would be nothing unusual.

It wasn't. Not at first. Alain and his pretty, dark-haired wife were charming and welcomed Holly with open arms, and as more guests arrived Holly and Jacques drifted into the enormous sun room stretching out from the drawing room.

A pianist was playing in one corner—there was to be a band later—and large full-length windows looked out on to the garden. The trees were alive with fairy lights and lanterns and these illuminated the impeccably kept smooth lawn and immaculate flower beds, although Holly caught sight of a child's brightly coloured tricycle lying on its side amidst all the perfection.

She smiled to herself, the small touch of ordinary humanity was comforting, surrounded as she was by Diors and diamonds. She was still smiling when her eyes were caught and held by the startled gaze of a young woman on the opposite side of the room.

It had been seventeen years since she had last set eyes on Christina in the flesh, but David and Cassie's foster daughter had included a photograph of herself in the letter she had written to Holly after David had committed suicide. Holly had written a polite note back to the other girl but declined the invitation to meet her, neither had she included a photograph, but it was clear Christina recognised her nevertheless.

Holly found herself shrinking inwardly, as though she was shrivelling from the panic and rush of memories which the other girl's face had called up. *It was impossible.* Christina, here? In France? In this particular home? What was she going to do? *What was she going to do?*

'What is it?' She must have looked awful because Jacques's voice was concerned, his eyes raking her face as he took her arm. 'Do you feel unwell?'

'Yes...'

'Do you want to leave?'

Yes, she wanted to leave, she had never wanted to leave somewhere so much in her life, but it was too late.

Holly remained quite still as Christina approached them, a sense of inevitability numbing the panic born of shame and fright. Just talk to her as you would anyone else, a voice in her head cautioned silently. Treat her as an old childhood friend you haven't seen in years. Jacques knows you were fostered in several homes; he won't think anything of this beyond mild surprise at such a coincidence.

When Christina had written to her she had hinted that she thought their foster parent might have hurt Holly as he had her but that was all. She clearly hadn't been sure. And it wasn't something you could discuss at a party anyway. There was no need for panic. None at all.

'Holly? It is you?' Christina seemed genuinely pleased to see her and Holly felt guilty for a moment that she didn't feel the same. She had forgiven Christina and the others for lying about her years ago—they had only been scared children manipulated by an evil man, after all—but there were too many unpleasant memories tied up with the smiling blonde woman in front of her. 'Oh, this is wonderful! I can't believe it.'

'Hello, Christina.' Holly knew the blood had drained from her face when she had first caught sight of the other woman but now her cheeks were burning. 'How…how are you?'

'Very well.' Christina didn't hesitate as she put her arms round Holly and hugged her for a moment, but Holly felt as though her arms were fixed to her sides by super-glue. And then, as Christina stepped back a pace, her face alight, she said, 'Oh, it's so good to see you, Holly, after all this time,' before her eyes flickered to Jacques in a manner which made it clear she was waiting to be introduced.

Holly swallowed. 'Christina, meet Jacques. Jacques, this is an old friend of mine from England. We…we knew each other when we were children.'

'Really?' Jacques was smiling politely as he shook Christina's outstretched hand but there had been the slightest of pauses when he scrutinised Holly's face before responding. 'It is good to meet a friend of Holly's,' he continued smoothly. 'Was she as beautiful a child as she is a woman, Christina?'

'Definitely.' Christina beamed at them both and Holly was conscious of thinking—ungraciously as well as un-fairly, she admitted silently—that Christina couldn't be as thick as she seemed. Surely she could see Holly wasn't exactly over the moon about renewing their connection?

It appeared not.

'I'm so glad I've seen you.' Christina seemed to have the impression the sentiment was returned. 'I wrote to you again after that first letter, you know, but the university returned it with ''not at this address'' written on the envelope.'

Holly nodded. Actually, she had written it. 'Well, here I am,' she said brightly, recovering a measure of composure. 'And here are you. Are you with someone?'

'My husband.' Christina beamed the hundred-watt smile again. 'Oh, here he is. Louis, this is Holly. You remember I spoke of her? This is my husband, Louis.'

The tall, slim man with dark eyes and grey hair was clearly twenty or so years older than his pretty wife, but he seemed very nice as he shook their hands and made the usual small talk for some moments. Holly was just thinking it was going to be all right, when Christina took her arm, drawing her slightly aside as she said, her voice low, 'I've wanted to see you again for so long, Holly. To...to say sorry as much as anything else. Both of us, John and I, knew we should have spoken up and told the truth about you instead of endorsing David's lies.'

'It's all right.' Holly spoke quickly. 'Forget it.'

'No.' Christina placed her hand on Holly's sleeve and it was all she could do not to shake it off and run away. She was terribly aware of Jacques at the side of her, and although he seemed to be deep in conversation with Christina's husband she wasn't sure he wasn't listening.

'The thing is, David was so good at manipulation and control,' Christina continued softly. 'He was doing the same thing to both of us but we never talked about it, not even to each other. It wasn't until I was older and everything happened with the youth club that I spoke out. And then John came forward too.'

'Christina, I don't want to talk about it.'

This time even Christina couldn't miss the tone of Holly's voice. The other girl stiffened for a moment and

then relaxed, shaking her head as she said even more quietly, 'I was like that once. Then with the court case my
mother came forward—I hadn't seen her in years—and
through that I found out my father was French, and
through my father I met Louis. I could have missed that.'

'I've met my mother and I don't like her,' Holly said
flatly, 'and my father was someone she had little more
than a one-night-stand with who already had several children with his wife. I'm not missing anything on that score,
believe me.'

'Holly, it really helps to bring everything out into the
open.'

'Christina, I'm glad things have worked out for you but
the past is the past—'

'Have you had therapy?' Christina interrupted her with
all the fervour of a true devotee of the treatment. 'Because
it really helps. I was so screwed up, but I started it after
David's death and I still go along once a month now. I've
got a marvellous therapist right here in Paris. I could give
you her name if you like.'

Holly didn't know if she felt better or worse when
Marguerite materialised at the side of them in the next
moment, the Frenchwoman's face smiling as she said, 'I
was looking for you two to introduce you but you have
found each other already. It is nice to meet someone from
home when you are getting accustomed to a new country,
n'est-ce pas?' she added directly to Holly.

Yeah, terrific. 'Very nice,' Holly confirmed tightly,
aware the two men had finished their conversation and
were looking at the three of them.

'And would you believe we know one another,
Marguerite?' Christina put in happily.

'No, really?' Marguerite's eyes were bright with
interest.

'It is a small world, as they say.' Jacques spoke at the side of them and then, as he took Holly's arm, he continued smoothly, 'But there are several people here who have not met Holly yet, so if you will excuse us...'

Had he heard anything? Holly glanced at Jacques's face as they walked away from the others but she could read nothing from the implacable countenance. However, he didn't whisk her away to a corner somewhere and start the third degree as she had half expected. Instead he did as he had said he was going to do and introduced her to more of his friends she hadn't yet met, as well as striking up conversations with several she had.

He hadn't been listening to Christina. The sick churning eased a little although curls of uneasiness remained. Everything was all right. All she had to do now was to avoid the other girl for the rest of the evening if she could.

In the event it was not hard. Jacques steered her from group to group, smiling, making easy conversation and taking care of things in such a way Holly found she only had to smile and speak in monosyllables, which was just as well considering the state of her shattered nerves.

Of all the places in all the world Christina had to pick this particular city in which to settle down, Holly thought wryly. And what were the chances of her husband knowing Alain and Marguerite? Millions to one. But it was no use dwelling on that. It had happened. She had been in Paris months now and gone to several parties and other social gatherings with Jacques and his friends, and she hadn't seen Christina before. It was probable she wouldn't see her again. Perhaps Louis was an associate or friend of Alain and Marguerite but not Jacques or his circle? She hoped so. She would question Jacques later about the other couple, but discreetly.

Soft piano music had been drifting about the downstairs

of the house since they had arrived, but once the buffet had been served and everyone had eaten a band moved in. Holly had found she couldn't eat a morsel, her nerves stretched like piano-wire, but if Jacques noticed her lack of appetite he didn't remark on it.

However, more than once she caught him staring at her, and his eyes were more intent and a clearer amber than she had ever seen them before, but then he would smile his slow, lazy smile and she told herself she was imagining things because of the turmoil her mind was in. It had been a shock seeing Christina; it had brought the past alive in a way which left an acidic taste in her mouth, but she didn't have to panic. Nothing was going to intrude on her new life here. It was a fool's paradise and she knew it at heart, but she clung to the hope right until the end of the evening.

Christina and Louis had already left but the other girl had done no more than wave her goodbye across the room, something which had caused Holly a pang of guilt before she had told herself it was for the best. Her attitude might have caused Christina a little disappointment but that was all. And the alternative—of sitting and talking about 'old times' or resurrecting the secret misery which had been life at the Kirbys'—was unthinkable.

Alain and Marguerite hugged her as she and Jacques left, extracting a promise from Holly that she would come to tea soon so she could meet their two children, and then they were out on the drive under the starry sky and the nightmare was over. Or so she thought. For about two minutes.

Jacques drove the car out of the drive, along the small lane which bordered two or three large houses, and then pulled into a parking place which was quiet and secluded and overshadowed by the branches of several huge evergreen oaks. He cut the engine, turning in his seat and draping one arm along the back of hers as his eyes narrowed on her wary face.

'Cerulean.'

It wasn't what she had expected him to say and she stared at him for a moment before she said guardedly, 'I'm sorry?'

'The colour of your eyes when you are disturbed about something. The blue becomes very deep and strong. I have noticed this before.'

Holly tried to think of something to say and failed utterly.

'Who was David, Holly?' His voice was quiet, even gentle, but she wasn't fooled. Her time had run out. He wasn't going to be fobbed off again, she could read it in his eyes. 'And what was his connection with you and Christina?'

'You were listening,' she accused weakly.

'Not as much as I would have liked,' he said grimly. 'Her damn husband kept talking about his golf handicap until I was tempted to find a club and wrap it round his head. But I caught the odd word here and there, a couple of which I did not like.'

'Oh?' She gave him a quick glance, then looked away again. His face was inscrutable and giving nothing away. 'Like what?'

'Just little words like therapy and court case along with this man's name,' Jacques said tonelessly, the very lack of emotion in his voice revealing how concerned he was. 'What was he to you and this other girl? Did you both go out with him, is that it? And he treated you both badly? He had some sort of problem obviously. Was he abusive, physically, I mean?'

'Please, Jacques.' She couldn't do this; she just could

not *do* this. She loved him so much but she wasn't what he thought she was. Inside she was such a mess, so mixed up and confused. He had no idea how terrified she was about loving him, of letting herself become vulnerable, open. And what would be a huge life-or-death type experience for her wouldn't mean the same to him. Sooner or later their affair would end and then what would she do? It was bad enough now to contemplate life without him, but if she gave herself to him, body and soul...

'No, enough! No more "please, Jacques",' he said harshly, so harshly her eyes shot to his face again. 'It is always like this, Holly. There are so many things that do not make sense, so many minefields where you are concerned. I do not understand what you want from me. If it had been any other woman I would have been sure the way you are was a ploy to keep me interested—one minute hot, one minute cold—the notion of give a wolf a taste and keep him hungry, *n'est-ce pas*? But you, you are not like that. This, at least, *this* I do know.'

'You don't know anything about me, Jacques. Not really,' Holly said painfully, aware as she said the words that he would be quite within his rights to blame her for that. He had told her so much about himself—his childhood, his early years as an adult, his hopes and fears and aspirations. He had been generous with his thoughts and emotions, he had shared most, maybe all, of what he was with her, and she had given him very little in return.

But he didn't accuse her. And when he spoke she realised he had not actually shared all of himself because she'd had no idea he was thinking along the lines his words revealed. 'I know enough to be sure I want you for my wife,' he said huskily. 'Whatever this man was to you, whatever happened, I am sure of this. I want to take care of you as he obviously did not—cherish you, adore you.

Why do you think I have not taken you to my bed before this? Why? Because I want to *marry* you, not have an affair or an open-ended modern relationship. I have had enough of those. I *love* you, Holly. Do you not understand this? And for my wife, for the mother of my children, I have waited. Waited until you trust me, until you allow yourself to take me into your heart and your head as well as your body. *Zut!*'

The oath was harsh, an explosion, and he breathed deeply for a moment before he gained control again. 'So many times I have been tempted to make you mine, and I could have done. Oh, yes, I could have done,' he said grimly. 'We both know this. Even today I made myself a promise that you would be in my bed tonight, that the waiting was over. But a relationship that is destined to go on for a lifetime should begin with absolute truth and trust.'

She stared at him, frozen outwardly but with her mind racing in despair. Until this very moment she would have sworn on oath that should Jacques ever say what he had just said she would fall on his neck in hysterical happiness. *Because she had known it could never happen.* She had been safe in lying to herself. Jacques liked bright, beautiful, successful women he could have a good time with—everyone knew that. Light-hearted flings, brief intrigues, passionate affairs that already had the stopwatch ticking the moment they began—that was Jacques's style. Nothing heavy, nothing serious.

But she believed him absolutely now. The seduction game was one thing but he wasn't playing games with her.

'I have often wondered if I would ever say those words to anyone,' he said after a long moment had gone by. 'I did not think they would look as you do if it happened.'

'I…I'm sorry.' What could she say? How on earth could she make him understand? It wasn't him who was at fault here, but she knew he was a man who, once having committed, would expect everything in return. And when it came—from her—it wouldn't be enough. *She couldn't be what he wanted, what he thought she was.* She could never fulfil his expectations. She didn't know how. And when he discovered that… 'I'm sorry,' she said again, her voice shaking.

'You do not feel the same.'

Feel the same? She adored him, she loved him with every morsel of her being, but how would she ever survive him leaving her if she gave herself to him? She was on first-name terms with rejection and exclusion, but this was something different. When Jacques left she wouldn't be able to go on.

She didn't know her eyes had filled with tears or that her face had mirrored her agony, so when Jacques took her cold little hands in his warm ones it was a surprise. She had expected him to shout at her, to tell her she was— oh, everything she feared he would see in her, she supposed. 'What did he do to you to make you look like that?' he murmured huskily. 'You do not still have feelings for him?'

'No, no.' Oh, the irony of it.

'Holly, you are breaking my heart. I cannot bear to see you like this.'

She was breaking his heart? It shattered the last of her fragile composure, which had taken a battering all night. *Her* heart was beating so hard it was reverberating in her chest, like the worst palpitations imaginable. Her body went rigid, her nerves at breaking point. 'Jacques, this isn't what you think.'

'No?' His voice was tight and very controlled. 'Tell me, *petite*. What am I thinking?'

'I...I can't explain.'

'You cannot or you will not?'

There was such a lump in her throat she didn't know how she managed to push the words over it. 'Can't. Please believe me. Can't.'

'Then where do we go from here? Do you see me as a friend, a benefactor, a business associate, what? Do you see me as a lover, Holly? A ship that passes in the night? Because sure as hell you do not seem to want anything more.'

How did she answer that? There was a quivering silence, but in spite of the fact she knew she was going to lose him she couldn't break it. She had been waiting for this moment since she had acknowledged she loved him, knowing it would come sooner or later. Now it was here she couldn't even begin to think clearly. She didn't understand herself, or how this barbed flirtation with Jacques had escalated into what was now facing her, but the facts were undeniable.

He wanted her to tell all. To open up all the past and the present with its goblins and horrors, and then trust him for the future. And she couldn't. She couldn't. End of story. End of her wonderful job, her dear little apartment, of Paris, the new life. End of Jacques.

Out of the chaos of her thoughts she suddenly made sense of one thing. She had to end this now. She owed him that if nothing else. She had to do what she should have done months ago and disappear.

'I...I resign.'

'*What?*' He was angry now.

'I resign from my job. Does that make it easier?'

'Oh, yes, Holly. That makes it all beautifully easy,' he

said with acid sarcasm. 'I now lose my textile technologist as well as my girlfriend. *C'est extra!*'

'Do you want me to work my notice?' she asked painfully.

'What I *want*…' He stopped abruptly, dark colour flaring under the chiselled cheekbones. 'Oh, to hell with it!'

What he meant was, to hell with *her*, Holly thought painfully.

She raised her head, a measure of bruised pride coming to her rescue as he glared at her, frustration in every line and plane of his body. He muttered something which sounded very rude in his native tongue whilst reaching for her in the same moment, cupping her head tightly in his strong hands and covering her mouth with his.

It was not a gentle or a tender kiss. Every ounce of his bitter disappointment and bafflement was in it, bewildered rage and pain evident as he pulled her against him. There was none of the restraint he had shown thus far; this was a man who had been driven to the very edge of himself and who sensed he was losing something precious.

And she didn't even fight him for one moment. The knowledge was there, hammering at her consciousness, but in seconds she was accepting his kiss hungrily, clutching at him as he levered himself over her.

His hands roamed over her body as his mouth ravished hers, but as she kissed him back with touching abandonment they became lost to the world, drinking in the scent of each other as they touched and tasted.

She couldn't let herself be taken over like this. The old fear rose but his caresses were evoking such sensual stirrings and delight that the fear evaporated, her body ignoring her mind's warning. A restless urgency was tuning her in to his every touch and sigh and all she knew was that she wanted him. Him, Jacques. No other man could make her feel like this and if she didn't make love with him she would make love with no one.

Her mouth was as hungry as his, her hands feeling the bunched muscles in his back as he crouched over her in the close confines of the car, and then suddenly she became aware of the change in him. He had become very still and he wasn't kissing her any longer.

'Jacques?' It was a whisper, and then, as he moved off her and into his seat again, Holly stared at him and saw his face was stiff and grim. 'What's the matter?'

'This is not the way it should be. Not for us. Not for you.' He made a sound low in his throat. 'I do not want to have this kind of an affair with you, damn it! I want to *marry* you and that is different. I want to wake up every morning and know you will be the first thing I see, and when I get home at night I want to know you will be there too. You understand? I want us to make a *life* together; is that so wrong? If we make love tonight I will still only have your body and not your heart, and it is not enough, Holly. It is not enough.'

'You wanted us to be lovers at the beginning,' she said, struggling to control the tears. 'So what has changed?'

'Me.' His voice was hollow. 'Is that not the greatest joke? It is I who have changed, *petite*. I love you and I will be damned if I will take you like this. I want you so badly it is driving me crazy, but I want more than this.'

'You want too much,' she said dully.

'Maybe.' He looked at her, his eyes narrowed and the amber light subdued and murky in the darkness. 'But that is Jacques Querruel, *chérie*. I can be no other way. I have never settled for less than exactly what I want.'

'An all-or-nothing guy?' she whispered painfully, closing her eyes to shut out his face as she lay back in her seat.

'If you like.'

'And if it turns out to be nothing?'

'I have never considered that an option and I do not intend to start now.' He turned the key in the ignition as he spoke, and as the car purred into action Holly averted her face so he would not see the tears spilling down her cheeks in a hot, salty flood.

CHAPTER EIGHT

'YOU aren't seriously telling me you walked out of that dream of a job, not to mention his life, and flew home without a word? That's just not *you*, Holly.'

No, it wasn't, but then she wasn't very sure exactly who she was any more, Holly thought wearily as she surveyed Lucy Holden over a steaming mug of coffee at Lucy's kitchen table.

'I wrote a letter explaining I couldn't stay,' she said flatly after a second or two had slipped by and it was clear Lucy was waiting for a response. 'And I enclosed the keys of the apartment and everything.'

'And that makes it all right? What about when you need a reference for another job?' Lucy bent down and whisked Melanie Anne onto her knee just in time to prevent her angelic-looking daughter from grabbing the cat's tail. The cat, realising its narrow escape, leapt onto Holly's lap, where it began to purr loudly after casting a superior glance at the wriggling baby who was now bellowing in frustration at being thwarted.

'I shan't ask Jacques for one,' Holly said definitely. 'In fact I shan't contact him again at all. It's best to make a clean break. Less painful for both of us.'

'Holly, I'm your friend.' Lucy surveyed her severely from bright blue eyes under a mop of blonde curls. 'And I'd just make the point you look the worst I've ever seen you in my whole life, and that includes the three weeks you spent with us when you looked as if you were at death's door.'

153

'Thanks.'

'I mean it. This guy, by your own admission, is offering marriage, and don't forget we're talking marriage to a millionaire here. That's got to be a bonus in anyone's book! And you've already said you care about him, so—' Lucy paused, thrusting a chocolate biscuit into Melanie Anne's podgy hand whereupon it was aimed immediately at the cat '—so I just don't see what the problem is here.'

Holly's stomach turned over but she had been expecting this. From the moment she had stepped foot in the apartment last night she'd known what she had to do. She had telephoned the airport and obtained an early-morning flight and then spent the next few hours packing and cleaning the apartment. After writing a letter to Jacques she had telephoned for a taxi at the unearthly hour of five in the morning, and had left the building in the pink haze of dawn.

After she had made the decision to remain in Paris when Jacques offered her the post permanently, she had notified the landlord that she no longer required her bedsit and had told him to pass on all her bed linen and towels and other incidentals to Mrs Gibson. It had been a furnished let so there had been no problem about storing furniture or anything like that, and Holly had already deposited a large box of miscellaneous personal items with Mrs Gibson when she'd first left for France, thinking that if the job did work out she could pick them up some time in the future.

And so she had arrived in England homeless but knowing there would be a welcome and a bed for her with James and Lucy. She had also known that if she threw herself on her old friends for sanctuary they deserved a full explanation, which would not be easy. She had never told anyone about David's attack and just how badly the social services had got it wrong.

She stared at Lucy now, and something in her face made Lucy say, 'What? What is it?' before adding, 'Look, I'm going to put Melanie Anne down for her nap and then we can talk properly. OK?'

'OK.' She wasn't looking forward to this but it had to be.

An hour and a box of tissues later the two women sat looking at each other after what had been an emotionally fraught sixty minutes for both of them. They had cried together and hugged a lot, which had been therapeutic for Holly, and now Lucy was saying, 'We always knew there was something more than you had told us. Oh, Holly, what a rotten time of it you had. I would kill anyone who tried to lay a finger on Melanie Anne.'

Holly smiled weakly at the vehemence in Lucy's voice. 'And I'd be right behind you in case you didn't finish the job.'

'I suppose it's no use my saying that you're fantastic and beautiful and a lovely person, and that all your fears regarding Jacques falling out of love with you are nonsense?' Lucy asked softly. 'That it's got every chance of being a forever story?'

Holly shook her head. 'I just can't be what he would want,' she said slowly. 'I know it, in here.' She touched her chest. 'I'd destroy us both with my insecurities and lack of trust in him, however patient he might try to be. And if he stayed with me out of pity...' She shook her head despairingly.

'Aren't you rather jumping the gun here?' Lucy said practically. 'You're assuming the absolute worst. What if you marry him and he's everything you want and you're everything he wants? It does happen, you know. Look at me and James.'

Wordlessly Holly shook her head again.

'Holly, you're brave and strong, so much stronger than you realise,' Lucy said passionately. 'And you say you love him with all your heart. Please, please don't throw this chance away. Just because the poor guy is loaded as well as handsome you can't hold that against him. And don't forget ordinary Mr Joe Bloggs is capable of infidelity as well as someone like Jacques.'

'Is that supposed to make me feel better?' Holly asked with a watery smile. And then, as Lucy went to say more, she held up her hand. 'Lucy, I know where you are coming from and I appreciate you and James more than words can say, but please, I've made up my mind about this. Can…can we talk about something else now?'

Lucy wriggled in her seat. 'Oh, *Holly*.'

'Please? And will you make me a promise that you or James won't try to contact Jacques or let him know where I am?'

'Of course we wouldn't.' Lucy looked horrified. 'I think you're crazy, and I wish you would change your mind, but I wouldn't dream of betraying your trust like that, neither would James.'

'Thank you.' Holly reached across the table and placed her hand on Lucy's arm for a moment. 'And you don't mind if I stay for a while till I find a job and a place to live? I'll pay board, of course—my bank balance is extremely healthy after the last few months—but I'd rather be with you and James than in a hotel or something.'

'I should think you would!' Lucy took a sip of coffee— their third pot since Holly had knocked on the front door two hours earlier—before saying, 'Stay as long as you want; you know we'd love to have you, and the guest-room bed is already made up.'

James expressed exactly the same sentiments when he arrived home later that evening, even before Lucy told him about Jacques and her hasty flight from France. Lucy waited until she and her husband were alone before she mentioned David Kirby, but the next morning James let Holly know he had the full picture in typical James fashion by giving her a big hug and stating grimly that some men ought to be castrated, before leaving for the university.

Holly watched him go fondly. She loved this couple and little Melanie Anne, and if she hadn't been feeling so utterly wretched she would have thoroughly enjoyed staying with them.

It was during the time Holly tackled the huge mound of ironing Lucy admitted had been growing for a couple of weeks—'I *loathe* ironing and I always put it off and put if off until it's mountainous, which then makes it worse!'—that she decided she was going to take a year or two off career-wise.

She'd get something completely different—waitressing maybe, or perhaps bar work or even working in a shop. She needed to chill out mentally and she couldn't face working in another office for ages. She didn't admit to herself here that if she tried for the sort of position she had trained for there was just the slightest possibility Jacques might be able to trace her, and Lucy made no comment when Holly told her what she had decided beyond raising quizzical eyebrows.

James and Lucy had left their apartment and moved to a small three-bedroomed terraced house in Wimbledon once Lucy's pregnancy was confirmed, but, even though James's job paid well and Lucy worked part-time at a local private hospital two days a week when Melanie Anne was at nursery, money was a little tight with Christmas approaching, Lucy confided once the ironing was done. How about if Holly left looking for somewhere to stay until after the New Year? That way they had a temporary lodger, which would help household finances enormously, Melanie Anne could get to know her Aunty Holly properly, and Holly wouldn't be all alone in a new bedsit for Christmas.

Holly rather suspected it was the last reason which was more on Lucy's mind than anything else, but in truth she had been dreading being by herself so soon after leaving Jacques. He was in every thought, filling her mind when she was awake and invading her dreams, and she had cried for hours the night before. She was glad she had told someone about David at last—in a way it had been a huge relief—but raking it all up again had been like salt on a raw wound. A few weeks with Lucy and James would be balm on her bruised and bleeding emotions. And so she had accepted Lucy's offer thankfully.

Two days later Holly secured a job in a local café that also doubled as a baker's and had its own shop. The hours were long and the work was tiring, and the staff had to be prepared to be jacks of all trades, but it paid well. The owners—a husband-and-wife team—were kindly employers who worked as hard as their employees, and the two other girls were pleasant and good-natured.

Holly knew she was lucky to have found such a position so quickly, and Lucy and James went out of their way to make her feel wanted and loved, but, nevertheless, she was so unhappy she felt as if she was living in a dark vacuum most of the time. Useless to tell herself things would get better, that she would adapt, that everything had turned out for the best—she seemed to miss Jacques more and not less as the days and weeks crawled by. But never, at any time, did she doubt she had done the right thing. Which was scant comfort in the circumstances.

Jacques would meet someone else, someone fresh and bright and beautiful, someone with no skeletons in the cupboard and without enough baggage to fill a ten-ton skip.

The week before Christmas Holly went to see Mrs Gibson and Mr Bateman, loaded down with presents for them and—of course—Mrs Gibson's cats. She spent a cosy Sunday afternoon with them in Mrs Gibson's bedsit, drinking tea and eating homemade coconut cake, and told them far more than she had intended to do about Jacques, due mainly to Mrs Gibson's persistent questioning.

Mrs Gibson, her bright orange hair toning perfectly with the big ginger tomcat draped in purring ecstasy round her bony shoulders like a green-eyed stole, thought it all wonderfully tragic and romantic, especially when Holly made them both promise to keep her whereabouts a secret should anyone enquire.

And at eleven o'clock the next morning Holly glanced up from the box of cream cakes she had just packaged for a customer and saw Jacques standing in front of her. The box fell unheeded to the floor and her hand went to her throat, and one of the other girls—who obviously thought she was about to faint—grabbed at her arm as she yelled for assistance.

'I...I'm all right,' she whispered, her gaze still locked with the amber eyes she remembered so well, the eyes that had featured in all her dreams for weeks. He was standing no more than six feet away, not moving, not talking, just looking at her. She blinked and then rubbed her eyes, but he was still there. How had he found her?

She wasn't aware she had spoken the words out loud,

but when he answered, saying quietly, 'Mrs Gibson telephoned me after you left yesterday. I've got to know her
quite well since you've been gone,' she was dumbstruck.

She was aware she was shaking uncontrollably and also
that Alice, at the side of her, was hugely interested in the
proceedings, but for the life of her she couldn't move or
speak.

He looked wonderful. Magnificent. But thinner, much
thinner, and older. She felt a rush of love surge through
her that was so almighty her head swam with it. Oh, my
love, my love. Why have you come? Why couldn't you
have let it be? And she forced herself to say, 'Please go,
Jacques.'

'Not on your life,' he answered steadily. 'Get your coat;
we have some talking to do.'

'I...I can't just leave; this is my job.'

He didn't point out that was exactly what she had done
before, which in the circumstances he thought showed
great restraint. He merely repeated very quietly, 'Get your
coat, Holly.'

'Do you want me to call Mr Bishop?' Alice was all
agog.

'Call whoever you like,' Jacques said pleasantly, still
with his eyes on Holly's white face.

'No, no.' This was turning into a farce. 'Tell...tell them
I've taken an early lunch break,' Holly said weakly to
Alice.

'Tell them they need a new assistant.'

'*Jacques.*'

'Yes, my sweet?'

Holly decided to get her coat. He was waiting by the
door when she emerged from the private quarters of the
business, arms folded across his chest and big body relaxed. Only he wasn't. She knew him well enough now

to know that the lazy pose was a sham. And Mrs Bishop was standing by the side of him, having returned from a visit to the bank. The pair had obviously been talking because Mrs Bishop said, somewhat dazedly, 'We shan't expect you in again today, Holly,' before giving Jacques a wide, warm smile.

How did he do that? Holly asked herself helplessly. He had obviously charmed the pants off the normally astute and very down-to-earth woman because Monday afternoons were always hectic, and Mrs Bishop wasn't usually so charitable in dispensing time off at the drop of a hat.

She had expected him to start the inquest as soon as they were outside, but he merely took her arm and walked her along the busy pavement. The shops were full of Christmas lights and decorations and the air was cold and sharp. Despite herself Holly felt heady with bitter-sweet joy at seeing him again, even though her heart was jerking in wild, panicked beats. He seemed very large and dark at the side of her, the big charcoal overcoat he was wearing increasing the impression of controlled masculinity. She nerved herself and glanced at him through her eyelashes. He had definitely lost some weight, she thought dizzily. It made him look even more ruthless, and sexier...

'Where are we going?' She forced the words out through the whirlwind in her head.

He didn't look at her, his voice cool and determined as he said shortly, 'Somewhere we can talk.'

'You shouldn't have come here.'

He pulled her into him slightly, shielding her with his body from contact with a group of noisy teenagers who were taking up most of the pavement. 'Yes, I should,' he said grimly.

They reached a long, sleek car that Holly rather suspected was a Ferrari parked expertly in between two family saloons at the side of the road. 'Get in.' Jacques had opened the door for her and she had no option but to slide into the leather-clad interior, her heart still thudding. She couldn't quite work out where he was coming from. He had every right to be furiously angry, but if he was he was controlling it well. But then he would, she reminded herself miserably. Control was Jacques's middle name.

'You're too slender.'

They had been driving for five minutes when Jacques spoke and Holly's heart kicked against her ribs.

'More beautiful than ever but too slender,' he said huskily. 'Haven't you been eating properly?'

'Have you?' she countered weakly.

'No, but then I wasn't the one who left.' Amber eyes flashed their golden light across her pale face.

'That doesn't mean...' She stopped abruptly.

'Yes?' he prompted softly.

'Just because I was the one who left doesn't mean I didn't care,' she managed faintly.

'You just did not care enough?' It was a rapier thrust straight for the heart and Holly reflected painfully that he hadn't lost his touch.

What could she say? She glanced at him again but the hard profile was looking straight ahead at the heavy lunch-time traffic now. 'It...it wasn't like that.'

'Maybe, maybe not, but I intend to find out exactly what is what before too much longer,' he said grimly. 'So accept that now and it will make things a hell of a lot easier for us both.'

Holly took a deep breath and prayed for a revelation on how to handle this. Nothing came. This time he wasn't going to be fobbed off and there was nowhere left to run. His face told her that. He was determined to find out why a relationship—a marriage—between them was impossible. Why she would fail him and in failing him destroy everything between them. Why she couldn't *trust* him. Because that was what all this came down to in the end. If she loved him so much, and she did, and she couldn't trust that he would continue to love her, that in itself would destroy his love.

She bit hard on her lip, her head feeling as though it would burst. One of her less sympathetic foster mothers had called her a nutcase once, and somehow—in spite of much worse insults from her peers at times—that had stuck with her, maybe because it had come from an adult. But perhaps Meg Connor had been right. Who else but a crazy woman would refuse Jacques Querruel?

'Eat first or talk first?'

'What?' She came out of the bitter maelstrom of her thoughts at the sound of his voice, and then said shakily, 'Talk.' Time had run out. She would tell him it all and then he would have to accept there couldn't be a future for them. Perhaps he wouldn't even want there to be after she had revealed the person she really was, deep inside. He could have anyone he wanted. Why would he bother with her?

'Good.'

He said nothing after the one cryptic word until they got to the open expanse of Richmond Park. Delicately proportioned, gentle-eyed deer were wandering under the trees in the far distance, and as he parked the car Holly thought how ironic it was that the final death blow to their future should occur in such beautiful surroundings. The blue winter sky overhead, the bare trees with their stark and majestic silhouettes and the red of the animals below added a poignancy to it all that made her want to howl.

Instead she steeled herself and turned to him, determined her control would match his. 'This wasn't a good idea, Jacques. It would have been far better to leave things as they were.'

'Really?' he replied, pinning her with that clear golden gaze that seemed to pierce straight into her soul. 'I disagree. But then perhaps some men would enjoy searching fruitlessly for weeks on end for someone who walked out on them without a word. Maybe they would get something out of doing the rounds of people they thought might be able to help them, of employing private detectives, of visiting eccentric old ladies every week in the hope that the object of their search might have made contact. Although, on reflection, Mrs Gibson was perhaps the only bright spot in a succession of long, dreary days. Because that's how things were, Holly. That's how I've been spending my time since you vanished.'

'I didn't expect you to do that,' she said in a tight voice. *Private detectives?* He had hired private detectives?

'Obviously not.' It was very dry.

His remoteness enabled her to inject a little attitude into her voice as she said, 'And what did you promise Mrs Gibson to make her rat on me anyway?'

'Rat on you?' He turned to face her, one arm on the steering wheel. 'Holly, I am not a gangster and Mrs Gibson is not a—what is the word?—stool pigeon.'

'That's two words.'

'She's neither.' He lifted her chin with determined fingers. 'Look at me, Holly, and listen. I want answers. I do not care if we sit here all day but I will have them. I have never pursued a woman like I have you, I have never trodden on eggshells for a woman like I have you, and I have certainly never waited for a woman like I have you. But enough is enough. You understand?'

He paused, moving his hands to cup her white face. 'I love you,' he said quietly, 'and I am going to kiss you.

Then I am going to ask you some questions and you will answer them.'

The kiss was a long one and at the end of it Holly knew her trembling would have communicated itself to him, pressed as she was against his hardness. He released her slowly, reluctantly, and then he said, 'Holly, who is David Kirby and what place did he have in your life, and that of Christina? And before you answer me I will tell you that I have made it my business to go and see Christina.'

She stared at him, wide-eyed and as white as a sheet.

'And she would tell me nothing,' he continued softly. 'Nothing at all. Neither would her husband. But I know this man hurt you both in some way and I want to know the truth. He is a spectre between us and I will not have that.'

She shut her eyes to block out his face. 'David Kirby was not a boyfriend or lover, as you imagined,' she said woodenly. 'I...I have never had a boyfriend...before you.'

His hands were still either side of her face and his warmth was soaking into her, making her realise how cold she was. But this was a coldness from deep within and nothing to do with externals.

Jacques did not move or speak for a moment and then he said, very gently, 'You still have not answered my question, *petite*.'

'I told you I was fostered from when I was a little baby, that I was with several families until I was old enough to look after myself? Well, that's true, but for the first eight years I was with a couple I looked upon as my parents. Oh, I knew they weren't, of course, biologically, but they were wonderful people. Then they got sick. I was sent to another home. David and Cassie Kirby's home. They were wealthy, good-looking, charismatic. Christina was fostered by them too, and a young boy named John.'

She jerked her head free now, opening her eyes and turning away from him to look blindly out of the window. 'So there were three of us in all and they showered us with toys and presents. Everyone thought I was lucky to be put with them. But I knew something was wrong, right from the beginning almost I sensed...'

She swallowed painfully, tears running silently down her cheeks. 'He came to my bedroom often. At first he just wanted me to sit on his knee. He'd read to me, things like that, and hug and kiss me goodnight, but...not as you should a child. Then one day when I'd been there a few months, when he thought I was under his control like Christina and the other child, he—' she took a hard pull of air '—he tried to rape me.'

She felt him jerk and then he took her into his arms. She didn't resist but neither did she look at him, burying her face in his chest. 'I fought him and eventually he gave up, but he told lies about me. He made Christina lie too. I was put with another family but I was scared and confused... Everything went wrong from then on.'

She could feel the slam of his heart against his ribcage and the rigid control he was keeping of himself, but she still didn't dare look at him. Her heart was thundering in her ears and she was terrified of what she would read in his face if she looked at him. Because she mustn't weaken in what she had to do.

And then his voice came, a low, rumbling growl. 'This man, this David Kirby. Where is he now?'

'Dead,' she whispered, rubbing at her eyes with her hand but keeping her head on his chest. 'There was going to be a court case, something to do with children at a youth club he helped out with. Christina came forward then and he…he killed himself.'

'Pity.' It was grim. 'I would have liked to meet him and do the job myself.' There was a pause and then he said, 'How old were you when that happened? When he killed himself?'

'I was at university.'

'So all that time you had been coping with this alone? Was it the reason you were moved from family to family?' he asked gently.

She nodded against his bulk. 'I was a problem child,' she said in a small voice.

He stroked his hand over the ruffled silk of her hair and then along her damp cheek. 'Look at me, *chérie*,' he said softly. And when she shook her head, he said tenderly, 'You were never a problem, this I know. Brave and plucky for sure, and strong and courageous, but this can be seen as defiance by the insensitive and ignorant.'

'Don't.' It was in the form of a small wail.

'Don't what?'

'I can't…' She raised her head now, her throat tight with the emotion she was battling to control. 'I can never be what you want me to be, Jacques. What you need. You must see that now?'

'What I see is a beautiful, fine woman.'

'Jacques, I can't live up to what you would expect of me. What you would have a right to expect of a wife. I told you, I haven't even had a boyfriend before, let alone a lover.'

'Because you were waiting for me,' he said softly. 'I told you before, *chérie*, it was fate who pointed us out to each other, and do not try to tell me that things would not be good between us in bed because I know different. I have held you, touched and tasted you. Trust me on this.'

'But that's just it.' She strained away from him. 'That's what I can't do.' He still didn't understand.

'Holly, I do not expect some sort of performance in bed,' he said patiently. 'Surely you understand this? Do you think I had not realised that you are not very experienced?'

'I don't mean about the physical side of our relationship,' she said miserably. 'At least, not just that. I don't know how to explain this.'

'Try,' he said wryly, 'before I go mad.'

'It wouldn't be so bad if I didn't love you, but I do, and…and if we did marry I'd be wondering all the time when you were going to tire of me. I've seen the way women throw themselves at you and sooner or later someone would come along… It wouldn't really even be your fault,' she finished weakly.

'Oh, thank you,' he said flatly. 'Not only am I a Don Juan who can't keep his hands off women and who would commit adultery at the drop of a hat, but now I am weak and spineless too?'

'I didn't say that.' It was coming out all wrong.

'That is exactly what you said, Holly. What do you expect me to do? I have made a great deal of money, I admit it, but through hard work and my own efforts. I do not intend to apologise for that. Neither can I help my physical appearance. You must take my parents to task for that. But my mind and my principles are my own and I happen to believe in fidelity within marriage.'

'But even if you didn't actually…do anything you would want to,' she said desperately. 'I'm not the one for you, don't you see? Your world is so different from mine—'

'*Holly.*' His voice was too loud and she watched him take a long pull of air before he said more quietly,

'*Chérie*, I can understand how what has happened has made you insecure and vulnerable—'

'No, it's not that,' she said thickly. 'You're not an ordinary man, Jacques, you're not, and I am very ordinary. It just wouldn't work. A brief affair maybe, but not marriage.'

'You are wrong, Holly,' he said quietly. 'So wrong. I am just as assailable as the next man, for a start, but you are an extraordinary woman. Quite extraordinary. And I do not want an affair with you, brief or otherwise. I want to marry you. To live with you as husband and wife. You have to believe me on this.' His voice was low but very intense.

Her stomach turned over. 'I can't,' she whispered, and soft though the words were Jacques recognised the finality in them.

He stared at her for a moment, his face darkening, and Holly knew he was trying to keep a hold on his temper. He looked angry; she had never seen him so angry. 'And I have no say in this?' he bit out grimly. 'Is that it? You are allowed to destroy both our lives and I am supposed to accept it? Well, I do not! I do not, do you hear? I am not going to apologise for being who I am and I cannot control whether other women find me attractive, damn it! But since I met you I do not even notice other females, and that's the truth. I only want you, now and always. I love you, Holly, and I want to marry you. I shall always love you. What the hell more can I say?'

'Nothing,' she said, her mouth trembling. 'It's not you, it's me. I know that.'

'Well, bully for you,' he said bitterly, his French accent all the more prevalent with the English-sounding phrase. 'What if I had been poor and ugly, what then? Would you have married me then?'

'Don't...don't be like this.'

'That should be my line in the circumstances, don't you think?' he said furiously. 'Holly, I'll give you all the time you need, reassure you every day for the rest of our lives if that is what it takes, but you cannot shut me out of your life and your heart. I'm in there now and I mean to stay. Your problems are my problems now; we'll deal with them together. It is not just you any more, don't you understand? What affects you affects me. You are looking on this as though we are two people and separate, but I do not see it that way. We are not talking about you or me—marriage is an us. We become one. You draw on my strengths and I draw on yours. I help you with your demons and you help me with mine.'

It sounded fine, in theory. 'You have no demons,' she said quietly, her head lifting in defiance. 'You know it. Yours were conquered years ago.'

'Every man, woman and child has things they need help with. I am not an island any more than you are. And that is how you have tried to live since you were eight, n'est-ce pas? But you cannot go on like this. Kirby is the past and he should be dead and buried in your mind as well as physically. If not he is still hurting you and you cannot live all your life with his sickness touching you.'

The concept shocked her and she looked at him as resentment and rage rose inside her. 'How dare you say that?' she said furiously. 'He has no hold over me, none at all.'

'Prove it.' The amber eyes were very dark, like burnt honey. 'Say you are prepared to take a chance on loving me, on being my wife. Say you will trust me if you cannot trust yourself. I love you with all my being, all my soul. You hold my heart in your hands. Marry me, Holly.'

There was a long silence and Holly couldn't speak. She

was aware that she was crying soundlessly, the tears streaming down her face, but he made no move to hold her or caress her and she knew why. This was decision time. A man like Jacques wouldn't keep asking; he had too much pride for that. He had bared his soul in a manner that was completely alien to him and he had given her all he could. But it wasn't enough. For right or wrong, it wasn't enough.

'No.'

There was another silence, which seemed endless, and then Jacques turned the key in the ignition and the engine growled into life.

It was over.

CHAPTER NINE

'NEW YEAR'S EVE. It doesn't seem like New Year's Eve somehow, does it?' Alice stretched bony arms and then tweaked down her bright red miniskirt, which had ridden up over her thick black tights. 'You doing anything special, Holly?'

'No.' Holly forced a smile. 'Unless you call babysitting my godchild special. Lucy and James have been invited to a neighbour's party so I said I'd stay with Melanie Anne. They protested but I wasn't going to go out anyway.'

Alice nodded but Holly could tell she wasn't on the other girl's wavelength. At nineteen years of age, Alice was still of the opinion that 'night' was spelt 'nightclubs' and the ultimate tragedy was staying in on a night when everyone else was partying.

'A group of us are going to Trafalgar Square.' Alice giggled, flicking back her Gothic black bob. 'You might see us on the news tomorrow night. You know, drunk and disorderly and all that jazz!'

'I look forward to it,' Holly said wryly, before another batch of customers claimed their attention and effectively finished all chance of conversation for the last few minutes the shop was open.

The bakery-cum-café was just a short walk away from James and Lucy's house, and as always during the ten minutes it took to reach their home Holly's thoughts focused on Jacques. It had been two weeks since she had seen him that last time and she'd ached for him every moment. The deep well of loneliness which had always been a part of her since she had left her first foster parents, Kate and Angus, had grown over the last days. She had hoped it would get better but instead it had got worse.

Christmas had been a nightmare, the worst part being that she had felt forced to put on a show of being heart-whole and cheerful for Lucy and James, and not least little Melanie Anne. And all the time the last conversation with Jacques had been going round and round in her head, beating at her brain until she had felt it would explode.

He had dropped her off outside her place of work that lunchtime without saying another word until she was on the pavement, where he'd joined her. Then he had taken her hand, his voice controlled and his face grim as he'd said, 'You can't shut me out of your heart and your head, Holly. Don't you know that yet? It's too late. Way, way too late.'

And then he had turned and left her and driven away in his expensive sports car. And she hadn't heard from him again.

All over Christmas she had been waiting for a call, even a visit, but there had been nothing. *Nothing.* Which was what she had wanted... Only it wasn't. But then the thought of making the sort of commitment he was asking for terrified her. How could she love Jacques as fully and unreservedly as he would expect, as he *deserved*, when she felt chained by so many fears and doubts? She couldn't, she told herself frequently. But then how could she live without him in her life now she knew him? She couldn't. And so it went on.

Every day since Christmas she had expected, with every tinkle of the bakery doorbell, to see Jacques standing there in front of her when she glanced up. But it hadn't happened. *He* hadn't happened. He had taken her at her word and disappeared out of her life, and she didn't know how she was going to bear it.

Tears misted the road in front of her and she blinked them away quickly. No self-pity, she told herself savagely. She had had her chance with Jacques and she'd blown it, and if she was being truthful she couldn't in all honesty say she wouldn't do the same again. Nothing had changed, not really. Nothing, it seemed, except Jacques's feelings for her, which it appeared he could put on and take off at will. And, that being the case, it proved her absolutely right, didn't it? But then she had known someone as proud and strong as Jacques wouldn't keep banging his head against the proverbial brick wall.

'Right, pull-yourself-together time.' As Lucy and James's house came into view Holly sniffed loudly and blinked furiously. Time to be happy-clappy again.

Circles of muted gold from the street lights were casting their soft glow on the pavement as she walked the last few yards, and there was already the nip of frost in the biting air. She had used to love nights like this, especially when there was the faint fragrance of woodsmoke in the air from a neighbouring bonfire like tonight, but now the clean, sharp night didn't move her. Would she ever feel remotely at peace again? She stood at the entrance to the three feet or so of paved front garden and lifted her face to the sky. It was pierced with stars and eternally beautiful.

'Holly? Is that you?'

The front door opening suddenly and Lucy's voice nearly made her jump out of her skin, and her heart was beating like a drum when she said, 'Of course it's me. What's the matter?'

'Oh, Holly. Quick, come in.'

There was a note in Lucy's voice which made Holly

fairly spring up the couple of steps to the hall, and then she stopped dead at the sight of Mrs Gibson standing in the doorway to Lucy's sitting room. Holly hadn't seen her old neighbour since Jacques's disastrous visit. She didn't bear the old lady any animosity—Mrs Gibson would have thought she was doing the best thing in telling Jacques where she lived and worked, Holly knew that, or else wild horses wouldn't have dragged the information from her. But she just hadn't felt like seeing anyone.

'What is it, Mrs Gibson?' It was clear the old lady was distressed, and normally she didn't budge more than a few yards from her home and cats. 'Is Mr Bateman all right?'

'Mr Bateman?' Mrs Gibson's scathing and expressive snort suggested extreme scorn. 'That man managed to put the dustbin lid down when Tigger was inside a few days ago. I had people combing the streets for him when he didn't come back for two days; he's lucky to be alive. How he didn't suffocate I don't know. And of course it would be the one time Mr Bateman remembered to weight the lid down with bricks. He was hungry and upset and he smelt to high heaven.'

Holly assumed Mrs Gibson was referring to Tigger in the last sentence. 'Oh, dear.' She shook her head sympathetically. 'Then why are you here?'

'Why am I...? Oh, yes, yes. How silly of me. That's Mr Bateman distracting me,' Mrs Gibson said, quite unfairly. 'It's that nice young man, Jacques, I've called about.'

Here we go. It was clear Mrs Gibson saw herself as the New Year goodwill fairy with a matchmaking hat on, Holly thought darkly, drawing on every ounce of patience as she said quietly, 'I'd prefer not to discuss Jacques Querruel, Mrs Gibson. We were seeing each other for a time but it is over. End of story.'

'Really?' Mrs Gibson nodded. And then, as Lucy went to speak, the old lady waved her to silence, before saying, 'I'm surprised at that. I know he thought a bit of you. "Milly," he said—did you know he called me Milly?' she asked Holly abruptly.

'Er—no, no, I didn't.'

'Oh, yes. The first afternoon he came to tea with me— when he was still searching all the hours of the day and night for you—we decided on Jacques and Milly. It's short for Millicent, of course.'

'Right.' Holly struggled to keep her voice in neutral. Mrs Gibson's tone had made it quite clear how she viewed the current situation and whose side she was on, and it wasn't Holly's. As far as Holly was aware, no one had ever had the temerity to address the fierce old lady by her Christian name—probably including the late Mr Gibson— but of course it had only taken Jacques an hour or two to charm Mrs Gibson into fluttering submission!

'Now, where was I?' Mrs Gibson glared at Holly and Lucy as though they had been the means of distracting her. 'Oh, yes, that's right. I was telling you what the dear boy said to me.'

'Mrs Gibson—'

'"Milly," he said—' Mrs Gibson completely ignored Holly's attempt to interrupt her '"—I know I have met the woman I want to spend the rest of my life with, and whatever it takes I shall find her again." What do you say to that, then?' she asked Holly confrontationally.

'Like I said, Mrs Gibson, it's over,' Holly said firmly.

'Lucy said you would say that.'

'And she was right.' And the fact that Jacques hadn't contacted her in any way since their last meeting seemed to suggest he'd got over her pretty quick too! Holly knew the thought which had tormented her day and night was probably totally unjust as far as Jacques was concerned, but it seemed as if a procession of beautiful, available females paraded themselves before her wherever she looked these days. On the TV, in advertisements, books, magazines—gorgeous, fancy-free lovelies who would be perfect for a young and handsome millionaire.

'So you wouldn't be interested in knowing about the dear boy's dreadful accident, then? Out of sight, out of mind, is it?' Mrs Gibson's bright, bird-like eyes were fixed hard on Holly's face.

'What…what did you say?' Holly's heart slammed against her ribcage with enough force to choke her breath.

'It happened early on Christmas Eve morning, of all days, apparently,' Mrs Gibson went on relentlessly. 'A collision with a car that had swerved onto the wrong side of the road to avoid a child who had run out in front of it. And of course these motorbikes don't give the sort of protection a car affords, do they? Mr Gibson drove one as a young man but I soon put a stop to that when I met him.'

'You're saying Jacques's hurt? He's not…?'

'Dead? Oh, dear me, no. Did I give you that impression?' Mrs Gibson asked without a trace of apology in her voice. Short, sharp shock treatment. That was what she'd decided on when she had finished talking with Jacques's housekeeper. This ridiculous situation had gone on long enough and Holly needed bringing to her senses. 'I understand he was unconscious for a good few days, which caused a great deal of anxiety for his family, but there, I mustn't bother you any more. You must be wanting your tea. I'll just get my hat and coat—'

'Please, Mrs Gibson…'

Mrs Gibson took pity on the young, white-faced woman in front of her then, her manner softening as she said quietly, 'I don't know a great deal more than what I have told you, Holly, except that I understand he is out of immediate danger. I only telephoned the number he had given me this morning, you see. I hadn't heard from him, which I thought was a little strange, considering he had promised to call by over Christmas.'

'He had?'

'Oh, yes. He was intending to spend the holiday in England.' Mrs Gibson stared at her meaningfully. 'Where his heart is. His housekeeper said he had only gone a short distance from the château when the accident occurred, however. I think the family would have liked to let you know but they had no way of contacting you, and of course Jacques was in a coma.'

Coma. Oh, God. Please, please, God, don't let him be badly hurt. 'Out of immediate danger'. What did that mean? He could be permanently disabled, anything, and they would still say that. *He could have died.* He could have died and she would never have known but for Mrs Gibson. Please, God, please help me to get to him quickly. Don't let him have a relapse or anything…

By nine o'clock that evening Holly was aboard a plane flying over the Channel.

She had spoken to Monique before she had left, and the housekeeper had immediately burst into tears at the sound of her voice, which had scared Holly to death. She had had the worst thirty seconds of her life, but once Monique had calmed down enough to talk to her it appeared Jacques was no worse and no better than he had been earlier that day when Mrs Gibson had telephoned.

'Severe concussion and two broken legs,' Monique had informed her tearfully when Holly had asked about Jacques's condition. There had been some internal injuries but the doctors seemed satisfied these were no longer a problem. Of course, he was still very ill and at this stage they were just taking it a day at a time. Nothing could be guaranteed...

The plane journey and cab ride to the private hospital on the outskirts of Paris forever remained a blur in Holly's memory. All she could think about was Jacques.

She had done nothing but push him away from the first moment she'd met him. She had rejected him, refused to trust him, failed him so badly she wouldn't have blamed him if he wanted nothing more to do with her after that last caustic meeting in England. *But he had been coming to see her.* Monique had confirmed what Mrs Gibson had intimated. He had set out early on Christmas Eve morning in order to be with her over Christmas. *To be with her.*

How could she have been so stupid? How could she have imagined, for one moment, that she could possibly live without him? If anything happened to him she would die, she would. She wouldn't want to go on living. This was all her fault. If she hadn't sent him away that day he wouldn't have been making the journey that had almost killed him. That still *could* kill him if something went wrong. What if the doctors had missed something? You read about that sort of thing every day in the newspapers. No one was infallible and the best of doctors were only human.

What if she got to the hospital and he had changed his mind about her after everything that had happened? After the accident? What if he now finally believed her when she said she couldn't trust him? She had believed it; she still did in a way. It seemed impossible that a man like Jacques would continue to love her forever and ever, but compared to him being taken permanently by death *now*, in the immediate future, everything else paled into insignificance.

When Holly arrived at the hospital she found to her surprise that she was expected, and as she was whisked along thickly carpeted corridors by a fresh-faced young nurse she blessed Monique, who had obviously telephoned to prepare the way.

Barbe was sitting waiting for her in the corridor outside Jacques's room, and his sister immediately leapt to her feet at the sight of Holly and opened her arms wide, giving her a big hug as she murmured, 'I'm so glad you've come, Holly. We all are. The rest of the family have gone home to sleep—we're all exhausted—but it was decided I remain and meet you.'

'Thank you.' It was more than she deserved. 'How is he?'

'He's got his head back, which is the main thing,' Barbe said with a weak smile. 'It frightened us, seeing Jacques so lifeless and still over the past days. He's always so full of energy, so vital, you know?'

Holly nodded. Yes, she knew.

'He's still sleeping most of the time but at least when he is awake he knows us now. As for his legs...it will take time, the doctors say, but hopefully they will mend, although the right one is very badly damaged. He may always have a limp.'

'Oh, Barbe.' The knot in the pit of her stomach was burning, stifling her breath and choking her. All she wanted now was to see Jacques. To sit with him, to kiss him, to love him. For as long as he wanted her. 'Does...does he know I'm coming?' she whispered thickly.

Barbe looked at her, a straight look, which, although

friendly, said more than any words could have done. She shook her head slowly. 'It seemed best to wait.'

In case she had changed her mind. Holly nodded at the other woman even as her mind told her Jacques's family had no idea of just how much she loved him. Which made them all the more gracious in their acceptance of her arrival at the hospital tonight. 'Can I go in?'

'Of course. I'm going home now, so give Jacques my love.'

The nurse had disappeared at some point, and now it was Jacques's sister who pushed open the door for Holly to enter the dimly lit room beyond, whispering as she did so, 'Monique has got your room ready at the château for when you leave here, OK?'

There were none of the tubes and drips Holly had mentally prepared herself for, just a large cage under the covers, protecting Jacques's damaged legs. She moved quietly forward, her heart accelerating, and then she was by his side of the bed, peering down at the sleeping occupant. It was Jacques and yet not Jacques. He was very still and she didn't think she had ever seen him still before, and very, very pale, almost grey-faced. His black hair fell across his brow in a way he would never have allowed normally, his long eyelashes lying on cheekbones that were starkly chiselled in the whiteness of the skin surrounding them. Holly felt as though her heart was being wrenched out by its roots.

Oh, Jacques, Jacques. Holly swallowed at the constriction in her throat, fighting back the tears which had been gathering behind a great dam since the moment she had seen Mrs Gibson. But she couldn't cry now, not here. He might wake up and she didn't want his first sight of her to be when she was weeping. But she loved him. So, so much. And she desperately wanted to believe they could make it.

She closed her eyes briefly, telling herself she had to be strong for him right now and that the future would work itself out, and when she opened them again Jacques was looking at her.

'Hello, my darling.' It was the first time she had ever used the endearment although she wasn't aware of it until much later. Her mouth began to tremble as he didn't respond in any way at all, simply staring at her with amber eyes that glowed dark gold in the dimly lit and expensively furnished surroundings. She bent down, brushing her lips lightly over his, and then, as she felt his arms come tightly round her, she found herself half lying across his chest as his mouth fastened on hers with a fierceness that belied his condition.

'I...I'll hurt you.' As she came up for air she tried to pull herself off him, only for his arms to tighten still more.

'I can't believe you're real.' It was a low murmur but the deep, sensuous voice was definitely all Jacques's. 'When I saw you standing there I thought I was dreaming again. So many dreams of you...'

He kissed her again, hard and long and not at all as a desperately sick man should kiss. Not that she'd kissed any.

'Jacques, I'm too heavy,' she murmured breathlessly.

'Impossible.'

'Your legs...'

'Damn my legs.'

Holly gave up and began to kiss him back, and it was much later when he finally let her go and she sat on the edge of the bed, both his hands holding on tight to hers and her eyes shining with tears. 'I'm sorry, I'm so, so sorry,' she whispered tremblingly. 'I should never have

sent you away and then this wouldn't have happened.'
She glanced miserably at the cage.

'You did not send me away, *chérie*,' he murmured just
as softly. 'I chose to go, to give you a little time to come
to your senses. I did not intend to give up, not then, not
ever. And it was my decision to ride the bike on Christmas
Eve, not yours. The accident could have happened at any
time, any place.'

'But it didn't,' she whispered, tears starring her
eyelashes.

'No, it did not.' There was a faint shadow of the old
smile on his face. 'But it brought you to me, *n'est-ce pas*?
So this is good.'

'How can you say what has happened to you is good?'
she said shakily. 'You could have been killed, and your
poor legs…'

'My poor legs will heal,' he said drily, so much the old
Jacques she felt a stab of relief. 'Certainly in time for our
wedding. And I do not intend to die for a long, long time,
petite. I will not leave you, OK? We will make old bones
together.'

'Oh, Jacques.' She hadn't realised she was crying, the
tears slowly dripping down her cheeks, or that Jacques
had hit on the consuming fear which had eaten her up
ever since she had realised how much she loved him.
Everyone she had ever cared about had been taken from
her in the past; why should the future be any different?

'Old bones,' he repeated softly, his eyes smiling at her.
'Because you are going to marry me, are you not, *ma
chérie*? I do not know how you knew I was here, and now
you *are* here I do not care who brought you to me. I told
myself, once I could think again, that I would be strong
over this. I would not call you to my side and blackmail
your soft heart with pity. I would wait until my legs were

my own once more and then walk, tall and sound, into your life again and make you marry me. Now you are here I see this was foolishness. All pride vanishes the moment I see your face.'

'I don't believe that for a second,' she said huskily.

'Then you have much to learn about me,' he said, and smiled. The smile which always had the power to turn her world upside-down. 'And I of you, no doubt. But we will have much fun in the learning, yes? Kiss me, Holly,' he added thickly.

She placed her lips on his mouth gently but then, as his mouth sought hers and he kissed her with a fierce, possessive ardour, locking her against him, she felt her senses reel. His hands cupped her face as his mouth demanded greater intimacy, his desire reassuring her more than any words spoken by the medical profession could have done.

His hands moved over her upper torso, sliding under her top and touching her with sensual, intimate caresses which made her gasp against his lips for long, rainbow-coloured moments.

A sound from the corridor outside had her pulling away. '*Jacques*, someone's coming.' She sat up, smoothing her dishevelled hair away from her hot, flushed cheeks as she said, half laughing, 'What will they say if they find us making love in your hospital bed?'

'That I can get out of this damn place sooner than they thought, I hope.' And then his eyes darkened as they searched her face. 'Do you believe me now?' he said levelly. 'Enough to marry me as soon as I can walk out of here? That will do to start with, *petite*. The rest will come in time. Time that will convince you I love you and want you and need you more than life itself. Is the running over, Holly? Are you here to stay?'

She nodded wordlessly, incapable of uttering a sound but her eyes speaking out her love.

'We'll make our own world, *chérie*. Believe me on this too. A world in which our children will know how much they are wanted and loved, and that they will never have to go through what you did. Our world will be safe and secure and strong.'

A sudden explosion of sound from outside the hospital made them both stop and listen for a moment. 'Fireworks,' Holly said tremulously, her hands tight in his. 'It's New Year's Day, Jacques.'

'A new beginning,' he said softly, his heavy lids making her realise that whatever he said to the contrary he was exhausted. 'Ours to make of it what we will. And we'll make it good, *petite*. *Merveilleux! C'est extra!* You agree?'

'You'll have to teach me French.' Her throat was dry with the enormity of what she was committing to. 'I can't have our children speaking their father's language better than I do.'

'This is true.' A bronzed hand lifted to her face. 'But be it French or English I want you to speak out all your fears, *chérie*, whenever you need to. Understand me on this. However many times a day you need me I will be there for you. I promise you this. I love you.'

'And I love you,' she said shakily.

'Then that is all we need.'

CHAPTER TEN

JACQUES and Holly were married on the lawns of the château on a brilliantly beautiful and frosty February morning two months later.

The doctors had advised Jacques it would be several months and well into the spring before he could walk again. He'd cut the prediction by more than half, but then, as Lucy whispered to James during the short service, he had had everything to get well for, hadn't he?

Holly looked radiant in an ivory Duchesse satin dress with an organza and satin train, over which she wore a satin cloak trimmed with clouds of soft, floating feathers. She carried a small, simple bouquet of baby's breath, and her face, framed by the hood of the cloak, was luminous with love for the tall, dark man at her side.

Mrs Gibson, as outrageous as ever in a bright lemon fun-fur coat and matching hat, declared Holly the most beautiful bride she had ever seen and even had a little weep, which allowed the ever-hopeful Mr Bateman to put a comforting hand round her shoulders. He grinned like a Cheshire cat for the rest of the day.

The bridal pair honeymooned first in the Caribbean, followed by a month or two at the Great Barrier Reef. By the time they returned home to the château in the summer Jacques was walking as well as ever he had and Holly had the bloom of a truly loved and satisfied woman. Jacques told her a hundred times a day how much he loved her and the dark shadows were being banished for good.

Time passed, time in which Holly opened like a flower to the sun of Jacques's adoration, and when first a daughter and then a son was born to them they felt blessed.

And then, early in the morning that heralded their tenth wedding anniversary, when they lay locked in each other's arms in their enormous bed, Holly stirred in her husband's arms. The night had been one of love, the warm glow of which was still reflected in her voice when she said, 'Jacques, we're so very lucky.'

'I know it.' His voice was a deep, soothing rumble above her head.

'And it could have been so different.'

'No.' As she raised her face to stare into the beautiful amber eyes he was smiling. 'I would not have let it be,' he said softly. 'I would never have given up, *petite*. You know this.'

'I want more children, Jacques.' And then, as he went to reach for her as his smile widened, she said quickly, 'No, listen. I mean it. I want to foster children, little ones in need of love and care. Children who have been hurt by life, children like I was. I feel ready for this now. I want to give them a chance in life, as many children as they let us have, because…'

'What?' He touched her face with his hand, his eyes gentle. 'What, my love?'

'Because they might not all meet a Jacques later in life. They need us *now* because you were right. Love is all anyone needs to come out of the darkness into the light.'

'No more shadows, *petite*?'

'Not a single one.'

'Then you are right, it is time.'

And together they made it so.

CITY CINDERELLA

by

Catherine George

Catherine George was born in Wales and early on developed a passion for reading which eventually fuelled her compulsion to write. Marriage to an engineer led to nine years in Brazil, but on his later travels the education of her son and daughter kept her in the UK. And instead of constant reading to pass her lonely evenings she began to write the first of her romantic novels. When not writing and reading she loves to cook, listen to opera and browse in antiques shops.

CHAPTER ONE

THE wind from the Thames came whistling up the cobbled street as he paid off the taxi. Aching in every bone, he hurried into the building and leaned against the wall in the lift, cursing the virus that had finally caught up with him. On the top floor he heaved himself upright when the doors opened, and with a groan of relief at the prospect of warmth let himself into the loft apartment he called home. He shrugged off his overcoat, dumped his briefcase on the pile of mail on the military chest in the hall, and, desperate for hot coffee with a slug of Scotch in it, opened the kitchen door. And stood rooted to the spot.

The kitchen's stainless steel and granite was immaculate, as expected. But it was occupied. A young woman he'd never seen in his life sat on one of the retro-style stools at his breakfast bar, tapping away at a laptop, her concentration so intense she had no idea he was there.

Before he could demand an explanation his sudden, hacking cough brought the stranger's head swivelling round, her eyes wide in utter dismay as she slid to her feet to face him.

'Mr Tennent?' she said at last, in a surprisingly deep, husky voice for someone only an inch or so over five feet. 'I do apologise. This is the very first time, I swear.'

Lucas Tennent remained standing in the doorway, staring at her blankly, his thought processes blunted by the dull pounding in his head. 'The first time for what? Who the devil are you?'

5

'I'm your cleaner.'

He blinked. 'My *cleaner*?'

She nodded, flushing. 'Thank you for the cheque you left for me today—unless you'd like it back now.'

'Why the hell should I want it back?' he said irritably, grappling with the fact that this was the E Warner who kept his flat in mint condition. Not elderly and aproned, but young, in jeans and skimpy sweatshirt, with soot-black curling hair skewered up in an untidy knot.

'Mr Tennent,' she said after a moment, eyeing him closely. 'You don't look at all well.'

'I feel bloody awful,' he snapped. 'But keep to the point. Explain about the laptop.'

'I was using my batteries, not your electricity,' she said defensively.

'My sole interest, of course,' he said with blighting sarcasm. 'Tell me what you were doing.'

Her jaw set. 'I'd rather not do that.'

'Tell me just the same,' he said relentlessly.

'Nothing criminal, Mr Tennent,' she said with hauteur. 'I'm—doing a correspondence course.'

'So where do you normally work on it?'

'In my room. But this week it's half-term. At the moment peace and quiet are in short supply where I live. So I did some work here today. But only after I finished your cleaning,' she assured him.

'Sorry I came home early to spoil your fun—' he began, the rest of his words engulfed in a sudden spasm of coughing. To his surprise, he was gently taken by the arm and led towards the breakfast bar.

'Sit there for a moment, Mr Tennent,' she said with sympathy. 'Do you have any medication?'

He shook his head, gasping for breath as he subsided

on a stool. 'No. I just need coffee. Make me some and I'll double your money.'

She gave him a withering look and turned on her heel, presenting a back view rigid with offence while she dealt with the machine guaranteed to turn beans into coffee at top speed. Lucas sat silent, chin on hands, diverted from the thumping in his head by the sight of E Warner tugging her sweatshirt down to cover an inch of bare midriff as she put her laptop to sleep and closed it before pouring the coffee.

'When I came in I thought I was hallucinating, Ms Warner,' he remarked eventually, as the scent of his best Blue Mountain filled the air. 'But a laptop seemed an unlikely accessory for housebreaking.' He took a relishing gulp of the strong, steaming liquid she set in front of him. 'Thank you. I think you just saved my life.'

She shook her head, frowning. 'Not really, Mr Tennent. You should be in bed.'

'I will be shortly.' He raised an eyebrow. 'Aren't you having any coffee?'

Her smile activated a dimple near the corner of her mouth. Which was a very enticing feature, he noticed—unpainted, full-lipped, and eminently kissable. The curves outlined by the sweatshirt were equally enticing... And the fever was obviously affecting his brain, he thought in swift disgust, hoping she couldn't read his mind.

'It seemed best to wait until invited,' she said ruefully.

Lucas nodded, then winced when the movement made his headache worse. 'Do please join me, Ms Warner,' he said formally. 'Or are you Mrs?'

'Miss.'

'What does the E stand for?'

'Emily.' She eyed him, frowning. 'Mr Tennent, do you mind if I touch your forehead?'

'Not at all.' He submitted to a cool hand laid briefly on his brow, and sat back. 'Diagnosis?'

'High temperature. You've got flu, hopefully.'

'*Hopefully?*'

'I meant rather than anything worse.' She hesitated, then bent to search in a backpack on the floor and came up with a packet of paracetamol. 'Will you take these? Two now and two tonight, and drink plenty of fluids.'

He stared at her in surprise. 'That's very kind of you, Emily, or do you prefer Ms Warner?'

'You pay my wages, Mr Tennent. Your choice.' She looked at her watch, then stowed her laptop in the backpack. 'I won't have any coffee, thank you. Time I was off. I'm taking the twins to the cinema.'

His eyebrows rose. 'Twins?'

'The children on half-term. Their father's my landlord, and I'm taking them off his hands for a couple of hours,' she explained. 'I did your shopping on the way in, so there's plenty of orange juice and fruit. Goodbye, Mr Tennent. I'll be in on Monday as usual.' She eyed him with concern. 'Is there someone who can look after you?'

'I wouldn't ask my worst enemy to risk this blasted bug. Which you could be doing right now,' he added suddenly.

Her shake of the head dislodged another hank of hair. 'I've already had flu this winter.'

'What did you do to get over it?'

'Went home to my parents to be cosseted.'

'My mother's asthmatic, so that's out of the question.' He shrugged. 'And otherwise I prefer to wallow alone in my misery.'

She pulled on her jacket and thrust her arms through the straps of her backpack. 'There's no point in calling a doctor if it's flu, of course. Not unless you develop something else, like bronchitis. But please take the pills—eight a day max—and drink lots of water. A good thing it's Friday, Mr Tennent. You'll have the weekend to get over it.'

'If I live that long,' he said morosely, and saw her to the door.

'Mr Tennent,' she said diffidently as he opened it.

'Yes?'

'I'm sorry.'

His bloodshot eyes narrowed to an unsettling gleam. 'Because I feel like death, or because you were caught in the act?'

Her chin lifted. 'Both. Please accept the coffee-making for free by way of recompense,' she added, and stepped into the lift.

Her mind occupied with Lucas Tennent, for once Emily Warner had no eyes for the view of the Thames as she crossed Tower Bridge. Up to now, the man she worked for had just been one of her four employers. He left a cheque every week for her wages, and owned a flat she'd give her eye-teeth to live in. But now she could put a face and body to the name the situation was different. He'd given her the shock of her life by catching her redhanded, of course. But her first startled glimpse of Lucas Tennent was rubber-stamped on her brain, partly because he'd looked so ghastly she'd been afraid he was about to pass out on her.

Oblivious of traffic noise and passers-by, Emily hurried back to Spitalfields, her mind busy with the physical details of the employer she'd never actually met before.

There were no photographs of him in his apartment, but because he did something in the banking world she'd visualised brains as well as brawn. In the flesh, Lucas Tennent was well over six feet tall, his windblown hair black as her own, possibly eyes to match, when they weren't too bloodshot to tell. His intelligence was self-evident, but it came combined with dark, smouldering good looks undiminished by even his current deathly pallor. And his Savile Row suit was no disguise for the musculature she would have expected, since it was part of her job to dust the rowing machine and treadmill up in the gallery. Emily sighed enviously. All that space for just one man. If she lived there she could work on her laptop to her heart's content under the gallery's pitched glass roof, which not only boasted sunblinds controlled electronically by temperature, but led on to a roof terrace overlooking the Thames. Perfect. And in total contrast to her solitary room on the second floor of a house owned by one of her brother's friends.

But it was a pretty room, and she was lucky to have it, she reminded herself as she reached the familiar cobbled street. Built originally for refugee Huguenot silk weavers in the seventeen hundreds, most of the houses in this part of Spitalfields had been painstakingly restored, including the one owned by her landlord. Nat Sedley was an architect with a London firm and a home in the Cotswolds. Originally he had bought the house in Spitalfields as a city base. But he now lived in it permanently, with only his two tenants for company, while his children remained with his estranged wife in the house in the country.

When Emily reached the railings which flanked the front door it flew open to reveal two excited six-year-olds lying in wait in the hall, ready and raring to go.

'They've been dressed for ages,' said their father, grinning in apology. 'I warned them you might want tea first but it fell on deaf ears.'

'I'll just dump my things and we're away,' Emily assured them, rewarded at once by beams from two faces so unalike it was hard to believe that Thomas and Lucy were brother and sister, let alone twins.

'I'll have supper waiting when you get back,' said Nat, as he saw them into a taxi. 'Now be good, you two, and maybe we can coax Emily to share it with us.'

By the time she'd brought the jubilant twins back to Spitalfields Nat Sedley had the promised supper waiting, and Emily not only enjoyed a family meal, but surrendered to pleas to stay afterwards until the twins were ready for bed.

'Thanks a lot, Em,' said Nat gratefully, as she made for the stairs later. 'You're a life-saver.'

She chuckled. 'That's the second time I've heard that today.'

Nat demanded details, amused when he heard she'd been caught red-handed at her laptop. 'But I'm sorry you were driven out to find quiet to work. I should have put your room out of bounds to the twins from the first. By way of a peace offering, fancy coming down later this evening for a drink?'

She smiled. 'Thanks, I'd like that very much.'

In the quiet of her room, Emily collapsed into a chair, suddenly weary. The outing with the twins had been great fun, but after a morning spent cleaning two apartments, followed by a couple of hours' solid slog on her laptop, the confrontation with Lucas Tennent had rather knocked the stuffing out of her. He'd had every right to sack her on the spot, too, which would have done serious damage to her finances. Lucky for her he'd been feeling so rough, otherwise he might not have taken her trespass nearly so well. She'd felt like Goldilocks caught by the bear. Emily chuckled. Wrong hair, wrong fairy tale. There were no fireplaces in Lucas Tennent's flat, but her role was Cinderella just the same. And she'd done no harm, other than just being there in his kitchen, where she wasn't supposed to be on a Friday afternoon.

But from now on her activities in Mr Lucas Tennent's flat would be restricted to the cleaning duties he paid her for. Emily frowned, wondering how he was feeling. He'd looked so ill she'd been a bit reluctant to leave him to fend for himself. Which was nonsense. If she hadn't stayed on for an extra hour or two she wouldn't have met him, nor known about his flu.

Emily took a reviving shower, dried her hair and treated her hands and face to some extra care, grateful to Nat for asking her down for a drink. Much as she despised herself for it, Friday evenings were still hard to get used to on her own. And to add to her pleasure, when she arrived in Nat's small, panelled drawing-room her fellow tenant, Mark Cooper, gave her a hug and shepherded her to the sofa to join his girlfriend, Bryony Talbot.

'Hi, Emily.' Bryony patted the place beside her. 'Come and sit down. Are you exhausted? Nat said you've been entertaining the twins.'

'And enjoying it. Evening all. How are you feeling now, Mark?' asked Emily. 'Recovered from your cold?'

He nodded, smiling smugly. 'Bryony kissed me better.'

Nat shook his head as he handed Emily a glass of wine. 'His own private nurse, lucky beggar.'

'But my medical skills don't come cheap,' said

Bryony promptly. 'He's buying me a *very* expensive dinner tomorrow night.'

Emily chuckled. 'Demand Claridges, at the very least.'

Mark winked at her. 'Flash your dimple at me like that, Emily, and I'll bring you back a doggy bag.'

'Gee, thanks!'

'Lots of strange bugs about where I earn my crust, though,' he commented, squeezing between his beloved and Emily on the sofa. 'Move up, you two.'

'Can't you sit on a chair?' complained Bryony affectionately.

'Much more fun like this, darling.'

Emily felt a stab of concern at Mark's mention of bugs. But Lucas Tennent was big enough and old enough to look after himself. And he could call on professional medical help if he became really ill; a thought which allowed her to relax in the stimulating company of people she liked very much. Mark rented the floor below hers in Nat's house, and along with Bryony had been a good friend when Emily, in urgent need of somewhere in London to live, had taken Nat up on his offer of a room. With two homes to keep up, her landlord insisted he could do with all the extra money he could get. Emily had scoffed at his idea of rent, which was ridiculously low for London. But Nat was a close friend of her brother, Andrew, and remained adamant. In the end she had pocketed the pride she couldn't afford, grateful for his help and generosity.

After a place to live, a new job had been the next priority on the agenda. When Emily moved into the room in Nat's house he had been trying for some time to find a suitable replacement for his cleaner, who wanted to retire. Because the elegant house was very old, and correspondingly fragile, he needed someone who would treat it with the care and respect it deserved. But when Emily proposed herself as substitute, at the same rate of pay, Nat thought she was joking at first. At last, when he realised she was in deadly earnest, he agreed with enthusiasm, and the moment Mark heard about it he begged Emily to take on his rooms as well. When it became obvious that Emily actually enjoyed cleaning, Nat asked permission to recommend her to one of his married female colleagues who'd just acquired a new flat in Bermondsey. The added job proved such a happy arrangement that Liz Donaldson soon suggested Emily kill two birds with one stone and also take on a friend's loft apartment in the converted warehouse across the street. And so what had been intended as a stop-gap before finding another secretarial job suddenly snowballed into a whole new career.

Emily's parents disapproved strongly, and friends thought she was raving mad. But in secret she was working to plan. The new job left her mind and imagination free to function separately from her busy, careful hands, and at the same time paid enough to provide financial backing while she tried her hand at writing a novel. Taken on the hop, she'd had to fib to Lucas Tennent, because not even her nearest and dearest had any idea what she was really up to in her spare time.

The plot of her novel was already mapped out, with some of the main characters automatically cast: villain and wicked witch no problem at all. But she'd had difficulty in conjuring up a charismatic central male. Nat was outrageously handsome, and Mark boyish-faced and charming. But, despite covert observation of both men as a possible role model, her hero had stubbornly refused to come to life. Then Lucas Tennent had caught her *in flagrante* with her laptop today, and wham, her main character had materialised right before her startled, guilty eyes.

After a couple of hours, much as she was enjoying herself in such convivial company, Emily resisted pleas to stay longer and went up early to her room. She sat down at her desk, booted up the laptop, and set to work on her novel. By the time she went to bed she felt tired, but very pleased with herself. Adding Lucas Tennent's physical assets to the previously bare bones of her central male character had provided her with exactly the charismatic hero she needed for her plot.

The moment Emily was dressed next morning the twins came knocking on her door. 'Hi, you two,' she said affectionately.

'Dad said we mustn't bother you if you're busy,' said Thomas in one breath, then smiled cajolingly. 'But please come down for coffee. We've got to go after lunch.'

'We'll miss you,' said Lucy, giving Emily a hug.

'But you'll be seeing Mummy today, sweetheart, so you won't need me. I bet she's missed you a lot,' said Emily, deliberately cheerful. 'Give her my love.'

Lucy's big blue eyes filled with tears. 'Emily, will *you* ask Mummy to be friends with Daddy again?'

'You can't ask Emily to do that!' said her twin gruffly.

Emily went downstairs with the children, wishing she *could* do something to help. But the Sedleys' private affairs were none of her business. She'd known them both a long time, it was true, but had no idea what sin Nat had committed that Thea found impossible to forgive. Nor did she want to know. Sorting out her own personal life was more than enough.

Emily enjoyed a lively half-hour with the twins, but

when they were settled in front of Saturday morning television Nat beckoned her into his kitchen and shut the door.

'Why has Lucy been crying?'

Emily looked at him squarely. 'She wanted me to ask Thea to be friends with you again, and Tom told her that wasn't on.'

His handsome face went blank. 'Are you going to do that?'

'Do you want me to?'

Nat was silent for a moment, then gave her a smile just like his son's. 'If I thought it would do any good, yes. But it won't.' He shivered a little. 'Forget it, love. Don't get involved.'

Emily eyed him with suspicion. 'Are you all right, Nat? Not coming down with something, too, are you?'

'Too?'

'Like Mark,' she said hastily.

He shook his head. 'I'm just dandy, other than taking my children back to the love of my life, who won't let me over the doorstep.' He forced a smile. 'You've had enough upset in your life lately without worrying about me, Emily. Enjoy your weekend.'

But before getting ready to go out Emily gave in to her prodding conscience and rang Lucas Tennent, who growled a response so hoarse it was obvious he was worse than the day before.

'Good morning,' she said briskly, 'this is Emily Warner.'

'*Who?*'

She bristled. 'Your cleaner, Mr Tennent. I wondered how you were feeling today.'

'Oh, right.' There was a pause. 'Actually, I feel bloody awful.'

'Have you eaten anything?'

A spasm of coughing blasted her ear before he spoke again. 'No,' he rasped. 'Not hungry.'

'Is your temperature still high?'

'Probably.' He gulped audibly. 'Oh, *hell*—'

Emily seethed for a moment after he disconnected, then told herself it was idiotic to feel offended. Even more so to worry about a perfect stranger. Especially one who couldn't remember who she was.

Mindful of Ginny, who always looked effortlessly right, Emily took time over her appearance, then went downstairs for a last hug from the twins before she set off for Knightsbridge to meet her friend.

'I say, darling, you look rather gorgeous today,' exclaimed Ginny Hart, when Emily joined her in the Harvey Nichols coffee shop.

'I like the "today" bit,' chuckled Emily, shedding the amber wool coat bought in the days when she still had a high-salary job. 'I try my best every day.'

'A bargain, that coat—matches your eyes,' commented Ginny, and eyed the clinging black knit dress with approval. 'Don't tell me you wear that kind of thing to scrub floors!'

'I don't scrub floors. My clients provide labour-saving devices. Like mops.'

Ginny sniffed. 'The tyrant who cleans for us demands extraordinary things. A new three-inch paintbrush to dust the skirtings, would you believe?'

Saturday morning coffee had been a treat enjoyed together in the days of flat-sharing, and a ritual kept to whenever possible since, despite marriage for Ginny and a relationship of a less binding nature for Emily.

'So what's new?' asked Ginny, after their order arrived.

'I met the man I clean for at last,' said Emily, raising her voice slightly.

'The mystery man on the top floor?' said Ginny, and bent her blonde head nearer. 'What's he like? Tall, dark and gorgeous?'

'Yes,' said Emily, giggling when Ginny's jaw dropped.

'*Really?* Not sinister after all, then. Frankly, I always thought it a bit iffy that he took you on without an interview.'

'You know perfectly well he took me on trust because Liz Donaldson gave me such a glowing reference.'

'As well she might,' Ginny frowned. 'But you're not going to do this kind of thing forever, surely?'

'Of course not. But for the time being I'm enjoying it. I work at my own speed in very pleasant surroundings. Especially Lucas Tennent's loft.' Emily looked her friend in the eye. 'Right now the work is good therapy for me.'

Ginny sniffed. 'And at least you're being paid to do it, unlike—' She held up a hand. 'All right, I'll shut up. Tell me about this sexy banker, then, now you've finally met up with him.'

Emily described the meeting in graphic detail, winning peals of laughter from her friend. 'Actually, he was very nice about it, Ginny. I can't help thinking about him, to be honest.'

'Because he's gorgeous?'

'*No*—because the poor man's ill with no one to look after him.'

Ginny ordered more coffee, then turned to Emily with a militant light in her eye. 'You say this man's no turn-off in the looks department, probably earns pots of money, and lives in a loft apartment overlooking the Thames. Come *on*, Em! There must be hordes of females panting to mop his fevered brow.'

'Bound to be. But apparently he'd rather wallow in misery alone.' Emily stirred her fresh coffee, frowning. 'Which he'll have to all weekend. I'm not due at his place again until Monday morning.'

'Good. See you keep it that way.' Ginny reached to touch Emily's hand. 'You're just beginning to get your life back together, so for pity's sake stop worrying about a man you hardly know.'

To change the subject Emily suggested some leisurely window shopping rather than spending another afternoon in the cinema, and as usual the time flew in company with Ginny, with no opportunity for introspection. But later, during the journey on the Tube and the walk to Nat's house, no matter how hard she tried to block him out, Emily couldn't help worrying about Lucas Tennent.

The feeling persisted during the evening. Emily worked for a while on her laptop, but because she'd based her main male character on Lucas Tennent the procedure was a washout as a way to stop thinking about him. At one point she even picked up the phone to ring him. But in the end she put it back without dialling and settled down to work instead. And eventually achieved such fierce concentration it was long after midnight before she closed the laptop and fell into bed.

Emily woke with a start next morning, hoping Lucas Tennent hadn't developed pneumonia in the night just because she hadn't troubled to check. And when he answered the phone she felt totally justified, because he sounded even worse than the time before. Before she could even ask how he was, he gasped something incoherent and rang off.

A couple of hours later, feeling like Red Riding Hood off to visit the wolf, Emily turned down the cobbled street towards Lucas Tennent's building, bag of shopping in hand. Cursing the nagging conscience which had driven her there, she rang his bell first then unlocked the door.

'It's Emily Warner, Mr Tennent,' she called. 'Your cleaner. May I come in?'

There was silence for so long Emily was sure he must be lying unconscious somewhere. But eventually Lucas Tennent materialised in the doorway to his bedroom. He'd looked ill enough at their first encounter, but now he looked ghastly, his ashen pallor accentuated by streaks of unhealthy colour along his cheekbones. His bloodshot eyes were underscored by marks like bruises, his jaw black with stubble, and his tousled hair lank with sweat.

'What the hell are you doing here?' he grated through chattering teeth, and wrapped his dressing-gown closer.

Emily flushed. 'You sounded so ill I was worried. I thought you might need—'

'For God's sake go away. I don't need anything—' He gave a frantic gulp and raced off, kicking the bedroom door shut behind him.

Emily glared at it, incensed. So much for her Good Samaritan act. Seething, she slapped the newspaper down on the chest, added a carton of fresh milk, and was halfway through the door with the rest of her unwanted shopping when a hoarse, repentant voice halted her.

'Miss Warner—Emily. I was bloody rude. My apologies.'

She turned to look at him. 'Accepted,' she said coldly. 'Goodbye.'

'Don't go for a minute. Please.' He leaned in the bedroom doorway, shivering. 'Though Lord knows you should run like hell, in case you catch this hellish bug. Sorry I snapped.' His mouth twisted in distaste. 'I took off because I had to throw up again.'

Emily thawed slightly and closed the door. 'In that case please get back into bed.'

'Not a very tempting prospect right now.'

'Did you perspire much overnight?'

His mouth twisted in distaste. 'Could we talk about something else?'

She hesitated, then took the plunge. 'Look, Mr Tennent, why don't you have a hot shower while I change your bed?'

He looked appalled. 'I can't possibly let you do that!'

'Why not? I would have done it tomorrow, anyway. It's one of the things you pay me for.' She smiled encouragingly. 'You'll feel much better afterwards—but don't get your hair wet.'

He eyed her in brooding indecision for a moment, then shrugged, went into his bedroom, took a T-shirt and boxers from a drawer, and shut himself in his bathroom. Emily stripped the crumpled linen from the bed, replaced it with fresh, fetched more pillows from the spare room, and did some quick tidying up. When Lucas emerged his face was still haggard, but it was free of stubble and he'd run a comb through his hair.

When Emily turned back the quilt invitingly Lucas shed his dressing gown and slid into bed to lean back against the stacked pillows with a heartfelt sigh of relief.

'Thank you so much,' he said formally.

She smiled in acknowledgement. 'I'll dispose of this lot, then I'll make you something to eat.'

'Please—no food!' he said with a shudder, eyes closed.

'Just some toast,' she coaxed, in the tone she used with the twins. 'How many pills have you taken today?'

He opened a morose eye. 'None. With my present problem it seemed a bit pointless.'

'If you eat something you'll be able to keep them down.'

'I doubt it,' he said despondently.

In the kitchen Emily made tea, toasted a slice of bread she'd brought, scraped a minimum of butter on it, cut it in triangles, then put plate and beaker on a tray and took it into the master bedroom.

'If you make friends with the toast I could scramble some eggs,' she offered.

'I'm not up to that,' he said with a shudder. He bit into the toast and chewed slowly, then took a second piece and ate it more quickly.

'Steady,' warned Emily. 'Not too fast.'

'It's my first sustenance for days!' But he ate the rest with more care. 'Toast never tasted so good,' he informed her, then inspected the steaming contents of the mug with suspicion. 'What's this?'

'Weak tea—kinder to your digestion than coffee,' she said firmly, and took two paracetamol tablets from the packet on his bedside table. 'Take these with it, and I'll make you some coffee later.'

Lucas swallowed the tablets obediently, then sipped the tea, frowning at her over the mug. 'You know, Miss Warner, this is extraordinarily good of you, but why are you here? You must have better things to do with your time on a Sunday?'

She shrugged. 'I had my very first dose of flu fairly recently, so I can appreciate how ghastly you feel. But I had my mother to look after me. I couldn't help feeling worried about you here on your own.'

He shook his head in wonder. 'You're pretty amazing to worry about a complete stranger. But now you are here, there is something you can do for me.'

'Certainly. What is it?'

'Indulge my curiosity. What made someone like you take to cleaning as a career?'

'Someone like me?' she said, raising an eyebrow.

'I'm damned sure you haven't always been a cleaner, so why do you do it?'

'I enjoy it,' she said simply.

'Fair enough.' He put the empty cup down and slid further under the covers. 'But what did you do before that?'

'Office work.' She got up. 'Right. I'll take those things. Try to sleep if you can. I'll stay for a while to see how you get on, then I must get back.'

'No laptop today?'

'Certainly not. Friday was a one-off, Mr Tennent.' She picked up the tray. 'Try to sleep.'

'Thanks, I will,' he murmured drowsily. 'What can I do for you in return?'

'Get better, please.'

Back in the kitchen Emily emptied the carton of soup she'd bought into a mug and put it in the microwave. She left the loaf in a prominent place on a board, placed the breadknife beside it and a dish of butter close at hand, then made herself some tea and sat on one of the smart stools at the bar, yawning. The late night was catching up on her. From now on, definitely no more writing after midnight.

She wrote instructions on the memo pad about the food she'd left ready, and after a moment's hesitation added her new, unlisted phone number. She tiptoed in with her note to find that Lucas Tennent, obviously feeling the effect of his disturbed nights, was out for the count. But he looked a lot better than the wild-eyed apparition of earlier on.

The house in Spitalfields was ablaze with lights in Nat's ground-floor section when Emily got back. Not brave enough to ask how things had gone with the trip to Chastlecombe, she let herself in and toiled up the two flights of steep stairs to her room, then put on speed when she heard her phone ringing. She unlocked her door and made a dash across the room, worried it was Lucas feeling worse. Then she stopped dead, every hackle erect, when a different, all too familiar voice began leaving a message.

'Pick up, Emily. I know you're there. We need to talk. Pick *up*.' There was a pause, then a soft chuckle. 'Don't be childish. Ring me.'

CHAPTER TWO

EMILY glared at the machine. The mere sound of Miles Denny's voice still tied her stomach in knots. But with cold animosity now. Once upon a time she'd been attracted to the sexy drawl he cultivated. Just as, according to Miles, her own husky voice had been an instant turn-on for him. But that had been in the beginning when he'd been moving heaven and earth to get her to live with him. Emily clenched her fists. With hindsight she found it hard to believe she could have been such a fool.

She had been working in a firm of commercial property consultants when Miles joined the company, and almost from the day they met he'd pursued her relentlessly. Firmly against inter-office relationships, Emily had held him off at first. But his persistence had been flattering, she'd been lonely without Ginny, and eventually, after wearing her down with months of persuasion, he'd won. But, once they were actually sharing a home, Miles' contribution to the running of it was minimal. In the evenings, while Emily cooked their meal and dealt with housework and laundry, he spent his time on the sofa, recharging his batteries in front of the television. Her only break had been on Friday nights, when Miles took her out for a meal.

How could she have been so stupid? she thought in disgust. Living together had soon shown her how little they had in common, and when Miles had taken to spending regular time with male friends after work Emily had thoroughly enjoyed the evenings with no dinner to cook and the television firmly turned off. Early to bed with a book had meant she was always asleep, or pretending to be, by the time Miles came home.

When it had become obvious that a good night's sleep was infinitely preferable to the lovemaking she'd found so disappointing with Miles, Emily had known it was time to move on. Deciding to tell him straight away, she'd waited up until he got home from one of his men-only evenings. And discovered why Miles had always been so meticulous about showering before sharing their bed. He'd reeked of musky, alien perfume and other scents Emily had identified with furious distaste.

The phone rang, bringing her back to the present with a bump. She tensed, eyeing the phone belligerently, but this time the message was from Lucas Tennent.

Emily seized the receiver. 'I'm here,' she said breathlessly. 'Is something wrong? How do you feel?'

'Not marvellous, but thanks to you, Miss Warner, there's an outside chance I'll live. Now I can string two words together without barking like a hound, I'm ringing to thank you.'

'Only too happy to help,' she assured him, eyebrows raised at the change in his attitude.

'I heated the soup, as per your instructions,' he went on. 'And even cut some bread, but I was too damn feeble to wrestle with the coffee machine so I made some tea. I didn't know I had any tea—'

'I bought it for you.'

'Then I owe you, Miss Warner.'

'You can pay me tomorrow, Mr Tennent. Is there anything else you need?'

'Just a morning paper as you come in, if you would. How do you get here?'

'I walk.'

'Where do you live?'

'Spitalfields. Would you like me to make lunch for you?'

'Don't bother about that. Just the sound of a human voice will do. Wallowing alone with my bug soon lost its appeal.'

Emily frowned. 'The Donaldsons are away, of course, but surely you have other friends who could call round?'

'The two most likely succumbed to the bug before I did—' He broke off to cough, and Emily waited until he was quiet before asking if there was anything else he needed.

'I can get it on my way in, Mr Tennent.'

'Call me Lucas.'

'Not suitable,' she said firmly.

'Why the hell not?'

'For obvious reasons.'

'If you mean because you work for me, that's rubbish,' he said with scorn. 'According to the great and good we live in a classless society these days.'

'It's nothing to do with class,' she said indignantly.

'You said choice of name was up to me,' he reminded her.

'I meant *my* name—' She stopped, wondering why she was making a fuss. 'Oh, all right, whatever you say.'

'Bravo. Now I can go happy to bed.'

'You should be in bed right now.'

'I was speaking figuratively. Apart from staggering out to the kitchen to make my supper, I haven't left my bed all day.' He coughed again. 'I trust you feel suitably sympathetic?'

'Of course I do. I was a fellow sufferer not so long ago, remember. Goodnight. I hope you sleep well. I'll see you in the morning.'

Emily had barely put the phone down when it rang again.

'At *last*, darling,' said Claire Warner. 'I've been trying to get you for the past ten minutes.'

'Hi, Mother. What's wrong?'

'Miles rang here half an hour ago, demanding your address.'

'*No!*' Emily groaned. 'You didn't tell him?'

'Of course not,' said her mother scornfully. 'I didn't even speak to him. Your father answered the phone and wiped the floor with him; told him to leave you alone.'

'Way to go, Dad,' crowed Emily, then sobered. 'Actually, Miles left a message here just now, too. He's got hold of my new number somehow.'

'Oh, *Emily*. Have you given it to someone he knows?'

'Only Ginny. But she wouldn't tell him.'

'I'm sure she wouldn't. How is she?'

'Fine. We had our usual little jolly together yesterday. Though she spent most of it lecturing me.' Emily explained about Lucas Tennent's flu.

Because Claire Warner failed to see why her daughter had to do the man's cleaning in the first place, let alone look after him now he was ill, she expressed wholehearted agreement with Ginny. 'For heaven's sake, child. It's not all that long since you were down with flu yourself. Amongst other things.'

'Temper, mainly.'

'You're certainly well shot of Miles Denny. I hope Nat hasn't put your name on his door!'

'Of course he hasn't. Nat lets me know if my presence is required when he's around, and Ginny rings me as she's coming down the street and I go down and let her in.'

'Terribly cloak and dagger—like living in a safe house.'

'Nat's house *is* safe.'

'You know what I mean!'

'You read too many crime novels, Mother. I just needed a place in London to get myself together for a bit. And Nat has provided it. I'm very grateful to him.'

'Darling,' said her mother, after a pause. 'Nat's a charming man, but—'

'Oh, *Mother!* Nat is Andrew's friend, not mine at all, really. And he's married to Thea and father to the twins. What on earth do you take me for?'

'At the moment, a very vulnerable girl,' said Claire Warner bluntly.

'I've learned my lesson, believe me.'

'No more men, you mean?'

'Certainly not. I'm off *Miles*, Mother dear, not men in general.'

But afterwards Emily felt deeply uneasy. If Miles had her phone number maybe he could track down her address, too—even have it already. Though if he was brass-faced enough to turn up in person he'd have to get past Nat, and possibly Mark as well, to get hold of her.

Emily had just got down to work on her book when the phone rang for a third time. She groaned in frustration, but at the sound of Ginny's familiar tones she cut through the message to answer.

'Hold it, I'm here.'

'Emily, thank heavens. You've been engaged forever. You'll never guess who came round here this evening!'

Emily sighed. 'I bet I can—Miles.'

'*Yes*. How did you work that out?'

'He rang my parents earlier, but my father gave him a very un-Christian ticking off, according to Mother.'

'Brilliant! That must have been before he came here, then. I was in the shower when he turned up, so Charlie left him cooling his heels in the hall until I deigned to appear.'

'Well done. What did he want?'

'Your phone number and address, of course.'

'You didn't—'

'Of *course* not. Even though he kept hammering away that it was a matter of life and death that he got in touch with you.'

Emily snorted. 'Not a hope.'

'My words exactly. He didn't like it one bit,' Ginny informed her with satisfaction. 'Took umbrage, big-time.'

'What happened then?'

'Charlie showed him the door.'

Emily giggled. Ginny's large husband was by nature imperturbable, unless someone was foolish enough to upset his wife. 'I don't suppose he physically threw Miles out?' she asked hopefully.

Ginny laughed. 'Next best thing. I doubt Miles will pay us a repeat visit. Let's hope he doesn't try to visit you, either. Has he ever met Nat?'

'No. Hopefully he never will, either.'

The idea of Miles tracking her down kept Emily awake for a while, but in the end she slept well enough, and woke with a feeling of anticipation she eventually identified—with alarm—as pleasure at seeing Lucas Tennent again. None of that, she warned herself, and went off to take a shower.

When Emily went downstairs later Nat was in the hall, about to leave for the day. He looked tired and pale, but not, she saw with relief, as depressed as he usually did after parting with the twins.

'How did it go?' she asked warily. 'I didn't like to barge in on you yesterday to ask.'

'The twins flew at Thea, and before she could say a word demanded that I stay for tea.' He smiled crookedly. 'To my amazement, their wish was granted. And the occasion went off surprisingly well, mainly because the twins dominated the entire occasion over the tea and cakes.' He shrugged. 'Who knows? Next time maybe Thea will ask me to supper.'

'Oh, Nat, I do hope so. By the way,' she added, 'my ex left a message on my phone last night.'

Nat's eyes narrowed. 'How the hell did he get hold of the number?'

'No idea. I just hope he doesn't ferret out the address, too.'

'Don't worry, Em. I'll deal with him if he does. Give me a photograph.'

'No can do. I burned them all.'

'Description, then.'

'About your height, but heavier, dark eyes and hair, toothpaste ad smile, and so full of himself you'll recognise him on sight.'

Nat grinned. 'You're still angry with him, then.'

'Livid!' She looked at her watch. 'Must go.'

'You look rather special this morning,' he said, giving her the once-over.

'Things to do after my morning cleaning session,' she fibbed. 'But I'll see to your place this afternoon.'

'Right, I must be off, too.' Nat gave her an evil grin. 'And don't worry, if Mr Denny comes knocking I'll throw him out, neck and crop.'

Emily set off for her normal working day with anticipation she firmly dismissed as utter nonsense. Lucas Tennent was feeling rough and needed company; she was merely the person willing to brave his germs. And to brighten him up she was wearing a newish yellow sweater with her jeans, and a touch of make-up. No big deal.

By the time the lift doors opened on the top floor of Lucas Tennent's building Emily had herself well in hand. She was the cleaner. Lucas Tennent paid her wages. For the moment he was feeling so rotten he needed a helping hand. So she would be brisk and efficient, hand over the paper, complete her usual cleaning routine, make lunch for him, then go straight home again.

Emily pressed the buzzer, unlocked the door and called her name. And this time Lucas appeared at once, haggard, the bloodshot eyes dark-ringed, but with a smile of greeting so different from the hostility of the day before it did serious damage to her resolutions.

'Good morning, Emily Warner. Good of you to come.'

'I'm always here on Mondays.' She handed him the paper.

'Thank you just the same. But be of good cheer,' he said, leaning in the doorway. 'No need to change sheets and force pills down my throat. I've performed both duties myself, already.'

'Well done.' She took off her jacket and put it on the chest. 'How do you feel?'

'Not wonderful. But better than yesterday.'

Which was obvious from the interest he was taking in her appearance.

'Back to bed now,' she said briskly. 'Read the paper while I tidy up.'

'Forget that. I need conversation. Come and talk to

me for a while—' Lucas broke off to cough, and Emily gestured towards his bedroom.

'Please go back to bed.' She went ahead of him to stack the pillows and turn down the newly changed covers. 'You should have waited for me to do this,' she said severely. 'Because you don't feel so marvellous now, do you?'

'No,' he admitted, and slid into bed with a groan of relief.

'Have you had anything to eat today?'

'I drank some milk.'

'Better than nothing, I suppose,' said Emily, and smiled her approval.

'Cute dimple,' he commented.

'What would you like to eat?' she asked, ignoring him. 'Eggs in some form would be best. Something light to start you off.'

'At the moment I feel too feeble to lift a fork. Later, maybe. When I've got over my exertions.' He eyed her irritably. 'For the moment just sit down and *talk* to me, woman.'

Objecting hotly to this form of address, Emily stood her ground for a moment, then sat down on the chair beside the bed. 'Oh, very well. What shall I talk about?'

'You.'

She grimaced. 'Boring subject.'

'I disagree.' He slid further down in the bed. 'Tell me what you did before the domestic engineering.'

'I worked in a commercial retail agency—I told you it was boring.'

'Emily, that sexy voice of yours could recite the phone book without boring me.' He threw up a hand at her scowl. 'Sorry, sorry. Go on. Tell me why you switched careers.'

She shrugged. 'I lived for a while with a man who worked in the same agency. When we broke up I moved out and packed in my job.'

Lucas lay watching her, his shadowed eyes alert with interest. 'Non-amicable parting, obviously. When was this?'

'Fairly recently. Now, how about that breakfast?'

His mouth twisted. 'I'm a bit wary of eating. It's bloody mortifying to keep dashing away to throw up.'

She nodded sympathetically. 'My mother got a leaflet about flu when I was ill. It said one must try to eat if possible. So will you try?'

'On one condition—that you keep me company while I do.'

'If you insist.'

'Not at all. I'm asking you nicely!'

Emily laughed and went off to the kitchen. When she returned to the bedroom with a laden tray she found Lucas waiting with barely concealed impatience, the daily paper unopened beside him. 'Sorry I was so long,' she said breathlessly. 'I'm used to cleaning your kitchen, but not cooking in it.'

'Which you shouldn't be doing at all,' he said irritably.

'Of course I should.' She laid a clean towel across his chest. 'Better use this now you've made the effort to change your bed.' She handed him a fork and a plate of scrambled eggs on toast, then feeling a little awkward sat down again. 'Salt, pepper?' she asked. 'I seasoned the eggs a bit, but you might want more.'

'They're perfect,' he said, tasting them. 'Now, entertain me while I eat. I can tell you're not a Londoner. Where do you come from?'

'Chastlecombe, in Gloucestershire.'

'Snap—same county,' he informed her with a grin. 'We're both country bumpkins, then.'

Anything less like a country bumpkin than Lucas Tennent was hard to imagine. Even lying in bed, haggard and feverish. 'Speak for yourself,' she said pertly, then bit her lip.

'What now?' he demanded.

'I keep forgetting.'

'Forgetting what?' His eyes narrowed. 'Oh, right. Me boss, you slave.'

Emily glared at him. 'I wouldn't put it quite like that!'

'I should bloody well hope not,' he said forcibly, and eyed his empty plate in surprise. 'That was good. Thank you.'

Emily took his plate to the kitchen, then returned shortly afterwards with two mugs of coffee. She handed one to Lucas, then resumed her place in the chair. 'You look a little better now,' she said with approval.

'I feel it.' He drank with relish, then settled back against his pillows. 'So tell me more, Emily. What course are you doing?'

She winced. 'I lied about that.'

'Did you now?' he said, eyeing her flushed face with amusement. 'So what exactly *are* you doing on that laptop of yours? Hacking into state secrets?'

'Nothing so exciting. I'm trying my hand at a novel. I make a sort of rough draft of the next bit in my head while I'm cleaning, then get it down on my laptop later. But if I hadn't been stupid enough to lie to you when you caught me,' she added bluntly, 'I wouldn't be telling you this. No one else knows, not even my family.'

'My lips are sealed,' he assured her, hand on heart. 'But why the secrecy?'

Her chin jutted. 'I experienced a pretty humiliating form of rejection recently. If—or more likely when—the manuscript's rejected, too, I'd rather no one knew about it.'

CHAPTER THREE

Lucas eyed her with respect as she got up to refill his coffee cup. 'You're a lady of surprises, Emily.'

She shook her head. 'Not really. All my life, until recently, I did everything by the book.'

'What happened then?'

'Miles Denny happened.' Emily sat down again. 'My family disapproved. They don't like him.'

'I don't either.'

She laughed. 'You haven't met him.'

'I don't have to.' He frowned. 'Emily, I've got a name, but you haven't used it yet. I thought we'd sorted that out.'

She gave him a fulminating look, and jumped to her feet. 'Right—*Lucas!* I'm going to clear up now.'

'Don't go yet! Please?' His eyes met hers with a persuasion she found impossible to resist.

'I'm still going to clear away and so on,' she said firmly, picking up the coffee tray. 'But I'll come back afterwards for a few minutes. Then you should try to sleep.'

'I can do that when I'm alone,' he said testily.

While Emily loaded the dishwasher later she fought a losing battle with her common sense. She'd achieved her aim in coming here to check on Lucas Tennent, feed him, and make sure he wasn't any worse. So she should go home once she'd finished her usual routine. But it was such balm to her dented ego to have a man like Lucas Tennent pleading for her company. Besides, she thought, brightening, it was all an aid to research. The more she saw of him, the more her fictional hero would take shape.

She paid the living-room some attention, made sure the kitchen was immaculate, then cleaned the bathroom in the hall to complete at least part of her usual routine for Mondays. Afterwards she brushed her hair, used a lipstick, then went to rejoin Lucas, who regarded her with bloodshot, accusing eyes.

'I thought you'd gone,' he said, his jutting lip so much like young Tom Sedley in a strop that Emily bit back a smile.

'What's so funny?' he demanded.

'You reminded me of someone.'

He scowled. 'Not the much-disliked Miles?'

'No. I'm very fond of this someone.'

'Who is he?'

'Son of my landlord.'

'One of the twins?'

'You remembered,' she said, surprised, and sat down in the armchair.

'I remember everything you've told me so far,' Lucas assured her. 'I've felt too lousy to read, or watch television, so I lie here and think about you.'

'Time I was going,' she said hastily, and got up, but he lunged swiftly and caught her hand.

'I was *not* coming on to you. I meant that you interest me.'

Her eyebrows rose. 'Is that a compliment?'

'It's the truth,' he said simply, and released her hand.

Appeased, Emily resumed her seat. 'By the way, Lucas, the new number I left for you is unlisted. My family have it, of course, and my closest friend, but—'

'Not Miles,' he said, nodding.

'That's the problem. He's got hold of it somehow. He rang me last night.'

His eyes narrowed. 'Did you speak to him?'

'No. I just listened while he left a message. He tracked the number down somehow. Now I'm afraid he'll find out where I'm living.' She shivered at the thought.

Lucas frowned. 'Emily, are you afraid of this guy?'

'Certainly not. I just don't want to see him again.'

'Why did you leave him?'

Her lips tightened. 'The usual reason.'

'Another woman?'

'One that I know of personally, but probably a lot more that I don't.' She shrugged. 'A boring little tale.'

He settled more comfortably against the pillows. 'Tell me about your family instead.'

Preparing to lie about some fictitious appointment, Emily hesitated. Lucas Tennent was enjoying her company. And she was enjoying his. But she had no illusions. Without his dose of flu none of this would be happening.

His heavy eyes narrowed as he watched her face. 'You're about to say you can't stay. Are you due at the Donaldsons'?'

'No, not today. But I should be going home.'

'Don't tell me we're back to this "upstairs, downstairs" garbage again?' he demanded irritably.

'You should be resting.'

'I can do that after you're gone.' He gave her a cunning look. 'I could pay you overtime.'

'Certainly not,' she snapped, bristling.

He grinned. 'Thought that would do it. Right, then. Stay for a while. Talk to me.'

Disarmed by the grin, Emily gave in, and at his prompting provided Lucas with a brief résumé of her

background—father a retired clergyman, mother a leading light in the local history society and devourer of
crime novels. 'A combination with drawbacks,' she said
wryly. 'Mother wasn't keen on my move to Spitalfields
because it was once a favourite haunt of Jack the Ripper,
though she's interested in the Roman skeletons found
there. I also have a brother,' she went on. 'Andrew is
head of the physical education department in the school
he once graced himself in company with my landlord,
Nat Sedley. They've been close friends ever since, which
is why Nat offered me a room in his house when I left
Miles.'

'And is your landlord married to the mother of his
twins?' Lucas asked casually.

'Yes. But there's a rift. Thea lives with the children
in their house near Chastlecombe and Nat lives alone up
here. But he desperately wants his life with Thea back.
He gets the twins on alternate weekends but it cuts him
to pieces to part with them every time. He's a colleague
of Liz Donaldson, your neighbour, by the way.' She
smiled a little. 'He interrogated her pretty thoroughly
about you before I was permitted to take the job.'

Lucas gave her a cynical look. 'Are you *sure* this man
still loves his wife?'

'Nat was merely acting on Andy's behalf to make sure
you were a suitable employer for the little sister.' She
smiled demurely. 'Happily, you passed muster.'

He laughed, then put a hand to his head, wincing. 'I'm
pleased I made the grade.'

'Is your head bad?' she said with sympathy.

'Only when I laugh.'

'I'll give you some more pills, then you really should
try to sleep.'

'If I do, you'll disappear.' He gave her a cajoling look.

'If I promise to sleep for a while will you stay this afternoon, and have tea with me later? In the meantime, put your feet up, watch television, or read. Take anything you like from my shelves. Another time,' he added slyly, 'you can bring your laptop and work here.'

'There won't be another time. You'll be better soon.'

'No, I won't,' he said promptly. 'I'm very ill.'

'In that case, you'd better call a doctor.'

'I don't want a doctor. I just want you to stay for a while. Though God knows I don't blame you for wanting to run,' he added with sudden self-disgust.

Emily eyed him in silence for a moment, then nodded reluctantly. 'Oh, very well. I'll stay until six, but then I really must get back, otherwise there'll be no point in going. I'm due at the Donaldsons' in the morning. They come back tomorrow.'

'Don't go back. Stay the night in my spare room. I meant it just now,' he added quickly. 'I'll happily pay the overtime.'

She gave him a scornful look, took two pills from his bedside drawer, poured bottled water into a glass and handed it to him. 'Every drop, please.'

He obeyed, then gave her a smile which unglued her knees. 'Thank you, Emily. I promise I won't mention money again.'

In contrast to the stark, minimalist effect preferred by the Donaldsons, Lucas Tennent's taste ran to uncluttered comfort. Because the converted loft gave maximum living space but presented a problem with storage, he'd solved it by investing in a collection of chests, some of them modern, others brassbound and antique. In places the old honey-coloured brick of the walls had been left exposed, in others plastered and painted amber, the few pictures hung on them modern, bright slashes of colour.

And in the short time she'd been working there Emily had come to love every inch of it.

Her only time spent in the vast, split-level living area had been to put it in perfect order as part of her cleaning routine. But now, while the washing-machine was on its dry cycle, Emily settled down on one of the deep, tempting sofas and began to read. Before long the words started to run into each other and at last she gave up, tugged off her shoes and curled up, her head on one of the cushions. She set a mental alarm clock to wake up after half an hour, so she could check on the invalid, but woke with a start to find Lucas Tennent looking down at her.

'I'm terribly sorry,' she said penitently, scrambling to her feet to put her shoes on.

'It was so quiet I thought you'd gone home after all, so I came to investigate.'

'You shouldn't be out of bed,' she scolded, and took his arm to shepherd him back, then dropped it again in alarm when she felt the heat of his skin scorch through the clothes.

'Do that again,' he said, grinning. 'I like it.'

Emily gave him an exasperated glare. 'If you'll go back to bed, I'll make tea.'

'Tea for two,' he said firmly, then turned away to cough.

'You see? Go back to bed—Lucas, *please*,' she begged, and flushed at the look he gave her.

'For you, Emily, anything,' he assured her and, still coughing, went off towards his bedroom.

She went to the kitchen to make tea and toast the crumpets she'd included in her shopping. When she took the tray into the bedroom Lucas was waiting, bolt upright against neatly stacked pillows in his newly tidied bed. His ashen face sported streaks of hectic colour, which worried Emily very much, but she smiled at him as she put the tray down.

'Feeling better?'

'Not a lot,' he admitted, and gave a rueful look at the dish of crumpets. 'I hate to be ungrateful, Emily, but I'm not hungry.'

'OK,' she said without fuss. 'Just the tea, then.'

He downed the tea thirstily, then lay back against the pillows as though the mere exertion of drinking had exhausted him. 'I feel so bloody feeble. Were you like this?'

'Yes. But my mother called the doctor, who gave me antibiotics for my chest infection. So I soon got better,' she added significantly. 'Look, Lucas, your temperature's up and I can hear you wheezing from here. You need a doctor. Do you have one I can ring?'

'It's just flu,' he said testily. 'I don't need a doctor—' He broke off to cough again and Emily handed him a box of tissues, then looked at him in question as the phone rang.

'Answer it, please,' he gasped.

Emily picked up the receiver and said a cautious hello.

'Alice Tennent here,' said an attractive voice. 'Is Lucas there?'

Emily gave the receiver to Lucas, who lay with sweat beading his forehead as he battled to control his cough. He croaked a hoarse greeting, then went off into another paroxysm of coughing and handed the receiver back. 'My sister—explain,' he gasped.

'I'm afraid your brother's feeling very unwell, Miss Tennent,' said Emily.

'Sounds as though he's dying! Has he seen a doctor?'

'He refuses to call one,' she said, defiant as she met

the glare in the invalid's eyes. 'And I'm pretty sure he's got a chest infection.'

'Right. Hand him over, please.'

Emily thrust the phone at Lucas, then watched in some amusement when he disagreed in violent protest with his sister before handing the phone back. 'She wants to speak to you,' he growled.

'Who, exactly, *am* I speaking to?' asked Alice Tennent pleasantly.

'Emily Warner, your brother's cleaner,' she said baldly, ignoring the look of impotent wrath on the invalid's face. 'I stayed on this afternoon because I was worried about your brother.'

'That's extraordinarily kind of you! Look, Mrs Warner—'

'Miss, actually.'

'Right. I've just told Lucas that if he won't behave I'll send Mother up to look after him. In which case she will certainly catch the bug herself. Naturally Lucas won't hear of that. I'd come myself but I'm ringing from Italy. Can you contact a doctor and stay with Lucas until he arrives?'

Emily had no hesitation. 'Of course, Miss Tennent. If the doctor thinks it necessary I can even stay the night.'

'How very kind. Thank you. That's a load off my mind. Now, put Lucas back on and I'll read the riot act.'

But this time Lucas was surprisingly acquiescent as he listened, eyes fixed on Emily. 'Did you mean it about staying the night?' he demanded as he handed the phone back.

'Of course I did.' She picked up the tray. 'Where will I find your doctor's number?'

'In the address book on my desk up in the gallery.' He mopped at the perspiration standing out on his forehead. 'I've only seen him once. Maybe he doesn't do house calls.'

'He'd better,' said Emily darkly.

She stated Lucas's problem to a receptionist, gave directions to the flat, then went back to Lucas, who by this time was looking ghastly.

'A doctor's coming shortly,' she told him.

'Dr Barnett?' he croaked.

'They didn't say. Probably whoever's on call.' Emily eyed him with misgiving. 'How do you feel?'

'Not great. It hurts to breathe,' he said hoarsely. 'I don't get it. I felt so much better earlier.'

Emily went into his bathroom, collected a towel, dampened a washcloth and went back to the invalid. 'I'll just wipe your forehead,' she said briskly.

'You don't have to do this,' he protested.

'No,' she agreed. 'But you'll feel better if I do.' She mopped him up, dried him off with the towel, poured water into a glass and handed it to him. 'Down the hatch.'

'I might be sick again,' he protested wildly.

'You're sweating so much you'll get dehydrated if you don't drink.'

He gave in and took a few sips of water, then gave her a wry, twisted smile. 'I bet you're sorry as hell you stayed behind on Friday.'

'Certainly not. I'm glad to help.' She looked him in the eye. 'How would you have managed otherwise?'

He smiled ruefully. 'A question I've been asking myself all day, Emily Warner.'

'I'm not sure how long the doctor will be,' she said. 'Otherwise I'd say another change of bedclothes was a good idea. But maybe it's best if you stay the way you are.'

'So he can see how poorly I am?' he mocked.

'Exactly.' Her tone was casual, but underneath Emily was worried. Lucas's forehead had been so hot the washcloth had steamed as she mopped him with it, reinforcing her fears about pneumonia. So far she'd functioned on common sense and her own experience, but committed to an overnight stay she felt in urgent need of professional advice.

'Lucas,' she said apologetically. 'I'm probably the only person you've met who doesn't own a cellphone. May I make a phone call?'

'Of course. Use this phone, if you like, or one of the others out there if you want privacy,' he said, his breath rasping in his chest.

She smiled her thanks, and stayed where she was to contact Nat.

'Hi, Emily here. I'm just letting you know I couldn't make it this afternoon, and I won't be back home tonight.'

'No need to clock in and out, Em,' Nat assured her.

'I know that,' she said, colouring under the sardonic gaze trained on her face. 'But I thought I'd better explain.'

'Much appreciated,' he said warmly. 'I'll see you when I see you, then.'

'Right. Apologise to Mark for me.' Emily put the phone down, her eyes defiant. 'My landlord,' she said shortly.

'Are you *sure* there's nothing going on between you—?' Lucas broke off, coughing, and flapped his hand at her in apology. 'Sorry. None of my business.'

She glared at him. 'I'll have to skip my other cleaning jobs this afternoon, and since living in Nat's house I've never stayed out overnight before. So it seemed like common courtesy to explain. But you're right—it *is* none of your business.'

He lay panting, his feverish eyes bright with amusement. 'That's better!'

'What do you mean?'

'You forgot the paid underling bit.'

'Oh.' Emily thrust her hair behind her ears. 'Sorry,' she muttered.

'Don't be. I like pushy women.'

'In that case, for heaven's sake listen to this one and just lie there quietly until the doctor comes.'

But it was almost two o'clock before the doorbell rang, by which time Lucas looked so ill Emily was secretly frantic.

'Dr Hall,' announced a brisk young woman when Emily opened the door. 'I came as soon as I could, but we're busy. How's Mr Tennent?'

'Not too good. Thank you so much for coming.' Emily led the way to the bedroom and ushered the attractive young doctor inside. 'Dr Hall, Lucas,' she announced, and hid a smile at his open dismay at the sight of a female GP.

'Sorry to bring you out, Doctor,' he said hoarsely, but the young woman shrugged as she took a stethoscope from her bag.

'Goes with the territory, Mr Tennent. Sit up, please.'

She hoisted up Lucas's T-shirt to give his chest and back a thorough examination, checked his pulse and his blood pressure, looked in his ears and down his throat, took his temperature, then sat down on the chair by the bed to write a prescription. She tore it off the pad, took a strip of bubble-packed pills from her bag and handed both to Emily.

'I'll give you a few antibiotics to start him off. You can get the script filled tomorrow for the rest.'

'Will I live, Doctor?' wheezed Lucas.

'It's just a respiratory infection, so if you follow the instructions, yes.' She turned to Emily. 'See he gets plenty of fluids, sponge him down if he gets too hot, and he'll need to take the pills at four-hourly intervals to start with. Right through the night, if possible. Tomorrow he can go on to four times a day.'

'Thank you,' said Emily. 'I'll see you out.' Once in the hall, out of Lucas's range, she confronted the doctor. 'Is there any danger of pneumonia?'

'I doubt it. Normally, Mr Tennent's obviously very fit, so once the medication kicks in he'll get better quite quickly.' Dr Hall eyed her surroundings curiously. 'What does he do for a living?'

'Works for an investment bank.'

'Ah. Long hours, lots of stress. Rather like my job— only much better paid. Make it clear that he won't be back at the grind until he's finished the antibiotics.'

Emily smiled awkwardly. 'We're not really on that kind of footing. I'm just his cleaner.'

Dr Hall looked taken aback. 'Oh—sorry. Is there someone else who can look after him?'

'Only me for the time being.' Emily eyed the doctor questioningly. 'Or do you think he needs professional nursing?'

'Not at all. If you're willing to look after him he'll be fine. I'd better be off; more calls to make.' She smiled. 'Good luck, then.'

'I'll probably need it! Goodbye, Doctor.'

Emily went back to the bedroom, poured water into a glass and handed Lucas the first of his antibiotics.

'What if I throw it up?' he gasped after he'd taken the pill.

'You won't,' she said firmly. 'Think positively.'

'Yes, Nurse.' He managed a smile. 'Bossy creature. Just like the doctor.'

'She looked very tired,' said Emily reprovingly.

'I'm very grateful to her,' he wheezed. 'To you, too,' he added. 'How can I repay you?'

She smiled awkwardly. 'I just need the money I spent on your shopping.'

Lucas looked appalled. 'Hell, of course you do. Fish in the top drawer of that chest for my wallet. Take what you want.'

Emily went out quickly, her colour high. But there was no point in false pride. She would look after Lucas Tennent for a while, but she couldn't pay for his food as well. She took the till receipt for the shopping from her bag and went into the bedroom. 'This is what I spent,' she announced, handing it to him.

'I don't want to see that, woman,' he rasped, tossing it away. 'Take whatever bloody money you need.'

Emily went to the chest, extracted a twenty-pound note from his wallet, took the exact amount of change from her own, and left it on the chest. 'I'll leave you to sleep for a while,' she said colourlessly, and turned to go.

'Emily,' said Lucas.

She turned. 'Yes?'

He smiled ruefully. 'Sorry I snapped.'

She looked at him levelly, noting the high colour and fever-bright eyes. 'I'll be charitable and blame your state of health. I'm in the kitchen if you want me.'

'Stay here with me, Emily—' He began to cough again, this time so violently she rushed across the room to hoist him upright, then gave him more water when the paroxysm was over. 'Please?' he gasped.

'Right,' she said, breathing almost as hard as Lucas as she stacked the pillows behind him again. 'I need some tea. But I'll bring it in here until you settle, if you like.'

He nodded wordlessly, his eyes expressing his thanks, and Emily relented, giving him a wry little smile. 'Would you like anything?' she asked.

'No. Just make your tea. God knows you deserve it—along with anything I possess that takes your fancy.'

'Just tea, thanks just the same.'

'Emily.'

'Yes?'

His heavy eyes held hers. 'This Miles of yours must be a raving lunatic.'

'Not really.' She smiled, deliberately activating the dimple. 'Just your average, standard-issue male.'

CHAPTER FOUR

BY THE time Emily got back to the bedroom Lucas had fallen into a restless doze. She tiptoed out again, filled with misgiving about the night ahead. Lucas Tennent's muscular frame carried very little spare flesh, and she was no weakling. But he was a foot taller and a lot heavier than she was. If he got out of bed in the night and collapsed, it wouldn't be easy to get him back in again. She shrugged philosophically. No point in worrying. Now she was stuck with her Florence Nightingale role she'd just have to manage, whatever happened. And in the meantime there was ironing to do. Normally the bedlinen went to the laundry, but at the present rate of turnover she needed to deal with it herself, and fast.

After a brief spell at the ironing board, Emily checked that Lucas was still asleep. She stood looking at him, decided he was safe to leave for a bit, and abandoned the ironing to run out for the rest of the antibiotics. While the prescription was filled she shopped for a few more basic supplies, then raced back to the flat to find Lucas leaning against the chest in the hall, his sunken eyes hostile.

'Where the hell have you been?' he barked at her.

She stiffened at his tone. 'Shopping.'

To her surprise he gave her a contemptuous glare, staggered back to his room and slammed the door.

Seething, Emily shed her jacket, took the bag of shopping into the kitchen, then marched into the bedroom to confront the invalid, who lay rigid in a bed like a rat's nest. 'I brought you the *Financial Times*,' she said, putting it down beside him.

'I didn't ask for it,' he snarled, and turned his head away.

Emily's fast-diminishing sympathy vanished completely. He didn't pay her nearly enough money for this.

'If you'll sit in the chair for a moment, I'll sort the bed out.'

'It's fine as it is,' he growled.

'You'll be more comfortable,' she insisted.

Swearing under his breath, Lucas heaved himself up, then groaned and sat with head in hands for a moment.

'Let me help you,' said Emily, putting a hand under his elbow, but he shook her off irritably.

'I can manage.' He lurched to his feet and swayed so precariously Emily put out a hand, but he gave her a ferocious glare, collapsed in the chair, and sat with bare, muscular legs outstretched, the breath ripping through his chest with a sound like tearing cloth.

Emily swiftly restacked the pillows, straightened the sheet, folded it down over the quilt and turned back a corner. 'In you get.'

'Why the hell did you put a sheet on?' he said irascibly. 'I get tied up in the bloody thing.'

'Because you're sweating so much,' she said, with what remnant of patience she could muster. 'I can change sheets and covers but I can't do much about the quilt itself, so the bed will stay fresher this way. Now you're up,' Emily added, 'how about a visit to the bathroom?'

Lucas lurched to his feet, eyeing her malevolently. 'I'm beginning to sympathise with the ex-lover. If you ordered *him* around like an army sergeant, no wonder he cheated on you.' He went into the bathroom and slammed the door behind him.

Fighting the urge to hurl something at it, Emily put her shopping away instead and made coffee. She laid a tray, and was about to take it into the bedroom, then thought better of it. Lucas might say he didn't want any coffee. In which case he might well get it thrown at him, invalid or not.

She knocked very pointedly on the bedroom door and went in to find Lucas sitting up against the pillows, scowling.

'You were out shopping for a hell of a long time,' he accused. 'What was so vital that you couldn't exist without it for even a day?'

'The rest of your antibiotics,' said Emily, and slapped them down on his bedside table. 'You were still asleep after I'd done some of your ironing, Mr Tennent, so it seemed a good time to make for the pharmacy before it closed. And, just for the record, I was out for less than half an hour. But I plead guilty to a bit of shopping while the prescription was made up. Frivolous stuff like bread, milk, and so on.'

Lucas's blank dismay was almost comical. 'Emily—' He got no further before a cough seized him, and it was some time before he could speak again. 'Hell, I'm *sorry*,' he gasped. 'I was afraid you'd taken off—and wouldn't blame you if you had.'

'I said I'd stay, so I will,' she said coldly. 'But only until tomorrow, Mr Tennent. Now, I've made coffee, so would you like some?'

He nodded, eyeing her with a look she couldn't quite identify. 'Emily, my crack about the ex-lover was way out of order. I apologise.'

'Forget it,' she said brusquely. When she returned

with a beaker of coffee, Lucas eyed it moodily as she put it down beside him.

'Aren't you having any?'

'Yes, Mr Tennent. In the kitchen, with a sandwich. Would you like something?'

'Yes, you can stop calling me Mr Tennent!'

'I meant,' she said, unrelenting, 'something to eat.'

'No, thanks. Unless,' he added, with the sudden, irresistible smile, 'you've got a slice of humble pie handy?'

But Emily, still smarting over the crack about the army sergeant, was immune to smiles by this time. 'I'll be back later,' she said curtly, and left him alone.

In the kitchen, she ate a cheese sandwich, drank some coffee, finished the ironing, then, in need of a break, went into the living-room to read her book. The combination of cheese, coffee and temper had given her indigestion, which made it hard to concentrate at first. But after a while she calmed down enough to follow the intricacies of the thriller's plot. It was half an hour before she went back to check on Lucas, who looked so ill by this time Emily forgot her anger as she laid a hand on his forehead.

'You're burning up,' she commented, worried. 'I'd better sponge you down.'

'You will not!' he growled.

'I'm just following the doctor's instructions.'

'I'll sponge myself down. Later.'

'Now,' she said inexorably.

Lucas glared at her. 'I'll do it next time I get out of bed.'

'Why won't you let *me* do it?' she said impatiently.

'For obvious reasons,' he said through his teeth.

'You mean because I'm your cleaner?'

'No!' he howled, then regretted it when it brought on another bout of coughing. 'Hell,' he gasped afterwards, lying back with an arm over his eyes. 'How long do these antibiotics take to work, for God's sake?'

'They'll function a lot faster if you co-operate.'

'Tell me what to do and I'll do it.'

'Stay where you are unless absolutely necessary, for one thing,' she retorted. 'How long were you hanging about in the hall before I got back from the shops?'

'Not long,' he muttered behind his arm.

'Too long, obviously. From now on, *Lucas*, will you just stay in bed? Please?'

He took his hand away to look at her. 'Yes, Emily. For you, anything. And I'm not just being bloody-minded. At least, not this time. My objection to the sponging is a man/woman thing. We standard-issue males have our pride.'

She smiled unwillingly. 'Can't you just think of me as a nurse?'

Lucas gave her a long, explicit look. 'Emily, angel of mercy you may be, but you're also a woman. And I'm very much aware of it. And now,' he added, resigned, 'I'm going to incur your wrath and get out of bed. I need to go the bathroom again.' His mouth twisted. 'This is all so blasted intimate. And in entirely the wrong way.'

'I feel as shaky as a newborn colt,' he said later, when he got back into the neatened bed. 'What were you doing before you came to check on me?'

'Reading.'

'You were a long time.'

'Half an hour.'

'Bring your book in here.'

'If I do that you won't sleep.'

'I won't sleep anyway. I need company. Your company.' A great shiver ran through him. 'God, I ache all over. I had no idea flu was as hellish as this.'

'As many as a thousand a day died of it about the time Victoria came to the throne,' Emily informed him. 'But *you* won't, as long as you're sensible. How about some soup?'

'Could we leave that until later? Just stay here with me for a while.'

She hesitated, then gave in. 'All right. But only if you try to sleep. I'll fetch my book.'

On her way back, Emily caught sight of herself in the hall mirror and eyed her reflection with distaste. Looking after an invalid was wearing. Or maybe it was just this particular invalid. Obviously never ill normally, Lucas Tennent was convinced he was at death's door. With a wry shrug Emily pushed her unruly curls behind her ears and went back to him.

'Emily,' said Lucas glumly. 'Now I've given it thought maybe it's not such a good idea for you to spend time in here with me.'

'Infection?' she queried, sitting down in the chair. 'Too late to worry about that. Besides, these days I take multivitamins religiously, as instructed by my mother. And she's right. They seem to work.' She gave him the smile which brought her dimple into play. 'If I get you some tomorrow will you take them, too?'

'Yes,' said Lucas huskily, his eyes on her mouth. 'Smile at me like that and I'll do anything you want.'

Emily turned her startled face away and tried to read. The book was gripping, and curled up on Lucas's sofa in his living room she'd been enthralled by it. But here in his bedroom it was different. Conscious in every fibre of the man in the bed, she kept her eyes glued to the book and forced herself to sit motionless for what seemed like hours.

Her tactics paid off. Lucas was dozing when it seemed safe at last to look, and Emily settled down to read in earnest. When she looked up again his eyes were fixed on her face.

'What is it?' she said at once.

He smiled drowsily. 'I was just thinking how reassuring it is to wake and find you here. But you look tired. Are you sure you're not catching this blasted bug, Emily?'

'Perfectly sure. So let's not go over that again,' she said briskly. 'Now, how about that soup?' She leaned over him to tidy the covers, but he dodged away.

'Don't,' he ordered.

'I just—'

'Just *don't*. In fact,' he added harshly, 'I've changed my mind. You'd better go home. I can dish out my own pills.'

She eyed him in exasperation. 'What's the problem *now*, for heaven's sake?'

'You are.'

Emily moved back, offended. 'I see.'

'You don't see at all!'

She looked down her nose. 'Whatever it is, Mr Tennent, I'm not going home. At least, not today. I'll remove myself from your presence, but I'll stay in the flat because the doctor thought it best and I promised your sister. But only until tomorrow. After that you're on your own.' She turned on her heel.

'Emily!'

She halted at the door, but refused to look round. 'Yes?'

'I know you think I'm an ungrateful bastard, but you'd be safer if you went home.'

Emily sighed as she turned to look at him. 'As I keep telling you, Lucas, I'm unlikely to get the virus again. Now try to rest. I'll be in to see you later.'

He turned his face into the pillow, muttering something unintelligible.

If it hadn't been for her assurances to Alice Tennent and the doctor, Emily would have taken Lucas at his word and gone back to Spitalfields. She was tired, and his mood swings were increasingly hard to take. She went back to the sofa in the living room, consoling herself that it was for one night only. After that the ungrateful wretch could doctor himself.

When Lucas had been left to his own devices for a while, Emily knocked formally on the bedroom door and put her head round it.

'You're still here, then?' he asked hoarsely.

'Brilliant deduction. How do you feel?'

'I don't ache so much,' he said with faint surprise, and smiled a little. 'Maybe I'll live after all.'

'Could you manage some soup now?'

Lucas thought it over, then nodded. 'What kind?'

Encouraged by his first glimmer of interest in food, Emily smiled at him in approval. 'Wild mushroom. I bought two cartons of the fresh kind when I was out.'

'Are you having some?'

'Yes.'

'No point in asking you to come in here while we eat, I suppose?'

'None at all.'

When Emily returned with a mug of soup and some fingers of dry toast Lucas was sitting up against newly stacked pillows, a smug look on his face.

'I saved you the trouble of tidying the bed,' he informed her.

'How kind,' said Emily distantly. She whisked a towel across his chest. 'What would you like to drink afterwards?'

'Whatever you're having,' he said virtuously.

She went back to the kitchen to heat her own soup, wondering how long the perfect patient act would last. Lucas was obviously feeling better after a rest, but from her own experience she doubted that would last as the evening wore on.

Beginning to feel the lack of a proper meal, Emily buttered some thick slices of bread to go with her soup. Afterwards she made a pot of tea, then took some in to Lucas to find he'd eaten everything.

'Good,' she said in approval. She filled a glass of water and gave him an antibiotic. 'This would be a good time to take some paracetamol, too.'

'Whatever you say,' said Lucas, obeying so meekly that Emily looked at him narrowly as she took the empty glass afterwards.

'I'm doing my damnedest to please you,' he said, looking up at her. 'Or hadn't you noticed?'

'Oh, yes. I'd noticed.'

Back in the kitchen, Emily frowned as she perched on one of the stools to drink her tea. This time last week she'd never met Lucas Tennent, yet here she was, looking after a stranger in circumstances so intimate they were normally the prerogative of a partner of some kind. Suddenly restless, she went up the open staircase leading from the breakfast bar to the gallery above. She gazed at the lights of the City for a while, looked up to count stars through the arched glass roof, then went back to the bedroom to find Lucas recovering from a coughing spasm.

'You may find this hard to imagine, Miss Warner,' he said, panting, 'but normally I get up early every morning, row on my machine for a while, then walk to the City. There, amongst other things, my working day includes in-depth research, followed by complex reports on shares to recommend to investors.' He glared at her in self-disgust. 'But right now my legs feel like spaghetti, and I can't even concentrate on the daily paper.'

'I know how you feel. I've been there. But don't worry. You'll soon be back to normal.' Emily looked at her watch. 'Try to rest. I'll be back later.'

Much later, she decided. When it was time for the next antibiotic and a hot drink. And after that he was on his own until two. She yawned and set the alarm on her watch, just in case she dozed off during the evening, then settled down on the sofa to enjoy her thriller in peace. She finished the book just before the alarm went off, got up, stretched, put her shoes on and went to beard the lion in his den. And found that now, when she wanted him awake, Lucas was fast asleep, his hair plastered in lank black strands on his forehead, the white T-shirt transparent with sweat.

'Lucas,' said Emily softly, touching his outflung hand.

He muttered, pulling his hand away, then opened his eyes. And smiled at her.

'Hello,' she said quietly. 'Sorry to wake you, but it's time for your medication.'

Lucas blinked, then heaved himself up, his nose wrinkling in distaste. 'Hell, I'm drenched again.'

Emily went to his chest and took out a clean T-shirt and boxers. 'You'd better sponge yourself down.'

He heaved himself out to sit on the side of the bed. 'At least the soup stayed with me,' he said brightening.

'Progress,' she agreed. 'Hurry up. I'll strip this lot off while you wash.'

Lucas got to his feet, took the change of clothes from her with a word of thanks, and made for the bathroom.

Emily stripped the bed at speed, dismayed to find that the quilt itself was damp. She put the bedlinen in the washing machine and, after a moment's thought, took the down-filled quilt to spread on the under-heated floor in the guest room to air. She borrowed the quilt from the guest bed, added the bottom sheet to conserve linen supplies, and returned to Lucas's bedroom with her spoils to hear the shower hissing in his bathroom.

Nothing to do with me, she thought, shrugging, and set to work. The bed was ready and waiting and the room tidy by the time Lucas emerged.

'I smelt like a polecat. I couldn't stand it,' he said flatly, rubbing at his hair.

'I can understand that,' she agreed, surprising him.

He raised an eyebrow. 'I thought you'd be yelling blue murder when you heard the water.'

'What's the point? I could hardly march in there and yank you out of the shower.' She gave him a militant look. 'But please tell me you own a hairdryer.'

'There's one in the chest in the guest room. For visitors' use,' he added blandly.

'Good. I'll get it. Put your dressing gown on and sit in the chair.'

His eyes gleamed. 'Are you going to dry my hair?'

'Only to make sure it's done properly. I flatly refuse to let you get pneumonia and put all my hard work to waste.'

Emily went off to search in the guest room chest,

which, like all the other chests in the flat, lay outside her normal tidying up jurisdiction. It came as no surprise to find a few items of female underwear in the drawer with the hairdryer. Probably the current girlfriend. Who had to be a very tidy creature. In the short time Emily had been cleaning for Lucas she'd never seen any traces of feminine occupation.

When she got back with the hairdryer Lucas submitted to her ministrations with such blatant enjoyment that Emily thrust her fingers through the layers of glossy black hair as rapidly as she could, keeping the dryer on full heat until Lucas protested.

'Steady on. I've only just managed to cool down.'

'You're done, anyway. Back into bed, please.' Emily thrust her own hair back from her shiny face.

'I feel a hell of a lot better after a shower. Why don't you have one, Emily?' said Lucas, eyeing her with sympathy. 'If you need a change of clothes, borrow something from the guest room.'

Emily stiffened, not at all happy to wear something one of his girlfriends had left behind.

'Ladies who stay the night with me,' he said, reading her mind, 'don't sleep in the guest room. But my sister keeps some things in there. Borrow what you like. Alice won't mind.'

'Thank you,' said Emily shortly, and poured water into a glass, then handed it to him with the pill. 'Would you like something to eat?'

'Please don't bother, Emily—you look worn out,' he said remorsefully. 'I'll be fine now. Have your bath.'

'How about tea and the inevitable toast afterwards?' she suggested, annoyed to find her throat thickening at the touch of sympathy. 'I fancy some myself,' she added, her voice even huskier than usual.

'In that case, thank you.' Lucas gave her a very serious look. 'Look, Emily, I know I'm an awkward swine half the time—'

'*Half* the time?'

He grimaced. 'Most of the time, then. But I deeply appreciate what you're doing for me.'

She gave him a stiff little smile and went off to the kitchen, feeling much too tired to cope with a Lucas Tennent who succeeded so spectacularly when he set out to please.

CHAPTER FIVE

EYEBROWS raised at the labels on Alice Tennent's underwear, Emily restricted herself to some lacy briefs, but otherwise made do with her own clothes. Later, showered and dressed, with hair curling damply over the towel round her shoulders, she went to see Lucas, who still looked haggard and sunken-eyed, but visibly less feverish.

'You're better,' she said, pleased. 'Fancy an egg on your toast? Or you could have honey, or jam.'

He thought about it, then shook his head in defeat. 'I'll pass on all three, thanks.'

'Egg for breakfast, maybe?'

'Never mind breakfast, Emily. May I have the pleasure of your company for supper tonight?' he said, and smiled.

Emily's knee-jerk reaction to the smile was to give Lucas Tennent anything in the world he wanted. 'Certainly,' she said, determinedly brisk. 'I shan't be long.'

'You're an angel,' said Lucas later, when she returned with a tray. 'This is perfect for me, Emily, but you should be eating something more substantial.'

'This is just what I want, too,' she assured him as she sat down. It was the truth. She was too tired to bother to cook, or eat, anything more demanding.

'Because I've worn you out,' Lucas said darkly.

'Not at all.' Emily licked her buttery fingers one by one, then stopped, her face hot when his eyes followed the procedure with a relish which made her toes curl. 'More toast?' she said, passing the plate to him.

'You have some, too,' he ordered.

'No more for me.' She got up to hand him the mug of tea.

Lucas took it with a word of thanks, his eyes on her face as she sat down. 'Get some sleep in the other room, Emily. I'll make sure I take the pills on time.'

'I wouldn't sleep if I did,' she assured him. 'So I'll set my alarm and we'll both get some sleep until it rings.'

Twenty minutes later Emily was settled comfortably on one of the sofas. She'd wrapped Alice Tennent's terrycloth robe round her in preference to staying in her clothes, added her own jacket as makeshift cover, and fell asleep almost at once. It seemed like only seconds before the alarm startled her into unwilling consciousness, and disorientated, cold, and only half-awake, she stumbled from the room and went to rouse Lucas.

He was deeply asleep, but to Emily's relief the covers were dry and his forehead free from sweat. She touched his outflung hand.

'Lucas.'

The thick black lashes lifted slowly on unfocused eyes. Lucas stared at her incredulously for a moment, then his eyes lit up and his arms shot up to pull her down to him. Almost in the same movement he rolled over and captured her beneath him, his mouth on hers in a kiss which paralysed her brain.

The hungry, expert mouth took complete possession of hers, kissing her into silence, his tongue invading and caressing, the sheer weight of him holding her body down as he stripped himself. His hands smoothed her robe away to find the warmth beneath, his fingers trailing

ribbons of fire over her skin, and she gasped at the exquisite sensation as he caressed her hard, expectant nipples and sent heat arrowing downwards to melt any last
shred of resistance. Lucas made a relishing sound deep
in his throat as she yielded, his caresses finding eroge-
nous zones Emily had never known she possessed. When
his fingers slid between her parted thighs to work their
magic on the concealed, throbbing bud, she gave a
choked little scream and reared up against him, and
Lucas, fiercely aroused, entered her with a smooth, practised thrust which pinned her to the bed. He captured
her hands, his eyes burning down into hers for an instant
while he held her impaled. Then he began to move, his
body urging hers to move with him, and for the next
few hot, surging minutes of urgent flesh on flesh, her
body responded with total abandon to physical possession so absolute that she clutched his shoulders in frenzy
when a powerful orgasm swept over her at last, engulfing
Lucas in the same shattering climax before he collapsed
on her as though he'd been poleaxed.

For a long, breathless interval Emily lay winded beneath his weight, her body vibrating with the throbbing
aftershocks of his lovemaking. But at last, desperate for
a deep breath, she pulled herself together and thrust
bunched fists at Lucas's shoulders. He rolled clear, trying to take her with him, but she shoved at him so violently he let her go, and without looking at him she
tugged at the dressing-gown until she was free. She
scrambled out of bed and stood up with her back to him,
body and hands shaking as she wrapped the material
around her and tied the sash viciously tight. Back still
turned, Emily managed to pour a glass of water, took a
pill from the pack, blindly thrust it towards Lucas, and
rushed out to make for the bathroom in the hall.

She locked the door and sat on the edge of the bath, hands thrust in her hair, breath still heaving through her chest as she fought for calm. I bet Florence Nightingale never had that problem to cope with, she thought, and began to laugh. And couldn't stop even when Lucas began hammering on the door.

'Let me in,' he bawled. 'For God's sake, Emily, calm down and unlock this door, or I'll break it down.'

His threat cut off her hysterics like a douche of cold water. She unlocked the door, turned on the tap in the washbasin and bent her head to splash her face. She felt a towel thrust into her hand and straightened to dry her face, and at last forced herself to face him.

Lucas looked pale and haggard, hair wild and eyes heavy, but in some indefinable way no longer as ill as before.

New cure for flu, thought Emily, and gave him a derisive little smile which stopped well short of her dimple. 'Do you know what my gut reaction to—to all that was?'

His mouth twisted. 'Disgust?'

'Regrettably, no. As was embarrassingly obvious.' She looked him in the eye. 'I'm a practical soul, Lucas Tennent. My first thought was money. Because I can't work for you now. And in my current financial situation that's bad news.'

'You mean all you can think of is *money*?' He frowned incredulously. 'I thought you were hysterical because you felt I'd raped you.'

Emily shook her head impatiently. 'We both know that what happened between us was nothing like rape. I—I co-operated with too much enthusiasm for that. Anyway, I thought rapists were motivated by anger.'

'Whereas the only one angry is you,' he said bleakly. 'Do you blame me?'

'No.' He thrust an unsteady hand through his hair. 'Not in the slightest. Is there any point in an apology, Emily? If so, I'll grovel.' He swallowed, his eyes locked with hers. 'I must have been dreaming of you. Then I woke up to find you there for real, and you know the rest. I was only half-awake at first. But that's no excuse. Once you were in my arms I couldn't have let you go if the roof had fallen in.'

'Maybe it's the antibiotics—' She glared at him. 'Please tell me that you took that one just now?'

'Of course I didn't,' he snapped. 'I was too concerned about you.'

'Then go and take it now, for heaven's sake.'

'If I do, will you come with me? To talk?'

Her anger drained away. 'All right,' she said listlessly. 'But only after I've had another bath.'

It was some time before Emily, fully dressed and more or less in her right mind, felt up to facing Lucas again.

'Before you ask,' he said swiftly as she went into the bedroom, 'I've taken the pill.'

'Good.' She moved the chair well away from the bed and sat down in it, legs crossed, trying to look relaxed. 'So what do you want to talk about?'

Lucas sat erect in the bed, his eyes holding hers. 'First of all, I apologise again, Emily. It's not a habit of mine to force a woman.'

She eyed him with scorn. 'Oh, come on, Lucas. You didn't force me. I was so sleepy it was more a case of taking me—and my body—by surprise.' She thought about it. 'More a revelation than a surprise, to be exact, especially the last bit. I've never had an orgasm before.'

Lucas looked thunderstruck. 'Never?' he asked at last.

'No. I've always faked it.'

'Surely that didn't go unnoticed?'

She shrugged. 'Miles certainly never mentioned it.'

Lucas shook his head in wonder. 'The more I hear about this guy, the harder it gets to believe you even passed the time of day with him.'

Emily sighed despondently. 'Whatever I felt for him didn't survive the first couple of weeks. But where we both worked everyone knew we'd bought a place together, and I wouldn't admit, even to myself, that I'd made such a disastrous mistake. My parents wanted me to marry someone else.'

'And Miles took you away from him?'

'Sort of. The relationship with Harry was already running out of steam, anyway. He's a solicitor. Lives in Chastlecombe. But when I came to work in London things sort of fizzled out between us. Then Miles came on the scene, in hot pursuit from the first. Very different from cautious, sensible Harry. But, alas, my savings were my main attraction for Miles.' She gave Lucas a wry look. 'I don't have much luck where men are concerned.'

Lucas moved to the side of the bed and leaned towards a suddenly wary Emily. 'Don't look like that. I'm not going to pounce on you again.' He reached for her hand. 'Let's clear the air. Where I'm concerned you needn't worry.'

'About what?'

'Money, for a start.'

She dropped his hand like a hot coal. *'Money?'*

'I meant,' said Lucas impatiently, 'that even if you never want to lay eyes on me again, you can still go on working for me if you want, because normally our paths never cross.'

'Oh, right,' she said dully.

'The other point I'm forced to raise is lack of protection.' His eyes held hers relentlessly. 'Though your only fear on that score where I'm concerned is possible pregnancy.'

She stared back in outrage. 'Isn't that *enough*?'

'Which means that you don't practise contraception yourself.'

'No. I'm one of the awkward ones. The pill disagrees with me.'

Lucas nodded briskly, then winced. 'I must remember not to do that.'

Emily jumped up. 'Please lie back. For a moment I'd forgotten—'

'That I'm ill?' He smiled. 'So had I. How about writing an article for the *Lancet*. New miracle cure for influenza.'

'It's not funny to me,' she snapped.

'Nor to me,' said Lucas quietly, his eyes steady on hers. 'It was miraculous, Emily.'

Secretly, she was in full agreement, but something about the way he was looking at her told her it would be dangerous to admit it. 'Please rest now. When I leave in the morning I want to know you're on the mend. And able to take care of yourself when I'm gone.'

Lucas held out his hand. 'Sit on the edge of the bed for a while, Emily. We haven't finished our talk.'

She shook her head and got up. 'No more talk, Lucas. I'm tired. And it won't be long before I'm back with the next dose of pills.'

'You don't have to,' he said at once. 'I can do that myself.'

'Possibly,' she retorted, 'but I'll be back at six, just the same. Goodnight.'

This time when Emily settled on the living room couch she felt jumpy and out of sorts, and so far from sleep that she gave up after a while and tiptoed into the kitchen for some water. She perched on one of the stools, chin in hands, then turned to see Lucas watching bleakly from the doorway.

'You look the picture of despair, Emily,' he said, coming nearer.

'Not despair, exactly.' She slid off the stool. 'I was just sorting things out in my mind.'

'What things?'

'Dates,' she blurted, then blushed to the roots of her hair.

Lucas reached for her involuntarily, and Emily leaned against him limply. 'When will you know?' he asked.

'End of next week. I'll find out how soon I can take a pregnancy test.'

Lucas tipped her face up to his. 'And give me the result straight away.'

'Of course.' She smiled faintly. 'Lucas, I certainly didn't bargain for all this when I decided to play Good Samaritan.'

'Enough to cure you of all charitable impulses in the future,' he agreed, and smoothed her unruly curls back in a gesture which made her throat thicken. 'Go and get some rest, Emily. I promise to take my pill at six.'

'I couldn't sleep if I did,' she said, backing away.

'Neither could I.' His eyes met hers. 'The memory of making love to you, Emily Warner, will give me insomnia for the foreseeable future.'

'I bet you say that to all the girls,' she said wearily.

'You couldn't be more wrong.' He shivered and Emily hurried to take his arm.

'Will you please go back to bed?' she scolded. 'I absolutely forbid you to have a relapse.'

'If I did would you stay to look after me?'

'Certainly not! Because you're going to be fine from now on. Though you might feel a bit down for a while,' she warned. 'I certainly did.'

'Without you on hand I'll be more than just down.' In the bedroom Lucas gave her a dark look as he slid beneath the covers. 'Are you really going to abandon me in the morning, Emily?'

'I have work to do,' she reminded him. 'But after I've finished at the Donaldsons' I'll look in on you before I go home.'

Emily made sure Lucas took the medication at six, then retreated to the sofa for an hour to worry about taking the morning-after pill neither of them had mentioned. If her intolerance to contraceptive pills was anything to go by, the effect of such a huge dosage of hormones would be unpleasant in the extreme. But better that than a possible pregnancy. Not that one solitary experience of love, sex, or whatever spin one put on the episode with Lucas, need necessarily result in a baby. And even if it did it wasn't the end of the world. She bit her lip. Who was she kidding? She couldn't bring up a baby in her room in Nat's house. The two flights of steep stairs alone vetoed that. She would just have to find somewhere else. Because for several reasons, her father's calling among them, she couldn't face the idea of returning pregnant and single to Chastlecombe.

At last Emily could stand it no longer. She got up, made use of one of the new toothbrushes Lucas kept in the main bathroom, then went into the kitchen to make coffee. Overcoming reluctance to face Lucas by the light of day, she put her head round his door and found him sitting upright against his pillows, reading the *Financial Times* from the day before.

'Good morning,' he said, abandoning the paper. 'You look shattered, Emily.'

'I'm never very bright in the morning,' she confessed. 'How do *you* feel?'

'A damned sight better than I did yesterday.' He sniffed the air. 'My olfactory powers are back to normal, for a start. Do I smell coffee?'

'I'll bring you some right away.'

'Bring yours as well and sit with me,' commanded Lucas. 'We need to talk.'

'Yes, we do,' Emily agreed. When she got back she handed him a steaming beaker, then sat down with her own. 'First, the morning-after pill,' she said baldly. 'I'd better find a doctor today and ask for one.'

'No way!' he said forcibly. 'Alice's flat-mate vomited for days after taking that, and still stayed pregnant. With your intolerance to contraceptive pills, Emily, God knows what a high-voltage dose of hormones would do. Leave the outcome to me. Please.'

'We don't know there's going to be an outcome yet,' she said irritably.

'True. But no morning-after pill. Emily, promise me.' His eyes met hers with such intensity that she nodded, secretly relieved to have the decision taken from her.

'All right, let's talk breakfast instead. How about some eggs?'

'Yes. If you have some, too. In here. With me.' Lucas lay back against his pillows, smiling with persuasion she couldn't resist.

Emily nodded again, afraid, as so often lately, to trust her voice. She picked up the tray and made for the door, clearing her throat. 'How do you want the eggs?'

'The way you like best,' he said promptly. 'What time are you due at the Donaldsons'?'

'They won't be back until late this evening, so I'll go over there after you've taken the next dose.'

'I'm perfectly capable of looking at a clock and swallowing the damned thing myself,' he informed her.

'Good,' she said, unmoved. 'From then on you'll have to.'

Emily returned later with a tray. She gave Lucas a glass of orange juice, then handed over his omelette and sat down to eat her own.

'Wonderful,' said Lucas indistinctly and peered at her plate. 'Yours is much smaller than mine.'

'I'm not the invalid in need of nourishment—careful, don't eat so quickly.'

'Yes, Nurse,' he said, and gave her a smile which made her heart contract.

'Perhaps you'll fancy something more filling later on,' she said huskily. 'I'll do some shopping while I'm out. What would you like?'

'If I'm to cope with it myself, something basic like soup,' he said, with a melancholy sigh.

'Can't you cook, then?'

'I can, if absolutely necessary. But at the moment I'm a bit deficient in the energy department—for cooking, anyway,' he added, looking her in the eye.

Emily jumped up to take his empty plate, her face hot. 'Right. Soup it is.' She looked around her in disparagement. 'Tomorrow you can retreat to the sofa for an hour while I sort this room out.'

'Tomorrow?' demanded Lucas, brightening. 'I thought you were abandoning me for good, today.'

Emily shrugged, resigned. 'I suppose I'd better come back tomorrow. But not for long,' she added, when his eyes, no longer bloodshot, gleamed like jet in satisfaction.

'I'll take whatever crumbs of your company you'll give me,' he said, with unconvincing humility.

She grinned and went off to the kitchen, sobering quickly as she made tea. This intimacy of sharing meals in the bedroom had to stop. It smacked too much of a relationship which didn't actually exist. And if there were any 'outcome' to the episode in the night, some share of the blame was hers. Lucas hadn't asked her to come round to look after him. She couldn't deny that the enforced intimacy of the past few days had done away with the employer/servant barrier she'd tried to put up between herself and Lucas Tennent. But the fact remained—whatever the outcome, they were still virtual strangers.

She went into the bedroom, gave Lucas his tea, then sat down.

'How do you feel?' she asked. 'Truthfully.'

'A lot better. Yesterday I thought I was dying. Today I'm very much alive.' He smiled at her. 'A combination of medical science and your tender loving care, Emily. No man could ask for more.'

'Good. I won't feel so guilty when I leave you on your own, then.'

His smile vanished. 'I'm going to miss you like hell.'

'Nonsense,' she said, getting up. 'Until last Friday you'd never set eyes on me.'

His eyes gleamed. 'Why can't I get my head round that?'

'Because you're under the weather. Once you're fighting fit and juggling with stocks and shares again, or whatever it is you do—'

'I'll still feel grateful to you, Emily. Nor will I forget,' he added.

She sighed impatiently. 'We're back to the "outcome", I suppose.'

Lucas stabbed her with a look like black ice. 'You don't have some hare-brained idea about keeping me in the dark, by any chance?'

'No.' Though she'd certainly considered it. 'I promised I'd let you know, so I will.' Her eyes flashed. 'But until then, could we drop the subject, please?'

'For the time being only.' Lucas eyed her moodily. 'Must you clean at the Donaldsons' today? You need a rest.'

'It won't take long to leave them a few supplies and make sure everything's shipshape for their return. I did their place thoroughly last Friday.'

His eyes gleamed. 'Eventful day, last Friday!'

Emily gave him a wry smile of agreement and got up to take their mugs. 'Stay in bed, please, Lucas. Take advice from an old hand. You might feel better right now, but leave it for a day or two before you're up all day.'

He scowled. 'I'll go raving mad!'

'Nonsense. There's a radio and a television in here, and a stack of books by your bed,' she said impatiently. 'Be sensible, Lucas. I'll bring you a daily paper when I come back to check on you.'

'How long will you be?' he demanded, looking so gloomy that Emily laughed at him.

'As long as it takes!'

She gave Lucas his pill, provided him with bottled water and orange juice, then went off to do some shopping before her stint at the Donaldsons' flat. After putting the supplies away there, she made sure everything was in order, watered the plants, left a brief note on the kitchen memo-pad to say Lucas had flu, then went back to him.

Emily let herself back into the flat as quietly as she could, put her shopping away, peeped into the bedroom, frowned to find it unoccupied, then gave a smothered screech when Lucas caught her in his arms, spun her round, and kissed her soundly.

'Don't *do* that!' she exploded, shoving him away with furious hands. 'Why are you out of bed?'

'The obvious reason.' He blinked suddenly and steadied himself against the chest at the end of the bed.

'You see?' she said fiercely. 'Crime doesn't pay, Lucas Tennent. I bet your head's spinning.'

'Yes,' he admitted meekly, allowing her to help him back to bed. The black eyes gleamed. 'But only from *your* effect on me.'

'You mean you're not as fit as you thought!' She stared down at him in an agony of indecision, then looked at her watch. 'I really must get back to Spitalfields now, Lucas, but if you can mange on your own this afternoon I'll come back later if you like.'

'And if I promise to keep to my own bed will you stay the night?' he said, with a look of such blazing relief that Emily, who had intended nothing of the sort, nodded, defeated.

'Oh, all right. But just for tonight.'

'But don't walk back, Emily. Take a taxi. I'll pay.'

She smiled wryly. 'You'll have to. My budget doesn't run to taxis.'

Before she went, Emily made some coffee and a sandwich and took it in to Lucas with strict instructions to remember his pill at two. 'I'll be back in time for the next dose.'

'I'll manage without you, somehow,' he assured her.

'Go home and have a rest, Emily. The shadows under those big eyes of yours are giving me a guilt complex.'

'You've got some, too,' she retorted, then grinned. 'But if my eyes look big I'm definitely not sickening for anything. According to my brother, I look like a hamster when I'm ill.'

Lucas let out a snort of laughter. 'Typical brotherly comment.'

'Time I went.' She wagged an autocratic finger. 'Once you've taken the antibiotics, have a good sleep.'

'I will, Nurse, if only to pass the time until you're back. And take some money for the taxi.'

'We'll settle up when I get back—'

'Take it now,' he ordered in a tone which sent Emily to the chest to take out his wallet. Lips compressed, she extracted a banknote and showed it to him.

'Right. I'm off.'

'No kiss goodbye?' he said, aggrieved.

'Certainly not! See you later.'

CHAPTER SIX

ON THE way back Emily bought a pregnancy test, and learned she had nineteen days to wait before using it. By which time it would be unnecessary. When she got to Spitalfields she trudged wearily up the two steep flights of stairs to her room, and found a red light on her answerphone. Certain it was Miles, but afraid to erase the message in case it was Lucas, she pressed the button and listened in angry frustration.

'Emily, this is Miles again. As if you didn't know. I need to talk to you. Pick *up*, Emily.' There was a pause. 'All right. Play it your way. But don't think you can hide forever.'

Why not? she thought furiously. She had nothing to say to Miles. Their parting had been so acrimonious she shuddered at the memory. The row between them had escalated to the edge of violence before Miles had gone rushing out of the flat that night. Afraid he might come back any minute, Emily had left a message on her boss's voicemail to say she was ill, and quit London immediately to drive herself and her possessions to Chastlecombe. By the time she'd arrived home in the small hours her fictional illness had become factual influenza, and as soon as she'd recovered enough to make conscious decisions she'd sent in her resignation. Apart from frantic phone calls to her parents' home, when he was told Emily wanted nothing to do with him, she'd heard nothing since from Miles until his messages on her new, unlisted telephone.

Emily erased the latest, rang to order a taxi for five-thirty, then changed her sweater for a T-shirt and went downstairs to make an overdue start on Nat's rooms. She worked steadily for a couple of hours, then went up to the first floor to perform the same service for Mark. Tired and hot afterwards, and filled with an overwhelming desire to crawl into bed, she swallowed a cup of black coffee instead. Once the caffeine had done its work, she packed an overnight bag, stood under a warm shower for a while, then went back to her room to treat her hair to some styling for once. She gathered it up into a loose, curling knot on top of her head, then paid detailed attention to her face. Yawning, she dressed in bronze velvet jeans and black sweater, pulled on black suede ankle-boots, added a vintage black velvet jacket snapped up in a church jumble sale, slung a long black mohair scarf round her neck, then took her belongings downstairs to wait in the hall for the taxi.

Light-headed with fatigue, Emily dozed on the short journey and woke with a start, blinking like an owl when the taxi stopped outside Lucas's building. She paid the driver, hoisted her bag, then went up in the lift and let herself into the flat. She went quietly into Lucas's bedroom to find him sitting in a chair in his dressing-gown, watching a newscast. At the sight of her he came to his feet with a smile of such unguarded delight that Emily felt a giant fist squeeze her heart.

'I'm back,' she informed him after a pause.

'So you are,' he said huskily. 'I've missed you.'

'Did you sleep?' she said breathlessly.

'Yes. Did you?'

'No. I had a shower instead.'

'Will you hit me if I said I did, too?'

She smiled ruefully. 'Not much point, now. How do you feel?'

'All the better for seeing you, Emily Warner.' He moved closer. 'You still look tired.'

'I had a few things to do,' she said, backing away.

'Working on your laptop?'

'No. Just a bit of tidying up.' Emily looked at her watch then took off her coat. 'I'll put this away, then I'll bring you a drink so you can take your pill.'

'I was just about to do that,' he assured her virtuously. 'Though I'm delighted you arrived early to remind me.'

'Back into bed, then.'

Emily hung her jacket up on a hook on the guest room door, decided the quilt needed to stay on the heated floor a bit longer, then went into the kitchen to put the kettle on to make a hot drink with lemon juice, honey and brown sugar.

'I thought you'd like this for a change,' she said when she took it in to Lucas.

He sipped experimentally and smiled in appreciation. 'Pure nostalgia. My grandmother used to make this when Ally and I were sniffly kids.'

Emily handed him the antibiotics. 'Chase this down with it and you'll soon be back to normal.' A thought which depressed. Normal for Lucas Tennent was light years away from normal for Emily Warner.

He gulped the pill down, took a swig of the drink, then waved her to the chair. 'Sit down and talk to me. I missed you.'

'You said you slept.'

'I did.' His sloe-black eyes locked with hers. 'But I would have slept better with you for company.'

Controlling a shiver of reaction, Emily sat back in the chair, making a conscious effort to relax. 'Do you think that's why I agreed to come back tonight? To sleep with you, Lucas?' she asked bluntly.

He shook his head, smiling. 'I know exactly why you came back.'

She stiffened. 'Oh?'

'Because you just couldn't bear the thought of leaving me all alone and ill.'

Emily grimaced. 'A bit saccharine. Pollyanna was no favourite of mine.'

'If I also said you're sexy as hell would you like that better?' he demanded, then laughed at the outrage on her face. 'I hope you never play poker, Emily.'

She got up, scowling at him. 'I'm going to do something about a meal.'

'I'll only eat it if you come in here and share it with me,' he said promptly. 'Whatever it is.'

Emily shook her head. 'I'll share it with you, certainly, but not in here. If you feel up to it, I suggest you get up for a while and have supper on a tray.'

Lucas eyed her narrowly. 'Does that mean you're never going to set foot in my bedroom again?'

'No, indeed. In the morning I'm going to give it a good sorting out,' she said briskly.

'Emily?'

'Yes?'

He gave her the bone-melting smile. 'Am I allowed to say you're a delight to the eye tonight?'

'Certainly,' she assured him, ignoring her pole-vaulting heart. 'By the way, I forgot to ask. Do you like salmon? The cold, poached variety?'

'As it happens, I do. But for you, Emily Warner, I'd eat anything!'

Emily left him to begin preparations for their simple meal, knowing full well that she looked good tonight.

She'd taken a great deal of trouble with her hair and face, and the clothes she was wearing were simple enough, but they were the kind she wore to go out with Ginny, or to join Nat and the others for a drink. Certainly not the clothes she wore to clean Lucas's flat. Nor the kind she could afford any more. Refusing to analyse her reasons for gilding the lily, Emily prepared tiny potatoes and green beans and put them to cook, then whisked a spoonful of horseradish into clotted cream to accompany the fillets of ready-poached salmon. She buttered slices from a ciabatta loaf, dusted a touch of cayenne over the cream garnish, then tested the vegetables for readiness.

She went into the hall and knocked on Lucas's door. 'Dinner ready in five minutes,' she called.

He came out at once, newly shaved, wearing a heavy sweater and khakis. 'I dressed for dinner,' he said, stifling a cough. 'Can't lie around in a dressing gown when my companion looks so delectable.'

His delectable companion flushed hectically. 'I hope you haven't tired yourself out in the process,' she scolded. 'Go and lie down on one of the sofas. I shan't be long.'

'Emily.' Lucas laid a hand on her arm. 'Relax. Please. I swear I won't jump on you again.'

'I thought we'd decided to drop the subject,' she muttered, face averted.

'We can't pretend last night never happened,' he said quietly, then turned her face up to his. 'But just for *this* evening let's forget I've been ill and you're only here because you promised my sister to stay. I enjoy your company, Emily, so for a couple of hours couldn't you at least pretend to enjoy mine?'

She gave him a very straight look. 'You know perfectly well that I don't have to pretend.'

'Is that why you came back?'

Emily gave him a wry little smile. 'I suppose it must be one of the reasons.'

Lucas had said no more than the truth. She *had* come back because she couldn't bear to think of him alone and ill—also because she'd promised his sister to look after him. But those were the high-minded reasons. The other motive was more basic. She'd just wanted to spend the evening with Lucas. Emily knew that this little interlude was a time apart from their normal lives. Once Lucas was better he wouldn't need her any more.

And pretence didn't come into it when it came to enjoying Lucas's company over the simple meal. It was fun to eat from plates on their knees, sitting together on the same sofa, and, because Lucas had been reading book reviews earlier, arguing amicably over the merits of various writers.

'This morning,' said Lucas, when he laid down his knife and fork at last, 'I wouldn't have believed I could eat a mouthful of that, let alone wolf it down.'

'Flattering to the cook,' commented Emily, finishing her own at a slower pace. 'Though cooking didn't really come into it. Anyone can do something like this.'

Lucas gave her a wry look as she got up to take his plate. 'Not in my kitchen, they don't. No one's ever made dinner for me here before.'

'Really?' Emily eyed him in surprise.

'Really. The ladies of my acquaintance prefer dining out. My sister included.'

Well aware that for a man like Lucas Tennent there would be no shortage of women in his life, Emily controlled an irrational pang of jealousy and went out to load the dishwasher. When she got back with a tray of coffee Lucas sprang up to take it from her.

'Steady,' she warned, as he swayed enough to make the cups rattle. 'Don't get up so suddenly. You're not fighting fit just yet.'

Lucas grimaced as he set the tray down on the low chest in front of the sofa. 'God knows how I'd be at this stage if you hadn't come to look after me.' He sat down and patted the place beside him. 'I suppose I couldn't have a brandy with my coffee?'

'Bad combination with antibiotics,' Emily said firmly, and handed him his cup. 'And no more of this tonight, either, or you won't sleep.'

Lucas leaned back, his eyes on hers. 'I probably won't anyway, with you in the next room.'

'Then I'd better go home.'

'If you do you won't sleep, either.'

'Oh? Why not?'

'Because you'll worry about me.'

His smile was so smugly triumphant that Emily couldn't control a giggle.

'Sophist!' she accused.

'Nevertheless, I'm right. You'd lose sleep over anyone you knew if you thought they were alone and ill.'

He couldn't be more wrong. Up to now, Emily had never experienced such overwhelming urgency to care for someone in the way she did with Lucas. Certainly not with Miles. A discovery which would have saved a whole lot of trouble if she'd made it at the start of their acquaintance.

'You'd better not stay up too long,' she advised him. 'Not for the first time.'

'But if I go back to my bedroom, that's it,' he complained. 'No more Emily.'

She leaned back in her corner, smiling at him. 'You can stay up until you take your last dose for today.'

'Gee, thanks! For that and for a great many other things,' he added, and eyed her musingly. 'Strange to think you've been sharing my flat with me all this time—more or less—without my knowing it.'

'Cleaning, not sharing, Lucas.'

'But you were the one making the place a pleasure to come home to, Emily. A pity I'm rarely home early, or we would have met before.'

She chuckled. 'When we finally did I wanted to sink through the floor. Did you think I was a computer-literate burglar listing your possessions?'

He shook his head, smiling. 'I thought I was hallucinating.'

'Actually, you were very forbearing, Lucas.'

'A good thing I was,' he said with feeling. 'Otherwise I would have languished alone and ill on my sickbed all this time without a soul to take care of me.'

'I doubt it. Your sister would have arranged for a nursing service.'

Lucas shuddered. 'A thought which makes me all the more grateful to you, Emily.'

She yawned suddenly. 'Sorry! I've had rather a busy day—' She stopped, flushing.

'I thought,' said Lucas suavely, 'that you went home to relax for a while.'

She looked down at her hands. 'I did eventually, but first I had work to do. I was already a day overdue with my other jobs—'

'So you spent the afternoon cleaning for your landlord!'

'And for Mark, too.' Emily's chin lifted. 'There's absolutely no point in glaring at me, Lucas. It's how I earn my living. At the moment, anyway.'

He scowled. 'In the circumstances, surely these guys would have let you off today?'

'Of course they would.' Not that she had the least intention of discussing these particular circumstances with either Nat or Mark. 'But that would have been taking advantage.'

'Do they know you're looking after me?'

'No. Sometimes I don't actually see either of them for days on end. And even when I do I don't have to explain myself to them.' Emily looked pointedly at her watch.

'Don't tell me,' said Lucas, resigned. 'You're about to blow the whistle.'

'It's not up to me, Lucas. If you want to stay up for a while after taking the pills I can't stop you.' She got up. 'I'll fetch you the pill and some water, and I'm leaving a flask of hot lemon drink by your bed in case you fancy it in the night.'

'Thank you—' His eyes narrowed. 'What flask?'

'Mine. I brought it back with me earlier.'

He shook his head in mock wonder. 'You're a paragon, Emily. Did you ever think of nursing as a career?'

'Not my kind of thing.' She smiled at him and went off to the kitchen, glad he had no idea that Lucas Tennent was the only man she'd ever met who brought out her caring instincts.

When she got back she was touched to find Lucas had made a nest of cushions in her corner of the sofa.

'Put your feet up and lie there for a while,' he ordered.

'Thanks, it looks so tempting I will.' Emily slid her boots off and curled up with a sigh of pleasure, fixing him with persuasive eyes. 'Lucas, you know all there is to know about me. Would I be overstepping the mark to ask about your background?'

He raised an eyebrow. 'You mean the mark between master and slave?'

'That's the one,' she agreed, smiling. 'If I cross my heart and promise complete discretion, will you give me a brief rundown on the life and times of Lucas Tennent?'

He shrugged. 'I'm not worried about your discretion. I can hardly be of much interest to your friends.'

He hadn't met Ginny, thought Emily drowsily, as he began to talk about his grammar school education, followed by a degree from Cambridge and an MBA. From the start, he told her, he'd been tunnel-visioned about acquiring the best possible technical skills to add to the flair and determination necessary to get on in his profession. He described how he'd begun in a lowly way in research at the investment bank that had offered him his first job, and after rising steadily through the ranks there, had been eventually headhunted by another much-respected banking institution.

'Its continued success in the global market is due to skilful alignment between ambition and resources. In short,' Lucas explained, turning to her, 'an outfit unlikely to crash—'

He smiled ruefully. Emily was asleep. Which allowed his eyes to roam at leisure over the sleeping face framed in escaping tendrils of glossy black hair, the rise and fall of her breasts under the clinging black jersey. Knowing he was to blame for the exhaustion which had finally overtaken her, guilt mingled with the pleasure he took in just looking at her. Filled with a protective feeling new in his experience with women, he got up slowly, careful not to disturb her, then stood frowning in indecision. It was a cold night. Electronically controlled heating or not, Emily would wake shivering at some stage if he left her where she was. Even go down with flu again. He rubbed his chin thoughtfully for a moment, then with infinite care he picked her up and stood still, cradling her in his arms for a moment until he felt steady enough on his feet to carry his sleeping burden.

Relieved to find he was more than capable of transporting one small female a relatively short distance, Lucas made for the guest room, then stood in the open doorway, cursing silently. There were no pillows, the bed was stripped and the quilt was on the floor. For all he knew, maybe he'd gone through his entire stock of bedlinen. And to his disgust he was fast running out of energy to go and check.

Only one thing for it, then. Lucas carried Emily into his own room and very carefully laid her on the bed she had tidied up at some stage during the evening. She muttered indistinctly and he hung over her, braced on his arms, willing himself not to cough. Eventually he straightened with care. Bad idea to collapse on top of her. From her point of view, anyway. But there was still the problem of whether to risk waking her by undressing her, or to leave her as she was. The sweater could stay. But the jeans fitted so perfectly they would be uncomfortable once she was tucked up in bed. Gingerly, he undid her waistband and slid down the zip, waited a moment, then tugged gently and to his relief found the velvet material had some kind of stretch incorporated into it, making it easy to pull off. She made a muffled, protesting sound as he achieved success, then settled into the pillow like a little animal getting comfortable in its nest.

Lucas stood still and watchful for some time. When Emily showed no signs of waking, he went into the bathroom to undress and buried his face in a towel to smother the cough that finally defeated him. When he came out Emily still lay motionless, out to the world, and, taking care not to disturb her, he stretched himself out on the far side of the bed. Resisting the overpowering urge to kiss her flushed, sleeping face, he reached out a hand to switch off the light, then pulled the covers over them and settled down to sleep.

CHAPTER SEVEN

EMILY woke to feel an arm round her waist, and breath hot on her neck, and let out a squeak of fright which woke Lucas up with a start. He snatched his arm away and shot upright, coughing.

'Emily, I can explain,' he panted, meeting her startled eyes. 'Don't be frightened.'

She pushed herself upright, thrusting her hair back from her face. 'I'm not now I know it's you. But for a nightmarish moment I thought it was Miles.'

Lucas let out a heartfelt sigh of relief. 'I was afraid you'd scream and run for your life once you woke up and found yourself in bed with me. But there's a logical explanation, I swear.'

But Emily was less concerned with logical explanations than the discovery that it felt perfectly natural to share a bed with Lucas.

'Don't you want to know why I brought you here?' he demanded. 'And before you ask, nothing happened other than sleep.'

'I know that,' said Emily, surprising him with her dimple. 'Unless you managed to put my clothes back on after you'd had your wicked way. Not counting the jeans, I appear to be fully dressed.'

'You fell asleep on the sofa last night,' he explained. 'I was afraid to leave you there in case you got cold, but when I carried you to the other room there were no sheets on the bed. By that time I was dead on my feet, so I brought you here, even at the risk of mayhem when

you woke up. I removed the jeans with great reverence,'
he added soulfully.

Emily chuckled, but, suddenly aware that whatever
reasons had made it necessary to share Lucas's bed last
night they no longer applied now it was seven in the
morning, she slid to her feet and made for the jeans
folded neatly on the chest. She turned her back on Lucas
and pulled the stretchy velvet up over sheer black tights.

'I've never slept in my clothes before,' she muttered,
embarrassed now. 'If you don't mind I'll have a quick
shower before I make you some breakfast.'

'I don't mind in the least,' he assured her.

Later, when Emily was dressed in the more everyday
denims and sweatshirt she'd brought with her, she
knocked on Lucas's door before going in.

'A bit late for formality, Emily,' he said, laughing at
her. 'Not much point when we've shared nearly every
intimacy there is in the past few days. The more romantic of them not of your choice, it's true, and the rest of
it certainly not mine. But in the short time since we met
we've come to know each other remarkably well.'

Too well in one instance, thought Emily. 'How do you
feel today?'

'Better,' he assured her. 'Apart from the odd cough
now and then, I'm definitely on the mend.'

'Good.' She smiled in approval. 'I'll bring your breakfast. Then later, when you feel up to it, you can transfer
to a sofa while I sort this place out.'

'And after that?'

'I'm going back to Spitalfields.'

Lucas slumped back against the pillows, his eyes accusing. 'Aren't you worried I'll relapse?'

'I can't stay here all the time, Lucas!'

'Why not?' he demanded. 'Are you supposed to be cleaning somewhere today?'

'No,' Emily admitted. 'Not today.'

'Then what's so urgent in Spitalfields that you have to rush back there?'

'My laptop, for a start. I'm not playing at writing a novel, Lucas. I should be working on it right now.'

'Fetch it and work here.'

She gave him a quizzical look. 'Are you really telling me that you can't manage on your own if I go home?'

'No, I'm not,' he admitted with reluctance. 'I'm not feeling totally fit yet, but I'm perfectly capable of heating soup and swallowing pills at the prescribed intervals.' The sloe-black eyes held hers like magnets. 'I'm asking you to stay, Emily, for the simple reason that I'll miss you like hell if you go.'

She turned away blindly and made for the door. 'I need coffee. I'll be back as soon as I can with your breakfast.'

This was getting out of hand. While she made coffee and put eggs to boil Emily made a firm resolution. From now on she wouldn't let those hypnotic black eyes persuade her against her better judgement. The situation was stereotyped enough. The patient dependent on the nurse. But she was not a nurse, and if she had any shred of common sense she would take off today after tidying Lucas's bedroom and come back only when she was due here next. In her official capacity as cleaner. Or, if she were really sensible, not come back here at all.

'Why the heavy frown?'

Emily whirled round, startled, to see Lucas, fully dressed. 'You're up,' she said idiotically, and he grinned.

'So I am. I had to clear out of my bedroom shortly, anyway, so I've come to eat here with you, in the kitchen.' He looked at her steadily. 'But if you object to the arrangement I'll take myself and my breakfast to the living room sofa and leave you in peace.'

Emily put her resolution on hold. 'Of course I don't object. Settle yourself on one of those stools and drink some orange juice while I make toast. I hope you like boiled eggs?'

It was fun to sit perched at the breakfast bar with Lucas, to share coffee and toast and even the eggs, since he insisted Emily ate one of them.

'What do you normally eat for breakfast?' she asked, dunking a finger of toast in her egg yolk.

'Just some fruit juice,' he admitted, following suit. 'Caroline, my assistant, provides me with coffee and croissants when I get in. What about you?'

'At home, under my mother's eagle eye, something like this.'

'And with Miles?'

Emily shrugged. 'I always left long before him to provide *my* boss with coffee and buns.'

'Was the boss man cut up when you left?'

'He said so. He replied to my resignation with a very kind, regretful letter and promised a glowing reference. He even asked me to call in and see him some time. But, for obvious reasons, I'm not going to do that. As far as I know Miles still works there.'

Lucas turned in his seat to give her a searching look. 'I've been thinking about Miles. Exactly why is he ringing you, Emily? Does he want to kiss and make up?'

She scowled. 'If he does he's out of luck. In fact, I'm amazed he wants anything to do with me.'

'Why?'

'Money.' Emily's smile was mirthless. 'My money. When we split up we had a huge row over it. Like a fool I'd given Miles my savings as part of the deposit on the flat. But that night when I asked for it back he said no chance, because he didn't want me to leave, and in any case I hadn't signed anything to prove I'd ever given him any money.' She glowered. 'Like an utter fool I'd trusted him. So I learned the hard way that co-habitation doesn't give a woman the same rights as mar-riage. Although I paid for our food and household bills while we were together, I didn't contribute to the actual mortgage repayments. And darling Miles had taken out the mortgage in his name only, which means I have no legal rights over the flat we shared and no hope of get-ting my money back.'

Lucas swore volubly. 'The bastard cheated on you *and* swindled you out of your money? Did you contact a lawyer?'

'Of course. My father got in touch with my solicitor chum right away. But in the end Harry advised us not to pursue it. In his opinion the costs of the case would have come to more than the nest egg I'd handed over to Miles in the first place. Anyway, by that stage I wanted to forget everything about him—*and* his wretched mort-gage. And how criminally stupid I'd been.' Emily stared malevolently into her cup. 'I'd saved some of my nest egg myself, but the rest came in presents over the years from my parents, who never have all that much to spare. I could kill Miles with my bare hands every time I think of it.'

Lucas's grasp tightened. 'Look, Emily, if the swine turns up and gives you any trouble at all, tell me right away. I'll sort him out for you.'

'I don't think he will, but even if he does find me in Spitalfields he'll have Nat to contend with first. And don't look like that,' she added impatiently. 'Nat would naturally be first on the scene. It's his house.'

Lucas slid off his stool and lifted Emily down and held her by the elbows, his eyes probing hers. 'If Miles gives you any hassle I'll get a lawyer friend of mine to take out an injunction against him.'

She brightened. 'That's a great idea.'

His grasp tightened a little. 'Tell me the truth. During this row of yours, did Miles get physically violent?'

'No.' Emily gave him a triumphant smile. 'I was the violent one, not Miles. At first that horrible night he just blustered, saying I was making a fuss about nothing. That boys will be boys. Tamara was just a fling. I was important to him.' She shrugged. 'I think his ego just couldn't take it when I said it was over. Then I demanded my money back and things got really ugly—lots of shouting. When he caught hold of me to stop me packing I grabbed his precious school cricket bat and told him to take his hands off me and get out, or I'd hit him for six.'

Lucas threw back his head and laughed. 'And how big is this idiot?'

'Almost as tall as you, but heavier. Why?'

He shook his head in wonder. 'Emily, you can't be more than an inch or so over five feet, and delightfully rounded though you are I was able to carry you quite comfortably last night. Yet this prince among men actually turned tail when you threatened him?'

'He certainly did,' she said, her eyes glowing at the memory. 'I was dying to hit him and Miles knew it. So he did the sensible thing and took to his heels.'

Lucas laughed delightedly and ruffled her hair. 'Vicious creature. I'm thankful I don't own a cricket bat any more.'

Emily surveyed him, head on one side. 'Should the need arise I'd take more subtle revenge in your case.'

'You already have.' He laid a hand on his chest with a theatrical sigh. 'You've stolen my heart.'

'Very funny!' she jeered. 'Now go and lie on a sofa while I clear away. Then I'm going to attack your bedroom.'

Emily was putting the finishing touches to it when the doorbell rang. 'I'll get it,' she called, and went to open the door.

'Emily?' said Liz Donaldson in surprise. 'I didn't think you came here on Wednesdays.'

'She doesn't normally,' called Lucas from the living room door. 'Sorry to be inhospitable, Liz, but stay where you are. I might still be infectious.'

'So I gather. I got Emily's note, so I came to drop the paper in and see if you needed anything,' said Liz, who was tall and fair, with a bright-eyed, intelligent face. 'But if Lucas is infectious, why are you braving his germs, Emily?'

'I had flu not so long ago, with all the same side effects, so hopefully it's the same virus and I'm immune,' said Emily, desperately trying to hide her embarrassment. 'Did you have a good holiday? If Lucas will go back to his sofa you could come into the kitchen. I'll make coffee.'

'Can't stop, thanks,' said Liz with regret. 'So who's been looking after you, Lucas? Alice?'

'No. She's on holiday in Italy—and under orders to keep my state of health from my mother.' Lucas smiled blandly at Liz. 'My bug brought me home early last Friday, which was a stroke of luck because I met Emily in person for the first time. She's been an absolute saint: so worried because I had no one to soothe my fevered brow that she's dropped in from time to time to check on me.'

Liz wagged a finger at him. 'I hope you've doubled her wages!'

'Good God, no. Emily goes berserk at the mere mention of money.' He began to cough and Liz ordered him back to his sofa, promising to check on him later.

'It was very sweet of you to take care of Lucas, Emily,' she whispered, as she made for the door.

'Not at all.' Emily went outside with her on to the landing. 'Look, I'm sure the subject won't arise,' she said in an undertone, 'but if you happen to talk to Nat don't let on that I've been looking after Lucas, please.'

'I'm not going in today, but when I do, not a word, I promise.' Liz gave her a sparkling look. 'Would Nat be jealous, then?'

'Heavens no. But he might well rat on me to my brother!'

When Emily went back to Lucas he cast a dark look at her outdoor clothes.

'You really are going, then.'

'Yes, Lucas.'

'It's raining cats and dogs. Call a cab.'

'Certainly not. I enjoy the walk.'

He thrust a hand through his hair in frustration. 'You'll ruin that coat. If you must walk borrow something of mine. You'll be swamped, but at least you'll be dry.' He went into the bedroom and returned with a black ski-jacket and held it out.

'Oh, very well.' Secretly not at all keen to ruin the vintage velvet, Emily shrugged it off and slid her arms into the parka, tugging at the elasticated wristbands to free her hands. 'It comes down to my knees,' she said, pulling a face.

'Since you're so pig-headed about walking that's all to the good,' he said, his eyes softening at her ludicrous appearance.

'Thank you,' she said politely. 'Now. Remember to take your pills at regular intervals, Lucas, and wash them down with lots of water. There's a flask of lemon and honey on the counter, and cheese, eggs, bacon and cartons of soup in the fridge—'

'Strangely enough,' he said caustically, 'I managed my life quite well before you came into it.'

Emily blinked as though he'd slapped her face. And Lucas leapt to take her in his arms.

'I'm *sorry*. Don't cry. Please.'

'I'm not crying—just tired,' she said huskily, holding him off. 'Bye for now. I'll see you on Friday.'

'*Friday?*' He glared at her, incensed. 'Why not tomorrow?'

'I'm busy tomorrow.'

'Slaving away for your landlord, no doubt?'

'And for Mark.'

Lucas gazed down at her, his eyes locked on hers in such intense persuasion she turned her head away in self-defence. 'You could come here afterwards,' he coaxed. 'And stay the night.'

'I could,' she agreed, 'but I'm not going to. Goodbye, Lucas.'

His hot protest changed to a sudden paroxysm of coughing. 'You see?' he gasped, when he could speak. 'The mere thought of your absence, even for a day, and I'm heading for a relapse!'

Emily refused to be moved. 'You'll be fine.'

But the effort to tear herself away from Lucas left her in a mood which matched the miserable, sheeting rain as she hurried back to Spitalfields. The hooded jacket

shielded her from the weather, but its warmth held a
scent so exclusively Lucas that at one point Emily almost turned round and went back. Instead she kept going, determined on time to herself to think rationally
about the future. Something she found impossible to do
in Lucas Tennent's company.

When Emily let herself into Nat's house she hung the
expensive padded jacket in the bathroom to dry, then
unlocked her door and put away the food she'd bought
on the way back. And at last checked her phone. But
there was no message from Lucas, nor, to her relief, from
Miles.

For once in her life Emily felt in need of a rest on her
bed before opening her laptop to get down to work. She
smiled a little. At least now she'd have a sizzler of a
love scene to describe. Life with Miles had been so disappointing in that area she'd assumed the fault was hers.
But Lucas had turned her preconceived idea about lovemaking on its head. Her eyes narrowed. Had that been
love-making? Or just red-hot sex? Either way, it had
been a revelation.

After spending almost an hour on her bed, something
new to Emily in the daytime, she made herself some tea
with the kettle that hid with a microwave and a tiny
refrigerator on shelves behind a wicker screen. She kept
basic supplies like tea and coffee in the cupboard underneath, but shopped as needed for anything more am-
bitious, and cooked it in Nat's kitchen during the day
while he was out. But not today.

She took her tea over to the table used as a desk,
plugged in the laptop, booted it up, and began to read
over what she'd written so far. The tea cooled, forgotten
beside her as she worked, but eventually she took a
break and checked her watch, wondering if Lucas had

remembered to take his medication. For heaven's sake, of course he has, she told herself crossly. But it was no use. With a sigh, she picked up the receiver and keyed in the number.

When an attractive—and unfamiliar—feminine voice answered, Emily disconnected hastily. Someone had obviously turned up at last to minister to the patient. Which, she informed herself savagely, was inevitable now he was better—and germ-free.

Furious at minding so much, Emily forced herself to forget Lucas and companion and settle down to work. And by the time she heard the evening noises of Nat and Mark getting home she'd made considerable progress. Pleased with herself, and suddenly hungry, she was filling rolls with cheese and salad greens when the phone rang. She waited, resigned, expecting Miles again, then tensed, her heart missing a beat when the message was from Lucas.

'Emily, I just rang to confirm that I've taken the pills, drunk pints of water and fruit juice and kept my coffee intake to a minimum. Ring back soon in awed approval—'

'I'm here,' she interrupted breathlessly. 'How do you feel?'

'Lonely.'

Emily scowled in silence.

'I know you rang earlier on,' he went on. 'You forgot to cover your electronic tracks. That was Caroline who answered, by the way.'

Caroline. His assistant! Emily revived. 'Did she remind you to take your pill?'

'You could have asked her yourself if you hadn't rung off. But Caroline came to deliver messages and talk work, not pills. And, wary of my germs, she cleared off

as soon as she could. What are you doing right now?'
he added abruptly.

'Nothing. I've just closed the laptop after a session on
the Great Work, and now I'm going to eat something. I
trust you are, too?'

'Yes, Nurse. Rather to my surprise, I'm quite hungry.
Liz called back this afternoon with some kind of cas-
serole I can heat in the microwave.'

'So I don't have to worry any more.'

'Were you worried?'

'The night you had a cough like a chainsaw, yes, I
was. Bloodshot eyes apart, you looked a bit lacking in
the red corpuscle department, too.'

He laughed. 'Half-dead I may have been, but I soon
came back to life under your care, Emily.'

Her cheeks flamed at the memory. 'Then please don't
waste my efforts. Keep taking the tablets.'

'It's going to be a long day tomorrow without you,
Emily,' he said, in a tone which badly undermined her
famous resolutions.

'Catch up on all the reading you never have time for,'
she advised briskly. 'Goodnight, sleep well.' Emily put
the phone down quickly, in case Lucas began persuading
her to spend time with him the next day. And in case
she said yes.

Emily rang her mother later, to report that she'd survived Lucas Tennent's flu unscathed—news received
with much relief by her mother, who went on to fire off
several barbed questions about vitamins and sensible eating before passing on Richard Warner's love to his
daughter and concluding with her own. To Emily's relief, there wasn't a word about Miles.

But when she rang Ginny later, her friend was plainly
worried to hear that Miles was still leaving messages.

'What on earth does he want? You didn't make off with his family silver, or something?'

'And me a vicar's daughter? Certainly not.'

'So how did it go with the gorgeous patient?'

'*Im*patient, you mean. As invalids go, he's the end.'

'Is he grateful to you?'

'Yes. Now he's better, anyway. He was very ill at one stage. I had to call a doctor.'

'Wow. He must have been pretty bad to want that.'

'Lucas didn't want it at all. Made a huge fuss. Fortunately his sister rang, read him the riot act, and asked me to arrange it.' Emily chuckled evilly. 'You should have seen his face when a woman doctor arrived.'

They went on chatting for a while, as they always did, before Ginny came to a halt because Charlie was due home. 'Emily,' she said, suddenly serious. 'You're all right, are you? Really, I mean?'

'Absolutely fine. Not a cough or a sneeze to my name.'

'I don't mean that.' Ginny hesitated. 'What I'm trying to say, with my usual consummate tact, is that you've just got over the break-up with Miles. So don't do anything reckless, Em. Please.'

Too late for warnings of that kind, thought Emily afterwards. Reckless didn't begin to describe her behaviour with Lucas Tennent. She should have resisted, protested, done *something*. But, from the moment he'd seized her in his arms, the warning signals from her brain had never had a chance. Besides, if she had put a stop to it all she might have gone through life with no experience of what sublime, earthy magic the act of love could actually be. She shivered at the memory. And didn't blame Lucas in the slightest, whatever the outcome. He hadn't asked her to come running to play nurse. A wry little smile played at the corners of her mouth and her eyes grew dreamy. There was no point in wasting time on regrets over an experience Lucas had described very aptly as miraculous.

Emily came back to earth with a bump. In future, she would avoid all contact with miracles and confine her charitable impulses to putting coins in collection boxes.

Time hung heavy for Emily for the rest of the evening. She felt too tired to open up her laptop, yet too restless to read. In the act of pouring boiling water on a teabag, she was seized by a sudden rush of panic and put the kettle down with an unsteady hand. It was imperative that she found *some* way to occupy her mind. Her cleaning jobs conveniently left her mind free to compose drafts for her novel, but they also left it free to worry about what fate had, or didn't have, in store for her.

CHAPTER EIGHT

THE following morning the phone rang in Nat's kitchen while Emily was finishing her usual cleaning routine. She went on mopping the floor, leaving the machine to pick up as usual, then looked up, her attention caught, when the message began.

'Nat, this is Louise Powell. I don't have your office number, or your mobile, and I don't like to ask Thea, but I thought you ought to know that she's ill—'

'Louise,' Emily broke in. 'This is Emily Warner. What's wrong? Can I help?'

'Emily?' said Louise, surprised, but too worried to ask questions. 'Can you possibly contact Nat for me? Thea just passed out on the kitchen floor. I've got her to bed now, but she looks absolutely ghastly.'

'Heavens, Louise, have you contacted her mother?'

'Away on a cruise. Always the way, isn't it? I've rung the doctor, and I can fetch Tom and Lucy from school this afternoon with my lot, and feed them, too, of course. Only too glad to help. But if you can get in touch with Nat I'd be terribly grateful.'

'I'll ring him straight away,' Emily assured her. 'Don't worry, Louise. I'll find him. Give me your number so I can let you know what's happening.'

To Emily's frustration, Nat's cellphone was switched off. She rang his firm's number, learned he was in an important meeting, and asked to speak to Mrs Donaldson instead.

'Right,' said Liz crisply, when Emily explained. 'I'll

105

haul Nat out at once. This is just the chance he needs. He can rush to Thea's bedside like a knight in shining armour. Perfect. Don't worry, Emily, I'll barge in there and get him to ring you back right away.'

'Bless you, Liz.'

Emily raced up the two steep flights of stairs to her own room just in time to answer the phone to a frantic Nat Sedley.

'Emily, for God's sake tell me what's wrong? Is Thea in hospital—?'

'No, nothing like that.' Breathless, Emily passed on the message and the phone number, assuring him that Louise Powell had promised to pick Tom and Lucy up after school.

'Right,' said Nat tersely. 'I'll ring Louise, then I'm off. I'll drive straight from here. Thanks a lot, Emily. I'll ring you tonight to keep you up to speed.'

Emily glared at the red light which had been winking on her phone throughout her conversation with Nat. Life had been so much simpler before the answer-machine her parents had insisted on. Refusing to pander to it, she made herself a cup of coffee and drank half of it before pressing the button.

'Emily, you haven't rung to ask how I am,' said a hoarse, aggrieved voice. 'In case you're interested, I passed a very restless night without you. I miss you.'

Emily reached out a hand to ring Lucas back, then changed her mind. She would be seeing him tomorrow. He could wait until then. Or rather, she could. Somehow.

After lunch, her cleaning sessions over, Emily opened her laptop and settled down to work. She took a deep breath and plunged into the love-scene, embarrassed to find her face hot and her pulse racing as she painted a verbal picture of the bliss experienced in Lucas

Tennent's arms. Her fingers flew over the keys as though possessed, then she stopped, groaning in frustration. She'd used his name. 'James,' she said through her teeth. 'The man's name is James, not Lucas.' She went back over the scene, so involved in the changes that she answered the phone without thinking.

'Success at last!' said a triumphant voice, but Emily slammed the phone down, waited until it rang again, and listened, resigned, while Miles began leaving a furious message.

'Answer me, God dammit. What the hell are you playing at, Emily? I just want my property back. So ring me. Now.'

Emily stared at the phone, mystified. What property? In her frantic hurry to get out of the flat she'd been forced to leave some of her own things behind, let alone make off with anything belonging to Miles.

To get some peace, Emily took the receiver off and put it on the table beside her so she could work undisturbed. And only put it back later because Nat was due to ring some time.

When it rang almost immediately, Emily seized it eagerly. 'Nat?'

'Sorry to disappoint you,' snapped a hostile voice.

'Oh.' She bit her lip. 'Hello, Lucas. How are you?'

'If it's of any interest, I feel better. Not wonderful. But better. I left a message earlier.'

'I know. I didn't ring back because—'

'Because you were waiting to hear from your landlord.'

'No.' Emily was silent for a moment. 'I had a quite different reason.'

'What is it?'

'I'd hate you to think I was taking advantage of—of our relationship because of what happened that night.'

'Ah. So you do admit we have a relationship,' he said triumphantly.

'I should have said arrangement. You the employer, me the cleaner.'

'Emily,' he said, his voice dangerously quiet. 'It's a good thing you're not here with me right now, or I'd wring your pretty little neck.'

'In that case,' she said lightly, 'I'd better not come to your place tomorrow.'

'If you don't, I'll leave my sickbed to fetch you.'

'You don't know my address.'

'Liz gave it to me.'

'You *asked* her for it?'

'Damn right I did.' Lucas's laugh sent trickles down her spine. 'She nobly refrained from asking why I needed it, tactful lady. But be warned, Emily, I know where you live.'

'Is that a threat?' she demanded.

'Just making sure you turn up tomorrow. As promised,' he said significantly. 'Goodnight. Sleep well.'

Emily was in bed when Nat rang with an apology for calling so late.

Thea, he reported, had been trying to fight off flu with over-the-counter medication in an effort to keep going for the twins. The faint had been the inevitable result of lack of food coupled with sleepless nights.

'How is she now?'

'Running a temperature, and so wretched, poor darling, she gave in without a word when I laid the law down about staying to take care of her, *and* my children.'

'You know, Nat, I'm sorry Thea's ill,' said Emily thoughtfully, 'but in other ways—'

'It's an ill wind, and so on,' he finished for her. 'One snag, though, Emily. Louise Powell told her you answered my phone today.'

'Only because I was mopping your kitchen floor, Mr Sedley!'

'Thea didn't know that, obviously. But apparently Tom and Lucy could talk about nothing else but you when they went back after half-term, so my wife asked me point blank if there was anything between you and me now, Emily.'

'*What?* I hope you convinced her that's utter nonsense, Nat Sedley.'

'Yes. In the end,' he said, an odd note in his voice. 'But only at the cost of a little white lie.'

Emily braced herself. 'What kind?'

'I was so determined to clear the decks with Thea that I said you were passionately in love with the new man in your life.'

'Thanks a bunch!'

'Don't worry. You don't have to produce him in the flesh. But I'd like our stories to match if you happen to talk to Thea.'

'Right.' Emily hesitated. 'Nat, what about the original problem? Is Thea coming round on that one, too?'

'Yes, thank God. We had a long talk this evening, after I put a jubilant pair of twins to bed. Let's just say I'll go happy to bed myself tonight.'

Wishing she could say the same, Emily spent a restless night, gave up trying to sleep at last, and with the aim of getting finished to be with Lucas as soon as she could, arrived so early at the Donaldsons' flat that Liz hadn't left for work.

'Goodness, you're an early bird, Emily,' she said, surprised. 'Ben's only just left. I'm agog to know what happened with Nat, so shoot. You won't be telling tales out of school,' she added, when Emily looked troubled. 'At the firm, all Nat's colleagues know the story. Besides, I've met Thea, even been to a party at their house in Chastlecombe. How is she?'

Emily explained the situation and passed on the news that Nat was staying on to look after his wife and children.

'But that's wonderful.' Liz raised an eyebrow. 'Why aren't you happy about it?'

'Because the original rift may be healed, but Thea's now got some crazy idea that Nat's interested in me, for heaven's sake.' Emily groaned in despair. 'And to convince her otherwise he told her I'm having a red-hot affair with someone else.'

Liz gave a shout of laughter. 'Poor Thea. She's almost pathologically jealous where Nat is concerned. Which is understandable. Thea's a honey, a wonderful home-maker and a brilliant mother. But pretty she's not. And Nat is quite the handsomest man I've ever laid eyes on. Don't let on to Ben I said that,' she added, laughing.

'I won't.' Emily hesitated. 'Look, Liz, I suppose I shouldn't be asking this, but do you know if Thea ever had reason to be jealous of Nat?'

'Absolutely not,' Liz assured her. 'The trouble started when Nat's PA left. Enter Melanie Baker—blonde hair, long legs and cleavage. She lusted after Nat from the first, but he wasn't having any. So when they worked late together one night Melanie tried to seduce him.'

'Wow! What did Nat do?'

'Promptly dispensed with her services. Whereupon Melanie, spitting fire, storms down to Chastlecombe and tells Thea she's been having a sizzling affair with Nat from the day they met. Sweet, unremarkable Thea took one look at this centrefold blonde and believed every word.'

'Instead of trusting her husband. Poor Thea. Anyway,' added Emily, brightening, 'according to Nat, every-thing's fine now, except for her crazy idea that he fancies me, of all people.'

'Not so crazy, Emily,' said Liz, getting up. 'You're attractive and female and you live in Nat's house—you know what they say about propinquity.'

'I assure you it doesn't apply in this case. Besides, Thea ought to know me better than that—' Emily was struck by a sudden thought. 'Oh, crikey. Once she's bet-ter, I hope she doesn't turn up on spec in Spitalfields to meet this lover Nat dreamed up for me.'

'If she does, there must be someone you can trot out for the purpose?' Liz grinned. 'I'd offer Ben for the role, but Thea's met him.'

After Liz left, Emily worked faster than usual in her hurry to see Lucas. When she was sure the flat was im-maculate, she locked up and ran across the cobbled street to the converted eighteenth-century warehouse she much preferred to the modern apartment block which housed the Donaldsons.

Strange, she thought, as she went up in the lift. After spending her childhood in a draughty Victorian vicarage she'd yearned for something modern and labour-saving when she went flat-hunting with Ginny. The one they'd rented was a bit poky, or bijou in brochure speak. But Emily had loved it so much it had taken endless persua-sion from Miles to coax her to leave it for the bigger, pricier apartment of his own choice.

But now she'd regressed a couple of centuries in her taste, both in Nat's house in Spitalfields and in Lucas's home, which, though a hip loft conversion, was part of an old, historic building. She loved both places. Which was silly when neither would feature permanently in her life. In fact, thought Emily gloomily, she would be forced to look for pastures new right away if Thea intended spending much time with Nat in London.

Before Emily could put the key in the lock Lucas opened the door, dressed in a Cambridge-blue sweater and vintage jeans. He looked very different from the irritable invalid of only days before.

'I heard the lift.' He smiled as he took the borrowed ski-jacket she held out. 'Hello, Emily.'

'Hi,' she said breathlessly. 'How do you feel?'

'All the better for seeing you,' he said softly, with a look in his eye which did serious damage to her resolutions. 'I missed you.'

'It's only been a couple of days,' she said, brushing past him to take off her jacket, but he was too quick for her and slid it from her shoulders.

'It felt a hell of a sight longer than that!' His lips twitched. 'Relax. I won't remove anything else.'

She ignored him and went off to the kitchen. 'If you'll sit in the living room I'll leave it until last,' she said briskly.

'Let's have coffee first.' He seized her waist and sat her on one of the stools at the bar. 'Like me, it's ready and waiting for you.'

This, thought Emily bitterly, wasn't fair.

Lucas slid on to the stool beside her and filled two mugs. 'There. While you drink that tell me everything you've done since I saw you last.' He gave her a challenging look. 'I presume you're still getting messages from Miles?'

'Why do you think that?' she asked, surprised.

'Because every time I ring the machine takes over for a while before you answer.' Lucas took her hand and stroked a finger over it. 'Tell me. Is that bastard frightening you?'

Not half as much as you are, thought Emily, panicking. 'He says I've made off with something belonging to him.'

'And have you?'

She shrugged. 'The only thing I can think of is the laptop. I gave it to him for his birthday, I admit. But I paid for it and still have the receipt to prove it, so he's out of luck if he wants it back.'

'If that's all he wants, give him the damn thing,' said Lucas irritably. 'I'll buy you another one.'

'Certainly not.' Emily detached her hand. 'Anyway, I'm not worried about Miles.'

'Then what's wrong? Tell me.'

'I can't,' she said, depressed. 'Most of it is none of my business.'

'But it's worrying the hell out of you, so get it off your chest. Or do you have to rush back to Spitalfields to minister to your landlord?' He grinned when she glared at him, then sobered. 'Seriously, Emily, come and sit down for a while and tell me what's wrong. You can trust me to keep it to myself, whatever it is.'

'I know that.'

When they were installed at opposite ends of the familiar sofa, Emily gave Lucas a brief outline of the trouble between Nat and Thea Sedley, and how the latter's illness had been the catalyst to bring them back together.

'Amazing thing, influenza,' commented Lucas. 'Without it, you and I might never have met, and in the Sedleys' case it's mended a broken marriage. I assume it is mended now?' he added.

'More or less.' Not without reluctance, Emily told him about Thea's suspicions where she was concerned.

'Can't say I blame her there,' said Lucas, looking down his nose. 'I share her point of view.'

'But you don't know Nat, whereas Thea's known *me* all my life.' Emily thrust her hair behind her ears in agitation. 'I would never dream of doing anything to harm her—or the twins.'

Lucas moved nearer to take her hand again. 'Emily, I refuse to believe your money was the only attraction for Miles. And you know damn well *I* don't find you a turn-off either. Thea Sedley obviously thinks her husband feels the same.'

'She doesn't any more,' said Emily gloomily. 'Nat's told her I'm violently in love with the new man in my life.'

'And who the devil's that?' he demanded, eyes slitted.

She shook his hand off impatiently. 'A phantom lover who doesn't exist.'

'Ah.' Lucas relaxed. 'So what happens if the suspicious Mrs Sedley turns up unexpectedly one day, thirsting for an introduction?'

'Lord knows,' said Emily despondently. 'Liz would have offered Ben's services, but unfortunately Thea knows him.'

'She doesn't know me.'

'It's no joking matter,' she snapped.

'Who's joking?'

Emily stared at him, startled.

'I mean it,' said Lucas casually. 'If the occasion arises I'd be happy to oblige. After all, there's no lie involved.' He touched a hand to her cheek. 'On one recent, unforgettable occasion I actually was your lover.'

Emily sprang up precipitately. 'Time I made a start,' she blurted.

For the next two hours Emily cleaned and polished and scoured, ignoring Lucas's frequent demands that she take a break, or stop altogether.

In the end he seized his state-of-the-art vacuum cleaner and thrust it in a kitchen cupboard. 'Stop it right now,' he said in a tone which brooked no argument. 'Or are you by any chance trying to solve our little problem by sheer physical exertion?'

She thrust damp hair from her forehead, her eyes widening as she realised what he meant. 'Are you serious?'

'It occurred to me,' he said grimly.

'Well, it didn't occur to me!' she spat at him. 'I was merely trying to get everything done as quickly as possible so I could get back where I belong.'

Lucas raised an eyebrow. 'After what you've told me about his wife, do you feel you belong in Sedley's house any more?'

Emily stared at him, stricken. 'No—I suppose I don't. I'd better start looking for somewhere else.' She glanced at her watch. 'It's past two. Shouldn't you be taking some medication?'

'In a minute. Let's have some lunch.'

'But I didn't do any shopping on the way in,' she reminded him, seized by the sudden urge to throw herself into Lucas Tennent's arms and cry her eyes out. Which was idiotic. There was nothing to cry about. She just needed sleep. 'Shall I dash out for something now?'

'Certainly not. I ordered in. For the moment you're going nowhere,' he said inexorably. 'Wash your hands, or whatever, then come and eat.'

When Emily got back from the bathroom she found a tray waiting on the chest in front of the familiar sofa.

'Not exactly a feast,' Lucas said, indicating the platter of sandwiches. 'But I thought the occasion merited a touch of ceremony.' He set this thumbs to the cork of a bottle of champagne, removed it neatly, then filled a couple of tulip-shaped glasses and handed one to her.

Emily took it with a dazed word of thanks, then followed his beckoning hand and sat beside him on the sofa. 'Champagne? What are we celebrating? Your recovery from flu, or is it your birthday?'

'Something far more important—an anniversary.' He touched his glass to hers. 'It's exactly a week, almost to the minute, since you and I met for the first time.'

Emily almost dropped the glass.

Lucas grinned. 'It's only a sandwich and a glass of bubbly, woman. And in broad daylight in the afternoon, at that. Hardly cause for panic.'

'I'm not panicking,' she lied, and gulped down some champagne. 'These look delicious,' she added brightly when Lucas handed her a filled plate.

'I would have preferred to take you out to dinner, but I thought you might lay down the law about behaving sensibly—'

'I certainly would!'

'I meant,' said Lucas, 'that you'd rage about relapses and so on. So we'll postpone the dinner date until you think the time is right.'

'Lucas,' said Emily patiently. 'This is lovely, and I'm flattered you went to so much trouble, but that's as far as it goes. I'm certainly not dining out with you.'

'Why not? It's just a way of saying thanks for all you've done for me,' he said, undeterred. 'Nothing more sinister than that.'

Surprised to find the argument had sharpened her appetite, Emily started on another sandwich and prepared to do battle. 'Pointless rather than sinister, Lucas. Because when you're fit and well, and back in the City, things will revert to normal between us. You the City Banker, me your cleaner. And never the twain shall meet and all that.'

'I thought we'd put paid to all that nonsense.' Lucas pushed his plate away and refilled their glasses. 'Are you by any chance a snob, Emily Warner?'

She stared at him in exasperation and waved a hand around. 'How do you work that out? You own this. I live in one room I rent for such a small amount it's tantamount to charity. How can I possibly be a snob?'

'Inverted variety.' He raised a sardonic eyebrow. 'Does Mrs Sedley know how little you pay for your room, by the way?'

Emily sniffed. 'I've no idea.' She drained her glass recklessly. 'You know,' she said, with a confiding air fostered by the champagne, 'it really hacked me off to think that Thea suspected me of—of—'

'Sharing her husband's bed?'

'I don't suppose she went that far!' Emily shrugged. 'If so, it's utterly ridiculous. I don't think of Nat that way.'

Lucas topped up her glass. 'If she's jealous of him, I take it Sedley's got a lot going for him in the looks department.'

'Liz says he's the handsomest man she's ever met.' Emily thought for a bit. 'How are you on movie stars?'

'Adequate.'

'Think of a young Robert Redford, only taller and even better-looking, if that's possible.'

'Good God!' Lucas eyed her askance. 'And you don't find Sedley attractive?'

'Of course I do, but not in the way you mean. Nat's

kind and nice and I like him a lot. I'm grateful to him, too. But to me he's just my brother's friend and not my type at all. I don't go for fair men.'

'In that case—' Without warning, he scooped her on to his lap and kissed her. 'Part of the celebration,' he whispered against her parted lips. 'If this is never going to happen again you can at least agree to a few kisses.'

'Because of your outlay on champagne?' she said rashly, and said no more for some time, returning kisses that grew so heated it was alarmingly obvious where they would lead if she didn't do something fast. But when Emily gathered her wine-blunted wits about her and tried to get free, Lucas held her tightly against his chest.

'I want you, Emily,' he said hoarsely.

'No!' She shook her head frantically. 'It's not going to happen again, Lucas.'

He tipped her face up to his. 'You don't want me?'

'No,' she lied in desperation. 'I don't.'

'You mean that?' he demanded.

'Yes,' she said woodenly, and his eyes hardened, the heat in them icing over so quickly she shivered and scrambled to her feet. She ran into the kitchen, almost tripping over her bag in her hurry to be gone.

'Wait,' said Lucas, catching her up in the hall. 'There's still a certain matter outstanding between us. Or have you forgotten?'

'Are you serious?' Emily threw him a scornful look. 'I never forget it for an instant, believe me.' She snatched up her coat, disdaining his help as she pulled it on. 'Certainly not enough to risk the same mistake twice.' She grabbed her backpack by the straps and made for the door, but Lucas stood barring her way.

'Emily. Please. If you find somewhere else to live let me know.'

'All right.' Her mouth dropped. 'Though, in the interests of the Sedley marriage, perhaps I'd better stay where I am for the time being after all. Otherwise, Thea might think her suspicions were right.' She looked up with a bright smile. 'Remember to finish the entire course of tablets, Lucas. You're obviously a lot better—'

'I'm glad you think so,' he said grimly, then took her hand. 'Have a good rest this weekend, Emily. I'll see you on Monday.'

She shook her head. 'No, Lucas. I'll wait until you start work again before I come back to clean. I'm sure you can manage until then. Unless you'd rather get someone else—'

'I don't want anyone else,' he said through his teeth. 'I want you.'

Emily gave him a despairing look and hurried out on to the landing outside the flat, feeling oddly hurt when Lucas closed his door before she even got into the lift.

Outside in the windy, cobbled street, Emily found that the champagne had given her a splitting headache and the straps of her backpack were cutting into her shoulders for once. And she was halfway back to Spitalfields before she remembered that Lucas hadn't given her the usual Friday cheque.

CHAPTER NINE

'FOR heaven's sake, Emily, you look terrible,' said Ginny, when they met as usual the next day. 'Are you in mourning, or something?'

To match her mood, Emily was wearing unrelieved black, the only touch of colour her eyes and a lipstick so bright she rarely used it on the mouth she considered too full for bright shades. 'I'm tired, that's all.'

'You're sure you haven't caught this man's flu?'

'Yes. It's just lack of sleep.'

'So what's keeping you awake at night?'

Not even to Ginny could Emily confide the real reason for her insomnia. Instead, she told her friend about Nat and Thea and the phantom lover.

Ginny chuckled as she dished out coffee and buns and gave Emily the gooiest. 'You look as though you could do with it. Are you eating properly?'

'Yes, Mummy!' Emily tucked into her cake, feeling better, as always, in Ginny's company. 'How's Charlie?'

'At a conference this weekend. At least, that's what he tells me.'

'Come off it,' jeered Emily. 'You know perfectly well Charlie's never looked at another woman since the day he met you.'

'Of course I do,' said Ginny fondly. 'This all came up unexpectedly. He had to take someone else's place. So how about coming round to our place to keep me company tonight? We can get a bottle of wine and a video and be all girly.'

Emily gave a fleeting thought to the work she'd meant to do on her novel over the weekend, but the prospect of a day away from her lonely room—and her telephone—was too tempting to pass up. 'I'd like that a lot.'

Emily slept better on Ginny's sofabed than she had for some time, and returned to Spitalfields late the following afternoon, surprised to find no messages for once. Her immediate reaction was sharp disappointment because Lucas hadn't rung, followed by relief because Miles hadn't either. Emily put out a hand to ring Lucas, then changed her mind and opened the laptop instead. She would recycle her emotions by transferring them to the central female character in her novel.

Next morning, Emily was on her way out of the Donaldsons' flat when the bell rang. When she opened the door as far as the safety-chain allowed, her heart skipped a beat at the sight of Lucas.

'Let me in, Emily.'

She took the chain off and turned away to pick up her bag. 'I'm just leaving.'

'I was afraid I'd missed you.' He stood just inside the door, looming large in the padded jacket. 'How are you?'

'Fine. How are you?'

'Only a few more antibiotics to go. I'll be back in work soon.'

'That's good.'

Silence fell, loud with things unsaid.

'Look, it's too soon for me to know yet, Lucas,' said Emily, cutting straight to the chase. 'I promised to let you know and I will.' She gave him a wry little smile.

'My father's a clergyman, remember. He brought me up to keep my promises.'

'Admirable habit,' said Lucas, relieving her of the backpack. 'I never knew my father.'

Emily's eyes softened. 'He died when you were little?'

'No. When Ally and I were small he just left home one day and never came back.'

She gazed at him in horror. 'Why?'

'When my mother thought we were old enough to understand, she told us he was a free spirit who felt stifled by marriage and fatherhood.' His jaw clenched. 'She was wrong.'

'About your father?'

'About me. I'll never understand how a man could do that. Just take off and slough off his responsibilities like so much unwanted baggage.' Lucas paused. 'Look, if you've finished here have some coffee at my place before you go back, Emily.'

'All right.' She made sure the door was locked behind them and followed Lucas into the lift.

'I rang you over the weekend,' he informed her.

'You didn't leave a message.'

'The idea was to speak to you, not to a machine.'

'I was with the friend I used to live with. Ginny and I still meet every Saturday morning, but this weekend her husband was away so I stayed the night with her. Though I don't know why I'm telling you this,' she added with sudden irritability. 'I don't have to report to you.'

Lucas smiled faintly as they reached the ground floor. 'True. But I was worried when I couldn't reach you.'

'Why?' she demanded, shivering in the wind which

funnelled down the street as they crossed the cobbles to his building.

'I was afraid you'd succumbed to my flu after all.'

'In which case, I would have been in my room.'

'You could have gone home to your mother for more cosseting.'

She shook her head. 'I'm keeping well away from Chastlecombe for the time being.'

The lift in the converted warehouse was bigger than in the modern building next door, but even so Emily felt hot and bothered by the time they reached the top floor. In such close proximity to Lucas every hormone she possessed clamoured in response to the warmth from his body and the familiar tang of the soap he used mingled with the clean male scent of his skin. When they went into his flat he dumped her bag down, shed his jacket and took her raincoat, as though they'd done this a hundred times before, then followed her into the kitchen.

'Shall I make the coffee?' offered Emily.

'If you like.' He gave her a straight look. 'I take it you're here with me solely out of pity about my defecting father?'

'Sympathy, not pity.' Which wasn't the exact truth. She'd come with him because she wanted—needed—to be with him, if only for a little while, before going back to her solitary room.

Lucas sat on a stool and leaned his elbows on the counter to watch her get to grips with the coffee-machine. 'Normally, I never discuss my father. But I told *you* the story, Emily, to make a point. Well, two points, actually.'

Emily threw him a curious look as she took porcelain mugs from a cupboard. 'Which are?'

'First of all, it seemed a good idea to kill this bee in your bonnet about the social difference between us. I'm well-educated, I admit, but that's because I've always worked hard and I've been lucky enough to win scholarships at the necessary stages. And these days I'm successful in my career. But you fell asleep on me the other night so I didn't tell the whole story. Unlike you, Emily Warner, I'm the product of a single parent family. When my father abandoned us we moved in with my grandmother and Mother had to go back to work to feed and clothe us.'

Emily gazed at him in horrified sympathy as she passed him his coffee. 'What did she do?'

'She'd been a legal secretary before her marriage, but to earn money straight away she worked in a shop before she finally landed a job with the local solicitor.' Lucas's mouth twisted. 'Ally and I used to cry for our father in the beginning, but in the way of the young we eventually forgot him. I was in my first year in grammar school before the lack of a dad was really brought home to me. Schoolboys can be cruel young savages.'

'Did your father ever come back?' said Emily.

'No. In true beachcombing fashion his free spirit eventually took him to a Pacific island so small and remote it took months for news of his death to reach my mother.'

'After all that time was she upset?'

'Inconsolable for a while.' His eyes hardened. 'She'd never stopped loving him.'

Emily finished her coffee, at a loss for something to say. Even on acquaintance as short as theirs, she knew that baring his soul was hard for Lucas Tennent. He would probably curse himself for it afterwards. Maybe her, too.

'I had another reason for telling you,' he informed her, picking up on her reaction. 'If you are expecting my baby, Emily, you can be sure I won't evade *my* responsibilities. No child of mine will grow up without knowing his father.'

'That's very high-minded and noble,' she commented after a pause. 'Doesn't the mother—me, in this particular instance—have a say in this?'

Lucas's eyes flickered in surprise. 'Well, yes, of course. But surely you want my support if the worst happens?'

Emily's unruly heart contracted painfully. She looked at her watch. 'Time I was off. Let me know when you go back to work and I'll come and sort this place out for you. Unless you'd rather find another cleaner—'

'To hell with the cleaning! We need to talk about the necessary arrangements if you're pregnant, woman,' he growled, intercepting her as she passed him.

'Let's leave all that until I know whether the *worst* has actually happened,' she flung at him. 'Goodbye, Lucas.'

'Emily,' he said, striding after her as she made for the door. 'I put it badly—'

'But *so* accurately. My sentiments, exactly.' Emily turned her back on him and got in the lift she was beginning to dislike, because lately she so often went down in it feeling utterly miserable.

When she got back, Emily was surprised to find Nat in the hall as she let herself in.

'I'm on a flying visit. Louise Powell's with Thea,' he

explained. 'She'll fetch the twins and stay with Thea until I get back. My presence is required at a meeting this afternoon, then I'll come here afterwards for some clothes and go back to Chastlecombe for the rest of the week.'

'How is Thea?'

'Better, but still pretty fragile, poor darling.' Nat's grin took ten years off him. 'But with my tender loving care she'll soon be right as rain.'

'I'd send her my love, but I'm not top of Thea's list at the moment,' said Emily glumly.

'Actually, she's come round on that subject now, even begged me not to tell you she'd been so silly.'

Emily brightened. 'I'm off the hook, then?'

'Not exactly. She's still asking for details of this dream lover of yours.' Nat grinned widely. 'I was pretty unimaginative—tall, dark and handsome was all I could come up with. Must run—see you later.'

Emily trudged up the stairs to her room, cheering up a little when there were no messages waiting for her. Miles had obviously given up.

With no need to clean for Nat that day, Emily decided to skip lunch until she'd done Mark's rooms, and put in a couple of hours before retreating upstairs for a shower. Afterwards, comfortable in pull-on pink jersey trousers and black cable sweater, Emily made a sandwich and drank some tea. While she'd been cleaning, thoughts of Lucas kept coming between her and the next instalment, but now, she ordered herself, opening the laptop, she would banish him by getting to grips with her story. She spent a long time editing what she'd written, then started on the next chapter. For a long time her absorption was fierce, but eventually it dawned on her that there was something going on downstairs. Emily opened her door to hear familiar voices raised in altercation in the hall far below, and flew, barefoot, down two flights of stairs, skidding to a halt in the hall when two male faces swivelled towards her; Nat's deeply embarrassed, the other rigid with offence.

'A slight misunderstanding, Em,' explained Nat. 'I've just tried to throw your visitor out. From your description I thought he was Miles Denny.'

'I'd better introduce you,' said Emily, her spirits rising so precipitously that she smiled brilliantly on both men. 'Nat, this is Liz's friend, Lucas Tennent, one of the people I clean for. As you've probably guessed, Lucas, this is Nat Sedley, my landlord.'

The two men eyed each other warily, then Nat's face broke into an apologetic grin as he held out his hand to Lucas. 'Humble apologies! A case of mistaken identity. Emily's brother gave me strict instructions to throw the ex-boyfriend out if he showed his face here.'

To Emily's relief, Lucas grinned back as he shifted a sheaf of flowers to the hand holding a carrier-bag so he could shake Nat's. 'No harm done. The flowers suffered the most.'

'Are they for me?' said Emily idiotically.

'Who else?' said Lucas, and thrust them at her. 'Perhaps you can salvage some of them.'

Nat's vivid blue eyes moved from one face to the other with interest. 'Look, I'm just off to Gloucestershire, so I haven't got time to give you a whisky by way of apology, but Emily can do that. She knows where I keep the drinks. Make yourself at home in my place, if you like—not, I assure you, that I object to gentleman callers in Emily's room.' He glanced at his watch and whistled. 'I'm late. Promised to be home by bathtime. See you.'

He grabbed a suitcase and went out at a run, leaving a tense silence behind him after he closed his elegant front door.

'Do you get many?' asked Lucas eventually.

'Flowers?'

'Callers.'

Emily shook her head. 'You're the first.'

Another silence.

'So what do we do now?' he asked. 'Do you want me to go?'

She looked down at the flowers. 'I'd better put these in water. Would you like that whisky Nat mentioned?'

'Damn right I would.' He smiled crookedly. 'It's not every day of the week I get mugged.'

Emily chuckled. 'I don't see a black eye.'

'No, fortunately. And it only got as far as it did because Sedley took me by surprise. I didn't anticipate ejection into the street the minute I mentioned your name!'

She smiled ruefully. 'Sorry about that. Nat's never met Miles. I just gave him a description.'

'Which obviously fitted me down to the ground.'

'Not really. You're both tall, dark and very—' She halted.

'Go on!'

'In Miles's case, very full of himself.'

Lucas looked offended. 'And is that how you see *me*?'

'No. Confident, maybe? Self-assured?'

'Better,' he conceded grudgingly. 'And is Miles prettier than me?'

'Heavens, no. You win by a length in the looks department.' She showed him into Nat's small, elegant drawing-room. 'If you'll wait here for a moment I'll just put these in water.'

Emily hurried along the hall to Nat's kitchen, thrust the sheaf of spring flowers into the kitchen sink, half-filled it with water, then rejoined Lucas, who was taking in his surroundings with interest.

'Your landlord has great taste,' he told her, then frowned as his eyes dropped to her feet. 'Shouldn't you be wearing shoes?'

'When I heard the fracas I ran down as I was.' Emily hesitated. 'Look, it was very kind of Nat to offer the use of his place, but—'

'You'd rather I left.'

'No,' she said impatiently. 'I didn't mean that at all. I don't have any whisky, but I can offer you some reasonable wine. Though you'll have to come up to my room to share it. Don't worry,' she added. 'My mother provided me with a chair comfortable enough for you to sit in.'

'I'm delighted.' He grinned. 'Are you all right without shoes, or shall I carry you up?'

'In your state of health?' she jeered. 'Be warned. These are serious stairs—two flights of them, and murderously steep.'

'Stairway to heaven,' he said promptly. 'If your room's at the top.'

'Corny!' Emily wrinkled her nose at him, then started up the stairs with a practised speed which had Lucas coughing by the time they reached the landing outside her room.

'Holy Moses!' he gasped. 'This place could do with a lift.'

'Inharmonious with early Georgian architecture,' she said loftily, and went through her open door, beckoning Lucas inside. 'Welcome to my eyrie.'

Like the rest of the house, the room was high-ceilinged, with beautiful plasterwork picked out in white against walls painted pale, authentic green.

Looking at the room as though he meant to memorise it, Lucas stood in the doorway, carrier-bag in hand, while Emily closed down her laptop, burningly aware of his physical presence. In black jeans and a brown leather windbreaker well-worn enough to match the bigger chair, he dominated her private space to such an extent she wished they'd stayed downstairs in Nat's place.

'Great room,' he said at last. 'Your taste in furnishing or Sedley's?'

'The paintwork had been done and the bed and wardrobe were already *in situ*. But Andy donated the chair and table I use as a work-station, the leather chair came from home, and I bought the other one in the antiques market near your place. It was a bit battered, but I found a biggish remnant of rose corded velvet to cover it—a bit faded, but I like that—and there was enough left over for the bed.' Enough, she told herself sharply, and gave him a bright, social smile. 'It's a bit of a surprise to see you here, Lucas, but now you are, do you approve?'

'Very much,' he assured her, and handed her the bag. 'I brought your coat back.'

'Thank you. Come in and close the door. You can put your jacket on the bed.'

Lucas's smile was wry as he removed the jacket to reveal a black roll-neck sweater. 'You know, Emily, when Sedley wouldn't let me in I thought he was acting on your instructions.'

She shook her head and hung the velvet coat in the wardrobe. 'I never expected *you* to come here.'

'I came to grovel, make my peace. Unfortunately, my olive branch got a bit mangled.'

'A soak in some water and the flowers will soon revive,' she said, suddenly feeling breathless. The room seemed to have shrunk in size now they were alone in it together. 'I'll open that wine.'

'Let me do it for you.'

Emily went behind the screen to take a bottle from her tiny fridge and collected glasses and corkscrew from one of her shelves. 'It's not champagne, I'm afraid.'

Lucas removed the cork and poured the wine into the glasses she'd set down on the crowded table. He handed one over and raised his own. 'To your beautiful eyes, Emily Warner,' he said, and tasted the wine.

'To your regained health,' she countered, and drank in turn. 'Do sit down.' She curled up in the smaller chair and Lucas settled himself in the larger one, taking such open pleasure in looking at her that she felt her cheeks grow hot.

'You look very appealing tonight.'

She stared at him in surprise. Her clothes were old and her face was as bare as her feet. The only thing she had going for her was newly washed hair. 'Thank you.'

'I obviously disturbed your work. Is it going well?'

'Surprisingly enough, yes.'

'Why surprising?'

'I've had a lot of distraction lately.'

'To put it mildly. Which brings me to one of the reasons for seeing you.' He gave her a straight black look. 'Emily, I know my choice of phrase was tactless in reference to our mutual problem, but I meant the worst for you, not for me.'

Emily sipped some of her wine, eyeing him over the rim of her glass. 'Very true. I'd be the one left holding the baby.'

His face darkened. 'As I told you, I won't shirk my responsibilities.'

'That's nice.'

'Nice?' He gritted his teeth, then leaned forward, his face urgent. 'If you'll only come to my place when I'm not there, how will you let me know?'

'I'll leave a note on the kitchen jotter.'

He scowled. 'Damnation, Emily, we're not talking groceries here!'

Her chin lifted. 'True. But it's not something I care to discuss over the phone, either.'

Lucas drained his glass. 'You're very calm about this.'

Then she was a fantastic actress. 'Not really.'

He got up to put the glass on the table and looked round at the room. 'If you are pregnant you can't stay here,' he said flatly.

'No,' she agreed. 'Imagine lugging a baby-buggy up those stairs.'

Lucas winced. 'You'll need somewhere else to live.'

Emily got up. 'I'll meet that particular problem—if there is one—when I come to it.'

He looked down at her in silence for a moment. 'I'm going back to work next Monday.'

'Are you fit enough for that?'

'I will be.'

'Then I'll come round to clean that morning, as usual.'

Silence fell between them, and at last Lucas put on

his jacket and took an envelope from the pocket. 'You should have reminded me,' he said huskily.

Emily flushed as she took a cheque from the envelope, her eyes wide when she saw the extravagant amount. Her head flew up. 'What's this for, Lucas? Personal services?'

'Don't talk like that,' he said angrily. 'If you count it by the hour, as we've always done, you'll find it comes out about right. I meant it as a token of appreciation for all you did for me, not an insult.'

Emily badly wanted to tear up the cheque and throw the pieces in his face. Instead she gave it back without drama, her hand steady instead of shaking with fury. 'Make a new cheque out, please. Just give me the usual amount I get every Friday. Or I don't work for you any more.'

Lucas glared at her, a pulse throbbing at the corner of his mouth as he took the cheque, screwed it into a ball, and hurled it into her wastebasket. In angry silence he took his cheque-book out, scrawled his signature and the amount she stipulated, then handed it to her.

'Thank you,' she said politely.

'Are you like this with everyone?' he demanded. 'Or only with me?'

'Like what?'

'In some ways you're the most difficult woman I've ever met.'

'Better than being the easiest,' she retorted, then wished she hadn't when his eyes lit with an unsettling gleam.

Emily swallowed. 'I'm sure you have things to do, so don't let me keep you.'

'You want me to go?'

'Yes.'

'You haven't thanked me for the flowers yet.'

'I'm sure I did.'

Lucas moved closer. 'But not in the way I hoped. I walked all the way here to see you, clutching that damn bouquet, only to get thrown out in the street for my pains, remember. You owe me, Emily Warner.'

'No, I don't.' She backed away, her mouth suddenly dry. 'And I've obviously given you the wrong idea by inviting you to my room.'

He shook his head. 'You made it clear this morning that you don't want me. Which makes no difference. I still want you.'

Too late she realised she had nowhere to go. Lucas had backed her up against the bed, the edge of which fitted nicely behind her knees. If he moved only a fraction, she would fall. She shivered as she pictured all too vividly what might come next.

'Just a kiss, Emily,' he whispered. 'As thanks for the flowers, or goodnight, or whatever reason suits you best—'

At the first touch of his lips on hers Emily's legs buckled. She sat abruptly on the bed and Lucas fell on his knees beside her, hauling her against his chest to kiss her with such force and hunger that she yielded to him, powerless to control her response.

'You see what you reduce me to?' he demanded roughly, raising his head a fraction. 'Does it give you a kick to see me on my knees?'

She shook her head wordlessly, and Lucas stared down into her flushed face for a moment as though expecting her to speak. When she remained silent he released her and got wearily to his feet.

'Time I went, obviously.' He pulled on his jacket and, utterly deflated, Emily scrambled to her feet.

'Thank you for bringing my jacket back.' She took in a deep breath and folded her arms across her chest. 'It's no use. I lied, Lucas. You know very well that I do—' She stopped, biting her lip.

'What?' he demanded, his face tense.

'Want you.'

He lunged towards her in triumph, but she held out fending arms. 'No, Lucas. It doesn't change anything. Even,' she added deliberately, 'if the worst comes to the worst.'

Lucas, abruptly still, gave her a look which raised the hairs on the back of her neck. 'What the hell are you saying? If you are expecting my child, surely you can't expect me to stay tamely out of your life?'

Emily met the look head-on. 'If we had created a child within a relationship it would be different. But in our case it was an accident I keep feeling I should have prevented.'

'How do you work that out? In that particular situation you didn't stand a chance, against me or any other man frantic to make love to you.' Lucas leaned against the door, arms folded. 'Tell me—purely as a hypothesis—if I hadn't been ill, and we'd gone through the accepted mating rituals of dining out and trips to the theatre and so on, before we finally became lovers, would you feel different on the subject?'

'I've no idea, because it doesn't apply in this case. If you hadn't been ill, it wouldn't have happened—any of it,' she said tartly. 'I'm just your cleaner, remember.'

'How could I forget? You keep reminding me often enough.' He looked suddenly tired. 'All right, you win.

But,' he added, his eyes spearing hers, 'keep your promise, Emily.'

'To tell you the worst?' she countered. 'I'll leave a note for you next Monday. I should know by then.'

Lucas gave her a long, hard look, hesitated as though he meant to say something, then, with a muttered curse, opened the door and strode out to race down the stairs at a rate that terrified her. Emily ran to watch him out of sight, but the street door closed so softly it was some time before she went down to make sure he'd gone. And, instead of allowing herself the relief of tears, she looked through Nat's kitchen cupboards to borrow a vase, rescued the undamaged blooms from the sheaf of daffodils and tulips, and carried the result up to her room. Which looked depressingly empty now Lucas had removed his forceful presence from it.

CHAPTER TEN

THE rest of the week dragged by. Emily seized the phone expectantly every time it rang, but it was never Lucas. Not that she had really expected to hear from him after sending him away. But she'd hoped. And missed him so badly by the end of the week that after finishing her Friday session at the Donaldsons' she gave in to impulse and ran across the street to see him. But turned away before she even reached the entrance to his building, afraid Lucas wouldn't even let her through the door.

Emily trudged back to Spitalfields, cleaned Mark's rooms, checked that nothing needed doing in Nat's, went early to bed to toss and turn through another restless night, then woke next morning to find that she was not expecting Lucas Tennent's child after all. Limp with relief, along with other emotions she put down to hormonal imbalance, she rang Lucas immediately, but her euphoria faded when his recorded voice told her to leave a message. Unwilling to entrust this particular piece of news to his answer-machine, Emily was forced to keep to the original, unsatisfactory plan of leaving a note for Lucas after her Monday cleaning session.

Ginny was visiting in-laws with Charlie, so with no Saturday morning rendezvous with her friend to brighten her day, Emily went shopping locally to pass an hour or two. Later, laden with bags, she treated herself to the rare indulgence of a fry-up in the Market Café to put off returning to her room.

From then on, Emily's weekend went rapidly downhill. Back in her solitary room, all set to put in a good few hours on her laptop now her worries were over, she experienced her first run-in with writer's block. After a frustrating session of scrapping every sentence the minute it came up on the screen, she gave up at last in disgust. Feeling headachey and out of sorts, she took her shopping down to Nat's kitchen and listened to his radio while she spent a more productive session making vegetable soup and her mother's special recipe for tomato sauce. Catering sorted for the immediate future, Emily made sure Nat's kitchen was pristine afterwards, consigned her pots of sauce to his freezer, ready for future pasta suppers, and took her container of healthful soup up to her room.

Afterwards, Emily stood at the window, staring moodily over the rooftops towards the backdrop of City towers as she wondered how to fill the rest of the day. One of the new paperbacks she'd bought or a session in front of the television were the only options in the ancient, empty house she'd never actually been alone in before. Mark was away on a course, Nat was restored to his wife and family and, worst of all, Lucas's recorded message was the only response to two more phone calls. She wished now that she'd agreed to go home for the weekend. But when her mother had suggested it Emily had been waiting for nature to inform her of her fate, too tense to enjoy a stay in the little cottage her parents had bought when they vacated the vicarage. But now everything was back to normal again it would have been good to spend time at home. Andy, his wife Bridget and their two small sons usually came to share the Sunday roast when Emily was down, and in her present mood she would have enjoyed their boisterous company. Instead, she was rapidly growing bored with her own.

Emily had never welcomed any morning more thankfully than the one which dawned the following Monday. She set off for her cleaning sessions with a feeling of escape, so glad to quit the elegant green walls of her solitary confinement that she walked briskly, revelling in the noise and bustle of traffic and passers-by. But when she left the Donaldsons' immaculate flat later her mood deteriorated as she crossed the cobbled street to Lucas Tennent's building. It would be strange, now, to work there in his absence. She'd given up trying to ring him over the weekend, which meant a note on his kitchen jotter. On her way up in the lift, Emily wondered whether to try for humorous and light or just to ask him to ring her.

But when Emily unlocked Lucas's door a note was unnecessary. He was in the hall, waiting for her. Without a word, he pulled her into his arms and kissed her surprised, parted lips with a hunger she responded to so fiercely she felt his heart thud against her as he yanked her up on tiptoe against his chest.

'Why are you here?' she panted, when she could.

'I'm waiting for you,' he said raggedly, and began kissing her again until Emily found the strength from somewhere to push him away a little.

'Aren't you well?' she demanded, touching a hand to his forehead.

'Now you're here I've never felt better,' Lucas assured her with a triumphant smile. He seized her by the waist and swung her round in a dizzying circle, then set her on her feet with a look of horrified apology. 'Hell, I'm *sorry*—'

'It doesn't matter. I'm not pregnant,' Emily blurted.

Lucas stood utterly still, the animation draining from

his face. 'When did you know?' he said conversation-
ally.

'Saturday morning.'

His eyes glittered. 'Two *days* ago? And it never occurred to you to contact me?'

Emily's chin lifted. 'Of course it did, but you weren't
around. I couldn't leave that kind of message on your
machine. So I thought I'd just leave a note today, as
promised.'

'Would you have preferred that to telling me face to
face?' he demanded.

'No. I'm very glad to see you,' she told him. Which
was an understatement. 'You haven't told me why
you're at home, by the way.'

'I decided to take more time off.'

'You could have rung to tell me.'

'Do you think I'm a fool, Emily? If I had you
wouldn't be here now.' His eyes narrowed, putting her
antennae on red alert. 'So. There's no outcome to worry
about, after all.'

'No.'

'You must be pleased.'

'Of course I am.' She looked away. 'If you'd rung me
over the weekend, I could have put you out of your
suspense.'

Lucas took her chin in his hand and raised her face
to his. 'You made it pretty plain that night that you
wanted nothing more to do with me. Did you really expect me to ring you after that?'

'No,' she said gruffly.

Lucas thawed enough to smile a little. 'I've been
away. I went down to visit my mother. The night I came
to see you I had some crazy idea about asking you to
go with me, but that didn't work out.'

Emily could have cried. After the endless, boring weekend she'd just endured it was painful to think she could have been with Lucas. Even if it had meant meeting his mother.

'I hoped you'd ring, because I wanted to explain things a bit better than I did last time.' She paused, searching for a way to make him understand.

'Go on,' he prompted.

She looked him in the eye. 'The thing is, Lucas, if I had been pregnant I couldn't have handled a relationship with you—of any kind—based on obligation.'

Lucas frowned. 'So if the worst had come to the famous worst, how would you have wanted things arranged? It would have been my child as well as yours. Even if you'd refused to have anything to do with me yourself I would have demanded a father's rights. Unless—' He stopped abruptly.

'Unless what?'

'You'd decided not to go through with it.'

Emily swallowed. 'A termination?'

'Yes,' he said tonelessly. 'Though that never occurred to me.'

She shivered. 'It never occurred to me, either. Good daughter of the vicarage that I am.'

'So you are. I'd forgotten that.' He rubbed a hand over his chin, eyeing her soberly. 'It would have made life doubly awkward for you if there had been a child.'

'Very true,' she agreed. 'I suppose I would have coped somehow; so would my parents. But I'm grateful it didn't come to that. Though if it had I'm sure you and I could have come to an amicable agreement of some kind. About the baby, I mean.'

'I'm glad you think so,' he said dryly. 'But, since there is no baby, where do we go from here?'

'What do you mean?'

'Oh come *on* Emily,' he said impatiently. 'After what happened the moment you were through my door, can you honestly deny the chemistry between us?'

'No, I can't.'

'Then no more of this nonsense about employer and cleaner.' He smiled evilly. 'Or I'll dispense with your services, Miss Warner.'

Her eyes narrowed. 'Would you really do that?'

'Damn right I would, if it was to my advantage.'

'That's not fair,' she said hotly. 'You know I need the money.'

'All's fair in love, Emily!'

'Love?' she snapped. 'Don't you mean lust?'

'I know exactly what I mean,' he cut back.

They stared at each other in hostile silence for a moment, then Lucas held out his hand. 'Come and sit down for a moment.'

'I need to make a start—' she began, then thought better of it. If he really was giving her the sack she wasn't working for free. 'On the other hand, Mr Tennent, if you are dispensing with my services I might as well get back to the jobs I'm paid for.'

Lucas grabbed her hand and pulled her along with him until they reached the familiar sofa.

'Sit,' he commanded.

Emily's eyes flashed fire, but in the end she perched on the very edge of the sofa, her back ramrod-straight.

'Good,' approved Lucas. 'Now listen.'

'If you really want to put an end to my cleaner/employer objections you can stop ordering me about, for a start,' she snapped, and he grinned and sat down beside her.

'That's my girl. Or do you object to the term ''girl''?'

She sniffed. 'It's better than your usual "woman".'

'I like the sound of that,' said Lucas, his eyes softening.

'Well, I don't—'

'I meant "usual". It implies continuity.' He took her hand. 'So let's sort this out. I am thirty-one, single, solvent, and with no significant female presence in my life at this moment in time other than you, Miss Warner. You are—how old?'

'Twenty-four, but—'

'Don't interrupt. You have recently severed all connection with the unspeakable Mr Denny, and unless you met someone new last week I take it there's no man in your life right now other than me.' Lucas leaned close. 'You've seen me at my worst—so no nasty surprises there—we both enjoy each other's company, and physically we're very definitely compatible. Are you with me?'

Emily eyed him narrowly. 'I'm not sure.'

He sighed impatiently. 'Short of handing you my curriculum vitae, Miss Warner, what other information do you need to convince you?'

'Of what, exactly?'

'God, grant me patience! Pay attention—'

'Woman?' she said sweetly.

Lucas disarmed her with a snort of laughter. 'How about "darling", then?'

'In preference to "woman", certainly. And I am paying attention. Do go on.'

'Thank you so much.' He rolled his eyes. 'I'm doing my damnedest to get you to admit that there's no reason why we shouldn't spend time together. Socially. No obligation involved, since you're so hung up on that. So do you?'

'Do I what?'

'Admit it?'

'I suppose so.' She eyed him uncertainly. 'Look, are you dispensing with my services, or not? I've lost the thread somewhere.'

He gave a growl of frustration. 'Back to the money again. Is that all you can think about?'

'Lack of it tends to focus the mind,' she said tartly. 'So have I got the sack?'

Lucas gave her a considering look. 'It all depends.'

'On what?'

'Whether you can work for me, and take my weekly cheque, and at the same time accept me as the man in your life.'

Emily gazed at him in silence, her heart beating thickly. 'I—I'm not sure, Lucas.'

His face darkened. 'About me?'

Emily shook her head, suddenly tired of pretending. 'I meant that if we do see each other socially it seems all wrong to take your money at the same time.'

His response to that was to pull her on to his lap and kiss her until her head reeled. At last, Lucas tore his mouth away and groaned, putting her away from him.

'What's the matter?' said Emily breathlessly.

He smoothed her tumbled curls, smiling ruefully. 'You know damn well—I want to take you to bed.'

She smiled at him challengingly. 'You could burn off surplus energy by helping me clean the flat instead.'

He shook his head. 'Not a chance. I've been away, so the place is still perfect from your labours last week. And you don't have to change the bed,' he added. 'I've already done that.'

'Have you, now?'

He leered at her. 'Your suspicions are perfectly correct, Miss Warner. I had every intention of carrying you off to it the moment you came through the door, and keeping you there for the foreseeable future.'

She grinned. 'Bad luck.'

Lucas bent to kiss her dimple, then went on to plant kisses all over her face, but stopped abruptly when he found tears on her lashes. 'Darling, what's wrong?'

'Nothing at all, now,' she said, sniffing. 'But I've had such a depressing week, Lucas. Ever since you left me, in fact. And this weekend I was alone in the house. Mark was on a course, Nat was with Thea, and Ginny was away with Charlie. So, as if Saturday wasn't miserable enough already, I didn't meet her for coffee as usual, either—' She stopped, her face suddenly hot.

'Miserable?' he asked sharply, his arms tightening around her. 'Why?'

'Hormones,' she muttered, ducking her head, but a relentless hand brought her face up.

'Tell me the truth,' Lucas ordered. 'Were you by any chance miserable because you *weren't* pregnant?'

'Of course not,' she said scornfully. Though she had been. For a split-second.

Lucas kissed the tip of her nose. 'Must you really go back to Spitalfields today?'

'Yes. I still have to earn my living. But I'll come back later.'

'And stay!' He kissed her by way of emphasis.

'You mean spend the nights here, too?' she said huskily, when he raised his head.

Lucas nodded, his eyes glinting. 'And I don't mean in the spare bed. It's always best,' he added virtuously, 'to make things clear from the start. I'd hate you to misunderstand my intentions.'

'Which are?' she demanded.

'Exactly what you think they are,' he said promptly, and gave her a smacking kiss totally different from before. 'It doesn't matter that I can't make love to you right now. I can wait. Somehow. But, just in case you've forgotten, I've recently been ill. I need you here with me, day and night, to complete my cure. I haven't been sleeping well lately.'

'Neither have I.'

'Why?'

'You know perfectly well why,' she said crossly, and tried to get up, but Lucas kept her firmly in place on his lap.

'So why the hell did you send me packing that night?' he demanded.

'Lucas,' she said patiently, 'at that point I could have been pregnant.'

He gave her a baffled glare. 'What's that got to do with it?'

'Everything.' Emily smiled at him coaxingly. 'Surely you can see my point?'

'No,' he said flatly, and ran the tip of his tongue round the outline of her parted lips before sliding it into her mouth, the kiss so arousing it won him a feverish response. But after a breathless, increasingly frustrating interval Emily pushed his hands firmly away.

'Stop! I can't think when you do that, and I need to get a few things straight, Lucas. I'm happy to come back later. Very happy,' she added with a smile. 'The rest of the week, too, if you want, in the time left over from my cleaning jobs. But I'm not going to sleep here.'

He stared incredulously. 'Why the hell not?'

'If I stay here at night it would be the next best thing to moving in with you.'

'What's wrong with that?' he said, and cupped her face in his hands.

'Try to understand, Lucas. My father tries desperately hard to be liberal, but it really upset him when I set up house with Miles. Dad would have liked to see me married first.'

'Which would have been a total disaster!'

Emily nodded vehemently in agreement. 'Dad knows that now, and is probably thanking God daily that there wasn't a wedding. My mother lives in the real world, so her objection was to Miles, not the cohabiting. But the thing is, Lucas,' she went on, 'I'm not going to upset their apple cart again right now by even appearing to move in with you.'

His eyes narrowed. 'You mean you'd hold out for a ring first?'

'Of course not,' she said scornfully. 'I simply want to give them—and myself—time to get over the last fiasco before trying anything like it again.'

'It wouldn't be a fiasco with me,' Lucas said flatly. 'So what exactly *do* you want, Emily?'

'To carry on with my life as usual, spend as much time as you like with you, but go back to Spitalfields at night,' she said, smiling.

'Stop coercing me with that dimple,' growled Lucas. 'What about your novel?'

'I'll take time off from that until you go back to work.'

He smiled indulgently. 'You realise that it won't make the slightest difference?'

'What do you mean?'

The black eyes gleamed with a look so explicit she caught her breath. 'To the precise nature of our relationship, Miss Warner. Go back to your room at night if you must, but no one will be fooled. Sedley knows already.'

'Knows what?'

'How I feel about you.'

'That's nice, because *I* don't!'

'Of course you do. I want you so much I can't sleep at night, Miss Warner.' And to prove his point Lucas kissed and caressed her to a pitch of longing that made it clear that making love would happen any time, or anywhere, the mutual need arose. 'You see?' he said hoarsely, raising his head. 'Everyone will assume we're lovers whether you stay here at night or not.'

'I know that!' said Emily scornfully. 'I'm not an idiot. But I'm sticking to my guns. Indulge me in this, please, Lucas. Or—'

'Or you won't even spend the rest of the morning with me,' he said, resigned.

'I have to get back right now, anyway,' she said, startling him enough to let her go when she jumped to her feet.

'*Why?*'

'Because I have my other jobs to do. After which I need a shower and a change of clothes.'

'In future keep clothes here. Though, personally,' he said, eyeing her, 'I find the dishevelled look *very* sexy. You look perfect to me.'

Because she knew her face was shiny, her hair had escaped from its moorings, and she was wearing jeans so old they were bleached nearly white, Emily eyed him with scorn.

'I mean it,' he assured her, then scowled. 'All right, have it your way. But no walking back. I'll call a cab.' He kissed her swiftly. 'Then, when you're ready, I'll come and collect you.'

'No, don't do that,' she said urgently. 'I'll come back on my own.'

His eyes narrowed. 'Why don't you want me to fetch you?'

Emily braced herself. 'You won't like it.'

'Tell me, anyway.'

'Miles came to fetch me in a taxi when I moved in with him. It was a weekend and there were people around from the other flats. We were waved off like newly-weds.' She eyed him warily. 'Mark will be back from his course this morning, with his girlfriend—'

'So what?' snapped Lucas. 'Do you think they'll care a toss that I'm taking you off with me?'

'*No!* I just don't want it to be like last time. I want everything different. Silly, I know, but I'm superstitious. Try to see it my way.'

'Chauvinist that I am,' he said with cold sarcasm, 'I can only see it from my own. You quite fancy an hour or two here with me now and then, as long as you can sneak away when your friends aren't looking. And I'm supposed to be grateful for that?'

'You're putting words in my mouth,' she said angrily.

'I prefer them to yours!' he snapped, his eyes so hostile she backed away. 'If we are to share our life in any way at all, I want exclusive rights on the arrangement— while it lasts—and I want it public, *darling*.'

The snarled, flippant endearment was the last straw. Emily gave him a look that should have felled him on the spot, then ran for her coat, snatched up her bag, and raced from the flat, banging the door behind her. In the lift angry tears streamed down her face, partly because there'd been no need to run. Lucas had made no attempt to come after her.

*   *   *

When the cab dropped a deeply miserable Emily in Spitalfields she forced a smile when she found Bryony on her way out. 'Morning, Nurse Talbot.'

'Hi, Emily.' Bryony beamed. 'I'm just popping out for a paper.'

'Enjoy your weekend?'

'You bet I did. I made full use of the hotel gym and spa facilities in the day while Mark worked his socks off, then we got together afterwards for the socialising. I didn't trust the females on the course!' Bryony winked as she went to the door, then turned. 'Oh, by the way, I let your brother in just now. He's waiting for you in your room.'

Emily blenched. '*Andy?* Oh, my God, something's wrong at home!' She took the stairs at a run, raced up the second flight, and shot through the open doorway to find a man stuffing her laptop into a sports bag.

'*Miles?* Put that down,' she shouted furiously.

'Emily!' Miles Denny spun round to face her, his dismay quickly covered by belligerence. 'I'm only taking what's mine.'

'Wrong. You're stealing,' she snapped. 'How did you find out where I lived?'

He smiled smugly. 'Ginny keeps an address-book by her telephone.'

'Snooping,' said Emily with disdain. 'But right now you're trespassing. I should call the police.'

He glared at her. 'If you'd returned my calls it needn't have come to this. I just want the laptop.'

'Well, you can't have it. It's mine. I paid for it, remember. I need it.'

'Hard luck,' he sneered. 'So do I.' He strode towards her, but Emily stood her ground.

'Put that down,' she ordered angrily.

'No chance!' He tried to brush her aside, but Emily fought with him, trying to wrench the bag from him, and after a panting, undignified struggle Miles shoved her away roughly at last, sending her sprawling on the bed. But by the time he was through the open doorway with his prize Emily was up and running. She flew across the landing, careering down to wrench the bag away so violently when she caught up with him on the second flight that she missed her footing, and with a scream crashed into Miles. He gave a despairing yell as he tried desperately to save himself, then went hurtling the rest of the way, to land with a sickening crack as his head met the beautiful tiles of the hall floor. The noise brought Mark bursting from his rooms to race down the stairs with a groan of horror when he saw Emily in a winded, crumpled heap, the sports bag clutched to her chest. He crouched to take it from her, his face so white Emily managed a wobbly smile. He heaved a great sigh of relief.

'Thank God! Are you all right? What the hell happened, Em? Who's the guy? Where do you hurt?'

'All—over. Is—is he dead?' she gasped, shivering.

At which point Bryony arrived back, took in the scene, and immediately switched to staff nurse mode. When a groan from the man on the floor indicated he was alive, she checked his vital signs, then gave Emily a thorough going over, her fingers gentle through the tumbled black curls as she encouraged deep breaths. 'I'll see to your brother in a minute. Did you bump your head?'

'No more—than—various other bits of me,' gasped Emily. 'My ankle—hurts most. I stuck my leg out to save myself.'

Bryony tried the patient's endurance not a little with

some expert probing. 'Not broken, but a bad sprain by the look of it. Best to have an X-ray to make sure—you may be concussed, too. We'll take you into hospital, love.'

'What about your brother?' said Mark.

Emily eyed the recumbent, groaning man with scorn only slightly tempered with remorse. 'That's not my brother. He was making off with my laptop—'

'*What?*' screeched Bryony. 'You mean I let a burglar up to your room?'

'Ex-boyfriend, not burglar. How is he?'

Bryony checked Miles's pulse again, then shrugged. 'He's concussed, but as far as I can tell he hasn't broken anything. Not even his neck.'

'Thank heavens for that. I'd hate to have his murder on my conscience. I didn't *mean* to push him down the stairs.' Emily smiled ruefully at Mark. 'Break it to me gently. Is the laptop done for?'

He retrieved the bag, took the machine out and opened it up. 'I can't be sure without switching it on,' he said, examining it. 'I'll check it later.'

Bryony returned her attention to the groaning man on the floor. 'What's his name, Em?'

'Miles Denny.'

'Right then, Miles Denny. Let's have a proper look at you.'

Miles surfaced groggily, ignored Bryony's orders to lie still, struggled upright, threw up copiously and passed out again.

'Yikes!' said Mark in disgust.

During the hectic few minutes that followed Bryony displayed sterling qualities of organisation. She rang for an ambulance, put a bag of ice on Emily's ankle, and with Mark's reluctant, green-faced help cleared up the mess and mopped up the patient while they waited. The paramedics who arrived knew Bryony from her job on the staff at the A & E Department at Guy's Hospital, and much joshing went on about busman's holidays while she gave them concise details of the fall. The unhappy Miles, fully conscious and complaining now, was soon strapped, complete with neck brace, to a stretcher and stowed in the ambulance. Bryony helped Emily inside after him, then jumped in herself for the familiar ride to the hospital.

'I'll do my best to get you seen quickly, Em,' she promised, and cast a worried glance at her as they set off. 'How do you feel?'

Emily gave her a wan little smile. 'Not great. But probably a whole lot better than Miles over there.'

'Nice fellow!' whispered Bryony in her ear. 'When I went up to your room for your bag I found he'd forced the lock and damaged the door while he was at it.'

Emily groaned in dismay. 'Nat won't be happy.'

'I doubt he'll worry over a few splinters.'

'Genuine Georgian splinters, circa 1727!'

Bryony grinned. 'Nat won't care a toss about that, now he's back with Thea and the twins.'

There was an urgent sound from the man opposite, and one of the paramedics caught Emily's eye. 'He wants to talk to you. But you keep that foot where it is, love. He'll have to shout across.'

'What is it, Miles?' asked Emily, craning her neck to see him.

'I'm sorry,' he gasped. 'Is the laptop smashed?'

Bryony glared at him. 'Of course it is. But *just* in case you're interested, Emily sprained her ankle.'

'Buy—her—new computer.' He managed a smile, then passed out again.

It was an hour later before Emily, X-rayed, strapped up and provided with a crutch, finally hobbled from the hospital with Bryony, who had made some enquiries in the meantime, at Emily's urgent request, and learned that Miles was concussed enough to be kept in overnight for observation, but there was no skull fracture.

'Ouch. I didn't think of anything as serious as that.' Emily pulled a face, then smiled warmly at Bryony in the taxi. 'I'm so lucky you were there this morning. You're a star.'

'Nah! As they say on television—just doing my job.'

When they turned down the familiar cobbled street Bryony told the taxi-driver to wait outside the house, and fetched Mark to help Emily from the cab.

'We'd better commandeer Nat's kitchen for the moment,' said Mark when they were inside.

'I'll make tea,' said Bryony, hovering as Emily made slow progress along the narrow hall.

'I need something stronger than tea!' protested Mark, and shuddered. 'It took years off my life when I saw you lying in a heap, Emily. My heart only kicked in again when you smiled at me.'

'Sorry about that.' She grinned at him, glad to sit down at the table.

But it was only after reviving hot tea, when the shock of the past couple of hours began to recede, that the full implications of the episode finally dawned on Emily.

'You know you can't go back to your room like that, Em,' said Mark, looking worried. 'I'd change places like a shot, but you'd still have to get up a flight of stairs to mine.'

'I'll have to go home, I suppose,' said Emily, shrugging.

'Easier stairs there?' asked Bryony, refilling her cup.

'Worse than here, if anything.' Emily thought with misgiving of the steep, open-tread staircase in her parents' cottage. 'I suppose I could beg a bed in my brother's bungalow for a night or two.' But, much as she loved her boisterous nephews, at the moment Emily felt desperate for peace and quiet. 'I don't see what else I can do. I'll ring Andy when he gets home.'

'You need a rest,' said Bryony, and exchanged a look with Mark. 'I think we should put her in Nat's bed for a bit.'

Her voluble protests brushed aside by the other two, Emily eventually gave in, on condition that Bryony helped her into Nat's bathroom first. 'I meant to shower the minute I arrived back, but Miles got in the way. Sorry to be a nuisance, but could you fetch me a change of clothes, too, please?'

'Of course. Tell me what you want and I'll pack a bag for you while I'm at it.'

By the time the shower was over, her hair was reasonably dry, and she was finally propped up under the quilt on Nat's bed, Emily was so limp with reaction she didn't care whose bed it was. 'I'm fine now,' she told her willing helpers. 'Take off and have some time to yourselves.'

Bryony suggested Mark run up to Emily's room for the book she was reading, and he hurried back to report that there was a message on her machine. 'Thought I'd better listen in.'

'Who was it?'

'Some bloke ordering you to ring him. Deep voice, no name.' Mark grinned and handed her his cellphone. 'Use this.'

Emily held the phone in her hand for a long time once she was alone, not sure that talking to Lucas was a good idea. He was probably still angry. And she hadn't changed her mind. She was determined to keep their relationship private so no one would know, this time, when it was over.

Emily keyed in Lucas's number, listened, resigned, to his recorded message, then gave a brief account of the fall that made it impossible to work for him for a while. She hesitated, said a forlorn goodbye and disconnected. At which point her body insisted on rest and she drifted into sleep.

She was jerked awake by an accusing voice and surfaced, dazed, to meet a pair of furious dark eyes glaring at her from a small, all-too-familiar face.

'What are you doing in my husband's bed?' demanded Thea Sedley.

CHAPTER ELEVEN

EMILY sat up, speechless with horrified dismay, which she saw reflected in Nat's eyes as he peered over his wife's shoulder. But before she could gather her wits to explain Bryony and Mark came hurtling downstairs to save her the trouble. Halfway through their story Nat went out to answer a peremptory rapping on the front door, and Lucas Tennent came into the bedroom like a whirlwind, brushed everyone aside and took Emily into his arms.

She clung to him convulsively, burying her face against his sweater, so giddy with relief she wanted to howl like a baby now there was nothing to cry about. 'Miles broke into my room, Lucas. He wanted the laptop—'

'To hell with the laptop!' Ignoring the fascinated onlookers, he turned her face up to his to kiss her, his mouth tightening when he saw the bruise on her cheek. 'In your message you said the bastard's in hospital. Pity—I'd like a word with him.'

Emily chuckled, her wet eyes suddenly dancing. 'No need to beat Miles up, Lucas. He didn't cause the bruises; I sort of bounced off him against the wall. I was the one who damaged *him*—and without a cricket bat this time, too.'

'God, you're a dangerous woman!' He kissed her again, then stood up. 'I'm taking you home.'

Home. Emily smiled up at him, liking the sound of that. 'OK. But first let me make some introductions. You know Nat, but this is his wife, Thea. And this is Bryony Talbot and Mark Cooper, my saviours.'

Lucas shook hands all round while Emily described how Bryony and Mark had come to her rescue.

'Bryony did all the work,' said Mark proudly.

'What a fright you've had!' To Emily's surprise, Thea came up to the bed and kissed her cheek. 'Sorry I yelled. Appearances were deceptive.' She smiled at Lucas. 'Nat said you were tall, dark and handsome.'

Lucas flushed, to Emily's deep enjoyment, gave Thea a mocking little bow, then thanked Bryony and Mark for their help. 'I can take over now.'

'You said you were taking her home, but where do you live?' asked Bryony bluntly. 'She can't use that foot for a while.'

'It's a top-floor apartment overlooking the river, with a nice comfortable lift instead of death-defying stairs. No offence,' Lucas told Nat with a grin.

'None taken.' Nat gave Emily a rueful smile. 'So all the precautions were in vain. Your ex-swain managed to get in after all.'

'He just rang the bell to ask for Emily, and I let him in,' said Bryony with remorse. 'He told me he was her brother, the wretch.'

'Talking of Andy,' said Nat, 'does your family know about this, Emily?'

She shook her head. 'I was going to ring Andy when he gets home from school, and ask for board and lodging for a bit—'

'You don't need that now,' cut in Lucas. 'You can ring your mother from the flat.'

'Where did you two meet?' asked Thea curiously.

Emily exchanged a gleaming look with Lucas. 'Like Nat, he employs me. I'm his cleaner.'

He shook his head. 'Not any more. Your cleaning days are over.'

'Only until my foot gets better!'

'We'll discuss it later,' he said firmly, and held out his arms. 'Up you come.'

'I can walk with the aid of my trusty crutch,' she protested, but Lucas shook his head.

'At the moment, I feel this overwhelming compulsion to hold you in my arms,' he said, not quite lightly, and won looks of warm approval from Thea and Bryony. 'Besides, you look a bit fragile.'

'So would you in my place,' she said, grimacing. 'Though it was Miles who fell down and broke his crown.'

'Good,' said Lucas with grim satisfaction. 'But did he really come here just to make off with the laptop?'

'Apparently.'

'Maybe he's left something on the hard drive,' suggested Mark. 'I checked it, and it seems to be working. You can play with it later to make sure, Em. I've put it with your bags in the hall.'

Nat went out to answer the door, then returned to say the taxi-driver wanted to know how much longer he had to wait. 'I told him you were ready to go, Lucas. Take good care of her,' he added.

'Don't worry; I will,' Lucas assured him.

Bryony helped Emily to her feet. 'All right, Em?'

'Thanks to you, Nurse, yes.'

'OK, Lucas; she's all yours.'

'That she is.' Lucas picked Emily up, went the round of the others so they could kiss her goodbye, then carried her outside to the taxi waiting on double yellow lines outside in the cobbled street. Nat handed in the crutch and bags, then stood with the others to wave them off, giving Emily a sense of *déjà vu*. So much for keeping Lucas a secret. Barring a different cast of extras, the scene was identical to last time with Miles.

Lucas eyed her face, reading her mind with accuracy. 'Your plan to keep me a secret backfired big time.'

'I don't care. I'm just grateful you arrived when you did.' She giggled. 'Thea had just discovered me in Nat's bed when you came charging in like the cavalry.'

He shook with laughter. 'Not your day, one way and another. Never mind,' he consoled her, taking her hand. 'I promise to make it better from now on. How do you feel after all your adventures, darling? Shall I put you straight to bed when we get home?'

'Good heavens, no!' Emily smiled at him cheerfully. 'Your sofa will do very nicely, thank you. In fact,' she added, 'I could even perch on one of the stools in the kitchen and supervise supper, if you like.'

'Unnecessary.' He gave her a smug look. 'When you left I was furious—'

'I noticed.'

'Don't interrupt. So I went for a walk to cool off while I planned my next course of action, which was to storm over to Spitalfields and carry you off over my shoulder if necessary. Being the practical type, I did some shopping on the way back to the flat so I could feed you after the kidnapping.' His jaw clenched. 'Imagine my reaction when I heard your message.'

'Thank you for coming to my rescue, Lucas.' Emily stretched a little, wincing when her ankle protested.

'I wanted to collect you in my new car,' he said with regret, 'but I knew there'd be nowhere to park near Nat's house, so I fell back on a cab.'

'What kind of car?'

'A new model Mini Cooper S,' he said, trying to sound offhand.

'Really?' Emily smiled, surprised. 'I would have thought something like a Porsche was more in your line.'

'Why?'

'It goes with the rest of you—the hip loft apartment, the job, and so on.'

'I do own something speedier for motorway journeys, also bought from new.' His face set. 'In my teens I had to wear blazers and shirts from the school second-hand shop. So these days I like my possessions brand-new.'

Emily was quiet for the rest of the short journey, and Lucas, his eyes concerned, put his arm round her and held her protectively. When they arrived at his building Emily would have given much to get inside under her own steam, but common sense told her that walking with a crutch would be a precarious business on a cobbled street. And there was no point in risking another injury. She'd had quite enough excitement for one day.

The helpful taxi driver parked as near to the entrance as possible, then brought the bags inside and put them in the lift while Lucas carried Emily in to set her down very carefully, holding her by the waist.

'Lean against me while I pay up. Keep the weight off your foot.'

Emily did as she was told, shivering a little despite the warmth of the lift.

'You're cold,' he said, hugging her close as the lift doors closed on the lavishly-tipped driver.

'Probably reaction. Bryony warned me about that.'

'Quite a girl, isn't she? Your friend Mark's a lucky man. Up you come,' he added as the lift doors opened. 'I'll soon have you safe and sound on our sofa.'

Emily felt a little warmer at the discovery that Lucas

shared her views about his sofa. Which, of course, didn't mean she was the only woman who'd ever sat there with him.

'That's a strange look on your face,' commented Lucas, as he carried her into the hall. He was breathing heavily by the time they reached the big, split-level living-room she loved so much. He lowered her carefully to the sofa, stacked cushions behind her, bent to give her a swift kiss, then straightened to heave in a deep breath. 'I'm out of condition. Now stay put,' he ordered. 'I'll get the bags in from the hall. Don't move a muscle until I get back.'

Emily had no desire to move any muscles, particularly those in the ankle stretched out in front of her on the sofa. She lay motionless, glad to be so comfortable after all the hassle, her only mobile feature her eyes as she looked around her at the uncluttered space of Lucas's living-room. The great advantage of any loft apartment was light. Lucas's was filled with it, even on a rainy day. And now she was going to live here. At least for a while.

'You look very thoughtful,' said Lucas, rejoining her. 'Ankle hurting?'

'Not much, now. But I must give Mother the news before she hears it from Thea.'

'Will she expect you to go home to recuperate?' he asked, frowning.

'In theory, yes. But their new cottage is actually very old, with open-tread stairs as steep as Nat's.'

'In that case, you're much better here with me. Ask your parents to visit you here instead. Your friend Ginny, too.' His lips twitched as he bent to pat her cheek. 'Don't look so stunned. It won't commit you to anything.'

'That's very kind of you,' said Emily, ignoring the last bit, 'but for the time being I'll just tell Mother I've hurt my ankle. She's never seen Nat's stairs.'

Lucas handed her his cellphone. 'Give her the number and tell her to ring you on that. Tell her you've borrowed it until the ankle's better.'

She smiled at him gratefully and reached for the crutch.

'What's the matter?' he demanded.

'I'm going to the bathroom, *and* I'm going to manage on my own with this,' she said firmly. 'You'll put your back out if you keep carrying me everywhere.'

'But I like the feel of you helpless in my arms!'

Emily made a face at him, and carefully got to her feet. Bryony had advised against trousers with a strapped ankle and, to make life easier, had eased Emily into a skirt and tunic in ribbed topaz wool, normally kept for special occasions. Because the skirt was long, the outfit called for boots or high heels, but with a single flat black loafer on her good foot Emily felt more like Long John Silver than Cinderella. She tucked the crutch under her arm and, with Lucas pacing beside her, flatly refusing to let her go it alone, she made with increasing agility for the bathroom, then closed the door in his face. Afterwards, Emily opened it to find him standing where she'd left him.

'We're back to the unromantic intimacy again,' she said, resigned.

'Works for me!' Lucas picked her up, ignoring her protests. 'Stop arguing, Emily. It's a waste of time.' He gave her a questioning look as he set her down on the sofa again. 'I've been thinking of what Mrs Sedley said to you. Is that really how you see me?'

She looked blank for a moment, then her eyes lit with

unholy glee. 'Oh, tall, dark and handsome, you mean?
That's Nat's description, not mine.'

Lucas looked so appalled she roared with laughter,
and reassured him that it was Nat's way of diverting his
wife's suspicions from his lady lodger. 'He said it was
the first thing that came into his head when Thea asked.
Which was before he met you, anyway,' added Emily,
and batted her eyelashes. 'But if the cap fits…'

To her surprise, colour rose in the lean, watchful face.

'Do *you* think it fits?' he asked casually.

'Like a glove, Mr Tennent. You're the archetypal answer to a maiden's prayer—' She halted abruptly, and
he frowned and took her hand.

'What's the matter? Are you in pain?'

'No.' She gave him an unhappy look. 'I keep thinking
of something you said. About a school uniform from the
second-hand shop.'

Lucas looked blank for a moment, then gently slid his
arms round her as comprehension dawned. 'Surely
you're not saying that *you* feel second-hand after Miles?'

'I didn't until I met you,' she said honestly, pleased
that he understood. 'I'd had boyfriends before, relationships that ran their course and ended amicably. But after
Miles I felt so grubby and humiliated.' She met his eyes
squarely. 'And you do seem rather fixated on the new
and unsullied.'

'Only when it comes to cars and clothes!' Lucas gave
her a swift, punitive kiss. 'Though, oddly enough, what
I feel for you *is* new. I've known quite a few women,
obviously. It would be pretty strange if I hadn't at my
age—'

'And with your various impressive assets,' she put in
slyly.

'As I was saying,' he said with severity. 'I've known

women in the past, and enjoyed their company both in and out of bed, with no strings and no harm done on either side. But you're different, Emily.'

'Why?'

His eyes locked with hers. 'Because I'm in love with you, of course. And because I can't think of another soul, barring Alice and my mother, who would have cared for me when I was ill. Admittedly, I've never *been* ill before—'

'I could tell!' said Emily, flippant to hide the great bubble of joy rising inside her.

'Because I made such a fuss?'

'Exactly.'

'But you still hung in there and got me through it. And in return I was idiot enough to risk getting you pregnant,' he added bitterly.

'I didn't think about risks at the time—or anything else,' Emily assured him. 'Making love with you put my thought processes out of action. I'd never experienced anything like that before. Especially the last bit.' Her eyes locked with his. 'Was that a fluke, do you think? Or will it happen next time, as well?'

Lucas let out a shout of laughter. 'Are you by any chance propositioning me, Miss Warner?'

'Purely in the interest of scientific experiment,' she said primly, then dimpled at him in a way which brought an abrupt end to the conversation.

'This won't do,' said Lucas, after an interval of kisses and caresses which quickly threatened to get out of hand. 'I said you were a dangerous woman. You're driving me insane.'

'Me, too,' she said with feeling, then blushed as her stomach gave a loud, unromantic rumble.

'Darling, you're hungry—and I haven't even given

you a cup of tea!' He jumped up in remorse. 'I'll make up for it right now. Just sit there while I do something about feeding you.'

'I'm coming, too,' she insisted, reaching for the crutch.

'Why?' he said, exasperated.

'I just want to be where you are,' she said simply.

Lucas scooped her up, holding her high against his chest as he kissed her in a way which made words superfluous. 'My sentiments exactly,' he said huskily at last, then carried her off to deposit her on one of his smart retro stools. 'Now, just sit there and watch while I switch on the oven.'

Lucas's idea of playing chef was to put together plates of cold, herb-stuffed chicken and Bayonne ham, served with salad greens and several kinds of cheese. The sole function of the oven, Emily discovered, laughing, was to heat a baton of French bread to accompany the meal.

'This is lovely,' she said indistinctly, when they were back on the sofa together.

'The food, or being with me?' asked Lucas, buttering bread for her.

'Both. I spent last weekend almost entirely alone, with my own home-made vegetable soup for every meal.' She made a face. 'I shan't want any more of that for a while.'

'I told my mother about you,' he said casually, startling her. 'Described how you came to nurse me in my hour of need.'

Emily put her fork down, her eyes wide. 'She must have been taken aback—that your cleaner came to the rescue, I mean?'

Lucas wagged an admonishing knife. 'I told her that your cleaning jobs finance you while you're writing a novel. She was impressed, and wants to meet you. When you're mobile again I'll drive you down for Sunday lunch.'

Emily gazed at him in silence.

'As I keep saying, it won't commit you to anything,' he assured her.

'You take a lot of women to meet your mother?'

'No. You'll be the first.'

The information gave Emily a rosy glow which lasted right through supper, though she firmly resisted when Lucas coaxed her to talk about her novel.

'You can read it when I've finished it,' she conceded eventually. 'But only when I'm satisfied with it myself. If I ever am.'

'If you're not, will you give up cleaning and go back to the work you were doing before?'

Emily shook her head. 'I don't want to do that any more. It pays well, and I'm pretty good at it. But I've been far happier with the way my life is now than I ever was at nine-to-fiving in an office. So, if the first novel doesn't turn out well, I'll just try again. I'm sure I can find an extra cleaning job to pay my way.'

'I've thought of something else you can do,' said Lucas casually.

'Really? What, exactly?'

'I'll get rid of this stuff, make some coffee, then I'll explain.' He smiled at her as he hefted the loaded tray. 'Be good while I'm gone.'

CHAPTER TWELVE

WHEN Lucas got back with the coffee, he found Emily with the laptop on her knees. 'I told you to be good,' he said, exasperated. 'Which didn't mean starting work the minute I turned my back.'

She smiled guiltily. 'After I rang my mother I just had to make sure the machine still worked, Lucas. And, as far as I can tell, it does. But I can't help wondering why Miles was so desperate to get it back. I checked when I first took it, of course, but his files were all empty.'

'There must be something lurking on it somewhere.' Lucas sat down beside her. 'Hand it over. I'll do a search.'

'But surely he'd have saved anything important on a disk?'

'I would. But he wasn't expecting you to steal it that night, so there must be something he didn't have time to transfer.'

But other than Emily's novel there was nothing until at last Lucas found a file hidden inside another.

'Bullseye! Our lad has a digital camera.'

Emily, sitting close to look, stiffened in horror when a photograph appeared, filling the entire screen.

Lucas swore volubly and lowered the lid. 'Don't look any more. I'll switch the bloody thing off—'

'No,' said Emily decisively. 'I might as well know the worst. Keep going.'

Three photographs filled the big screen one by one. The studies were of three muscular, nude young men, their smiles provocative as they postured for the photographer. Two of them were strangers to Emily, but the other one delivered sandwiches to the firm she'd once worked for. Where Miles was still employed.

'Get rid of them, please,' she begged.

'Done.' Lucas wiped the laptop clean of everything other than the embryo novel, took it up to his desk on the gallery, then returned to the sofa. He filled cups with strong black coffee and gave one to Emily. 'You need this, darling. You're white as a sheet.'

She drank the hot, fragrant liquid down, reviving as the warmth spread through her. 'How could I have been such a fool?' she said at last. 'Though I wasn't the only one. I was warned about Miles by more than one friend at the firm. His reputation as a womaniser was well-publicised.'

Lucas took her empty cup and put hard, protective arms round her. 'A deliberate smokescreen to keep his proclivities in the closet? Though he isn't the first to feel attracted to both sexes.'

Emily leaned against him gratefully. 'No wonder he would never let me use the laptop. He always kept it in work. But he had it with him when he got in that night, and after the row, when I got violent, he was in such a hurry to take off he left it behind. Poor Tamara,' she added ruefully. 'Miles deliberately let me think he'd been with her that evening.'

'Preferable to the truth.'

'But I could have confronted the girl.'

'He banked on your not believing her if she denied it.'

'You're right.' She leaned her head back to look at Lucas. 'The firm we both worked for is a tad on the conventional side, so he wouldn't want anything getting out to affect his career prospects. It seems my money wasn't my only attraction for Miles. I was his cover, too.'

'And if he's in his right mind again by this time he's probably sweating blood because you still have the blasted laptop,' said Lucas, rubbing his cheek over her hair.

'Actually, he's not,' said Emily with regret. 'In the ambulance Bryony was so angry he hadn't asked about me she told him it was smashed. The smile he gave me must have been relief, not remorse.'

'I could pay him a visit to put him in the picture,' Lucas said grimly.

'Ugh! Don't talk about pictures.'

'If you feel like that, get rid of the blasted machine.'

'Certainly not. I paid good money for it.'

'I'll buy you another one.'

Emily shook her head decisively. 'I can't let you do that.'

'Yes, you can.' He smiled down at her. 'Where's the harm in a present?'

'If you give me cheques *and* buy me presents I'll feel like a kept woman!'

'Hold the thought. Because I am going to keep you.' Lucas stroked her cheek. 'You look tired. You should be in bed.'

'Cuddle me a bit first?'

He drew in a deep breath, his hands sliding beneath the clinging wool tunic as he kissed her. 'Is this what you mean by cuddling?' he demanded against her mouth.

'Whatever it is, I like it,' she whispered, kissing him with such fervour they were soon lying full length together on the sofa, caressing each other into a state of arousal which forced Lucas to pull away at last.

'I'd better take you to bed,' he panted.

She nodded with enthusiasm, licking the tip of her tongue round her swollen lips as she put herself back together.

Lucas clenched his jaw. 'I meant the spare bed!'

'Of course.' She gave him a wicked little smile. 'But I'm afraid you may have to help me undress later, if I get stuck.'

He growled something under his breath. 'Right. Up you come, then.'

'No,' she said firmly. 'I must start fending for myself. I'll call if I need you.'

Lucas jumped up, pushing the hair back from his damp forehead. 'Then for God's sake be careful.'

'Just give me ten minutes. Have a drink, or something.'

'Good idea,' he agreed, his face tense as Emily disdained his aid as she reached for the crutch and got to her feet.

'I'll leave my shoe,' she said, and began a careful progress to the bathroom, leaving Lucas to pour himself a finger of Scotch instead of chasing after her, as he so very obviously wanted to.

Emily hurried through her preparations for the night, removed her clothes, laid them neatly on the chest, slid into bed, and waited.

It seemed a long time before she heard Lucas open the door of the guest room.

'Emily!' he roared. 'Where are you?'

'In here.'

He strode into the master bedroom, then stopped dead when he found her in his bed with the covers drawn up to her chin.

'Ah,' he said, swallowing. 'Of course. I'll take the

other room. Better for you here, with a bathroom close to hand.'

'For heaven's sake, man,' said Emily impatiently. 'Get your kit off and come to bed.'

'Darling,' he said in desperation. 'I can't *do* this. I'm not superhuman—'

'Lucas.' She smiled slowly, bringing her dimple into play. 'In case you're missing the point, I'm doing my darnedest to seduce you!'

He started throwing off his clothes before the words were out of her mouth. He dived into bed and took her into his arms, his breath leaving him in a rush when he found she was naked.

'You undressed yourself,' he accused, sliding a hand over her breasts. 'I was looking forward to giving you a helping hand.'

'I like the one you're giving me now,' she gasped. He laughed deep in his throat and kissed her fiercely, his hands on her bottom to pull her hard against him as her lips opened in welcome and her tongue answered his with caresses of its own.

'I don't want to hurt you—your ankle,' he said hoarsely.

'You won't,' Emily assured him, and felt the muscles of his back tense as her fingers caressed them, digging a little in demand, desire bright and hot inside her as their kisses grew wilder.

'Slowly,' panted Lucas, putting her away a little. 'I was in too much of a rush before. This time I want you to experience every nuance of pleasure possible.'

'You were half-asleep last time,' she said, shivering as his mouth closed over a hard, expectant nipple.

'Not for long.' Lucas raised his head to gaze down

into her glittering eyes. 'And this time I'm very much awake, so pay attention.'

'If you keep the light on,' she said breathlessly, 'you'll see my bruises.'

'And kiss them better.' Lucas drew the covers down until he could see all of her, bruises and all. 'This is part of the deal, darling. I want to see you. I want you to see me. To use all the senses. To touch.' He kissed her mouth as he caressed her breasts. 'Taste.' He took a nipple into his mouth and she moaned, trying to pull him close, but he shook his head, gazing down at her from the tumbled black curls over every part of her body, which grew taut and flushed, her nipples standing proud, as though he were caressing her with his hands, instead of just his glittering, possessive eyes.

'To hear?' she demanded at last, shifting restlessly beneath the tactile gaze.

'God, yes! The sound of that husky little moan sends me crazy,' he said roughly, and kissed her, his lips and tongue taking full possession of hers before his mouth moved down her throat to descend slowly and tantalisingly over her breasts and stomach until he reached the delta between her thighs, and she arched like a strung bow as his tongue played havoc with a part of her unused to such ravishing attention.

Emily lay limp in his arms afterwards, and Lucas held her close, moving a gentling hand down her spine.

'Not a fluke, then,' she said gruffly. 'Or doesn't it count that way?'

'All ways count if they give you pleasure.' He moved over her until he lay propped with his thighs between hers. 'Just to be in total contact like this is a pleasure in itself.'

Her breathing quickened as her eyes locked with his.

'But that,' she whispered, 'is because we know it's just the overture to what comes next.'

She felt him tense in response, his body poised over hers, and slid her hand down between them to caress the part of him which rose, hard and ready in her grasp. 'Now,' she said fiercely, and Lucas obeyed, entering her with a long, slow thrust that pierced her entire body with sensation so intense she gave a sobbing moan. He began to make love to her with a slow-burning control that she responded to with such passionate fervour his control gave way at last to breathless, thrusting frenzy, which brought them to almost simultaneous release and left them gasping in each other's arms as the aftershocks died away.

'I'm getting good at this,' panted Emily, once she regained the power of speech.

Lucas grinned and eased himself on to his back, taking her with him to lie in the crook of his arm. 'It won't work with anyone else,' he warned.

'I know.' Emily heaved a deep, relishing sigh. 'I really thought it was my fault, Lucas.'

He smoothed her damp curls back from her forehead. 'With Miles?'

'Yes. Because it was so—so sort of perfunctory and disappointing.' She looked up at him, smiling ruefully. 'And all the time it was just because I was the wrong gender.'

'Whereas you suit me in every way there is,' said Lucas with emphasis.

'Then that's all that matters.'

'You mean that?'

'Yes.'

'In that case, could we rewind to the point, earlier

today, when I mentioned that I was in love with you, Miss Warner?'

She nodded, flushing. 'I'm in love with you, too, Mr Tennent. Which is a bit frightening.'

'Why?'

'Because we've known each other such a short time.'

'There are no hard and fast rules in relationships, darling.' Lucas bent his head to kiss her. 'Say it again.'

'I love you,' she muttered, ducking her head, but he brought her face up to his.

'I love you, too. So what shall we do about it?'

'I thought we'd just done something quite earth-shattering about it! At least, it was for me.'

Lucas's arm tightened round her. 'For me, too. So much so that I'd hoped to repeat the experience as soon as is humanly possible. But it isn't yet.'

'Isn't what?'

'Possible. You're dynamite, Miss Warner. And, as I said before, I'm not super-human.'

Emily smiled at him. 'You are to me, Mr Tennent.'

'In that case, you're one of a kind, so I'd better hang on to you—' He stopped abruptly. 'Darling, in the heat of the moment I forgot to ask. How's your ankle?'

'Throbbing a bit,' she said, surprised, then grinned. 'But every other part of me was throbbing so much just now I didn't notice.'

Lucas gave a shout of laughter and hugged her close. 'I'd expected to toss and turn all night, thinking of you on the other side of the wall. Instead—' He paused.

'Instead?' Emily prompted.

'We made magic together,' he said softly, a note in his voice which brought her arms round his neck in passionate agreement.

After a while Emily pulled away, a resigned expression on her face. 'And now, alas, I must interrupt this magic moment to request my crutch. Plus my dressing-gown from my bag.'

'Borrow mine,' said Lucas, and slid out of bed to pull on his jeans.

Emily got out of bed, flushing with embarrassment as she tried to balance naked on one foot. Lucas laughed, kissed her, wrapped her in his robe, then scooped her up to deposit her in his bathroom.

'I'll fetch your bags. Shout when you want me.'

Emily put her weight on her good foot to wash her hands afterwards, and eyed her flushed face in the mirror, surprised to find she looked much the same as usual. Her mouth was red, and obviously much kissed, and her eyes were a bit heavy, but they gleamed like the amber earrings she kept for special occasions. Otherwise, the most ravishing experience of her entire life had left no visible mark.

She told Lucas so as he carried her back to bed.

'Did you expect to see a scarlet ''A'' branded on your forehead?' he said, amused.

'Doesn't apply—we weren't committing adultery.'

'No. We were making love,' he agreed as he slid into bed. 'And I do mean *love*, Miss Warner, not lust. There's a difference.'

'I know.' Emily sighed with pleasure as her body fitted to his as though custom-made for the purpose. They lay together, completely at peace for a comfortable interval, then something occurred to her. 'In all the excitement, I forgot. Earlier you mentioned some other kind of job for me.'

Lucas nodded. 'I did.'

Emily pulled away a little so she could see his face. 'What kind of job? Cleaning at your bank?'

'Hell, no,' he said, appalled.

'What, then?'

Lucas eyed her warily. 'It's not a job exactly.'

'What, then?'

'First,' he said tantalisingly, 'a question or two. When you found you weren't expecting my baby you said you were relieved. Why, exactly?'

She stared at him. 'I would have thought it was obvious.'

'Tell me just the same.'

'For one thing, I really didn't fancy the role of single mother. I couldn't have stayed at Nat's place, and I wouldn't have wanted to go home to my parents. And, quite apart from that, all this would never have been possible.'

'All this?'

'Being here with you, making love with you, having you in my life in any way at all, other than financial support I couldn't have refused. Of course I was relieved. But at the same time, Lucas,' she added, smiling, 'utterly astonished that an experience like that *didn't* result in a baby.'

He let out a deep unsteady breath. 'You certainly know the right things to say to a man, Miss Warner.'

'Actually, I don't. I'm not into flattery.'

'*I* was disappointed,' he said abruptly.

Emily drew away in dismay. 'When we first made love?'

'No! This morning, when you told me you weren't expecting my baby.'

Emily gazed at him in disbelief, her eyes like saucers.

'It's the simple truth,' he assured her, then raised an eyebrow at her change of expression. 'What?' he demanded.

'When I found out, I was disappointed, too—but only for a second or two,' she added honestly. 'But it really amazes me that you were.'

'It amazed me for a while, too. I'd never given fatherhood a thought before.' He smoothed a caressing hand over her stomach. 'Which brings me back to the subject of your future employment. I need a mother for these unborn children of mine. Since you're the only woman in the world I want for the post, Miss Warner, will you accept?'

Emily looked at him in silence for a moment or two, then saw a pulse throbbing at the corner of his mouth and realised that Lucas wasn't sure how she'd respond. 'Yes, please,' she said, her voice even huskier than usual. 'Do you need references?'

Lucas drew in a deep breath. 'No. But before you accept the post there's something you have to do first,' he told her, his voice not quite steady.

'What is it?'

'You have to marry me.'

'*Marry* you?'

Lucas propped himself up on an elbow to look down at her stunned face. 'Emily Warner, you said yes a minute ago.'

'I didn't know what you meant!'

'I've never proposed before, so I obviously didn't get it quite right—' He halted, frowning down at her. 'Wait a minute. You mean you were ready to take me—and these mythical children of mine—without a wedding first?'

'Yes.'

'Even knowing your father's views on the subject?'

Emily gave him a startled look. 'I clean forgot about that. I just wanted to say yes to whatever *you* wanted.'

'My darling girl!' He dived down beside her and took her in his arms. 'So you do love me.'

'I said I did,' she said tartly. 'What else do I have to do to convince you?'

Lucas pretended to consider. 'First you kiss me.'

'That sounds easy.'

'Then you put your arms round me.'

'Like this?'

'Perfect.'

She wriggled closer. 'Now what do I do?'

'Use your imagination,' he said unsteadily.

Emily's imagination proved astoundingly fertile for someone who, up to meeting Lucas Tennent, had considered the entire concept of lovemaking over-rated.

'Are you—convinced yet?' she demanded at one stage, her only answer a devouring kiss as Lucas slid home between her parted thighs and Emily strained him close, her body answering his as she tried to prove to him beyond all doubt how much she loved him. And knew she'd succeeded when he gasped in elation as the earthy, transient glory finally overwhelmed them.

The week that followed was hectic. Emily had grown quite agile with her crutch by the time her parents came to the flat for a celebration lunch everyone much enjoyed after Lucas had formally requested, and been granted, the hand of the Reverend Richard Warner's daughter in marriage. Claire Warner, it was obvious, took to her prospective son-in-law on sight, and to Emily's relief told her in private that her father was equally pleased with her choice.

The next celebration was a party with a guest-list which included a jubilant Ginny Hart, and husband Charlie, along with the Donaldsons, Bryony, Mark, Nat and even Thea, who came up to London for the occasion. And at the weekend Emily, minus crutch, but stiff with nerves, went with Lucas to collect his sister from Heathrow. Alice Tennent, all bronze skin and sun-streaked hair, courtesy of the Italian sun, embraced her brother and Emily with equal enthusiasm, so delighted at the news that she talked wedding plans non-stop with Emily as Lucas drove them down to the house he'd bought for his mother in a Cotswold village near enough to Chastlecombe to invite Emily's family for lunch.

Emily felt rather dazed on the journey back to London that evening.

'Are you tired, sweetheart? Ankle hurting?' asked Lucas.

'No. Neither. I just feel I'm in a dream and I'll wake up any minute. Your mother's lovely, Lucas, and Alice is a kindred spirit, as I'm sure you could tell. I hope they both like me.'

'Of course they do,' he said, laughing. 'And even if they don't it doesn't matter a damn, because *I* like you. I like you a lot.'

Emily grinned at him. 'I like you a lot, too.' She paused. 'But I'm very glad your mother took to me, just the same.'

'When we had a minute together before we left she told me she was delighted. Relieved, too.'

'Relieved?'

'Because I work in the City, Mother was always afraid I'd marry some frightening, power-suited female in the same line of work.'

'Whereas I've never frightened anyone in my life.'

'I wouldn't say that. You've put the fear of God into Miles Denny more than once!'

'Don't remind me!' Emily shuddered. 'This time I really thought I'd killed him. Thank heavens his skull is thick—but never mind Miles. I'm just glad your mother liked me.'

'She knows that with you I'll have the kind of marriage she never had herself. She wants the same for my sister, too.'

'Does Alice have someone in her life?'

'She's never short of male company, but so far no one significant.' He grinned. 'Ally thinks it's wonderful that I'm marrying my angel of mercy.'

Emily chuckled. 'I'm no angel, Lucas.'

'For which—at certain times—I'm passionately grateful,' he said, in a tone which took her breath away.

By the time Lucas returned to his job in the City, Emily was mobile again, and to please her parents went down to Chastlecombe to spend the month before the wedding with them before taking up permanent residence in Lucas's flat. She spent the weekends with Lucas in London and back home during the week, in the time left over from wedding arrangements, Emily worked on her novel. And found that writer's block was a thing of the past.

'I probably shouldn't be staying here so near to the wedding,' remarked Emily, the Sunday before.

'Why not?' demanded Lucas.

'My superstitions again, I suppose.'

'Because of bloody Miles!'

'I just don't want anything to go wrong this time.'

Lucas moved closer on the sofa and scooped her close against him. 'Nothing,' he assured her, 'will go wrong. I wouldn't dare let it, because Ally will kill me if she can't wear the hat she's bought.'

Emily giggled and relaxed against him. 'It's going to

be a long, long week until Saturday. I'll miss you,' she said, sighing.

'Not as much as I'll miss you,' he said gloomily. 'I'll be so haggard from insomnia you won't recognise me when you come down the aisle.'

'You'll just have to wear a gardenia in your button-hole so I don't marry the wrong man.'

'Fat chance of that.' He laughed and got up, pulling her to her feet. 'Bedtime.'

'It's only a little after ten!'

'I get up early,' he reminded her, then caught her close and kissed her. 'Which, as you know perfectly well, is nothing to do with it.'

It was a wrench to part with Lucas early next morning. Emily clung to him as they said goodbye, as though they were parting forever.

'I'll ring you tonight—and every night,' he said huskily. 'Take care of yourself, please. Don't fall down any more stairs.'

She nodded dumbly, trying to smile, and Lucas kissed her again, then with reluctance broke away. 'See you in church, darling.'

On the way down to Chastlecombe by train later Emily tried hard to dispel the uneasiness she felt as each mile took her farther away from Lucas. There was absolutely no reason for it, she told herself irritably. Her mother had everything well in hand for the small reception, a ravishing dress hung in her wardrobe at the cottage; the result of an expedition to Knightsbridge with Ginny, and this time next week she would be on her honeymoon.

Doing her best to shake off her blues, Emily hugged her father when he met the train and chatted brightly to him on the drive back to the cottage, where she found her mother in the kitchen, making preparations for dinner.

'You look tired,' Claire Warner told her daughter. 'Sit there and watch, darling. Richard, you can make some tea, if you would.'

Emily did as she was told, enjoyed the meal later, and afterwards spent half an hour talking to Lucas on the phone. But once she was in bed, sent there early by her mother to get a good night's rest, she tossed and turned for most of it, her fey mood back in full force once she was alone.

For the next couple of days Emily tried hard to throw off her mood and show enthusiasm for the preparations, but halfway through the week, glad to escape for a while, she told her mother she had to make a swift trip to London for a few things she'd forgotten to pack for the honeymoon.

'Stay the night with Lucas, then,' said her practical mother. 'No point in wearing yourself out with two journeys.'

When Emily let herself into the familiar loft late that afternoon she realised, with a pang of disloyalty, that already it felt far more like home than her parents' cottage. In the master bedroom all was tidy, with Lucas's luggage standing by the bed, waiting to be packed. Emily took off her coat and kicked off her shoes. She would do something about a meal later. She let herself down on the bed, clutching Lucas's pillow to her chest, and surrendered to an overwhelming desire for sleep.

Emily woke reluctantly, fighting with whoever was trying to take the pillow away from her.

'Darling, wake up,' said Lucas, something in his voice cutting through the fog of sleep.

Emily sat up, smiling guiltily. 'I know I should have rung to tell you, but—'

'Never mind that.' He sat down beside her, his eyes searching as he took the hand wearing the ring they'd chosen together. 'Tell me what's wrong, Emily. Have you changed your mind?'

Now she was fully awake Emily saw that Lucas was as white as his shirt. 'About marrying you? Absolutely not!'

'Thank God for that,' he said, relaxing slightly. 'Forgive me for pointing out the obvious, darling, but you're not supposed to be here. Luckily, I rang the cottage before I left for home tonight, so I knew you'd made a sudden decision to come to London for the day.'

She nodded. 'There's something I have to tell you. Before the wedding, I mean.'

'You're worrying the hell out of me,' he said with sudden violence. 'For God's sake, tell me!'

'Sorry. It's just that I'm pregnant,' she said baldly.

'Pregnant?' Lucas stared at her blankly. '*How*? After what happened the first time I've taken every care not to put you at risk again.'

'I went to see Dr Hall on my way here today, Lucas; the one who came when you were ill. She said I'm six weeks pregnant.'

They gazed at each other in silence.

'So it happened that night, after all,' said Lucas slowly. 'But I thought—'

'So did I,' said Emily. 'The usual signs appeared, as I told you, but nothing like normal, which I put down to the shock of the fall. But I knew something was wrong. If you remember, I was very clingy when you left on Monday morning. I felt so off-colour I thought I was sickening for something. Then, after supper last night, I was beginning to pack for the honeymoon and found the pregnancy test I'd never used. When it showed positive I thought I'd better get someone to confirm it, so I made an appointment with Dr Hall and came on here to give you the news.'

Sudden comprehension dawned in Lucas's eyes, and he pulled her into his arms and held her cruelly tight in silence.

'Aren't you going to say anything?' said Emily after a while.

'I'm too busy thanking God you didn't find this out sooner,' he said hoarsely, and kissed her hard. 'Otherwise you wouldn't be marrying me on Saturday, would you? I'd just be a signature on some child-support agreement!'

She shook her head, burrowing closer. 'I can't imagine that, now.'

'Good.' He tipped her face up to his. 'Then you'd better bow to the inevitable, bride-to-be. The wedding's definitely on.'

'Alice would kill you, for a start, if she couldn't wear the hat,' agreed Emily unsteadily.

'If your brother hadn't already saved her the trouble!'

They collapsed on the bed together, half laughing, half not, and held each other close in silent thanksgiving for a while.

'I couldn't have done it, anyway, Lucas,' said Emily eventually.

He propped himself on an elbow to give her a searching look. 'Done what, exactly?'

'Kept to my obligation hang-ups.'

His eyes lit up. 'Thank God for that. But why not, darling?'

'Because I fell head over heels in love with you the

first moment I saw you.' She grinned. 'Red nose and hacking cough included.'

'And, ill though I was, I wanted to grab you off my kitchen stool and make love to you there and then,' said Lucas, inching nearer.

'Did you really?' she said, starry-eyed, then sighed heavily. 'But there's something else I ought to confess, too.'

'Oh, God,' he groaned. 'Go on. Tell me the worst.'

'I've based the hero of my novel on you. Do you mind?'

He fell flat on his back in relief. 'Not in the least— as long as he's tall, dark and amazingly handsome, and the story has a happy ending.'

'All of the above,' she assured him. 'In my fairy-tale, Cinderella will firmly ignore all half-baked principles and marry her prince. If he uses sufficient persuasion.'

Lucas rolled over to kiss her. 'I'm no prince, darling.'

'True. But you're *very* good at persuasion.' Emily wriggled closer. 'I could use some of it now. And I don't mean friendly persuasion, either.'

'Good. Because the red-hot passionate kind is the only thing on offer,' her bridegroom informed her.

'Bliss,' sighed Emily, and smiled up at him with such love in her eyes that Lucas closed his for an instant, then kissed her again.

'I know the happy ever after bit is supposed to start after the actual wedding,' he said huskily, 'but for me it began almost from the moment I surprised you in my kitchen, Cinderella.'

'Same for me,' she assured him happily. 'Thank goodness you went down with flu!'

MANHATTAN MERGER

by
Rebecca Winters

Rebecca Winters, whose family of four children has now swelled to include three beautiful grandchildren, lives in Salt Lake City, Utah, in the land of the Rocky Mountains. With canyons and high Alpine meadows full of wildflowers, she never runs out of places to explore. They, plus her favourite holiday spots in Europe, often end up as backgrounds for her novels because writing is her passion, along with her family and church. Rebecca loves to hear from her readers. If you wish to e-mail her, please visit her website at: www.rebeccawinters-author.com

Don't miss Rebecca Winters' exciting new novel, *The Lazaridis Marriage,* out in July 2007 from Mills & Boon® Romance.

CHAPTER ONE

"UNCLE Payne?"

Thirty-three-year-old Payne Sterling glanced up from the screen of his laptop in time to see his favorite niece Catherine come flying in the study. He doubted her feet touched the ground.

His fiancée followed at a little slower pace in her wheelchair. Both women seemed panicked by something.

"You've got to see this!"

Catherine looked and sounded frantic as she thrust a paperback book at him.

"Easy, sweetheart."

Puzzled, he took it from her, then gave it his full attention. To his surprise he discovered it was a romance novel of all things entitled *Manhattan Merger,* by Bonnie Wrigley.

Below the title was a picture of a man holding a woman in his arms. They were standing in the office of a New York City skyscraper where the Manhattan skyline was revealed in the background.

Upon a second look he realized it wasn't just any office.

Or any man...

Even though it wasn't a photograph, it was like looking at himself in a mirror.

He stared at it for a full minute in stunned disbelief.

"Promise you won't tell mother I've been reading these, Uncle Payne. The thing is, over the last year I've noticed that quite a few of the men on the covers resemble you. But this one *is* you," Catherine's voice trembled. "Even his hairline is the same shape."

He could see that.

"She's right, Payne!" Diane cried out anxiously. "This man has your build and dark brown hair. It's the same length. Everything is like you, even to the exact hue of your blue eyes. That's why I told Catherine she had to show this romance to you."

Both of them had lost color.

"He's even dressed in the same kind of suit and shirt I've noticed you wear to work before, Uncle Payne! And that view out of those same kinds of windows is exactly what you see when you walk in your office. The person who did the cover has to know a lot of private things about you.

"Look!" She pointed to some items. "See that picture of a ship passing in front of a lighthouse? You have a similar picture hanging on your office wall! And what about that little picture of a bulldog propped on the desk?"

Payne had recognized those details at once, but he hadn't wanted to say anything for fear of alarming either of them further.

The fact that he'd hired an architect to incorporate the old lighthouse at Crag's Head into a home where he'd been living for the past few years had set off more warning bells.

He eyed his fifteen-year-old niece whose hair was the same pale gold as his sister's. "Have you read this yet?"

"No— As soon as I showed it to Diane, we decided to bring it straight to you!"

"You did the right thing."

Somewhere he'd heard it said everyone had a look-alike. Possibly more than one. Maybe this was a fantastic coincidence, but he couldn't take any chances. Not after what had happened at Christmas.

"Where do you get these books, Catherine?"

"One of the maids reads them first, then gives me a bunch. When I'm through, I return them to her."

"Which maid?"

"Nyla."

"Catherine really shouldn't be reading books like this, Payne," Diane declared. "Whoever is responsible for putting you on the covers probably read a lot of trashy romances at a young age and can no longer distinguish between fantasy and reality."

"There's nothing trashy about them," Catherine defended quietly. "They're exciting stories about people falling in love. You learn so much and go so many places. I think they're wonderful! If you or mom would ever take the time to read one, you'd be hooked too."

Diane's eyes sent him a private message that indicated her strong disapproval.

"Listen, Uncle Payne—don't be angry with Nyla. I don't want her to get into trouble. She's the one who said I ought to bring it to your attention!

"If you say anything to mom and dad about this, they'll make me stay with grandma and grandpa the next time they take a trip. Nyla might even lose her job."

He shook his head. "I'm not going to jeopardize her position here. On the contrary, I want to thank Nyla for aiding and abetting you in your latest reading frenzy. It has brought something to light that needs to be dealt with right away."

Diane trembled. "This could be another crazed woman who's been following you around without your knowledge. There's no question she's been in your office, Payne. I'm afraid for you."

His fiancée had every reason to be terrified.

Less than six months ago Diane Wylie had taken a stalker's bullet meant for him and was now condemned to a wheelchair—perhaps permanently.

Consumed by guilt, Payne moved around the desk and hunkered down at her side. Reaching for her hand he said, "I don't know what to believe at the moment, but if this is another demented wacko, I'm going to find out. You two stay here. I'll be back soon."

He stood up, stroked his niece's pale cheek, then grabbed the romance off the desk and strode out of his brother-in-law's study. A few minutes later he caught up with Nyla in the kitchen enjoying afternoon tea with some of the other staff.

Her expression sobered when he showed her the romance and asked where she'd bought it.

"I get them through a book club, but you can find copies people have already read at the used book store in the village. It's called Candle Glow Books. They have everything."

"Thank you, Nyla."

"You're welcome. I might as well tell you, I've seen your face on other covers, but your hair and eyes were always different. Until this book came in the mail, I thought it was just one of those amazing coincidences.

"I suggested Catherine say something to you about it. The likeness to you is startling! So's the story."

The story too?

Without wasting more time he pulled out his cell phone and called security to meet him around the back of his sister's house.

Since the age of seventeen, Payne had been the victim of half a dozen stalking incidents which had been brought to an end through police intervention.

But last December between Christmas and New Year, a psychotic woman had managed to penetrate the Sterling compound on Long Island's South Fork. Whether she came by water or managed to get past the guard at the gate, no one knew.

At the time, the Sterlings were having dinner for the Wylies who'd invited them to their home for brunch earlier in the day. The Wylies lived on the North Shore of Long Island and had enjoyed this exchange tradition with the Sterlings for many years.

Prior to the Christmas holidays Payne had been out of the country a great deal and had spent most it working at his office where he could catch up on the paperwork in solitude.

While immersed, his mother called him upset because he'd missed the Wylies' brunch. Could she at least count on him for dinner, and would he please bring Diane who was in the city shopping? If she could fly back with him, then no one would be late.

Knowing how much his mother cared about these things, he agreed to come and bring Diane with him. As the two of them were walking from the car to the front porch of his parents' home, the demented intruder had emerged from the bushes. The thirtyish-looking woman claimed to be in love with Payne. If she couldn't have him, no other woman could either.

Payne saw the glint of metal in time to push Diane aside before the gun went off, but the stalker had poor aim. To his horror the bullet struck Diane in her lower back before he could knock the lunatic to the ground. The horrific experience had changed all their lives.

Diane had clung to him all the way to the hospital. In the fear that she was going to die, she'd told him how much she needed him, how much she'd always loved him.

He'd had no idea of her deep feelings for him. He'd never been interested in her that way, but at that point it didn't matter because he couldn't have abandoned her in the state she was in.

Several months later she still couldn't walk though she retained some feeling in her legs. The doctors told her they'd done all they could do and suggested she go to a clinic in Switzerland reputed to have success with her kind of spinal injury.

Afraid of failure, Diane had flatly refused to consider it and wouldn't be consoled. At that point Payne took stock of his life and decided that if he proposed marriage, she might be more inclined to get the help she needed.

But after their engagement was announced, she seemed to retreat further into herself, unwilling to discuss going to Switzerland. Worse, she'd developed an almost irrational fear of the two of them being shot again.

In order to reassure her, Payne had made certain new security measures had been added to protect her and the Wylies as well as everyone on the Sterling estate. His fiancée now had twenty-four-hour protection.

As for Payne, four security men accompanied him wherever he went on business. A helicopter took him to his office in Manhattan. If he had to fly overseas, he used his private jet. When he had to drive somewhere on Long Island, one of the security men chauffeured him in a bulletproof limousine with one-way glass windows.

En route to the used bookstore in Oyster Bay, he handed the novel to the retired Navy SEAL, Mac, who'd been his personal bodyguard for the last three years.

"What do you make of this?"

Mac took one look and whistled. His gray eyes darted to Payne in puzzlement before he gave it back to him. "How come *you're* on the cover?"

"That's what I intend to find out."

While the driver looked for Candle Glow Books, Payne opened the novel to the copyright page.

Red Rose Romance Publishers, Inc., Second Avenue, New York, New York.

His eyes narrowed. He'd never heard of it, but that location was east of Central Park near the Turtle Bay Grill where he often met with overseas clients.

It appeared the book had been published two months ago.

That meant whatever party was responsible for his picture being on the cover had possessed knowledge of him long before the publication date. Most publishing houses had up to three or more years of books waiting to go to press.

There was a disclaimer.

Any characters, names or incidents in this book do not exist outside the mind of the author.

Like hell!

A grimace marred Payne's features.

He turned the book over to read the blurb. By the time he'd digested the second sentence, his body had broken out in a cold sweat.

Secrets?

Powerful, dashing New York billionaire Logan Townsend, is hiding a painful secret from his fiancée and family.

"Good Lord," he whispered.

When he's involved in an accident in the Canyonlands of the American West, Dr. Maggie Osborn discovers what that secret is.

Unbeknownst to him, she puts her life in danger to save his.

But secrets have a way of getting out.

It isn't until Logan returns to New York that he learns Maggie is keeping one from him.

On the verge of sealing the most vital merger of his existence, he's torn between duty and desire.

Upon reading the last line, Payne felt as if someone had just walked over his grave. Convinced nothing about this book was an accident, he rolled it up in his fist.

He would willingly litter the island page by page to be rid of it. But for several obvious reasons he couldn't do that and was forced to sit there while he attempted to contain the savage impulse.

Sam, the security man at the wheel, turned down an alley, then came to a stop at the rear of the used book store in question. Two of the security men, John and Andy, jumped out to enter the shop ahead of Payne.

It was near the closing hour on a Tuesday evening in June. The timing couldn't have been more perfect if he'd hoped to avoid a lot of unwanted attention.

When the all clear was given, Mac covered Payne's back as they got out of the limousine and went inside the claustrophobic shop. It was a maze of cubbyholes and narrow aisles. With novels stacked to the ceiling everywhere he turned, there was no doubt this was a paperback lover's paradise.

The eyes of the older saleswoman behind the counter lit up at his approach. "Mr. Sterling— Good evening! I'm Alice Perry. It's a real honor to have you in my store." She extended her hand which he shook.

"It's nice to meet you, Ms. Perry," he answered back.

"What can I do for you?"

He handed her the novel which would never lie flat again.

She took one look at it and her gaze lifted to his with excitement. "I *knew* this was you!" she cried. "Every romance reader who's come in here lately has been talking about it."

Payne groaned. "According to my niece, there are other novels besides this that appear to have my likeness on the cover."

"Oh there are!" she blurted. "But *this* one…"

So neither Catherine or Nyla had exaggerated anything. The news was going from bad to worse.

"At this point there isn't a copy of *Manhattan Merger*

to be had anywhere on the Atlantic seaboard. My phone's been ringing off the hook with book dealers wanting copies! Those people lucky enough to have purchased it when it first came out are holding on to it for dear life.

"I kept copies of it and those other books for myself and my daughter who helps me run the shop. Perhaps before you leave you'd be willing to sign them? We'd be so thrilled if you would."

"I'd be happy to oblige, *if* I'd given my permission to appear on their covers."

Her smile faded. "I don't understand."

"Neither do I, Ms. Perry. That's why I'm here, to try and solve this mystery."

"You mean they just went ahead and used your picture?"

"I don't know, but I'm going to find out." He had to tamp down hard on his anger. "May I see them please?"

"I only have four left. They're locked away in the back room until a book dealer from Connecticut arrives on Friday. He's a collector and is going to pay me five thousand dollars apiece for them. Give me a moment and I'll bring them out."

"Only five thousand?" Mac said in a teasing whisper as the woman disappeared.

Ignoring the aside, Payne wandered over to the nearest bookshelf marked Mysteries. It was crammed with titles by various authors and sorted according to the alphabet. He pulled one out, curious to see what kind of cover was on the front.

The photograph had captured a busy street scene

somewhere in London. A quick look at the copyright page gave the name of a British publisher.

He moved to another section marked Upbeat Romances published in Los Angeles. Their covers were done in cartoon caricatures.

"Here we are."

He reshelved the book and joined the woman who'd laid the four books out on the counter for him. At first glance, he was horrified.

It was his face all right.

One of them depicted him as a Norseman with a flowing mane of white-blond hair, hazel eyes, bulging thighs and biceps twice his size. The book was called *Roald's Bride.*

Another showed him as a Castilian prince in royal ceremonial robes with pitch-black hair and eyes entitled, *Her Prince of Dreams.*

In the third book, *Undercover Love,* he was a gray-eyed Royal Canadian Mountie in full red dress uniform wearing a hat that covered his hair.

The Star Grazer was the last book. It portrayed him as a man from the future with auburn hair and brown eyes.

On all of the covers he had his arms around a beautiful woman. It appeared the same person had done the artwork.

"That's some life you lead," came another crack from Mac, sotto voce.

Payne made no response as he looked at the spines. All four were a product of Red Rose Romance Publishers, and had been printed within the last year.

"How many publishers put out paperback romances besides Red Rose?"

"Dozens of companies throughout the world, but the ones on my shelves come mainly from the United States, England and Canada. Red Rose produces the most every year by quite a margin."

"Have you seen my face on the covers of any romances other than Red Rose?"

"No."

That was the only good news so far. He could hope Red Rose was a mom-and-pop outfit that probably didn't have a large distribution base. "Do you have your romances sorted by publisher?"

"Yes."

"Will you show me where the romance section is?"

She laughed. "It's practically the whole shop except for the mysteries and science fiction here at the front."

He tried hard not to reveal his shock. "Why don't we try the Red Rose section first."

"Follow me, Mr. Sterling."

She led him a fourth of the way back. "It starts here and goes to the rear of the store."

His eyes widened in incredulity. "*These* are all Red Rose Romances?"

"Yes. Their company has nine different lines depending on what kind of romance you're looking for. Of course these are only the English versions. Their books are published in over a hundred languages. Something like that."

A hundred! That meant—

"We keep a few copies in Italian and Russian for the occasional visitor," she added.

He wondered how many times Catherine had been in here that her mother didn't know about. Payne loved his sister Phyllis, but like their mother, she didn't approve of a lot of things.

With her high-brow taste in the arts, music and literature, he doubted she'd ever had the curiosity to read a paperback romance. He couldn't help but wonder if Diane disliked them on principle too.

Or maybe she'd read a few when she was a teenager and refused to admit to it. He'd like to know.

In Payne's mind it would make Diane a more real person if she'd gone against her mother's wishes the way Catherine had done, and could own up to it…

"How far do some of these books date back?"

"Red Rose has been in business at least forty years that I know of."

Forty years?

He studied the voluminous amount of reading material. Evidently someone besides Nyla and Catherine had been gobbling these up by the thousands for at least four decades.

That was a long time… Too long not to be a reputable company.

"You'll find their books listed under the separate headings hanging from the ceiling over each section. There's something for every taste."

"So I see," Payne muttered.

A Touch of Romance, A Touch of Passion, A Touch of Espionage, A Touch of History, A Touch of Babies, A Touch of Royalty, A Touch of Sci-Fi/Paranormal, A Touch of Cowboy and *A Touch of Humor.*

"You're welcome to browse as long as you like."

"Thank you."

Since she'd pulled all the books with his likeness from the shelves, there was no point in sifting through the mountains of romances. The mere thought staggered the imagination.

However he did take a book from each section to examine the covers. All of them had been done as a painting rather than a photograph. He carried them to the counter.

"I'm going to buy these nine books. The four you're keeping I'd like to borrow for twenty-four hours." He pulled a credit card from his wallet. "Add $20,000.00 to my bill. When the books are returned, you can credit it to my account."

She shook her head. "I trust you to bring them back, Mr. Sterling. There's no charge."

"Thank you."

He put his credit card away and pulled out a hundred dollar bill. "You've been very helpful," he said, sliding it toward her. She started to make change but he told her not to bother.

"This is much too generous."

"Humor me, please," he said with a smile.

"If you insist. After all these years, it's so exciting to meet the legendary member of the Sterling family!"

Payne had heard that comment one too many times in his life. However it would do no good to remind the woman that his place in the scheme of things had happened because of an accident of birth. Her place had been determined the same way.

Furthermore, he got up in the mornings, worked hard,

suffered, agonized and bled before going to bed at night, just the way she and everyone else did on the planet.

Her gaze searched his. "I do hope this turns out to be an honest mistake for all concerned."

"My sentiments exactly." Otherwise another nightmare had begun.

She bagged the books and handed the sack to him. He tucked *Manhattan Merger* inside the opening.

"I promise you'll get these back. Thanks again, Ms. Perry."

"You're welcome."

"Let's go," he murmured to Mac.

Once they were ensconced in the limousine, he phoned Drew Wallace, his attorney, and explained what had happened. They planned to meet at Crag's Head as soon as Drew could get away from an important dinner engagement.

Pleased Drew could come on such short notice no matter the hour, he told him he'd send the helicopter for him. This was one meeting that needed to take place tonight under strictest privacy.

When he returned to his sister's house, he discovered Diane in the backyard looking through some wedding magazines. Catherine was using doggie treats to make their family's golden retriever do tricks.

Though Payne loved all his nieces and nephews, he'd always had a special feeling for Catherine. Her heart melted for the less fortunates of this world whether they be animals or people.

Out of all his sister's children, Catherine was the one who'd taken her brother Trevor's death from leukemia the hardest. When she came into her inheritance, he had an idea she'd give it all to research in an effort to find a cure.

Since the shooting, his niece had attached herself to Diane, determined his brunette fiancée would walk again one day. Catherine's desire to make that happen had endeared her to Payne as nothing else could have done.

While Phyllis and Trent were away with their three older children, Payne's niece—who'd begged to stay behind—had been helping Diane and her mother with plans for their wedding. It was scheduled for August first.

Without Diane's knowledge Payne had already cleared his calendar so he could take Diane to Switzerland for the month. They would spend their honeymoon at a special hospital reputed to perform miracles on patients with Diane's type of injury. He was going to get her there no matter what.

After climbing out of the limousine, he handed Mac the sack before approaching his fiancée. Though her light brown eyes still looked haunted, she broke into a smile when she saw him.

He gave her a quick kiss on the lips knowing what he had to say would disappoint her, but it couldn't be helped.

"This problem with the romance cover needs to be dealt with. I'm afraid our plans to go into New York for dinner have to be put on hold."

"Somehow I knew you were going to say that."

"Drew's meeting me as soon as he can."

"That's good."

"After we've finished talking, I'll call you. In the meantime, Sam will run you home."

He pushed her wheelchair to the limousine, then lifted her into the back seat. Catherine and the dog ran over to say goodbye while John folded up the chair and put it in the trunk.

"Promise you'll phone later and tell me what's going on?"

He couldn't look at her in this condition without being aware of her near lifeless legs. Though he might not have pulled the trigger, he was the reason she couldn't walk.

"You know I will." He gave her hand a squeeze, then shut the limo door.

"'Bye, Diane," Catherine called to her.

As the car drove off, Payne put an arm around his niece and walked her toward the house. He needed to get his laptop. "I want to thank you for being so good to Diane."

"I want her to get better."

"So do I." *So do I.*

"She's decided she'll never walk again, but I told her that's crazy because she still has feeling in her legs. I won't let her give up! Even if she doesn't want to go to that clinic in Switzerland, you have to take her, Uncle Payne."

He held the door open for her and the dog. Once they'd entered the house he said, "That's my plan."

"While you were in the village, she broke down crying and said she didn't want to go through another operation when it wouldn't do her any good."

Payne gritted his teeth. "I'm afraid seeing me on the cover of that book has brought back the horror of what she went through at Christmas."

"Then all the more reason for her to fight with everything she's got to get better!" Catherine blurted. "At least her doctor hasn't said her case is hopeless. It's not like what happened with Trevor," her voice wobbled.

"You're right." He kissed her forehead. "I love you for caring so much. When your mom asked me to look in on you while they were in Mexico, I was happy to do it. Tell you what— I'll free up some time tomorrow afternoon and take you and Diane sailing."

"She doesn't like to sail."

Payne had an idea something unpleasant had happened between Catherine and Diane. "What's wrong, sweetheart?"

"Nothing," came the quiet response.

"You can say that to anyone but me."

His niece looked up at him with soulful blue eyes. "Diane got after me about reading romances. She said they're a waste of time and don't reflect real life."

Until Payne had a chance to read *Manhattan Merger*, he would reserve judgment.

"You shouldn't take her disapproval to heart. She's a little down right now."

"I'm not. She's been like this since you got engaged."

His brows knit together. "Like what?"

"Let's just say she has a hard time tolerating me when you're not around."

"That's not true, Catherine. She cares for you enough to have wanted your help with our wedding plans."

"She only asked me because you hinted it might be a good idea while mom and dad were away. I never told you this, but two years ago at that Fourth of July party on the yacht, Linda and I figured out Diane was in love with you when she told us to run along and leave you two alone.''

After what Catherine had just told him, he realized his perceptive niece understood a lot more about his fiancée than he'd given her credit for.

With so much on his mind at the time, Payne had been oblivious to Diane's interest in him. If he hadn't left his office that night... But all the what-ifs in the world weren't going to change the situation that had shattered lives and dreams.

After finding his laptop in the study he said, ''Why don't you ask Linda to come sailing with us tomorrow, Diane or no Diane.''

''Really?'' Catherine's face broke into a sunny smile. ''Thanks, Uncle Payne. You're the greatest!'' She stood up on tiptoe to kiss his cheek. ''I'll invite her when we get together later.''

''You do that. See you later.''

''Okay. Come on, Lady.''

Before he left the house to join Mac in the other limo for the short drive ride to Crag's Head, he watched the dog follow her up the stairs. The Sterlings loved their animals. Payne was no exception, but after his bullmastiff Bruno had died, he'd decided not to get another dog.

Since moving into his new home, he was gone too much. It wouldn't be fair to keep a pet when he was away a lot of the time. They needed constant love and attention.

When he joined Mac in the limo he confided, ''A few days ago I told Diane I missed having a dog and planned to get her one for a wedding present so she wouldn't be so lonely when I'm overseas. Apparently that's the last thing she wants, even though I pointed out it could serve as a guard dog too.''

"It's not really surprising when you consider her mother's allergy to them," Mac murmured back. "Your fiancée didn't grow up around animals."

Payne rubbed the bridge of his nose. "Diane claims she's been in love with me for years, but since our engagement she's begun to realize how little we have in common. I'm afraid I'm not the perfect man she thought I was."

Mac eyed him frankly. "Don't hate me for saying this, but someone should have warned her about the old saying, 'Be careful what you pray for. You might get it.'"

"You're scary, Mac."

"How so?"

"You just took the words right out of my mouth. Last night she broke down and admitted she doesn't like my home." Mac grimaced. "Instead of a dog for a wedding present, could we build an English manor along the lines of her parents' home?

"I reminded her that as an only child she would inherit her family home one day, and could spend as much time as she wanted there after our marriage."

Mac didn't say anything. Neither did Payne.

After leaving his sister's sprawling New England style home which was reminiscent of many homes in the Hamptons, he craved his eyrie at Crag's Head.

Money could buy a lot of things he would never want, and it had brought him more pain than he'd ever thought possible. But if he could be grateful for one thing, it had allowed him to turn his ideas for the old lighthouse standing on family property into a sanctuary of primitive beauty and isolation.

Payne was an engineer, not an architect, but he'd known what he'd wanted the moment he'd glimpsed Le Corbusier's Chapel of Notre Dame Du Haut at Ronchamps for the first time.

Using a sculptural style rather than rectilinear, the famous French architect had created two curving walls of white-washed rough masonry that met beneath a dark roof.

Incorporating those same elements with the lighthouse, Payne's home stood like a piece of sculpture on the headland overlooking the Atlantic. The randomly punched out windows of the walls gave him all the privacy and all the view he could ever want.

He liked being able to walk around while he studied where he would lay massive fiber-optic cables in a place as difficult as New York's labyrinthine underground.

The urban fiber networks were one of the least-developed pieces of Internet infrastructure throughout the world. Payne had always considered it a market of vast potential.

Pleased to have been responsible for putting five million kilometers of glass thread in the ground already, he was now selling rights to individual strands of fiber outright. World carriers and corporations were coming to him every day asking for more.

When he'd had the place built, he hadn't yet met the woman he'd wanted to marry. If he'd given it any thought at all, he'd imagined that when the right one came along, she'd love it as much as he did.

Last night he'd promised Diane he would add some interior features to the second floor to make it less austere and fortress-like.

As for the lighthouse portion of his house, it had been transformed into an open workspace. It was here in his inner sanctum he used the thick rounded walls to spread out his huge maps of the tunneling beneath major American and European cities.

Considering he was in negotiations for the rights-of-way to dig in fifty more markets by next year, there was no way of gauging where it would lead in future years. But it ensured he wouldn't run out of problems to solve. That's what he loved to do.

That's why he was taking Diane to Switzerland, even if he had to drag her there. And if working with those doctors didn't produce a cure, he'd heard of another one who ran a clinic for injuries to the spine in Norway.

If Payne had already figured out how to unearth dazzling riches lying in mud beneath the streets of New York, Paris and Rome, surely he could find a way for Diane to walk again!

"Betty?" he called to Mrs. Myers. She and her husband lived in to look after his house and do light housekeeping. "I'm expecting Drew Wallace later tonight. When he gets here, let him in my study, will you please?"

"Of course. Would you like something to eat before he arrives?"

"How about a sandwich."

"Coming right up."

Taking advantage of the time, he sat back in his easy

chair, adjusted the floor lamp light and began reading *Manhattan Merger.*

The opening line grabbed him by the throat.

Logan Townsend wasn't in love with his fiancée.

From that point on it was like walking through the minefield of his own psyche where his deepest thoughts and feelings were exposed at every unexpected turn. By the time he came to the last page and closed the book, his hands were literally shaking.

He recalled something Catherine had said before he'd left for Crag's Head.

Diane got after me about reading romances. She said they're a waste of time and don't reflect real life.

How wrong could Diane have been!

If Payne could be thankful for one thing, it was that Catherine hadn't read the story yet. It would bring her even more pain.

Once more the painting on the cover leaped out at him, underscoring his shock that this book with his picture was in circulation.

"Payne?"

At the sound of Drew's familiar voice, he levered himself from the chair. Only then did he realize he'd been too riveted to the well-written story to notice Betty had brought him a tray of food some time ago. Unfortunately his appetite had left him.

"I'm glad you're here."

"Good grief. You look like you've seen a ghost!"

"I wish that were the case. A ghost I could deal with," he muttered grimly.

Payne handed him the book. "I just finished reading it. No one, and I mean *no one,* could have reached down into my soul to pull things out the way this author did. I'm talking secret thoughts and feelings here.''

His attorney took it from him and studied the cover. ''There's no doubt about it. The person who did this artwork used a picture or photograph of you. Let's see the other books.''

Payne emptied the sack onto his desk. Drew examined the covers of all the books.

When he eventually looked up he said, ''Every day of life your picture appears somewhere in the newspapers or tabloids. The public has free access. That means you'll always be a target for unsolicited attention.

''But to find a painted picture of you on the cover of a book without your express written permission is a legal matter, never mind that the person responsible might or might not be a stalker.''

''So you don't believe this could be a coincidence?''

Drew pursed his lips. ''You have an aura that goes everywhere with you. Whoever did this painting caught your essence as well as the outer shell. I've a hunch this person has met you before, probably at your office.''

Payne agreed, still haunted by the story. ''I doubt the artist and the author are the same person, but I suppose it's possible,'' he theorized. ''Regardless, something needs to be done right away. My niece and fiancée are terrified.''

''With good reason,'' his attorney came back. ''I admit I don't like this either.'' His thick brows met in a frown. ''Rest assured I'll look into it first thing in the morning, then get back to you. I'll take these with me.'' He scooped up the books and put them in the sack.

''I promised the woman at the bookstore she'd get the

four books back with my picture on them by Thursday at the latest.''

''No problem.''

Payne walked him to the north door which led to the pad where the helicopter was waiting. ''Thanks for coming tonight.''

''It was my pleasure. The sooner we find out if we need to call in the FBI, the better.''

As he closed the door, Payne wasn't sure anything earthly could help. Not when the author knew things about him no one knew but God...

CHAPTER TWO

LORRAINE Bennett, known to most people as Rainey, had just set everything up to paint when her phone rang. It was only eight-twenty a.m.

Since she paid extra on her phone bill to avoid taking telemarketing calls, she figured it was Barbara Landers, one of the secretaries who worked for Mr. Goldberg, Rainey's boss at Global Greeting Cards.

Barb was the same age as Rainey, and single. They'd hit it off the first day they were introduced. Since then they'd often eaten lunch or dinner together.

Through Barbara, who was a native New Yorker, Rainey had met a lot of her friends at weekend parties. A couple of guys had already asked her to other parties and films.

Ken Granger, another guy who lived in her building and was clerking for a law firm, had taken her to dinner several times. Rainey's mother didn't need to worry that her daughter lacked for a social life.

Stepping away from the easel, she walked over to her desk and picked up the receiver.

"Rainey Bennett Fine Art Studio."

"Rainey? It's Don Felt again."

"Oh— Hi, Don!"

He was the head of the art department at Red Rose Romance Publishers. Only yesterday he'd phoned her about a new project, and had already faxed her the art-work sheets she needed to get started.

Between commissions from Global Greeting Cards and Red Rose, she had more work than she could handle at the moment. But of course she would never say no to a new project. This was her life and her livelihood!

"Sorry to bother you this early."

"This isn't early for me. I've already had my morning run in the park. What can I do for you?"

"Could you give me the name and phone number of the agency in Colorado you used for the male model on that sensational cover of *Manhattan Merger*?"

Her gaze clicked to the wall where she'd hung her oil paintings. Rainey was flattered that five out of the eight she'd done with him as the hero had already been sold to the authors who'd written the books featuring him on their covers. The ninth was in the beginning stages.

She had to admit those paintings *were* sensational even if she said so herself. However it was the *man* on the covers who made them so riveting. Rainey had only been the vessel to put him there.

"I didn't find him through a modeling agency, Don."

The artist in Rainey had been drawn to the face and body of a stranger whose rugged male beauty made her want to put him on every cover she did for Red Rose Romance.

It seemed the sales on those books had been phenomenal. The company had sent her red roses several times congratulating her for her excellent work.

Even better, the company had increased her salary to the point that she'd finally been able to move to New

York and live on what she made doing artwork for them and the greeting card company.

"So—this masculine heartthrob who is setting hundreds of thousands of female hearts aflutter around the world is a figment of your imagination?"

"No." She sucked in her breath. "I'm afraid even my psyche couldn't dream up anyone that gorgeous."

"Then he must be a boyfriend you've been keeping secret from me."

She chuckled. "Don't I wish. To be honest, I have no idea who the man is."

After a slight pause, "Then how did you get permission to paint him?"

"I didn't. About two years ago I saw him in a photograph. His looks were so incredible, I found myself sketching him every time I went near my drawing board."

"Whose photograph?" he asked without preamble.

"My brother's."

"Do you still have it?"

"It was never mine to take. The only reason I happened to see it was because I was helping my mom clean his bedroom before he came home to go back to college.

"You know me and how I work. I often get ideas from people I see on the street or in a photo or some such thing. Later on if a face haunts me enough, I end up sketching it from memory.

"That's what happened in this case. A third of the covers I've painted for Red Rose have been done without models."

"I know, and there's never been any kind of problem. Maybe there isn't now."

She gripped the receiver a little tighter. "What's wrong, Don?"

"Possibly nothing. The legal department sent me a memo asking for the information."

She blinked. "Legal department... Do you know what this is about?"

"Not yet. But since you admit you saw this face in a photograph, humor me and talk to your brother."

"Don—you don't understand. The man in that picture was simply one of a group of vacationers. Craig is a whitewater river guide. Every summer he takes dozens of groups on float trips down the Colorado, and always gets a picture of them at the place where they put in.

"This is his sixth year. He must have close to a hundred group photos lying in a box in his bedroom closet. I have no idea how old that picture even was."

"Are they dated?"

"Probably. I wasn't paying any attention at the time. He plans to open up his own sporting goods store one day soon and use them for wall decor along with trophy fish and elk he's had mounted. He might remember something unique about a particular trip, but I doubt very much he could recall a name."

"Will you ask him anyway? Then get back to me with the information A.S.A.P.?"

"It's the end of June, Don. He's been running rivers for the last three weeks. All I can do is leave a message at Horsehead Whitewater Expeditions. That's the company Craig works for.

"They'll get word to my brother to call me, but it might take anywhere from a few days to a week before I hear from him."

There was another silence that increased her nervousness.

"Tell you what," Don murmured at last. "I'm going to contact the legal department and find out why they're asking questions. Then I'll get back to you. Will you be there for a while?"

"Yes. I'm finishing up the painting for the cover of *The Bride's Not-So-White Secret,* and will send it over to your office by courier the day after tomorrow."

"Excellent. I'll look forward to seeing it. Expect to hear from me soon."

After they'd clicked off, she returned to the painting in question propped on her easel. Unfortunately the reason for Don's phone call had taken the zip out of her morning.

Instead of reaching for the brush to fill in the last bit of lace on the bridal gown, she walked over to the painting she'd done for *Manhattan Merger.*

There he was. The embodiment of her dreams come to life on a piece of canvas:

Rich dark brown hair that looked vibrant to the touch.

Nordic blue eyes that seemed to envision things no one else could even imagine.

Rugged facial features denoting a life of hard work, sacrifice and triumphs.

The build and stance of a conquerer beneath his business suit. Someone who dared to explore new frontiers.

A man who hadn't yet been transformed by a woman's love…

Perhaps because his total *persona* had enchanted her, she'd managed to breathe life into him. Enough life that she'd just been told this particular cover had taken first prize among all the covers on romance novels published by the various companies in the U.S. over the last twelve months.

The romance writing industry was going to present her with an award in August. Bonnie Wrigley, the author, would also receive an award for writing *Manhattan Merger,* chosen the best romance novel from the Touch of Romance line.

Much as Rainey was thrilled by this honor, she coveted this particular rendering of the man in the painting too much to part with it.

When Bonnie Wrigley had made inquiries to the art department for its purchase, Rainey had told Don it wasn't for sale. But she'd urged him to tell Ms. Wrigley that if it happened Rainey was the artist chosen to do another cover for her, she could have that painting for a minimal fee.

The phone rang again. Rainey rushed to answer it.

"Don?"

"No. It's Grace Carlow, the senior attorney in the legal department at Red Rose Publishing. I just got off the phone with Don and decided to call you myself."

Though the window air conditioner worked well, Rainey felt perspiration bead her forehead.

"Thanks for getting back to me so fast. I have to admit I'm a little anxious."

"After talking to Don, I think we're going to be all right. Where are you?"

"Near Eighty-Sixth Street and Lexington."

"That's good. Can you be at my office by ten?"

Rainey's green eyes widened. "You mean today?"

"Absolutely. The sooner we put out this fire, the better."

That didn't sound good.

"I'll explain when you get here. Come to the second floor. Make a left. I'm at the end of the hall."

The line went dead.

With heart pounding, Rainey showered and dressed in a straw colored wraparound skirt and pale blue cotton top. She brushed her gilt-blond hair which had been styled in a feather cut, slid on sandals and flew out the door of her furnished studio apartment.

There was no elevator, however the stairs were carpeted. She hurried down three flights to the entrance of the pre-World War II building, calling out hello to several people who lived there.

She'd been lucky to find a place this close to the Metropolitan Museum. Her rent might be horrible, and the landlord didn't allow pets which forced her to leave her dog behind with her parents. However this was a once in a lifetime opportunity.

If things didn't work out and her commissions fell off, she'd go back to Colorado. But she didn't anticipate that happening anytime soon.

So far the conversation with the attorney had sounded the only discordant note since she'd moved here four months ago.

After living in a small town all her life, she felt tiny walking between the skyscrapers. New York was like being in a different universe with every race and type of person represented. She loved the explosion of humanity amid the famous landmarks. Rainey loved the smells and sounds.

She loved Manhattan.

There was a pulse throbbing here. She was now a part of it. That's what made every day exciting.

Until today.

Since the phone call she'd had this awful pit in her stomach.

What if she'd done something so terrible, her happiness would be taken away?

Fear made her walk faster.

She entered Red Rose Publishers and took the stairs to the second floor. After reaching the end of the hall she entered the legal department and walked over to the front desk.

"I'm Lorraine Bennett. Grace Carlow is expecting me."

A young female receptionist told her to go on back to the first door on her left. Rainey complied.

"Good! You're on time." The attorney waved her inside. She was a tall, big-boned woman who was probably in her early sixties. She wore a white pantsuit with a black and white houndstooth print blouse. From the crown of her upswept blond hair she pulled down her glasses and studied Rainey for a moment.

"How old are you?"

"Twenty-seven."

"You don't look a day over twenty-one. Lucky you. Call me Grace." She smiled and extended her hand which Rainey shook. "Sit down."

Rainey took the chair opposite her desk. "I take it I've painted a celebrity by accident."

The woman made a funny noise in her throat. "Ever heard of the Sterling bank of America?"

She bit her lip. "Who hasn't?"

"Ever heard of Sterling Shipping lines?"

Rainey's body started to feel heavier in the chair. She nodded.

"Ever hear of U.S. Supreme Court Justice Richard Sterling?"

"Yes," Rainey whispered.

"Ever hear of Senator Phyllis Sterling-Boyce? Ambassador Lloyd Sterling? Rear Admiral Daniel Sterling?"

Her eyes closed tightly for a moment. "Of course."

By now Rainey was squirming.

Grace handed her a recent publication of *World Fortune Magazine*. "The whole lot of them don't even count compared to *this* Sterling."

Rainey took one look at the man on the cover and gasped.

King of Glass New York Billionaire-soon-to-be-Trillionaire Payne Sterling discovers ancient burial ground while mucking about with fiber-optic cable in his underworld kingdom close to Wall Street.

She read the caption twice before she studied the man in hard hat and jeans resting against an enormous cable.

Like pure revelation she understood why she'd been so drawn to him that she'd felt compelled to put his face and body to canvas.

"Oh boy." Rainey's voice shook before she handed the magazine back to Grace.

The attorney eyed her with compassion. "Oh boy is right. He's the embodiment of one of the sons of the Earl of Sterling who left England for America to build an empire of his own."

She tapped the cover. "This one shuns publicity like it was the plague of mankind, but he's so damned attractive it still comes after him, innocently or otherwise."

She winked at Rainey who groaned out loud.

"Cynthia Taft, the newest attorney to join our staff, handled *Manhattan Merger* while I was on a leave of absence. She came to us from Los Angeles and probably didn't catch the likeness because Payne Sterling is a celebrity in a very different pond than that of Hollywood.

"When I returned, I noticed his likeness on the cover and brought it to Claud's attention. However he said not to worry about it because there'd been no trouble with the other covers. What was done, was done, and this wouldn't be the first time an artist had unwittingly painted a cover that resembled a real person."

"Except that I did draw his face from memory," Rainey admitted.

"According to Don, you do that quite often."

"Yes."

"As I told you on the phone, I think we're going to be fine, but it will take the rest of the day to prepare our case."

Her pulse raced faster. "Case?"

"His attorney has already filed papers with the court. A judge is going to hold a closed door hearing tomorrow at two o'clock, so we have our work cut out."

"What?" Rainey cried out aghast. "You mean he's suing me?"

"You, the author Bonnie Wrigley and Red Rose Publishers."

"Good heavens—"

Grace's eyebrows lifted. "Don't forget you're dealing with a Sterling. The name moves mountains. But not to worry. He won't win.

"By the way, who's the person at Global Greeting Cards who will give us an affidavit to the effect that you haven't put Mr. Sterling on any of their products?"

That was easy. "Saul Goldberg."

She nodded. "I know Saul. Good man. All right. First things first. If we can get your mother and brother here in twenty-four hours, let's do it. Red Rose will be paying their expenses."

"Mom could come. But I don't know if it's possible to reach my brother in time."

Grace eyed her intently. "Try. Mr. Sterling's attorney, Drew Wallace, is the best there is if you know what I mean. He's pulled this in the hope of catching us unprepared, but we'll show him."

Rainey admired the other woman's grit. Though she didn't know anything about Grace Carlow, she had an idea the attorney was actually enjoying this.

"I'll have to phone the company Craig works for and see if they can find him. My mother knows the number."

"As long as you're phoning her, tell her to bring that photograph with her. One more thing. Don said you do preliminary sketches before you start your paintings. Where are your drawings of Mr. Sterling?"

She gave Grace a sheepish glance. "The old ones are stored at my parents' home."

"Do you have pictures of them on disk?"

"No, only the finished portraits. Those disks are at my apartment."

"I see. Tell your mother to bring the drawings too.

When you get back to your apartment, burn the *new* ones!'' she fired.

Rainey could weep for the sketches she'd done of him in cowboy gear as recently as three days ago. Sketches that would never appear on another book cover.

''Use my phone while I have a talk with Cynthia who's trying to track down Bonnie Wrigley. I'll be back in a minute to depose you.''

As soon as Grace left the room, Rainey hurried around the desk to call home. It was only quarter after eight in Grand Junction. Her father was a dentist and had probably left for his office already. He would have to get his partner to cover for him so he could drive her mom to the Denver airport with the requested items.

Later in the year, after all his little patients were back in school, her folks had plans to fly out to New York. They were going to spend time taking in the sights, then rent a car and drive Rainey through New England to see the turning of the leaves.

As it stood, her mom, and possibly her brother, were going to get an unexpected sneak preview of New York from the inside of a courtroom.

''Good news,'' Grace announced ten minutes later. ''Bonnie Wrigley will be at our office in the morning. How are things on your end?''

''Mom will fly in tonight with the items we need. The company Craig works for knows where he is and will get back to my father. Dad will call your office to let us know what's happening.''

''Excellent. What do you want for lunch? They have great goulash and cheesecake at the deli down the street.''

"That sounds good."

"Are you a coffee drinker?"

"No. Water or juice is fine."

She nodded before buzzing her secretary.

"All right." Grace sat forward with her fingers interlinked on top of the desk. "What Mr. Wallace will do is try to show that Red Rose Publishers willfully broke the law by using his client's likeness on the covers for monetary gain without obtaining his permission.

"He's asked us to bring the figures on the sales of those books to show that revenues went up when his client appeared on the covers."

"This is all my fault," Rainey whispered, feeling more and more ill by the moment. "He should be taking *me* to court, not the company."

"We're a family here at Red Rose. We defend our own, and we'll prove it was an honest mistake. The worst to happen will be that we're barred from using Mr. Sterling's likeness on any more covers.

"It's a shame, really," she added. "Though he's responsible for developing a whole new world-wide infrastructure, ninety-nine percent of our romance readership has no idea that Mr. Payne Sterling exists. All they care about is the man on those covers who is drop-dead gorgeous."

Rainey averted her eyes. "He is that."

"And you're the remarkable artist who brought him to breathtaking life. *Manhattan Merger* ranks among the ten bestselling novels ever put out at Red Rose. That speaks highly for you and Bonnie Wrigley who wrote the terrific story in the first place. Red Rose is lucky to have both of you on the team."

"Thank you. I hope you'll still be saying that when the hearing is over."

"I'm not worried. The truth will set us free, my dear. Why don't you start by telling me the process you went through from the moment Don phoned you about *Manhattan Merger* until you shipped off your painting to New York. Don't worry about dates. He has already supplied me with everything I need in that regard."

Without preamble Rainey explained how she worked up a project. Grace interjected a question here and there. Lunch came and went. Still they talked. At three the phone rang through to Grace's office.

It was Rainey's father on the phone to tell her Craig's company had flown him to Las Vegas by helicopter and he would be arriving at JFK airport before midnight.

Grace's eyes lit up at that news. "Your brother will be one of the key witnesses in your defense. I couldn't be more pleased to know he's coming. This is going even better than I expected."

"If you say so," Rainey murmured.

"I do. Tomorrow morning we'll assemble here at eight-thirty in the conference room down the hall. I'll rehearse what's going to happen and prepare your mother and brother for the kinds of questions Mr. Wallace will ask during cross-examination. Your job will be to perform for Mr. Wallace."

Rainey frowned. "What do you mean?"

"I have a hunch he'll show you a picture of a man or woman you've never seen before, then ask you to sketch them from memory. He'll supply you with a sketch pad and pencils."

"That won't be a problem."

"Of course not."

"What should I wear?"

"The outfit you have on is fine."

Rainey got up from the chair. "Thank you so much for your help. I'll never be able to pay you back."

"This is part of my job."

"I'm still grateful to you. See you in the morning."

On the way back to her apartment, Rainey stopped to buy food and flowers before hurrying home to clean and get things ready for her family.

Her mother arrived by taxi at seven p.m., her brother at eleven. He'd come with his backpack and bed roll which turned out to be a blessing. Her mom could use the hide-a-bed and Rainey would sleep on the futon.

She would have given anything if their reunion could have happened under different circumstances. The idea that a New York billionaire was suing her and Red Rose Publishers was like her worst nightmare.

Before they all went to bed, Rainey sorted through the pile of photographs to find the one that had gotten her into so much trouble. When she finally came across it and showed it to her brother, he remembered the man, but not the name.

"What was he like, Craig?"

"He was in a group of twenty people. I do recall he was congenial, fascinated by everything and seemed totally at home on the water."

"Nothing else?"

"There is one thing that stood out," her brother murmured. "When I take people on a float trip, I mentally pick someone in the group I could count on to help in an emergency. He was the one I chose. Most people panic a little at some point on the river, but he never did.''

After hearing Craig's testimonial, Rainey couldn't equate the man she'd painted with the person who could bring financial ruin to so many lives.

Grace had done her best to reassure Rainey things would be all right, but she had a hard time believing it. During the night she'd broken down sobbing. So, apparently, had Bonnie Wrigley who'd shown up in the conference room the next morning with drawn features and puffy eyes.

This was the first time they'd met each other. The minute the two women saw each other, they went out in the hall to commiserate in private.

At this point Rainey's guilt had increased a hundredfold. If it hadn't been for her cover, there would be no suit. Now poor Bonnie was going to have to explain how she dreamed up *Manhattan Merger*, where she got her ideas.

Before long Grace summoned them back to the conference room. The morning flew by while she coached everyone. After lunch was served, their entourage of twenty people left in taxis for the courthouse on Broadway.

When Rainey arrived with her family, it seemed to her there were an inordinate amount of security guards stationed outside the building. To her surprise, even more were positioned inside.

Several guards escorted her and her family to the designated courtroom where she saw more guards in place.

Though she might not be wearing handcuffs or leg chains, Rainey felt like a criminal. By the time they were seated down in front on the right side of the courtroom, she thought she would lose her lunch right there.

Grace came in with Cynthia Taft, the other attorney. They brought a look of calm as they took their places at the table in front of Rainey. Still she wasn't comforted. When she glanced at Bonnie, the other woman shook her head as if to say she couldn't believe this was happening.

Rainey couldn't fathom it either. There was an air of unreality about the entire situation.

Yesterday she'd gotten up motivated and happy, then received a phone call that had changed her whole life in an instant.

Immersed in pain, Rainey didn't notice the arrival of the opposition until Craig whispered to her.

She turned her head to see two men in dark business suits walking down the left aisle toward the table. Her gaze fell helplessly on the man from the photograph. The one whose looks and vitality had caught her artist's eye as no other man had done before.

He was tall and powerfully built, just as she'd remembered from the photograph. Yet he moved with careless male grace. It was one of those intangible traits you had to be born with.

The pool of genes that had come together to form the gorgeous man known as Payne Sterling was remarkable enough. When combined with the spirit that lived inside his body, he radiated a dynamism that made him much more attractive to her in person.

Afraid to be caught staring, she averted her eyes. It galled her to realize she could still be having these kinds of thoughts about him when he was the reason they were in court now.

''All rise.''

Shocked to hear the bailiff's voice, Rainey lifted her head in time to see the judge enter the courtroom and take his seat.

''The court of New York County, New York, is now in session. The Honorable James E. Faulkner, Supervising Judge of New York City, is presiding.

Supervising judge of New York? Rainey's legs trembled.

''You may be seated.''

CHAPTER THREE

THE judge adjusted his glasses.

"The case of Sterling versus Red Rose Romance Publishers et al has come before the court in an emergency show causing hearing. All who testify will be sworn in.

"Mr. Drew Wallace, Counsel for the Plaintiff, will make opening remarks, followed by opening remarks from Ms. Grace Carlow, Chief Counsel for the Defendants."

Long ago Payne had learned the trick of staying focused. Never look at the opposition when inside the courtroom, but stare them down outside of it. That strategy had served him well in his business dealings. It would serve him even better in this particular circumstance.

The possibility that there might be a stalker within these walls never left his mind. After the experience of tackling that lunatic too late to protect Diane, he had no desire to look into the face of another psychotic woman with the potential to do harm.

This moment hadn't come soon enough for him or his family. He exchanged a private glance with Drew before his attorney got to his feet.

"Your Honor—Ms. Carlow—my client wouldn't have pushed for an emergency hearing without just cause. Six months ago he and his fiancée were entering his parents' home when a stalker shot at them. His fiancée is now in a wheelchair and may never walk again.

"Besides this tragic event, there have been half a dozen other stalking incidences in my client's past where police had to be called in and people arrested and prosecuted. It's all a matter of public record which I've submitted to the court.

"Two days ago my client discovered he was the man on the cover of a Red Rose Romance entitled *Manhattan Merger,* which I shall enter here in evidence as Exhibit One. The painting was done without his knowledge or permission." He handed it to the bailiff who took it to the judge.

"Apparently eight covers have been created with his likeness, all without his knowledge or permission. As you can see by the title of this particular story, it takes place in New York City. If you'll read the blurb on the back, it mentions a New York Billionaire who has an accident in the Canyonlands of the American West.

"In reading the novel, my client became alarmed by the amount of similarities to his life and that of the protagonist's.

"I have never been the victim of a stalker, but my client and his loved ones have already paid an enormous price because of the behavior of some crazed people in our society.

"My client has asked for a hearing to determine if this is a case of art imitating life to an uncanny degree, or if there is something more sinister behind so many incredible coincidences.

"Should today's hearing prove the latter, he wants

this dealt with before anyone else gets hurt or killed. On
that note I defer to Ms. Carlow.''

Payne gave Drew a satisfied nod.

''Your Honor, I speak for myself and everyone present when I say that we deeply regret Mr. Sterling's pain
and suffering. The legal department at Red Rose
Romance should have caught the problem when the first
painting for *The Star Grazer* was shipped to our office.

''I noticed a likeness to Mr. Sterling in his facial structure and body type then, but the hero came from the
future. He had red hair and brown eyes. I assumed it
was a coincidence. It wouldn't be the first time a hero
or heroine on one of our covers happened to resemble a
real person.

''When the second painting of *Her Prince of Dreams*
arrived, I again saw similarities though the hero had
black eyes and black hair. However I still didn't feel
concerned enough to say anything.

''It wasn't until Ms. Bennett had painted *Manhattan
Merger,* that I could see the hero did indeed personify
Mr. Payne Sterling. I believed it was because she'd
placed him in a contemporary New York setting with
the kinds of clothes a man in his position would wear
to his corporate office.

''At this point I brought it to the head of the company's attention. Mr. Finauer said not to worry about it
because there'd been no problem with the other covers.

''Though I can understand and sympathize with Mr.
Sterling's alarm, as the attorney for Red Rose Romance
Publishers, may I assure the court and Mr. Sterling that
there is no stalker in this room as will be borne out in
testimony.

"To save the court's time I've already supplied a list of witnesses in the order in which they will appear in this court. I've given the same list to Mr. Wallace, and have indicated home addresses, phone numbers and job descriptions."

The judge nodded. "Then this court will proceed. Ms. Farr, please take the witness stand."

While the bailiff administered the oath, Payne could see that a sizable group from the opposition had assembled. Red Rose's attorney had come prepared. He would give them that much credit.

"Ms. Farr," Ms. Carlow began, "state your full name and job description."

"My name is Margaret Farr. I'm the head editor for the *Touch of Romance* line at Red Rose Publishers."

"How long have you been at Red Rose?"

"Fifteen years."

"Tell us about your relationship with Bonnie Wrigley, the author of *Manhattan Merger*. Give the court an idea of the process."

"Bonnie's first manuscript came through the slush pile ten years ago. It was a wonderful book and I phoned her to tell her we were going to publish it. Since then she has written twenty-seven novels for us. *Manhattan Merger* was her twenty-fourth book. It was written for a promotion called 'Urban Tycoons.'"

Urban tycoons?

"Will you explain what you mean by a promotion?"

"Every month we put out six books in the *Touch of Romance* line. One or two of these books are usually part of a promotion or theme that has particular appeal for readers around the world. I made the suggestion to

Bonnie that she write to the Urban Tycoon theme. She came up with *Manhattan Merger.''*

"Thank you, Ms. Farr. You can step down. I'd like to call Bonnie Wrigley to the stand."

To Payne's surprise the woman who was the next witness looked to be in her late fifties. Somehow he couldn't see her as a stalker, but he didn't suppose age mattered if a person were that unstable.

"Ms. Wrigley? Tell the court where you live."

"Spokane, Washington."

"Is writing a full-time career for you?"

"No. I'm a full-time Spanish teacher and write on the side."

"How long have you been a teacher?"

"Twenty-six years."

"How long have you been a writer?"

"Since I was twelve, but I didn't get published until ten years ago."

"Tell the court how you came up with your idea for *Manhattan Merger.''*

"When Margaret asked me if I'd like to write a book about a big tycoon, I decided he would have to be a billionaire because millionaires are too common these days.

"Since I'd already done several millionaire stories with European heroes who'd come from titled backgrounds, I thought I'd feature an American with ties to the English aristocracy. Someone whose family had amassed a fortune in real estate and shipping on the East Coast and had created a world bank.

"I decided he would have to be plagued by a problem that his billions couldn't fix.

"I thought, what if this billionaire has been diagnosed with leukemia? What if he decides to take a two week trip away from his fiancée and family to get his head on straight before he tells them what he found out during a routine physical exam? They think he's gone on another of his business ventures.

"As the blurb says, he has an accident in Canyonlands and is flown to a Las Vegas hospital where his secret is discovered by the attending physician who falls in love with him.

"I pictured her as a hardworking, dedicated young doctor who hasn't had time for men until now. Realizing the hero needs a bone marrow transplant, she asks everyone on the staff to give blood to find him a donor.

"When it turns out she could be a donor, the transplant takes place. It isn't until he returns to New York that he learns she helped save his life. When he confronts her, she tells him she did it because she loves him, but never wanted him to know because he's engaged to someone else.

"He confesses he was already in love with her before the transplant took place. As soon as he returned to New York, he broke off his engagement. Now he's proposing marriage. It's a Manhattan merger she can't turn down, not when they're joined body, blood and soul."

"Thank you, Ms. Wrigley. You can be seated. Mr. Felt? If you'll take the stand please."

While the third witness was sworn in, Payne leaned toward Drew. "When you cross-examine the author, ask her why she picked ties to the English aristocracy, how she happened to put in the part about archaeological sites. Why did she choose leukemia?"

Drew had already been making notes and nodded.

"Mr. Felt? How long have you been head of the art department at Red Rose Publishers?"

"Twelve years."

"Tell us what you do. Take us through the process when you handled *Manhattan Merger*."

"As soon as a manuscript has been cleared for publication, the art department asks the author to fill out a form telling the theme of the book, the description of the hero and heroine, a short synopsis and a summary of several scenes that might look good on the cover.

"When we receive these sheets, we make a phone call to a freelance artist who does original oil paintings for Red Rose covers. We inform them we are sending information to help them create a painting that will sell books and please the author. We also send a printout of the manuscript for them to read.

"*Manhattan Merger* was handled like any other manuscript. I phoned one of our artists, Lorraine Bennett, about the project. She was free to go to contract on it. Our department sent her the filled out forms and the printout. She did the painting. When it was finished, she shipped it overnight courier to our office."

"Thank you, Mr. Felt. You can step down. Will Mr. Goldberg please take the stand?"

So far Payne hadn't heard anything to sway him either way. The artist was the person he wanted to tear apart with his bare hands. She would follow the next witness being sworn in.

"Mr. Goldberg?" Ms. Carlow began. "Tell the court where you work and what you do?"

"I'm the Vice President of Global Greeting Cards in New York."

"How long have you been with that company?"

"Nine years."

"Do all of your employees work in-house?"

"No we contract freelance writers and artists to produce the bulk of our inventory."

"Is Ms. Lorraine Bennett one of those artists?"

"Yes."

"Tell us the nature of her work."

"We send her the words, and she creates the art."

"Does she do portraits or people?"

"Neither. Her work is restricted to nature, flowers, wooded scenes, brooks and bridges, dogs and cats, that type of thing."

"How long has she worked for you?"

"Three years."

"Thank you, Mr. Goldberg. That will be all. Will Ms. Bennett please come to the stand?"

Payne answered some questions Drew had written down for him, then lifted his head. When he caught sight of the woman with the gilt-blond hair taking the oath, he felt a rush of adrenaline.

"I've seen that face before, Drew!"

"Where?"

He shook his dark head. "I don't know."

It was a fresh looking face. Wholesome. Attractive. So was the rest of her.

While he sat there staring at her, he racked his brain trying to remember.

"Ms. Bennett? Please tell the court where you live."

"In Manhattan."

"Have you always lived in New York?"

"No. I was born and raised in Grand Junction, Colorado. I only moved here four months ago."

Colorado—

Payne had once done some skiing there, but that was years ago. If she'd only been in New York since February, then she'd done all the covers of him while she'd lived in Grand Junction.

So how in the hell did she know what his office looked like? He knew for a fact she hadn't been to his suite when he'd been there or he would have remembered.

"Did you ever visit New York City previous to moving here?"

"No."

"How long have you worked for Red Rose Romance?"

"Four years."

"We know you're employed by Global Greeting Cards too. Before you started freelancing, what did you do? Give us your background."

"I graduated from Colorado State University in Fort Collins, Colorado, with a B.F.A. in Art Education. That included an internship in Castiglion Fiorentino, Italy. After graduation I was hired to teach art at a high school in Grand Junction."

"How long did you teach?"

"Six years."

Ms. Bennett didn't look old enough to have been a teacher to a bunch of rowdy high school students for that long a time. Boys that age raged with hormones. With a woman so attractive and shapely, he could just imagine the drawings they'd generated of her. Drawings she would never know about.

"Will you tell the court how you prepare when you're doing a cover for a book?"

"As soon as the art sheet information arrives, I read it carefully, particularly the theme. That's where all the emotion is centered. After that I read the novel and take a few days for the elements of the story to solidify in my mind. During that reflective period, I do research on the background details of the suggested scenes.

"Slowly the characters come to life for me. Sometimes I can picture him or her in my mind. When that happens, I start sketching like mad.

"Other times I study models from agencies until I see one that encapsulates my vision of the character in question. At that point I make an appointment for them to sit for me.

"Every day of life I see beautiful, interesting, fascinating faces in the crowd, in a photograph. Once in a while there will be a face that won't leave me alone.

"A certain bone structure, smooth olive skin, the lines of experience around a compelling mouth, piercing black eyes, the shape of an eyebrow black as a raven's wing— I find myself drawing this face weeks or even months later. Sometimes it ends up on the canvas."

"Tell us what happened when you painted the cover for *Manhattan Merger*."

Payne's gaze had been riveted on her classic features. There was a subtle change—a tension in her demeanor as soon as the attorney mentioned *Manhattan Merger*.

"The minute I read the novel, I knew who was going to be the male on the cover. I'd used him on seven other covers, but never as a contemporary American hero who is one of the powers that be in the corporate world.

"It was as if Bonnie Wrigley had written that novel with him in mind. Like the glass slipper that only fits Cinderella's foot, the melding of the right words and art can be a spiritual experience. That's how it was with *Manhattan Merger.*"

"Did you use a model?"

"No. I'd seen the man in a photograph while I was helping my mother clean my brother's room."

"Did you know who he was?"

"No. But he had the spirit of a Renaissance man who could achieve anything. That's what was needed for the cover of this story to make it throb with poignancy. Imagine the reader falling in love with this extraordinary man so far ahead of his time, so endowed with superb male attributes, only to find out he's dying of a disease he's powerless to stop."

A stillness went out over the courtroom Payne could feel.

"Thank you, Ms. Bennett. You may be seated. If Mrs. Ellen Bennett will please come forward."

Drew turned his head, eyeing Payne with an enigmatic expression. His attorney wasn't the only one who'd been thrown a curve. Payne didn't know what in the hell to think.

"Mrs. Bennett? Please tell the court who you are and where you live."

"I'm Rainey's mother. My husband and I live in Grand Junction, Colorado."

"Do you work?"

"I'm a housewife, the hardest work I know."

Payne covered his face with his hand to hide his amusement.

"What does your husband do for a living?"

"He's a dentist."

"Do you have more than one child?"

"Yes. A son, Craig."

"How old is he?"

"Twenty-five."

"And your daughter?"

"Twenty-seven."

Twenty-seven—Payne couldn't believe it.

"You heard your daughter testify she saw a man in a photograph, the same man who ended up on the covers of eight romances. Will you please tell the court the circumstances of that day?"

"Yes. Rainey had come over to the house from her apartment to help me spring houseclean Craig's bedroom. He's a packrat. While we were cleaning under his bed and straightening his closet, we found boxes of his memorabilia. Frankly, everything was in a mess.

"We decided to separate his belongings into piles and put them in separate baskets that could be stacked. Rainey found the photographs he'd been collecting over the years of his river running experiences."

The Colorado River—

Was that where Payne had seen her face?

"As she was placing them in one of the baskets she said, 'Oh mom—you've got to see the incredible man in this photograph!'

"I looked where she was pointing and had to admit he really was something. But knowing my daughter, I realized she was struck by things beneath the surface too. That's what makes her such a remarkable artist.

"She studied the picture a little longer, then put it away with all the other pictures. I never heard her mention him again. To my knowledge, she never went near Craig's closet again. In truth, neither of us would want to!"

In spite of the seriousness of the situation, Payne chuckled at the remark. He glanced at Drew. The other's man lips were twitching.

"Thank you, Mrs. Bennett. You may be seated. We have one more witness, Your Honor. Will Mr. Bennett please come to the stand?"

The blond Colorado River guide who'd shown Payne such a fantastic time two summers ago was the last person he expected to see in this courtroom. But there he was, bigger than life, reaching the witness stand in a few athletic strides.

When he turned around, Payne found himself looking at the male version of Ms. Rainey Bennett. Now he had his answer. Payne couldn't imagine a better looking brother and sister.

Unfortunately Craig Bennett's appealing white smile was missing. Dressed in a suit rather than cutoffs and T-shirt, he looked older, less approachable as he took the oath and sat down.

"Mr. Bennett? Please tell the court where you live, what you do for a living."

"When I'm in Grand Junction I live with my parents. During the summers I live in Las Vegas or on the Colorado River where I work for Horsehead Whitewater Expeditions."

"Tell the court the nature of your work."

"I'm a river guide for people who want to take a float trip down the Colorado River."

"How many trips do you take a summer?"

"Dozens."

"Does this involve individuals or groups of people?"

"I take as few as four, or as many as twenty at a time."

"Do you see anyone in this courtroom who has taken a trip down the Colorado with you?"

"Yes. My mom, my sister and the man sitting over there." He nodded in Payne's direction.

"Do you know his name?"

"I do now. At the time he used another name which I don't recall. Something like Vince or Vance."

"Vince," Payne whispered to Drew.

"Do you remember taking a picture of him?"

"I always snap a photo of my group where we put in the river."

"Your Honor?" Ms. Carlow interjected. "I have that picture with me and would like to enter it in evidence as Exhibit Two."

Payne watched the bailiff hand it to the judge. He studied it for a moment.

"Mr. Bennett?" opposing counsel continued. "Did you ever discuss this man with your sister?"

"Never."

"Did she ever bring him up to you?"

"No."

"Did you know she was making sketches of him from memory?"

"No."

"Have you ever read any of the romance novels with her paintings on the covers?"

"I would never read a romance novel period."

Strike two against the male of the species.

"Thank you, Mr. Bennett. You may step down. That's all I have to present at this time, Your Honor."

The judge's gaze swerved to Drew. "Mr. Wallace? Do you wish to cross-examine?"

"I do, Your Honor."

"May I remind the witnesses you are all still under oath. Go ahead, Mr. Wallace."

"If Ms. Wrigley will come forward again please?" As soon as the older woman took her place he said, "How many times have you visited New York City?"

"This is my first time."

"My client is curious to know why you picked English royalty, why the East Coast, why banking?"

"I'm a genealogist. I've researched most of my ancestors who came from England. They were all as poor as church mice. However when you dig back in those old English lines, you come across fascinating information about the families who descended from kings, lords, earls and the like to build new fortunes in America.

"Every time I come across information like that, I keep it in a special research file for my writing. Most of the wealthy arrivals had banking and shipping interests. Upon reaching our shores, it was common for them to buy large tracts of land on the East Coast."

"I see," Drew murmured. "When you filled out the art sheet, did you suggest Ms. Bennett put the picture of a ship and lighthouse on the wall of the hero's office?"

"No."

"What about the dog in the picture?"

"No."

"Will you explain why you inserted a scene in your book where the hero comes across an ancient burial ground and has it designated as an official archaeological site?"

"Yes. When Frontenac came to the Eastern seaboard on an exploration expedition for the King of France, he discovered this was a land filled with the bones of hundreds of thousands of men, women and children who'd died in great battles of extinction long before the white man came here.

"The State of New York is really one massive burial ground. Every so often a farmer is digging in a field and finds the remains of bodies thrown in haphazard piles, the points of their weapons of war still embedded in their bones.

"In *Manhattan Merger* my hero heads a corporation that develops land, but he's a man who respects the first inhabitants of this land. That's why I have him heading a foundation for the preservation of all ancient artifacts, mounds, burial grounds, observatories found in New York."

"Did you know of the name Payne Sterling when you wrote your novel?"

"I had no knowledge of his name or existence until yesterday when I received a phone call from the company attorney, Ms. Carlow."

"One last question. Why leukemia?"

"Years ago our daughter died of leukemia. That was something my husband and I couldn't fix. It was the first thing that came to my mind when I was considering what kind of illness to give my hero.''

"Thank you, Mrs. Wrigley. You may be seated. If Ms. Bennett will please take the stand one more time.''

While Payne sat there mulling over Ms. Wrigley's answers, the adorable looking artist whose figure transformed the skirt and blouse she was wearing, walked to the front of the courtroom and sat down.

"Ms. Bennett? You've done seven other covers with this man's picture. Why is that?''

"Red Rose Romance has nine lines of books. Each line has a different readership. Of course there are crossovers, meaning people who read more than one line.

"If a certain face is popular, it is used more than once because it sells more books. Every time this man's face appeared on a cover, the sales climbed, so I was asked to do more pictures. I've been told *Manhattan Merger* is the biggest seller to date.''

"How did you happen to put a ship on the wall of the hero's office?''

"It seemed logical that a man whose ancestors crossed the ocean and built a shipping empire would have such a picture to remind him of his heritage and his love of the sea.''

"How did you happen to paint that particular ship?''

"I did research to find the right kind of vessel for the time period Ms. Wrigley mentioned in the book.''

"Why the lighthouse too?''

"One of my favorite living artists is Thomas McKnight. He did a surrealistic painting of a lighthouse on Nantucket. I adore that painting.''

Payne happened to love that painting too.

"While I was working on the cover for *Manhattan Merger,* a lighthouse just sort of slipped in there while I was painting the ship."

"Explain the reason you put a dog in the picture on his desk."

"In Ms. Wrigley's novel, there's a part where the hero has just found out he's dying of leukemia. Memories of his past life flash through his mind. One of them is running along the beach with his dog when he was a boy.

"This hero is a loner by nature. Obviously his dog meant a great deal to him. That's why I painted it in."

"Did Ms. Wrigley mention the breed?"

"No."

"Then why a bulldog?"

"For years I've had an English bulldog named Winston, after Winston Churchill, my favorite figure in history. At present the dog is staying with my parents until I can find a place that will allow pets.

"While I was doing the painting for *Manhattan Merger,* Winston happened to be sitting on one of the kitchen chairs watching me. He was so darling, I put him in the picture without even thinking about it."

Incredible. Absolutely incredible. Payne could only shake his head.

"Ms. Bennett, you testified that you'd never been to New York before you moved here. You also testified you went to school in Italy. Did your flight involve a stop in New York?"

"No. I took a nonstop charter from Denver to Frankfurt, Germany, and from Germany back to Denver when school was over. You can contact the art department at Colorado State to verify everything."

"Thank you. Will you tell the court the location of the eight paintings with my client's likeness?"

"Five of the authors have bought the paintings from me. I own the other three, one of which is *Manhattan Merger*. They're hanging in my apartment."

"According to the testimony we've heard, you only saw my client in a photograph for a few minutes, then painted him from memory."

"Yes."

"If Your Honor will permit, I'll ask the bailiff to give this sketch pad and pencil to the witness."

The judge nodded.

"Now if Your Honor will assist me by picking another person in the photograph from Exhibit Two? Show it to the witness. Let her study it for a moment, then ask her to draw this person from memory."

Payne whispered an aside to Drew. "If Ms. Bennett can pull this off, then we have no stalking case, thank God."

"Amen," Drew muttered.

First five, then ten minutes went by while the room sat in frozen silence waiting for her to finish her drawing. Payne watched her face and body change expression several times. Her concentration was almost as disarming as her femininity.

Finally she looked over at the judge and rendered him the sketchbook. He studied it and compared it to the photograph.

"You not only have a photographic memory, Ms. Bennett, you're a very gifted artist."

"Thank you."

"You may step down."

He signaled the bailiff to take the sketch and photograph to Drew. An impatient Payne was forced to wait until he could examine both items for himself.

"Good grief—" he blurted when Drew moved aside. "It's Mac— She's done a perfect likeness of him!"

"Her talent is remarkable." Drew turned to the judge. "I have no more questions of these witnesses, Your Honor."

"Ms. Carlow? Do you wish to make your closing remarks now?"

"Yes, Your Honor. I believe the facts speak for themselves. In future, Red Rose Publishing will require every artist to use licensed models for their covers. Needless to say, Mr. Sterling's likeness will never appear on another cover of a Red Rose Romance.

"I instructed Ms. Bennett to bring all drawings and disks with Mr. Sterling's likeness to this court. They can be turned over to him, or Red Rose can destroy them. Whatever the court wishes.

"It's worth noting that the cover of *Manhattan Merger* won first prize out of all the romance covers printed in the United States within the last twelve months.

"Ms. Wrigley also won first prize for the best *Touch of Romance* novel for *Manhattan Merger.* Both women were going to be honored at a banquet this fall.

"Under the circumstances they'll forego those awards in order to spare Mr. Sterling any unnecessary publicity or exposure. Our company will instruct the people at the U.S. Romance Author/Publisher Convention to pick two other winners.

"As for the books already in print and shipped out

through the book club, it would be impossible to judge how many readers would know the man on the cover is Mr. Payne Sterling.

"Your Honor?" she said after taking a drink of water. "Would it be permissible to ask how Mr. Sterling came to find out his likeness was on the cover of *Manhattan Merger?*"

The judge looked at Drew. "Mr. Wallace?" he prompted.

Payne nodded when Drew turned to him for permission.

"His sister's daughter reads romances and noticed the likeness. So did the maid who's also a romance reader."

Ms. Carlow smiled. "Thank you, Your Honor."

"Is there anything else, Counselor?"

"No."

"Very well." The judge looked at Drew. "Mr. Wallace? Are you ready to make closing remarks?"

"Yes, Your Honor. The extensive amount of testimony provided by the defendants has ruled out any hint of stalking violations which was my client's primary fear.

"My client could wish the published books with his likeness on the covers weren't in the public domain. However in view of Ms. Carlow's assertion that my client's likeness will never again grace a future Red Rose Romance cover, another fear has been removed.

"At this time my client and I would like to thank the court for hearing this case in such a timely manner. I also wish to congratulate opposing counsel for the outstanding defense she prepared on such short notice."

After Drew sat down, the judge removed his glasses.

"I too want to compliment both parties for conducting yourselves in a professional manner. This is an unusual case to come before the court."

Payne suddenly heard a voice cry out from the other side of the room.

"Your Honor?"

"Yes, Ms. Bennett?"

"Could I say something?"

"Go ahead."

"If I had been Mr. Sterling, I would have brought this case to court just as he did in the hope of preventing another tragedy. But Red Rose Publishing is not to blame. Neither is Bonnie Wrigley.

"I—I'm the one who painted him without permission and brought him more grief unknowingly," her voice trembled. "Ignorance is no excuse. I'm the guilty party. I feel so horrible about it, I don't know how to begin to make restitution.

"If there's to be a severe financial punishment, let it be on my head, no one else's."

"Thank you, Ms. Bennett. I do believe you've learned an important and necessary lesson in the early stages of your brilliant career. You never know who the stranger in the crowd or the photograph might turn out to be.

"A priceless gift like yours is going to have to be used with care in the future, as you've discovered. Call it destiny or fate, you happened to paint the one man whose phenomenal success in life has made him vulnerable to the ugliest elements in our society. The tragedy that befell his fiancée should never have happened.

"It is also unfortunate that no one at Red Rose Publishers caught the problem in time to rectify it.

However Ms. Carlow has assured the court that the company will require its artists to use licensed models from now on. A very wise move which will prevent unwanted occurrences like this from happening again.

"As for Ms. Wrigley's scholarly researched fiction novel which paralleled Mr. Sterling's life to a great degree, testimony has proved it to be one of those inexplicable coincidences. Counsel for the plaintiff said it best. 'Art imitating life.'

"In conclusion, the court has listened to testimony and finds no evidence of evil doing or intent to do evil on the part of Ms. Bennett, Ms. Wrigley or Red Rose Romance Publishers.

"Opposing counsels can get together to decide on disposition of drawings, disks, paintings, books already in print that can still be pulled, books that are still awaiting translation for foreign markets, et cetera."

The judge pounded his gavel. "Case dismissed."

CHAPTER FOUR

THE second the judge left the courtroom, Rainey was so relieved she leaped from the chair to hug Grace Carlow. The attorney dwarfed her five foot six inch body.

"It turned out as I knew it would, my dear."

"Only because of you," Rainey half sobbed the words. Relief swept over her in waves.

"Rainey's right," Bonnie chimed in, giving both of them a hug. "Without your confidence, I would have had a coronary before we ever got off the phone."

Grace smiled. "It's over, and the lesson we've learned has been instructive for the company."

Rainey nodded.

"We also learned something else, ladies." She cocked an expressive brow.

"What?" Rainey and Bonnie were both wiping their eyes at the same time.

"Mr. Sterling only has one sister. It means Senator Sterling-Boyce's daughter and maid read our romances. That's the kind of inside information guaranteed to make Mr. Finauer's day."

Rainey had never met the CEO, but she'd heard that when he erupted, everyone felt the shock waves. If this case had gone the wrong way...

"All's well that ends well, honey."

"Oh, mom—" Rainey turned to embrace her mother and brother. "Thanks for flying to my rescue on such short notice and bringing everything. The outcome would have been very different without you two!''

Craig gave her a hug. ''Congratulations on your big honor, even if you can't accept the award.''

''Thanks.''

''Trust my sister to pick the *one* billionaire face in the crowd,'' he teased.

She groaned, still shuddering from nerves which had been playing havoc with her emotions over the last twenty-four hours.

Her brother grinned. ''I guess I'm going to have to break down and read *Manhattan Merger* to find out why Mr. Megabucks felt so violated.''

''We'll never know all the things about Bonnie's novel that upset him so much. But it wouldn't hurt you to read a really fantastic relationship book with a powerful emotional punch.'' Rainey sniffed. ''Maybe it will give you insight into your less than satisfactory love-life.''

''How come it hasn't helped yours?'' he whispered.

''It has! Reading romance novels has taught me to wait for the kind of man I want for my husband. He just hasn't come along yet.''

''Ms. Bennett?'' a deep unfamiliar male voice sounded behind her.

She whirled around, but felt like she was still reeling after she'd come to a stop.

The man she'd drawn, painted and dreamed about so many times was actually standing in front of her, up close and too personal for her to breathe normally.

With a sense of déjà vu her gaze traveled over his rugged male features. There were strain lines near his eyes and mouth that hadn't been there two years ago.

Lines put there by a stalker who'd crippled this man's fiancée...

No doubt those creases had deepened further as a result of finding himself on the cover of *Manhattan Merger,* a book that paralleled his life to such a degree, he'd not only felt violated as Craig had said, he'd felt threatened.

"I would give anything if I could undo the pain and suffering I've caused you and your fiancée—" she blurted. Her smoky green eyes glistened with tears that trembled on the tips of her velvety black lashes.

"Please tell her how sorry I am to have been the person who turned your lives into another nightmare. I can't even imagine how terrible that experience must have been for both of you and your families."

"It was. I won't lie to you about that."

His honesty was as devastating as his dark blue gaze which traveled over her features with an intimacy that made her tremble.

She averted her eyes. "It's a helpless feeling to know you've done something you can't undo—like trying to recapture the air from a balloon. If I could turn the clock back, knowing what I know now—" she half moaned the words.

"Amen," he muttered with an unmistakable echo of pain revealed in that one word. It haunted her. "My attorney will be calling Ms. Carlow about the paintings of me still in your possession."

She nodded. "Naturally you'll want proof that everything has been destroyed."

"Excuse me for interrupting, Ms. Bennett," his attorney broke in on them. "I need to talk to my client."

"Of course." Her eyes lifted to Payne Sterling's once

more. "Thank you for not pressing charges against the others...or me. I'll always be grateful," her voice throbbed. "God bless you and your fiancée."

She turned away from him, feeling much worse than before because he was no longer just a memory from a photograph. The reality of his physical presence, plus the pain she felt emanating from him, had combined to squeeze her heart with fresh guilt.

"What did he say to upset you?" Craig whispered as he and their mother walked her out of the courtroom.

"Nothing. I just feel horrible for causing him and his family more pain."

"It wasn't intentional and he knows it," her mother assured her. "Let's be glad it's over. Since Craig and I have to fly back home in the morning, shall we celebrate your victory and take a ferry to Staten Island if it isn't too late? It's something I've always wanted to do."

"That sounds like a good idea, mom." Anything to get her mind off of Payne Sterling for a while. "We'll grab a taxi out in front of the court building and head for the terminal. If I remember right, the ferries leave often during rush hour."

"When we get back, I'll treat us to dinner," her brother offered. "Where shall we go?"

"There's a great sushi place on Bond Street." She'd said it to tease Craig. His proclivity for beef was well known.

When both he and her mother frowned on cue, Rainey laughed. "Just kidding. I'll take you guys to Del Frisco's. It's the best steak house in Manhattan."

"Now you're talking."

They moved outside the building to hail a cab. "I'm surely glad you've lived around here long enough to know your way around, Rainey,'' her mother confided. ''You love it, don't you.''

''On the whole, yes. But the masses of people can be daunting at times. To live here permanently would require a lot of money if you craved isolation and privacy.''

''Luckily we have that for free in Grand Junction,'' Craig said before letting out an ear-piercing whistle. It did the job. One of the taxis whizzing by came to a quick stop.

Rainey climbed in after her mother. Then Craig got inside and pulled the door closed after him.

She leaned forward to address the driver. ''Whitehall Terminal, please.''

As the taxi started up again, Rainey noticed Payne Sterling and his attorney, both in sunglasses, leave the courthouse surrounded by a group of men all in business suits. They got in a limousine with tinted windows.

After the accident that had left his fiancée paralyzed, Rainey imagined he would always be well guarded. How horrible to be a target everywhere he went. She shuddered.

Her brother eyed her with concern. ''Are you all right?''

''I'm thankful he didn't press charges, but I still feel awful about what I did.''

''As the judge said, there was no evil intended. Chalk it up to one of your exciting experiences in the Big Apple. Someday you'll look back and laugh about it.''

''I hope so.''

''Craig's right, honey. I'm sure Mr. Sterling's relief that neither you or Bonnie Wrigley was a stalker has caused him to forget about it already.''

"Even if that's true, he has to live every moment of his life with the knowledge that his fiancée is in a wheelchair because of a demented woman who imagines herself in love with him."

"That's the downside of being a man with a name like Sterling, and a bank account that could fund the homeless forever."

Rainey bowed her head. "Grace told me he already does that."

"Does what?" her brother asked.

"He's a philanthropist. According to her he has set up many charities including a foundation for the homeless. I know he does it for tax purposes, but I'm pretty sure she told me all those things to reassure me he's compassionate too."

"He seemed like a good man to me when I took him rafting down the river. No wonder he used the name Vince. It's the only way he can have any anonymity."

She buried her face in her hands. "I still can't believe I picked him to paint."

"I can," her mother drawled. "So can all the millions of women who will mourn when he's not on any more romance covers."

"Mom—" Craig laughed. "I can't believe you just said that."

"You'd have to be a woman to understand."

"Is dad aware of your secret fantasy?" he teased.

"There are several things he's better off not knowing."

"Don't tell me you read those romances too?"

"Rainey and I have been enjoying them for years. You were always too busy devouring your hunting and fishing magazines to notice."

At this point Rainey couldn't help chuckling. Her mother's comments had managed to lighten her mood.

"It looks like we've arrived," Craig muttered, sounding miffed by their mother's confession.

On the whole Rainey found that men seemed uncomfortable by the thought of romance novels and heroes. It was very strange since statistics showed that men had fantasies about women on a daily basis.

Rainey lifted her head in time to see her brother pay the fare. They piled out of the taxi into a horde of people coming and going from the ferry. It happened to be the *John F. Kennedy*.

Craig pulled out his pocket camera and snapped a picture, then herded them toward the terminal for their tickets.

Being with her family until they left for the airport the next morning prevented Rainey from dwelling on the whole disturbing incident with Mr. Sterling. Her long talk into the night with Craig about his business plans had kept disturbing thoughts of him at bay.

But once she'd waved them off in a taxi headed for the airport, memories of him came rushing back with a vengeance.

To stem the tide, she straightened her apartment, did a wash and scoured the bathroom. When everything was neat and clean, she showered and dressed in cutoffs and a T-shirt. After going downstairs for her mail, she was ready to get back to her painting.

An hour later she'd finished the lace on the wedding gown. The cover for *The Bride's Not-So-White Secret* was done.

She called the courier service to schedule a pickup for Monday morning. Now she could start on the next project for Global Greeting Cards which had come in the mail.

No sooner had she put the receiver back on the hook to get busy and her phone rang. She assumed it was Ken. He'd asked her to go to a jazz concert with him tonight in Greenwich Village and was probably calling to set up the time.

"Rainey Bennett Fine Art Studio."

"Hello, Rainey."

"Grace—" She clutched the receiver a little tighter for fear something else was wrong.

"Relax, my dear. All is well. Claud Finauer couldn't be happier with the outcome."

Relieved to hear that news, Rainey let go of the breath she'd been holding.

"For your information I had a call from Mr. Wallace a few minutes ago. If it's convenient, someone will be coming by your apartment within the hour for your paintings of Mr. Sterling. I wanted to make certain you were home."

"I'll be here. Tell them to buzz me from the foyer so I can let them in. I'm on the third floor."

"Good. I'll call you next week. We'll go out for lunch."

"I'd like that." Grace was a fascinating personality.

"So would I. Talk to you soon."

The minute they clicked off, Rainey walked over to the paintings and removed them from the wall. After dusting the frames off, she placed them next to the door.

It was a wrench to have to give up the one for *Manhattan Merger*. Not that she couldn't do another painting of him from memory. But it would be different the second time around because she'd seen him in person.

If she did do any new sketches, they would show a man embracing his wheelchair-bound fiancée. His eyes and rugged features would reveal intense suffering...

While she waited for the runner from Mr. Wallace's law firm to arrive, Rainey opened the manilla envelope. It appeared she was to design a series of cards that said "Goodbye—Enjoy your trip!" in various languages.

Having lived in Italy, she reached for her sketch pad and began playing around with some ideas that immediately sprang to mind. Soon her hillside in Tuscany began to come alive like the pieces of a patchwork quilt.

She drew in one of those charming farmhouses with the tiled roof. No one could see inside it, but her imagination allowed her to dream of two people madly in love. They stood at one of the windows overlooking their own spot of heaven. Twilight revealed two bodies entwined.

As Rainey stared into space, she realized she'd been envisioning herself in Payne Sterling's arms. It wasn't the first time this had happened. She feared it wouldn't be the last.

Disturbed by thoughts she had no right to entertain, she threw down her pencil and got up from the desk.

It was a good thing all physical evidence of him would be gone in a few minutes.

But not from her mind.

An overwhelming compulsion to look at him one more time drove her to the door of her apartment. She reached for her favorite painting.

The more she studied it, the more she realized the person who'd gone down the Colorado with her brother seeking adventure bore little resemblence to the man she'd faced in the courtroom.

Rainey finally put it back with the others.

How tragic to think the woman he'd fallen in love with could no longer run into his arms. Talk about cruel.

She tried to imagine herself in his fiancée's place. How hard it must be for her to want to do everything for him, to share everything with him when she—

The buzzer sounded from the foyer, interrupting her tormented thoughts. She spoke through the intercom. When she'd ascertained it was the runner, she told him to come up.

A half minute later there was a rap on the door. She opened it expecting to see a college-age person. Her greeting stuck in her throat to find a huskily built man blocking her exit. He was in his late thirties and wore casual clothes.

"Ms. Bennett?"

"Yes?"

He looked beyond her to the apartment itself, as if he were casing the interior. Sensing something wasn't right, she was about to close the door when another man came up behind him dressed in a business suit.

"I'll take it from here, John."

The second Rainey saw who it was, the breath rushed out of her lungs. Maybe she was hallucinating.

The all-seeing blue eyes of Payne Sterling seemed to take in every detail of her face and body before their gazes locked.

"I'm here for the artwork, Ms. Bennett, but I'd like to talk to you first." His cultivated male voice permeated her bones. "May I come in?"

Rainey couldn't believe this was happening. Thank heaven she'd done her housecleaning earlier that morning.

"Yes. Of course."

Once he'd stepped inside and shut the door, he dominated her tiny studio apartment.

"Would you like to sit down?" Even to her own ears she sounded breathless.

His glance darted to the sketch on her desk. "I can see that I've interrupted your work, but I don't plan to be here that long. I've come to ask a special favor of you."

Rainey gulped. "If you're worried about the other paintings, I'll phone those authors who purchased them. When they hear what happened, they'll send them back to me."

He shook his dark head. "Forget them. My concern lies in making my niece and fiancée feel secure. They're the ones who panicked when they saw my likeness on the cover."

His hands went to his hips, underscoring his compelling masculinity. "I'd like them to meet the artist. Between you and me, I'm confident we'll be able to dispel their fears that you're a threat to me or anyone else."

She was stunned by his request.

For one thing, she'd never imagined seeing him again. For another, it brought home the fact that she'd unwittingly terrorized two innocent people who loved him and needed reassurance.

No matter his reasons for asking this favor of her, somewhere in Rainey's psyche she knew she should say no for her own self-preservation.

What was it she remembered about the cycle of temptation?

First you allowed the thought to enter your mind. Then you began to fantasize about it. From there you started making plans. Finally you found yourself acting on those plans.

The man she now knew as Payne Sterling had been in her thoughts for two years. Since court she'd entertained certain intimate fantasies about him. If she agreed to his request, it meant crossing that precarious line into the "making plans" phase.

What really shocked her was how much she wanted to make plans with him, even though it meant meeting his fiancée. Was she some kind of masochist?

Clinging to one last thread of common sense she said, "They're welcome to come here to my studio."

"It would be easier for my fiancée if I take you to them."

Of course. The apartment didn't have an elevator. What was the matter with her?

"I'd like to surprise them with good news," he continued. "It'll be the best medicine of all."

But not for me Rainey's heart cried. Help—what should she do?

"When were you thinking of us meeting?" She fought to keep the tremor out of her voice.

"As soon as possible. Perhaps this evening after we've both finished work for the day."

This evening?

A shiver of excitement passed through her body.

"I see." She bit her lip remembering it was Friday and she had a date with Ken.

"By your hesitation I assume you're not free."

His eyes held hers. She could sense his urgency and the accompanying disappointment.

"I—I'll change my plans," she stammered. "After the pain I've put you and your family through, it's the least I can do."

Ken would forgive her when she told him it was a legal matter. He above all people would understand.

The only person who didn't feel right about the whole situation was Rainey. Not when her attraction to this man was so intense.

"Thank you, Ms. Bennett. Have you ever flown in a helicopter?"

Her pulse started to race. "Yes. My brother's friend runs a helicopter service in Las Vegas. He's flown me over the Grand Canyon several times."

"Good. I'll send the limo for you at four o'clock. We'll leave from my office as soon as you arrive. Do you have plans for tomorrow?"

"Work—" she blurted, throwing herself a lifeline. "I'm behind becau—"

"Because I forced you into court," he finished for her. "Bring it with you and anything else you'll require for an overnight stay, including a bathing suit."

Oh no.

Rainey averted her eyes. She was terrified he would see how excited she was at the prospect of going anywhere with him...of spending time with him.

And his fiancée, a little voice nagged. *Never forget that, Rainey Bennett.*

When she felt recovered enough to meet his glance, she discovered him studying her prized serigraph of the Nantucket Lighthouse painted by Thomas McKnight. It hung next to her own paintings, the few that hadn't yet been purchased by the authors of those books.

He suddenly turned in her direction, catching her staring at him. She didn't look away, but heat scorched her cheeks.

"Would you bring your dog's picture when you come?"

She shouldn't have been surprised he'd seen the small framed photo perched on her desk. He noticed everything. What intrigued her was the reason why he'd made the request.

"All right."

Their eyes held for a brief moment. "I'll see you later."

In an economy of movement he gathered the paintings and went out the door. Unable to help herself, she watched until he and the same security man named John disappeared from view.

After shutting the door she leaned against it, wondering if she was in the middle of one of her dreams about him. But six hours later she knew everything was real when John and another security man appeared at the door. They helped her to the limousine with her bags.

Insulated by glass that allowed her to look out without being seen, she enjoyed being chauffeured to the Financial District even though it was rush hour. Once they arrived in the underground parking of the Sterling building, she was whisked by private elevator to the penthouse.

When the doors opened to Mr. Payne's office suite, Rainey couldn't control the gasp that escaped her throat. It was like walking into her own painting.

Her dark-haired hero looked up from his massive oak

desk and said, "Since seeing the cover on *Manhattan Merger,* I've had the same reaction as you every time I've walked in my office."

Rainey stood there speechless.

Her gaze darted from the small framed photo perched on his desk to the painting of a ship passing a lighthouse.

"No," she whispered in disbelief.

It hung on the only wall not made of glass, just the way she'd set things up in her painting.

And then there was the dynamic billionaire himself.

Dressed in the expensive-looking blue suit he'd worn to her apartment earlier, it could have been the same suit she'd put on him in the painting. Behind him loomed the Manhattan skyline, astonishingly similar to the one she'd painted for the cover.

Still in shock, she watched as he got out of his swivel chair and brought her the small picture from his desk.

"I'm afraid to look," she confessed in a shaky voice as he closed the distance between them and handed it to her.

One glance at it and her green eyes flew to his. "This dog—the face—it looks like Winston!"

He nodded. "Meet Bruno, my trusty bullmastiff."

"I don't believe it," she murmured, starting to feel light-headed. The picture slipped to the lush carpet.

Suddenly she felt a hard-muscled arm go around her. He ushered her to the nearest leather chair.

Their faces were almost touching. She could see the alarm in those unforgettable blue eyes, feel his breath on her cheek. "You went so pale just now. I'll get you some water."

In the next instant he'd returned and put the cup to her lips.

She drank every drop hoping he would move away from her, but to her consternation he hunkered down next to her after she'd finished.

He was too close— He smelled too good— She couldn't think, let alone breathe.

"Better now?" The concern in his deep voice was too much.

"I—I'm fine. Thank you." She stood up abruptly in an effort to separate herself from him.

The picture was still lying on the floor. Needing something physical to do in her chaotic state, she walked over and picked it up. To her relief the glass hadn't broken. At last she had the answer to why he'd requested she bring her picture of Winston along.

She put it back on his desk before turning to him. "Mr. Sterling—"

"Surely we're beyond the formalities," he broke in. *No! We aren't! We can't be!*

"My name is Payne."

I know. I don't dare use it.

Her body was trembling. "I swear I've never been in your office before!"

Lines marred his rugged features. "After your testimony in court and the way you almost fainted just now, you think I don't know that?"

She put a hand to her throat. "I don't see how I could have painted everything so true to life! There's such a thing as coincidence. But *this* is something else…"

"My feelings exactly."

Rainey shook her head. "I'm not one to believe in an out-of-body experience that brought me to this office."

"Nor I."

She stared at him once more. "I'm frightened. How do you explain something like this happening?"

He rubbed the back of his neck before eyeing her through narrowed lids. "The judge said it. Some things can't be explained. You just have to accept them."

"But your fiancée probably won't believe I haven't been stalking you. *I* wouldn't!" Warmth rosied her cheeks.

His expression grew solemn. "That's why I want you with me when we tell her and Catherine the true situation."

"Your niece?"

"Yes."

"How old is she?"

"Fifteen."

"Are you two close?"

"Very," he whispered. "I shouldn't have favorites, but when you meet her, you'll understand why."

Rainey moaned. "I have to assume they've both been to your office."

He nodded. "Catherine, many times."

"When they saw the cover, they must have been petrified. I'm so sorry—" Rainey blurted.

"Don't you think you've beaten yourself enough?" There was an edge to his tone that silenced her. "Let's agree it's been a hellish week for everyone concerned and get out of here."

By now he'd reached the elevator and stood there a male entity of barely suppressed energy waiting to break free of the confining walls of his office.

Her heartbeat accelerated to a sickening pitch. Since coming to this office, being touched by him, she felt a stronger connection to him than ever.

This was wrong, all wrong. Yet she found herself taking one step, then another, toward him.

Her conscience screamed at her to beg off with some excuse before it was too late.

Still she kept going.

The doors closed, sealing her inside with him. So much for listening to the nagging voice that told her she would live to regret this.

They rode to the roof where his helicopter sat waiting.

She should stop this madness now, before things went any further. But the temptation to go where he led was greater than any force she'd ever known.

He walked to the helicopter with her and helped her get in. The security man she'd drawn in the courtroom for the judge followed them at a short distance. He climbed in behind her.

After fastening the seat strap, she realized she'd become an eager participant in a plan that could lead to her destruction. Yet one look at Payne Sterling sitting in the co-pilot's, so alive and vital, and no power on earth could tear her away.

The whir of the rotors drowned out the last death gasp of her conscience. There was liftoff.

Rainey was being carried beyond the point of no return.

CHAPTER FIVE

AFTER court, Payne had decided to spend the night at the penthouse working. In phone calls to both Catherine and Diane, he'd told them they could stop worrying. All would be explained when he arrived at Phyllis's on Friday evening.

He'd made arrangements for Diane to be picked up and driven to his sister's home where they'd have dinner. The two women had no idea he was bringing a guest.

Catherine would be delighted.

Diane would be disappointed the two of them weren't going to be alone. But her relief when she met the artist and found out Rainey was no stalker would go a long way to help make up for it.

More aware of the woman seated behind the pilot than he wanted to be, Payne let Mac do the honors of orienting her during the flight. But they were nearing Crag's Head now.

He turned his head in her direction. "We'll be putting down shortly. From there it's a short drive to my sister's house."

Rainey nodded her well-shaped head whose hair gleamed a silvery gold in the late afternoon rays of the sun. He could tell she was loving every minute of the ride. Her eyes were drinking in everything.

So were his.

He couldn't seem to get enough of her charming profile or the mold of her body in the attractive yellow sundress with the white short-sleeved jacket she was wearing.

On impulse he told his pilot to circle Crag's Head before landing. The stark whiteness of the remodeled lighthouse against the vivid blue of the ocean never failed to thrill him. He wondered what her artist's eye would make of the view.

Her reaction wasn't long in coming.

When the helicopter dipped toward his property, she cried out in awe, turning her head every which way to keep it in sight. The pilot swung around, giving her the full treatment.

"Oh—" she exclaimed again in what sounded like absolute delight. "It resembles Le Corbusier's chapel at Ronchamps I once visited. Yet it's a lighthouse too. The integration is pure genius. It's the most fabulous thing I've ever seen!"

Her shining green eyes fused with his. "Is it a museum? Can you go inside?"

Her ecstatic response pleased him in ways he didn't dare contemplate. "I think it could be arranged."

The comment produced a grin from his pilot who circled lower to land on the pad.

"You mean we're going to go inside *now?*" She sounded incredulous and so excited he could feel it in every atom of his body.

As they touched down, Payne unstrapped himself to help her out of the helicopter. When her arm brushed against his chest by accident, it felt like a lick of flame.

At the same time he breathed in the delicious scent of

spring flowers drifting around her as it had done in his office. The fragrance enticed rather than overpowered.

Sam and Andy had already pulled up in the limo to meet them. Payne cupped her elbow as he made the introductions. "I'm going to show Ms. Bennett around, then we'll leave for my sister's."

He didn't miss the speculative glance Mac gave him before the men started transferring bags and paintings from the helicopter to the limo.

Mac had every reason to look surprised. Payne guarded his privacy with a vengeance. No outsiders. Only family, Diane's family, his security people, the Myers and Drew Wallace were allowed. To the rest of the world, Crag's Head was off limits.

By bringing Rainey here, Payne had broken his own rule, another aberration that didn't bear close scrutiny.

Her gaze continued to study the exterior as they walked toward the north entrance. "This is your home," she said in a quiet voice. "The lighthouse should have been my first clue."

"Yes."

"How do you bear to leave it?"

He sucked in his breath. "I ask myself that question every morning when I climb in the helicopter."

She paused in front of the door, eyeing him with a directness he found exhilarating. "Now it's clear to me where the king of glass does his inspired thinking. Your office is simply a place where you get everyone else to carry out your business."

How did she know so much?

He cocked his head. "You read *World Fortune Magazine?*"

"No. Grace Carlow showed me the article so I'd have some idea of the man I'd be facing in court."

Her mouth suddenly curved into a haunting smile. It said she understood the forces that drove him.

The woman had second sight. Her painting was already proof of that.

"Shall we go inside?"

Her expectant expression gave her away. "I can't wait."

Payne's lips twitched before he used his pocket remote to gain entrance. Mrs. Myers met them in the foyer. She covered her surprise well at seeing him with another woman besides Diane.

"Betty? This is Rainey Bennett, an artist from Grand Junction, Colorado, now living in New York. As soon as I shower and change, we'll be driving to my niece's for dinner."

"Would you like something to drink while you wait, Ms. Bennett?"

"No thank you."

"What about you, Mr. Sterling?"

"Nothing for me either."

"If there's anything I can do, let me know."

"Thanks, Betty."

When she disappeared he turned to his guest. "While I'm upstairs, make yourself at home. I won't be long."

Fifteen minutes later he came back down knowing exactly where to find her. Sure enough she'd rolled a stool over to his underground map of Los Angeles. She was so deep in concentration she didn't hear his footsteps when he entered this portion of the house.

It took the ringing of his cell phone to bring her head

around. She got up from the stool. "How long have you been standing there?"

"A few minutes." He checked the Caller ID. It was Diane. He put the phone back in his pocket. "I do believe you find those maps as fascinating as I do."

"Fascinating isn't even the word. To tunnel under a city not knowing exactly what you'll find must provide the same kind of thrills experienced by an explorer or an astronaut."

"It's a world of rats and muck," he muttered.

"And ancient artifacts," she added. "Between you and Frontenac, the stories you could tell!"

Her reference to Bonnie Wrigley's testimony made him smile. "I have to admit it's exciting when we find something."

"Ooh I'd love to be with you the next time you come across an old burial mound."

There she went again, infecting him with her unique brand of enthusiasm. "I'll keep that in mind."

An impish smile broke out on her face. "You don't fool me. You're no ordinary engineer. It's obvious you love making sense out of a bewildering maze like this.

"When I was studying art at the university, I had to take some architecture and mechanical engineering classes as part of the curriculum. I was pulled a lot of ways back then before I ended up going for my fine arts degree.

"The fact is, I almost changed majors and went into engineering. The kind you do is probably the most challenging of all. It's another world down there under the streets. I marvel at the way you have figured it all out and then put your vision to paper.

"You see what nobody else sees and know how it's going to work. It's miraculous. What I'd give to work alongside you and learn from you."

Her vivacious eyes wandered over him.

"To know what can be connected to what, and make it function means you'll never run out of new challenges, you lucky man. Do you know how many people would kill to love their work the way you do?"

"You mean the same way you love yours?" He moved closer to her, enjoying their conversation more than he'd enjoyed anything else in years.

"I enjoy what I do," she said. "But I don't wake up every morning surrounded by this sea and this sky. I really can't find the words, but you already know them because you were the first one to visualize everything.

"There's so much beauty of shape and flowing line integrated with the lighthouse, it makes me want to cry." Tears clouded her exquisite green eyes. "If you knew me better, you'd know I cry a lot," she confessed on a self-deprecating laugh. "That's the way beauty affects me."

Payne could relate. Right now he was looking at someone incredibly beautiful both inside and out.

"While the pilot circled your home, my mind's eye began making sketches. Now that I've been inside, it won't stop. I promise I won't put anything to paper, but if you see me experiencing symptoms of withdrawal within the next twelve hours, have some compassion."

He burst into full-bodied laughter. Payne couldn't remember the last time that had happened. He couldn't remember ever enjoying a woman this much before. They related on a level that needed no words.

It felt good. She made him feel good. Too good.

He felt...alive.

"Mr. Sterling?"

Mrs. Myer's voice jerked him from certain private thoughts that were both exhilarating and alarming in their implication.

"Yes, Betty?"

"Your niece is on the house phone wondering where you are."

He hadn't even heard it ring. "Tell her I'll be there within ten minutes."

"Yes, sir."

"We'd better go so you don't keep them waiting any longer," Rainey murmured.

She was right.

But Payne didn't want to go.

He wanted...

No.

Don't say it, Sterling. Don't even think it.

"Are you hungry?" he asked as they started for the hallway.

"I'm getting there."

Payne had been *there* since the first moment he'd seen her in the courtroom. He recognized all the symptoms of an appetite that was growing out of control.

He should have sent Mac for the paintings, but some irresistible force had propelled him to Rainey's apartment door instead. That same force had prompted him to manufacture a reason to see her again.

And after tonight, what then?

The answer was simple. There couldn't be an after.

Tomorrow his pilot would fly her back to the city.

Andy would make certain she was driven to her apartment. Payne would destroy all evidence of Ms. Bennett's brief appearance in the scheme of things.

With her gone, his newly fabricated life since the shooting would once again resume its required pattern.

But even as he rehearsed those thoughts in his mind, his hand came in contact with her silken-clad skin. Somehow her dress had ridden up while he was helping her into the back of the limo.

Both their bodies trembled from the contact before she scrambled to the other side of the limo with a speed he hadn't thought possible.

His body tautened. She was as aware of him as he was of her.

"Is your niece caught up in politics like her mother?"

The innocuous question came after they'd left the parking area on the north side of the house. With Mac and John inside the car, she couldn't have chosen a better topic.

"No. She'll be a philanthropist one day."

"Sounds like she takes after her uncle."

"Hardly. Catherine was born compassionate."

"What a rare and wonderful trait that is. I'm looking forward to meeting her."

Payne stared out the window with unseeing eyes. Like water cascading to the pool below, Catherine would gravitate to Rainey. Like Payne, she wouldn't be able to help herself.

"Tell me about your fiancée. Does she have a career?"

He'd wondered when Rainey would get around to Diane.

"Her background is English literature. Until the accident she worked for a magazine put out by Blakely College, her alma mater."

"I'm impressed. Blakely's a prestigious women's college. I had a friend who tried to get in. She was a straight-A student with lots of other credentials going for her, but she was still turned down."

He nodded. "It's very competitive. What happened to your friend?"

"She ended up at Vassar."

They both started to chuckle at the same time.

This was something new for him. To be with a woman who could read his mind, who laughed and found joy over the same things. Whose thoughts were bound to his, especially during the silences.

Phyllis's house came into view.

Too soon their ride was over. Now he would have to share Rainey, then let her go. She would take all the sunshine with her.

Though she hadn't left yet, he could already feel his desolation. It shook him to the foundations.

"Uncle Payne!" His niece hurried across the back lawn with Lady at her heels. "We thought you'd never get here!"

She opened the limo door to hug him. Then her gaze caught sight of the surprise he'd brought with him.

"Catherine Boyce? Meet Rainey Bennett."

"Hello— It's nice to meet you," his niece said with a friendly smile.

Rainey smiled back. "I've been looking forward to meeting you, Catherine. You've got an uncle who's crazy about you."

"I love him too."

"Sweetheart? Rainey's the artist who painted those romance covers including *Manhattan Merger*. Since you're the one who brought that particular book to my attention, I thought you'd like to meet her. She'll be spending the night here as our guest."

"You're kidding." Her light blue eyes stared at him. "You're *not* kidding."

Her gaze flew to Rainey's once more. "*You* did the pictures of Uncle Payne?"

By now Mac held the door open for Rainey while the other men took the bags and paintings in the house.

His guest remained in the seat. "Guilty as charged."

"You're an amazing artist."

"It's not true, but thank you."

"Nyla's not going to believe it."

"Who's Nyla?"

"She's been with our family for years. When she's through reading her monthly mailing of romance novels, she gives them to me. The cover on *Manhattan Merger* worried her enough to say something about it. I couldn't believe how much it looked like Uncle Payne, so I showed it to him."

A shadow darkened Rainey's expressive features. "I'm sorry it frightened all of you so much. You have no idea how badly I feel."

"It's over," Payne declared. "I've assured my niece there's nothing to fear. Why don't we go inside and eat dinner before it's ruined."

Within seconds they'd alighted from the limo and the three of them started toward the back door of the house. Payne paused midstride because Lady had made

Rainey's acquaintance and was now enjoying a nice scratch behind the ears.

With her tail wagging in excitement, it appeared Ms. Bennett had just acquired another admirer.

"I cooked hamburgers and potato salad for us, Uncle Payne. You should have told me you were bringing company. I would have made something special."

Rainey caught up to them. "Hamburgers have always been a favorite around my house," she spoke up. "In fact my brother still lives on them. If you tried to feed him something like chicken cordon bleu, he'd slip it to our dog."

Catherine laughed. "What kind do you have?"

"An English bulldog."

"Oh how cute. Uncle Payne once had a bullmastiff."

"I know. I saw the picture of him on his desk. The two dogs' faces look a lot alike."

"What's his name?"

"Winston."

"Of course. Winston Churchill. How funny."

"I agree." Rainey chuckled. "There are moments when my dog looks just like him. Once Craig bought a cigar and put it in Winston's mouth while I took the picture."

They both laughed.

"I'd love to see that!" his niece said.

Rainey's eyes swerved to Payne's. "I have a picture in my purse."

"Can I look?"

"Of course." Rainey opened her handbag and handed her the framed picture showing Winston with the cigar.

Catherine broke into more laughter. "This is hilarious. He's darling!"

"I think so too. He's the dog I put in the painting. Just being with Lady makes me homesick for him."

His niece darted Payne a relieved glance before handing the picture back to Rainey.

"Lady's one of the reasons I didn't go to Mexico with my family."

Payne put his arm around Catherine's shoulders. "What's the other reason?" He knew there had to be one.

"It probably has to do with a boy," Rainey inserted. "I can remember missing a few trips to hang around my brother and his friends."

Catherine smiled without saying anything. It was as good as an admission. She opened the door so they could all go inside the house.

Being an artist obviously made Rainey an excellent judge of human nature. But being around her had knocked him off base until he didn't recognize himself anymore.

He took a fortifying breath. "Where's Diane?"

"I left her on the west patio. We'll be eating out there."

"Good. Why don't you show Rainey where to freshen up while I go find her."

"I'll be happy to. Come through here, Rainey."

"Your home is fabulous, like walking into a page of *Architectural Digest*. And it's so big! My studio apartment could fit in this one room alone."

"Where do you live?"

Their voices grew faint as Payne made his way to the

patio. He would love to eavesdrop on their conversation, but Diane was waiting.

"At last!" she cried when she saw him in the doorway. "I tried to reach you on the phone."

I know.

She wheeled around the table and lifted her arms to him. "It feels like two years instead of two days."

He wished to heaven he could say the same thing back to her, but he couldn't. It wasn't in him. All he could do was give her a quick kiss and hug.

As the opening line of *Manhattan Merger* had stated, Logan Townsend wasn't in love with his fiancée.

Payne wasn't in love with his fiancée either.

He'd never be able to say the words she wanted to hear.

Guilt and the need to find a cure for her had prompted his proposal of marriage. He'd told her he would take care of her and protect her. He owed her that much.

The grand plan was to help her walk again. Since their engagement he'd been working toward that goal with a single-mindedness he wouldn't allow anything to overshadow, especially not Diane's defeatist attitude.

What he hadn't counted on was Rainey Bennett entering his life.

"Are you sure everything's all right?" Diane asked when he straightened.

After pushing her wheelchair back to the table, Payne sat down next to her and reached for her hand.

"As I told you on the phone last evening, you don't need to worry anymore. To prove it, I've invited someone to dinner who will put any fears you have to rest."

Her face closed up. "You brought company here?"

"Yes. Catherine will be out with her in a minute. Her name is Lorraine Bennett. She's a freelance artist from Grand Junction, Colorado, who designs greeting cards and does paintings that appear on some of the covers for Red Rose Romance. She's the one who painted me."

"She confessed to it in court?"

"Yes. But when you hear the whole story, you'll understand it was an honest mistake."

Her eyes flashed in anger. "How could it be an honest mistake when she did it without your permission?"

"It's complicated. You'll just have to trust me."

Diane's hand clutched his. "I wish you'd asked me before you issued your invitation."

"It's because of your reaction right now that I didn't," Payne explained in a calm voice. "When the hearing started, I felt exactly like you. I was convinced someone would be arrested by the end of the day. We can thank God the reverse was true."

Her lips tightened. "For once I think you used the wrong judgment by bringing her here."

Payne happened to agree with her, but not for the same reasons she was thinking.

"I had another motive in mind, aside from the hope that meeting her would help you and Catherine to forget this incident."

"What motive?"

"Ms. Bennett feels terrible for what happened. It might help her to recover faster if she can see we bear no malice."

"She *should* feel terrible."

Payne knew it was her helplessness that made her less forgiving than she would otherwise be.

"Try to put yourself in her place, Diane. Throughout the hearing she felt the burden of being the one who not only implicated herself, but the author and the whole company."

She let go of his hand. "Why don't you find out what's keeping them? The sooner dinner is over, the sooner she'll be gone and we can be alone. I need to talk to you about our honeymoon. I've decided where I want to go and it's not Switzerland."

"Let's discuss this later."

"It'll be a waste of time, Payne."

He grimaced. "Until we've done every earthly thing possible to help you, you don't have the right to say that. I'll be back in a minute." In a few swift strides he left the patio.

"Payne—"

He could hear her calling him back, but for once he refused to give in to her tears.

CHAPTER SIX

WHEN Rainey saw Payne in the kitchen doorway, his whole expression had undergone a change. He was gripped by some dark, powerful emotion held barely in check.

The difference in him was so startling, she almost dropped the plates of freshly cut fruits and vegetables she was holding.

"What's going on in here?"

Catherine must have noticed the difference in him too, but all she said was, "We're bringing the food right now, Uncle Payne. I was just introducing Rainey to Nyla. She's going to eat with us so she can hear everything that happened in court."

"Aye, aye, Captain."

Payne's comment provoked a laugh from his niece who carried the platter of hamburgers out of the kitchen. But Rainey had an idea Catherine wasn't fooled by his sudden playfulness. Neither was Rainey.

She followed them to the patio. Nyla brought up the rear with the salad she'd taken from the fridge.

If Rainey hadn't already been to Payne's home, she would have thought the Boyce's house and view of the ocean was the most beautiful sight she'd ever seen.

Everything was picture perfect against the twilight backstop.

Payne took his place behind his fiancée.

That one defining gesture set the boundaries in concrete for Rainey. What had transpired before this moment was history. Whatever happened from here on out belonged to someone else's future. Rainey was simply a spectator passing through.

"Rainey Bennett? May I present my fiancée, Diane Wylie."

"How do you do, Ms. Bennett."

The other woman spoke first and held out her hand. Rainey moved around the table to shake it.

She and Diane were probably the same age. The attractive brunette had that girl-next-door look. To Rainey's eye she seemed the type her brother might date rather than—

Rainey forced herself to stop with the speculation. Payne Sterling meant nothing to her. He couldn't!

"I'm so thankful for this opportunity to meet you, Ms. Wylie. You'll never know how sorry I am for putting all of you through more anguish."

Payne's fiancée studied Rainey out of intelligent brown eyes before letting go of her hand. "Payne said it was an honest mistake, so it's best forgotten. I'm afraid his concern over my welfare has caused him to impose on your time."

"It's not an imposition!" Rainey blurted. "We've just come from his office. I almost had a heart attack when I saw how similar everything was to my painting. Anyone would be suspicious.

"After what you've suffered, I wanted to meet you in person and assure you I meant no harm. I hope in time you can forget it."

"Rainey? Do you want to come and sit between Nyla and me?"

Rainey could have hugged Catherine for smoothing a

difficult moment for her. She took her place, determined to avoid any eye contact with her host.

No more thinking about him.

"The hamburgers and potato salad are the best, sweetheart," he said after all of them had settled down to eat.

"Thanks. There's more in the kitchen."

"Everything's delicious," Rainey declared. Since meeting Diane Wylie, she'd lost her appetite but forced herself to eat in order not to hurt Catherine's feelings.

The dog brushed against Rainey's leg.

"Is it against the rules to give Lady a nibble? She's looking up at me with soulful eyes."

The teenager smiled. "You can feed her some strawberries."

"Oh good." Rainey let one drop. Lady snatched it before it reached the ground. She dropped a couple more. "Winston likes these too, but he hates grapes."

"Lady hates limes."

"I should think so." She chuckled.

"Why don't you tell us how you happened to paint my fiancé?"

Rainey had been waiting for that question. Before she could say anything, Payne rose to his feet.

"Just a minute, Rainey," he said, moving to the door. "First I want to get your brother's photograph and your artwork." Seconds later he returned and propped the fourteen-by-twenty inch paintings on some of the extra chairs.

Nyla and Catherine got up to study them. "I didn't know you did full-size paintings like these for the covers," the maid exclaimed. "They must take a long time."

"A lot of work goes into them because I do sketches

first until I know exactly what I want the finished product to look like.''

Nyla turned an animated face to Rainey. "It's exciting to have you here. To think you've done all those wonderful paintings. You're a fabulous artist.''

"You are!" Catherine cried.

"Thank you.''

"Nyla? Will you hand me the one of Payne in his office, please?''

"Here you go.'' The maid removed the dishes and placed the painting in front of Diane.

She examined it for a minute, then lifted her head to scrutinize Rainey. "Did you get permission to paint this woman?''

Payne's attorney was the person Rainey had expected to be adversarial, not his fiancée. But then Mr. Wallace wasn't the wheelchair-bound woman desperately in love with his client.

Rainey took a steadying breath. "Yes. She's a licensed model I've used in several covers. But sometimes I paint from memory. That's how I happened to draw Mr. Sterling.''

Without preamble she spent the next ten minutes telling the same story she'd related in the courtroom. Combined with Payne's explanations regarding Bonnie Wrigley's testimony, they covered all the essentials.

Rainey let her see the photo of Winston. Between that picture, her brother's photograph and Payne's assertion that Rainey's apartment contained a serigraph of the Nantucket Lighthouse, she hoped Catherine and Diane were satisfied.

"Because of this experience, the judge ordered that

all the artists at Red Rose Romance work with licensed models from now on.''

''I should think so,'' Diane muttered.

''I'm fairly certain they do anyway.''

''Why not you?''

''Because there are times when I can't find the right model for what I want to convey. As I explained, sometimes a face in the crowd or a picture jumps out at me. I don't even know it's happening.''

''You mean like my fiancé's.''

''Yes,'' Rainey answered honestly.

Old fears had been put to rest. Now there was a new one.

The other woman believed Rainey was interested in Payne.

What better way to expose Rainey than force a confrontation which would embarrass her in front of him and his niece?

Little did Diane know she had nothing to fear from Rainey. Now was the time to prove it.

''Because I'm an artist, I can't help looking at every face a little differently than most people do. Mr. Sterling is handsome in a rugged sort of way, but so are a lot of men. Some of the male models are breathtaking.''

Nyla nodded. ''You can say that again!''

Bless you, Nyla.

''It's what I read in a person's face that makes it memorable. Mr. Sterling's exudes character, confidence, hard work, struggle, determination, a passion for life. All those qualities combine to make him stand out as a heroic figure, artistically speaking.''

''Whoa! Uncle Payne—'' Catherine smiled at him. ''Did you hear all that?''

"I did," his voice grated.

Ignoring him, Rainey put Craig's photograph in front of Diane again. "Take another look at your fiancé."

Now Rainey was the one forcing his fiancée to co-operate when it was the last thing Diane wanted to do.

"See the way he's staring at the formations above the river? His eyes appear to be looking beyond them at something else the rest of us can't see. You can tell his mind is caught up in an inner vision. *That's* what makes him an arresting figure.

"That's why I suddenly found myself sketching him weeks later. He seemed perfect for certain novels I was sent. When *Manhattan Merger* came along, it was almost a spiritual mating of man and story."

The other woman's dark brows puckered. "When you're such a fine artist, why do you go to so much trouble for an inconsequential romance?"

Rainey had been waiting for a comment like that to surface. It was only natural for a woman like Diane. She'd never read a paperback romance and dismissed them as so much drivel.

"Millions of women will tell you they find them irresistible. Therefore it matters to the publishing company that their vast readership keeps coming back for more.

"Speaking from a personal note, it means everything to the author that the hero and heroine on the cover do justice to her superbly crafted relationship novel.

"That's *my* job.

"If I've done it right, the romance reader escapes even further into the story."

"I can vouch for that," Nyla piped up. "I still read the book if the cover's bad, but when it's a good one, it makes it even more exciting."

"Especially like that novel with Uncle Payne as a Viking! It was such a good story I checked out some books at the library about the Norsemen."

Rainey nodded. "It was written by a male author who's a Scandinavian history buff. I did the same thing as you, Catherine, and went to the library before I started to paint.

"You'll never know how much fun I had with that cover because the author had based Roald on a true historical figure. The clothes I put on him were the same ones on display at a museum in Norway."

"It was thrilling all right," Nyla murmured, "but I think I liked your cover of Mr. Sterling on *The Baby Doctor's Baby* the best."

"Oh, Uncle Payne—the little baby you were holding was so sweet."

"Is that right," he drawled.

Rainey forgot the promise she'd made not to look at him. Their eyes met. His were smiling. They filled her with warmth. She hurriedly glanced at Catherine.

"That was Matt, my best friend's baby boy."

"You just wanted to squeeze him," Nyla said with a sigh. "I can still see those big dimples and adorable blue eyes."

"Someday I want a baby that looks just like him."

"Let's make that about ten years away, sweetheart."

"*Uncle Payne—*"

Everyone laughed except his fiancée whose gaze remained leveled on Rainey.

"How did you happen to end up painting covers on romance novels of all things?"

"One day while I was in the media center of the high school where I taught art, I came across a book called

Writer's World U.S.A. I started looking through the pages at the hundreds of publishing companies that use artwork.

"On a whim I sent out queries. Sometimes I got an answer back. Sometimes not. A few times I was asked for a sample of my work.

"To my delight, Red Rose Romance asked to see my portfolio. I sent in my disk and they hired me. I was hired by Global Greeting Cards the same way."

"You're very talented."

Diane sounded tired. Not only of the subject, but physically worn out.

"Thank you, Ms. Wylie. Once again, I'd like to apologize for the pain I unknowingly caused you. I hope you'll be able to get past this."

"I already have," she muttered. "It's obvious you meant no harm. I wish you luck in your future endeavors."

"I want the same thing for you. Have you set a date for your wedding?"

"August first."

The words cut like a knife through Rainey's heart. "That's not far away."

"You're right," Payne broke in. "Diane and I still have an important matter to decide. If you'll excuse us, we'll say goodnight." He rose to his feet.

"See you tomorrow, sweetheart. That was a terrific meal." He kissed Catherine's cheek.

"Goodnight, Ms. Bennett."

"Goodnight," Rainey whispered.

"Nyla?" He patted the maid's shoulder. "Don't ever change."

The second he wheeled his fiancée into the house,

Catherine turned to Rainey. "If I brought you some paper, would you do a picture of Lady?"

Rainey wanted to hug her for making the request. The announcement of Payne Sterling's imminent marriage had come as a greater blow than she would have imagined.

When Rainey got upset, she always turned to her drawing board for solace. Right now she was in agony.

"I'd be honored. In fact while we were eating dinner, I sketched her in my mind."

"You mean it?" Catherine looked stunned.

"Yes. I've already given the drawing a title."

"What?"

Nyla looked equally curious.

She winked. "You'll see."

Both of them smiled.

"I'll find you some paper and a pencil!" Catherine cried.

"There's no need for that. The art case next to my overnight bag has everything I'll require."

"I'll get it!"

Lady raced after her.

"She's a darling girl," Rainey murmured as Payne's niece disappeared inside the house.

The maid nodded. "You're coming here this evening has made her happier than I've seen her in a long, long time."

"Why do you say that?"

"Her younger brother, Trevor, died of leukemia last year. She took it harder than the oth—"

"*Leukemia*—"

"Oh...I didn't realize you didn't know. I guess I

shouldn't be surprised Mr. Sterling didn't tell you. Too many similarities between the book and his life.''

''Dear God, Nyla.''

''It's been a difficult year. First his nephew's death, then Ms. Wylie's horrible accident. He's determined that she'll walk again, but she fights him so. I'm afraid Mr. Sterling has had about as muc—''

''Here you go.''

Catherine reappeared so fast, Nyla didn't get the opportunity to finish what she was going to say. Rainey was still so shaken by the news of another tragedy befalling the Sterling family, she felt ill.

Bonnie Wrigley wouldn't believe it when Rainey phoned to tell her that Payne's nephew had died from leukemia.

How many more uncanny coincidences were waiting to come to light Rainey didn't know about yet?

Nyla's revelation cast a new twist on the old adage about truth being stranger than fiction. Chills ran through Rainey's body.

With trembling hands she opened her case and removed the items she would need.

''Do you want Lady to pose for you? I can make her sit still for a few minutes.''

''Thanks, Catherine, but it won't be necessary.''

''Do you mind if I stand behind you and watch?''

''Of course not.''

Lady plopped down next to them. She might not know what was happening, but she acted as if she did. The retriever had a beautiful head.

It didn't take long for the drawing to come to life. Pretty soon Nyla, who'd been taking dishes in the house, came back out to join Catherine. "Will you look at that…"

"I don't see how you do it."

"Believe me, Catherine, neither do I."

"It's a gift," Nyla stated.

"One that landed me in a lot of trouble," Rainey's voice shook.

"Uncle Payne's forgiven you. Otherwise he would never have brought you home with him."

"Well, now that I've apologized to Ms. Wylie, we need to destroy those paintings so she won't ever be reminded of them again."

"Destroyed?" they both cried at once.

"Yes. That's what the judge ordered. If you'd dispose of them, Nyla, it will save Mr. Sterling having to deal with any more grief."

"You're right. If it's a legal matter I suppose now's as good a time as any to take care of them."

"Thank you, Nyla."

While the maid picked them up and carried them into the house, Rainey finished fleshing out the drawing. In the top left-hand corner she put, "To Catherine." Down in the right-hand corner she titled it, then wrote the date and her initials.

"There." She carefully removed the sheet of paper and handed it to Catherine.

The teen held it at both ends. "The Beggar." She broke into laughter. "That's perfect! I *love* it! I'm going to have this framed and put it above my bed. Excuse me while I show it to Nyla. Then I'm going to run it upstairs so it won't get damaged."

Alone for the moment, Rainey glanced at her watch.

It was quarter to eleven. They'd been out on the patio for a long time.

She got up and put everything in her case including her brother's photograph. The picture of Winston went back in her purse. On the way indoors she met Nyla.

"Where will I be sleeping tonight?"

"Up in the guest room next to Catherine's. I'll get your overnight bag and take you there."

"I'd appreciate that, but before we go, I have another favor to ask."

"What is it?"

"Could you manage to bring me a photograph of Trevor without Catherine finding out?"

The maid eyed her with a knowing expression. "You bet. There's one she carries in her wallet. It's her favorite. I'll get it."

Within fifteen minutes everyone had said goodnight. By the time Rainey had prepared for bed, Nyla returned with the photo.

Thankful for an important project that would help keep her thoughts off Payne and his fiancée, Rainey got started on the picture. Instead of using a pencil, she decided to work with her pastels. She wanted this gift to be perfect.

In the snap, Trevor appeared to be nine or ten years old and bore a strong resemblance to his sister. Several times throughout the night tears rolled down Rainey's cheeks to think he'd had to die so early in life.

At five in the morning she was finally satisfied with her work. She'd depicted him and Catherine sitting out on the back lawn. Lady lay at their feet with Catherine's arm thrown loosely around her brother's shoulders.

After putting the pastels away, Rainey climbed into

bed exhausted. But two hours later and sleep still hadn't come. She'd sopped her pillow and couldn't stand to lie in bed any longer.

Meeting Payne Sterling had changed her in ways she was terrified to contemplate.

Though his fiancée might not be the warmest person, after what had happened to her, Rainey couldn't fault her for anything. She had courage to get on with her life, to marry the man of her dreams.

Why would Rainey want to torture herself by hanging around a few more hours just to be with him one more time when his devotion to Diane Wylie was unquestioned. Heavens—they would be married in another month!

If Rainey didn't take control of herself and the situation right now, then there wasn't that much difference between her and the stalker who'd put his fiancée in the wheelchair.

Calling on her inner strength, Rainey straightened the bed, got dressed and hurried downstairs with her cases. A man she hadn't seen before was sitting on a chair in the hall reading a sports magazine. He lifted his head.

"Good morning, Ms. Bennett. My name is Stan."

"Good morning."

How could Rainey have forgotten nothing went on in the Sterling's world without the presence of security?

"Is there someone on the Boyce staff who would drive me into the city? Mr. Sterling was going to have me flown back to New York later in the day, but I've just had a phone call that has forced me to change my plans. I need to leave now."

"Of course. I'll have a limo brought around back for you."

''Thank you. At some point you'll have to inform Mr. Sterling, but would you please wait a while? I happen to know he's with his fiancée and it's a Saturday morning. I'd hate for him to be disturbed over a matter as trivial as my transportation. She appeared very tired last night.''

The security man hesitated briefly, then nodded. While he got on his radio phone, Rainey walked through the house to the back hall and let herself outside.

To her surprise there was a strong wind coming off the ocean. It filled the air with salt spray. Judging by the overcast sky, the sun might not make an appearance at all.

She would love to be at Crag's Head enjoying the elements right now. But that magnificent place and the man who lived there were forbidden to her.

You need to remove yourself from temptation and fly far away, Rainey. Much farther than your studio apartment.

By the time the limo had rolled around, she'd made up her mind to move back to Grand Junction. Coming to New York had been the biggest mistake of her life.

CHAPTER SEVEN

PAYNE walked in the back door of his sister's house at five after eight, ready for a morning swim in the ocean with Catherine and Rainey.

To his surprise Lady didn't come flying down the rear entrance hall to greet him. With a guest as exciting as Rainey to talk to, his niece had probably stayed up late last night and was sleeping in.

Rainey might still be in bed too, but Payne had a hunch she was an early riser. Somewhere in the house he imagined her hard at work on her latest art project.

In the hope she might be out on the patio where they'd had dinner, he headed in that direction. When he discovered everything was locked up tight and she was nowhere in sight, a keen sense of disappointment swept through him.

Maybe she was in the kitchen eating breakfast with the staff. But he quashed that thought the moment he spied Stan, one of his sister's security people, drinking a cup of coffee by himself.

When the other man saw him, he put down his mug. ''I was going to call you in a little while.''

Stan didn't have to say another word for Payne to know something had gone on he wasn't going to be happy about. Like the fact that Rainey was no longer on the premises.

''When did Ms. Bennett leave?''

"About an hour ago. Jed drove her back to the city. She asked me not to bother you since she knew you and Ms. Wylie were together."

"You're supposed to bother me. That's part of your job!" Payne bit out in a rare show of anger because Rainey's charm was so potent, she'd managed to con even a pro like Stan.

Payne shouldn't have cared. It shouldn't have mattered she'd slipped away without his knowing about it. But it did matter. Even more than he'd imag—

"Uncle Payne?"

At the sound of his niece's subdued voice he wheeled around. Both she and Nyla were standing in the doorway with Lady.

"I'm afraid it's my fault Ms. Bennett left in such a hurry this morning," Nyla murmured.

"Come and look," Catherine urged him.

On leaden feet, Payne followed them into the main dining room where he glimpsed a sheet of art paper laid out on the table.

Nyla stood at his other side. "Last night I happened to say something to Ms. Bennett about Trevor's illness because I thought she'd already been told about it. You know, after reading about the hero who had leukemia.

"I never saw anyone look as devastated as she did when she found out. Before she went to bed she asked me to bring her a photograph of him. *This* is the result."

Catherine put a hand on his arm. "I found it in the guest bedroom this morning."

He walked over to see Rainey's handiwork.

One look at the picture done in pastels and his throat almost closed from too much emotion. She'd caught it all. The love, the sweet, tender bond between brother and sister.

"It's so beautiful it hurts," Catherine whispered.

It *was* beautiful. It *did* hurt because everything Rainey drew or painted was driven by heartfelt emotions.

In the next instant his niece was sobbing quietly against Payne's shoulder. "How did she know Trev and I used to spend time out in back with Lady?"

"I guess that's part of her great talent." There didn't seem to be any other explanation.

Nyla's eyes went suspiciously bright. "She felt so badly for upsetting your family, it's evident she wanted to leave all of you with a gift that would bring you happiness. What a wonderful person she is. I've never met anyone like her."

Neither have I.

"She did another picture for me, Uncle Payne. I'll get it."

As he watched Catherine hurry from the room Nyla said, "I don't blame Ms. Bennett for setting off early. I'm sure she's anxious to forget this whole unpleasant business and move on."

Payne couldn't argue with that. After putting Rainey through the hell of a courtroom hearing, he'd forced her to face Diane who did nothing but patronize her all evening. Furthermore he'd had no right to bite Stan's head off because Rainey had reached the point where she couldn't take any more.

"You're going to love this one too." Catherine entered the dining room with another sketch in hand. He took it from her.

"'The Beggar,'" he read the words aloud. Incredibly,

Rainey had caught the special pleading expression in Lady's eyes while she waited with exaggerated patience and politeness for something to eat.

"She's left you some real treasures," Payne murmured. He put the sketch on the table next to the other picture and looked around. "Where are the paintings?"

"Rainey asked me to dispose of them."

He shot Nyla a piercing gaze. "She *what?*"

"Don't worry. I couldn't bring myself to do it. They're in my room."

"I can always count on you. Hold on to them for me. I'll get them later."

"You bet."

Adrenaline surged through his veins. If he didn't expend his excess energy soon, he'd explode.

"Catherine? Put your suit on and we'll take a swim."

"I'm already wearing it under my clothes."

"Then let's go."

"I'll have breakfast waiting for you when you get back."

"Nothing for me, Nyla," he said, "but thanks for the offer."

Forty-five minutes later he and Catherine came out of the ocean and took turns throwing a stick for Lady to fetch. Unfortunately Payne's swim had done nothing to improve his mood which was as stormy as the elements.

His niece appeared to be deep in her own thoughts. There was little conversation until they started back to the house.

"I didn't know the hero in *Manhattan Merger* almost died of leukemia, or that the author lost a child to it. Have you still got the book?"

"Yes."

"I want to read it."

"You're sure?"

"More than ever. I don't see how Diane can say that romances don't reflect real life."

"She would change her tune if she read one." Reading Ms. Wrigley's novel had been a revelation to him.

"But that's the problem. I don't think she ever will."

"Then it's her loss."

Somehow he had to find a way to break through Diane's defenses so she'd go to Switzerland. He couldn't think beyond it.

"Are you going to spend the day with her?"

"No. I have work at the office. She and her mother are overseeing the bridesmaids' fittings. What are your plans?"

"Linda and I are going to play tennis with a bunch of friends. Later I think we'll see a movie."

"Sounds fun. Be sure and take your cell phone with you so we can keep in touch."

"I will." She looked up at him. "Uncle Payne?" By now they'd reached the back lawn.

He sensed her hesitancy. "What is it?"

"When mom and dad get back, I'd like to invite Rainey over for dinner so the whole family can meet her. Would that be okay with you?"

His heart pounded like a sledgehammer. "Of course. Why do you ask?"

"Diane doesn't like me, and I could tell she really didn't like Rainey."

Tell me something I don't already know.

"Don't worry about it."

"After you're married, I hope you'll still come over a lot."

"No one will ever keep me away from you, sweetheart."

Payne gave his niece a hug before climbing into the limo. Mac followed and shut the door.

"Take us home, Andy."

On the short drive to Crag's Head, Payne phoned his pilot and told him to get the chopper ready. He'd be taking off for the city within twenty minutes.

During his talk with Catherine on the way back from the beach, a strange feeling had come over him. Something he couldn't explain. But it all had to do with Rainey and her precipitous departure from the Sterling compound. Suddenly he felt it imperative to catch up with her.

It was close to noon when he alighted from the limo and entered her apartment building. He pressed the button and waited for a response. If she wasn't home, he'd wait outside in the limo as long as it took until she showed up.

He was ready to buzz her again when he heard static and then a man's voice said, "Yes?"

Payne froze in place. "Is this Lorraine's Bennett's studio?"

"Yes."

He struggled to keep from erupting. "May I speak to her?"

"Who is this?"

The urge to knock the man to kingdom come was growing stronger by the second.

"If she doesn't answer within five seconds, I'm coming up to find out why," Payne thundered.

"I'm here, Mr. Sterling," Rainey answered sounding out of breath.

His brows furrowed. What in the hell was she doing with a man in her apartment this early in the day unless… The pictures that ran through his mind filled him with feelings too primitive to describe.

"We have to talk. How soon will you be free?"

"I thought you and your fiancée were—never mind, it doesn't matter. Just a minute, please."

Apparently she'd left his sister's house to rejoin her lover. Out of all the reasons he'd imagined for her disappearance without telling him, Payne would never have thought it was because of a man.

But then he remembered that she'd had other plans the night before and had canceled them in order to accompany Payne. How long had this relationship been going on?

"It's all right. You can come up now."

The minute he heard the click of the door, he opened it and took the stairs three at a time to her floor. He found her standing outside her apartment with the door closed trying to appear at ease, and failing.

She also looked so damn fresh and innocent in a white cotton top and tan jeans, he found her utterly desirable. His heart slammed into his ribs.

"Aren't you going to introduce me to your friend?"

"He went back to his apartment."

How convenient.

"If this was a bad time, why didn't you just say so? I'd have come by later."

"You're a busy man, Mr. Sterling. Since you took the time to drive over here, I didn't want you to be put out by having to come back again."

She was hiding something from him.

"It would have been nice if you'd tried to be this thoughtful by staying put at my sister's house until you were flown home."

She didn't move a muscle, but she couldn't prevent the blush that swept up her neck into her beautiful face.

"I was brought up to believe a good stay is a short stay. Last evening I did all I could to make your fiancée and niece feel better about what happened. When I woke up this morning, I could see no reason to prolong my visit."

"*I* can give you one."

Her hands rubbed the sides of her hips in a gesture she probably wasn't aware of. She didn't look quite so sure of herself now. "I-Is something else wrong?"

"I'm afraid the hallway of a busy apartment building is hardly the place to carry on the conversation I have in mind."

Color stained her cheeks again.

"Would you prefer to come downstairs and sit in the limo while we talk?"

"No—" she cried softly, putting a nervous hand to her throat.

"I can go to my office and come back later in the day if that would suit you better."

"Please don't do that." She sounded panicked.

"Then what *do* you propose? If you were planning to spend the day with the man upstairs, just say so. We can talk tomorrow."

"No," she whispered. "You can come in for a minute."

For a minute?

She darted inside and left the door open for him.

After crossing over her threshold, it took all his strength not to slam the door as he shut it. When he turned around, one look at her denuded walls and desk, and his body went cold.

"It looks like you're in the process of vacating the premises," his voice grated.

"Yes." There were several boxes on her couch already packed. She hurriedly moved them to the floor. "There. Now you can sit down."

He stayed where he was. "Are you moving in with him?"

She bit the soft underside of her lip in a betraying gesture that beguiled him.

"I don't mean to be rude, but I hardly believe that's anyone's concern except mine."

"It'll be my niece's when she tries to invite you to a family party once her parents get home on Monday and you can't be located."

Her gilt-blond head reared. Her eyes had gone that smoky green color again and looked haunted. "You mustn't let her do that!"

His breath caught. "After giving her back a sense of her brother with that magnificent picture she'll treasure all her life, do you honestly think she won't do whatever she can to thank you?"

"I'm glad if she liked it, but—"

"But what?" he demanded.

"I won't be here next week."

Good Lord. He knew what was coming before she said it.

"I—I'm flying home to Grand Junction tomorrow."

Payne felt as if a stalker's bullet had just pierced his heart. "You were going to leave without saying goodbye?"

"We said it last night."

"I distinctly heard you tell me goodnight," he reminded her.

She averted her eyes. "I know you think I'm running away to lick my wounds because of what happened at the hearing, but you'd be wrong," her voice trembled. "The hearing actually did me a favor because it brought my brother to New York."

The faster she talked, the more she revealed her nervousness.

"We haven't spent time together like we used to. While he was here, we talked all night. After next week Craig won't be running any more float trips. He's getting ready to open his own sporting goods company. It's been his lifelong dream.

"The bank gave him the loan and he's found space in a good location. Though he's got help, he could use a lot more."

Payne's hands formed into fists. "So you've suddenly decided to do the honors."

"I have some savings," she went on explaining, "and don't need to accept any more work for a while. I want to help him get set up."

"You're an artist! A fabulous artist. You moved to New York to follow your own dream."

"I never planned to live here forever. This was an experiment. An adventure. Nothing more."

"Does your brother know what you're about to sacrifice for him?"

"N-not yet. I'm planning to surprise him."

"I don't believe you."

"What do you mean?" She sounded angry, but anger masked fear.

"You're not running to him as much as running from something. Admit it!"

By now she was standing at the window looking out, ostensibly so she wouldn't have to face him.

"Please go, Mr. Sterling. When you see your niece, tell her goodbye for me, and let her know I'm happy she liked the picture."

"She loves both of them. The whole family will be delighted when they lay eyes on 'The Beggar.' Creating those masterpieces must have kept you up all night."

Payne hadn't been able to sleep either.

Still she said nothing.

He shifted his weight. "I'm not leaving this apartment until I learn why you planned to disappear without a trace."

Time lapsed before she said in a low voice, "You're going to make me say it aren't you."

Another surge of adrenaline electrified his body. "Say what?" he prodded.

Rainey turned her head in his direction wearing a solemn expression. "Your fiancée knows you've been to my apartment," she began in a throbbing voice.

"She knows I've been to your office, that I've ridden in your helicopter. She knows I've been out to Crag's

Head. After last night she knows I was an overnight guest in your sister's home.

"If I were your fiancée, I could handle all of it knowing everything was the result of the hearing. But any more contact, even a whisper of it, and I would feel...threatened."

He took a step closer. "If you think moving back to Colorado removes that threat, then you're very much mistaken. You could go to the ends of the earth and it wouldn't make any difference."

"Then you haven't done enough to make her feel secure in your love," she fired back.

Unable to respond to that remark without incriminating himself he said, "She'll never feel secure about anything until she can walk again. There's a clinic in Switzerland that might be able to help her, but she refuses to let me take her."

Upon that remark Rainey rested her body against the edge of the desk. Her head was lowered.

"I can understand why. It would be so hard to go there on a thread of hope and then find out not even those doctors could help."

"Diane still has some feeling in her legs, Rainey. There's a chance she could walk again. Otherwise the doctors wouldn't keep urging her to go for a consultation and exam."

Taking a calculated risk he said, "This morning while Catherine and I were swimming in the ocean, an idea came to me that could change Diane's mind. You corroborated it moments ago when you talked about her feeling threatened."

That brought Rainey's head up. He had her full attention now.

"Instead of putting your career on hold for your brother who still has no idea what you're planning, how would you like to do something that could result in Diane throwing away that damn wheelchair?"

A stunned expression broke out on her face. "If I thought I could help, naturally I'd do it, but I can't imagine what it would be."

Rainey Bennett—I'm going to hold you to that.

"Last evening you told me you'd give anything to work alongside me."

She shook her head. "I was carried away. You know that."

"You meant it, Rainey. So I'm proposing that you move into my home at Crag's Head and expand your artistic talents by making my maps for me. It'll be a merger financially beneficial for both of us."

An explosion of green sparks lit up her heavily lashed eyes.

"Until you came along, I never trusted anyone else to do them. With your help I'll be free to travel without the worry that I'm getting behind on the technical end. In this business I have to set up new markets before the competition does.

"In return, let's pray Diane is so threatened by your presence in my life, she'll agree to go to Switzerland and learn to walk again if only to be able to face you on an equal footing."

"You can't be serious!" She sounded aghast.

"I never say what I don't mean. You have to understand something about my fiancée. No one has more pride than Ms. Diane Wylie of the North Shore.

"Her condition is so shocking to her, it's come between her and her friends, her work on the magazine. She helped on my sister's last senatorial campaign. Once upon a time she had aspirations to go into politics herself. All that drive has vanished. She's not the same person she used to be."

Rainey's eyes shimmered with unshed tears. "That's so tragic."

"It is," Payne murmured. "No human being deserves to suffer like she has.

"Last night I felt her pain because she used to be vital and vivacious like you, with a hell of a lot to contribute. If I thought she could be that way again, I'd move heaven and earth to make it happen."

"I'm sure you would," she whispered.

"Since Trevor's death, Catherine's been working on Diane. In her own sweet way she's tried to remind her that there never was any hope for her brother, but there is for Diane. Still my fiancée hasn't responded.

"The first signs of fight I've seen in her were last night while you were enchanting everyone." Enchanting me. "Catherine was a different girl because of you, and Diane knew it.

"With your cooperation, maybe Diane will get so angry she'll end up begging me take her to Switzerland. She's a competitor at heart. That's why I believe this will work. I could have roamed the earth and never found a more worthy opponent than you."

After a significant pause he said, "If your answer is no, then I'll leave here and you'll never have to worry about dealing with me again. If it's yes, you'll have the satisfaction of knowing you tried to help another human being get back her life.''

Rainey couldn't have looked more dazed.

''I realize it's a lot to ask. I have no right. I do a lot of things when I don't have the right, but it's the way I'm made.''

The silence lengthened.

Summoning every vestige of willpower he possessed, Payne walked out of the apartment with a vision indelibly impressed of her standing there looking tormented.

But not tormented enough to call him back.

With that crushing realization, he headed for the staircase.

The thought of life without Rainey Bennett sent him into a despair so black, he didn't remember going down the three flights of stairs to the foyer. Mac and John stood somewhere in the periphery waiting for Payne to climb in the back of the limo. Doors opened and closed. It was all a blur.

''Payne?''

''What is it, Andy?''

''Ms. Bennett is on the sidewalk motioning for you to put down your window.''

Being told that Rainey had followed him all the way to the street was like his body freefalling thousands of feet only to be yanked as his chute suddenly opened.

With lightning speed he levered himself from the car, still trying to catch his breath.

Dozens of people were walking back and forth, but as far as Payne was concerned, he and Rainey were the only two people in existence. She couldn't very well avoid his gaze though she was trying.

"You wouldn't be standing here if the answer weren't yes. Shall we talk about it in the limo, or upstairs?"

She moistened her lips nervously. "When would you want me to start?"

"Now."

"So soo—"

"I have to leave for Paris on Tuesday morning. Therefore I'd like to go over my maps with you this weekend and show you how I work."

"But my apartmen—"

"I'll help you bring down the things you'll need for the weekend. On Monday we'll arrange for you to meet with movers. You can put anything in storage you won't require while you're living with me."

"I'll have to be here for the courier to pick up my latest painting."

"We'll do that and I'll take care of your lease."

"No—I've already made an installment agreement with the super."

Payne decided to let her have that victory for now. Early on he'd learned that when he was on the brink of a major takeover, he pounced when the tiny window of opportunity presented itself. The little things could slide.

"I—I won't need your help with my bags. If you'll wait here, I'll be back down as soon as I can."

"Take all the time you want." *I'm not going any-where without you.*

Payne recognized she craved privacy to say goodbye to the man who'd been in her apartment earlier. Little did the poor devil know Rainey would be out of permanent circulation the moment of liftoff.

While he waited, he phoned his niece.

"Hi, Uncle Payne!"

"How are things?"

"Great!"

That was the most enthusiasm he'd heard out of her in a long time.

"I invited my friends over to see Rainey's drawings. Now they want her to do pictures of them and their pets so they can give them to their parents for Christmas presents. Do you think she would do it if they paid her?"

He smiled. "Knowing Rainey, she wouldn't take the money."

"I'm sure you're right, but that's a lot to ask when she has two other jobs."

"Tell you what. You can ask her yourself tomorrow."

"Did you invite her out to the house again?"

"No. I asked her to accept a full-time job with me. She said yes, and she'll be moving into Crag's Head where she'll work on my maps."

There was a prolonged silence.

"Uncle Payne...does Diane know?"

"Not yet. I'll tell her tonight."

"That's going to hurt her a lot."

"I'm hoping it'll make her angry."

He could hear her brain working. "You *want* her to be jealous."

"I want her to walk again. Maybe if she gets angry enough, she'll do something about it and consider going to that clinic in Switzerland."

Another pause. "Does Rainey know why you've asked her to come to work for you?"

"Yes. She wants to help Diane too."

"So do I."

"You already have. You're a sweetheart. I'm sure Rainey will enjoy your company, especially when I'm out of town. You can show her around, make certain she knows where to swim safely."

"Do you think she likes to sail?"

"I guess we're going to find out. Come on over in the morning and have breakfast with us."

"Will Diane be there?"

"I'll invite her. Let's hope she won't be able to stay away. Have fun this afternoon. I'll see you in the morning."

After ending the call, he made one more to his pilot to alert him they'd be flying back to Crag's Head soon.

Two hours later he experienced the sensation of déjà vu when his housekeeper met him and Rainey in the foyer.

"Mrs. Myers? Ms. Bennett has agreed to come to work for me. For the time being she'll be living here. Let's put her in the bedroom with the view of Phantom Point."

Rainey's mouth curved upward. "That sounds intriguing."

"It is. Sometimes you see it, sometimes you don't. Shall I take up your bags now, Ms. Bennett?"

"Please call me Rainey. I'll carry them."

"You're going to find out my new assistant has an independent streak," Payne murmured.

"That's fine with me as long as you call me Betty."

His housekeeper liked to keep things formal. For her to make a concession like that meant Rainey had already won her over.

"It's a deal."

"We're going to get busy in my study, Betty. When you have a moment, will you bring us some lunch?"

"Coming right up."

Payne was eager to sit down with Rainey and explain how he put his crude drawings together into one blueprint. With her intuitive eye, she would bring her own expertise to streamline the process and make innovations.

After a moment's consideration he pulled out a tube housing the drawings of Paris he'd already begun work on. While he was laying them out on the large worktable, his cell phone rang. A check of the Caller ID confirmed it was Diane.

His eyes flicked to Rainey. "I have to take this call. Go ahead and see what you make of everything."

It was like a giant jigsaw puzzle. He couldn't help but be curious how long it would take her to fit each piece together.

Moving a few feet away he answered the phone. Now that he had Rainey firmly entrenched beneath his roof, it was time to follow through with the rest of his plan.

CHAPTER EIGHT

RAINEY slept, but it was fitful. At dawn she stole from the queen-size bed to half lie in the window seat and contemplate the vast Atlantic from her bedroom high above the water. As morning broke to the sounds of gulls, she remembered something Craig had said in an attempt to comfort her.

Treat the whole experience with Payne Sterling as part of your adventure in the Big Apple.

He didn't know it then, but her brother had dispensed the best advice he could have given her. That was exactly the way she was going to look at her situation from here on out.

A marvelous adventure. The kind she enjoyed living with the heroine inside a romance novel until the very last page when she closed the book.

There *would* come a last page with Payne. Until then, what were the odds of meeting an exciting, brilliant New York billionaire-soon-to-be-trillionaire in her lifetime? Of working temporarily as his live-in assistant in his hideaway which was an architectural treasure?

Maybe a gazillion-to-one?

She leaned out the window to inhale the tangy sea air and enjoy the ocean breeze. The humidity curled the ends of her hair. Her skin, so used to the dry climate of the Colorado Rockies, felt soft and smooth.

By some quirk of fate, she and Payne had been

brought together at this moment in time. It wouldn't last, so why go on torturing herself about it?

Why not be the catalyst that might rouse his fiancée from debilitating fear so she could walk down the aisle to the man waiting for her at the altar?

What were the odds of Rainey ever playing a major role in someone else's rescue again?

The answer was, never.

"Good morning, Ms. Bennett!"

Rainey looked down to see her host walking up the beach in cutoffs and a T-shirt looking like a contemporary Jane Austen hero.

"Why if it isn't Mr. Darcy!"

His hands went to his hips. The next thing she knew he was laughing up at her. She found herself laughing with him.

Careful, Rainey. Don't let him guess the very sight of him turns your bones to liquid. Keep things light.

"If it was your intention to go about startling all the young ladies, you can consider you've accomplished your objective, sir."

"My Dear *Miss* Bennett—if I startled you, it was because you were hoping I would happen to come along at this precise moment to catch you in, shall we say, flagrante delicto? so you could be pretend to be startled."

"Oh my, Mr. Darcy. Rumors of your monumental ego combined with your insufferable arrogance have been greatly understated. Isn't it a good thing you're in love with yourself since it's probable no one else would ever be able to love you quite so well."

More laughter rumbled out of him, the deep, rich male kind.

Suddenly Rainey heard clapping. "Well done, you two. Jane Austen is alive and doing just fine at Crag's Head."

Rainey looked to the right and caught sight of Diane. "She wrote one of the great romances, don't you think, Ms. Wylie?"

"She wrote several. I found *Persuasion* her most compelling."

The mention of that particular title sounded cryptic and introduced a different mood into the tenor of the morning. Rainey could tell Payne was equally affected.

Persuasion was what was needed to get her to that clinic.

"I understand we were all going to have breakfast when you arrived. Excuse me and I'll be right down." She tore herself from the window, unwilling to put herself through the agony of watching him greet his fiancée.

Yesterday he'd worked with Rainey all afternoon and into the early evening. The rapport between them had been uncanny. She couldn't believe how well things had gone, what a remarkable teacher he was.

Being with him, she'd been unaware of time passing. It had almost killed her when seven-thirty rolled around and he'd excused himself to go pick up Diane for dinner. At some point in the evening Rainey knew he would inform his fiancée he'd hired Rainey to come to work for him.

Since Rainey hadn't seen him until he'd been walking along the surf moments ago, it was anyone's guess how Diane had reacted to his news.

Judging by her unexpected appearance on the path just now, his plan seemed to be working to some degree. She'd plunged right into the thick of things, staking her claim in front of Rainey.

His fiancée had a lot of demons to fight besides her fear that another woman was interested in her fiancé. The last thing Rainey wanted to do was hurt her. All she could do was follow Payne's lead and hope it caused the kind of reaction that would force Diane to get past her psychological block.

Rainey pulled clothes from the closet and drawers. The temperature had dropped to the low seventies prompting her to dress in a pair of white pleated trousers and a yellow cotton pullover.

With a good brushing of her hair and an application of coral lipstick, there was nothing more to do but join them. She left the bedroom not knowing quite what to expect, but realizing that Diane was waiting for her.

The dining room off the study had its own glorious view of the ocean. Payne and Diane had already started to eat.

His gaze flicked to Rainey's. So much vital masculinity for breakfast made her heart race. "Help yourself to anything you want at the buffet."

"Thank you."

It looked like the housekeeper had outdone herself. Rainey poured herself some orange juice, then went for the sausage and eggs, her favorite breakfast.

"Come and sit down."

Said the spider to the fly?

The other woman's smile was benign enough. Yet Rainey did her bidding with a prickling awareness that

Diane had been geared for a confrontation since Payne had dropped his bombshell.

"How did you sleep, Ms. Bennett?"

Payne covered Diane's hand. "Since we're all going to be seeing a lot of each other from now on, let's get on a first name basis."

Fearing she might choke on her juice, Rainey put the glass back down. "To be honest, I was so excited to be right here on the water, I stayed awake most of the night. It's quite heavenly."

"No other woman apart from Mrs. Myers has ever slept at Crag's Head before."

His fiancée had just fired her first salvo.

"It must be thrilling for you to know that after August first this will be your home, Diane. The design transports you to another realm, yet you're firmly planted on a headland with a whole ocean at your feet. I think you're the luckiest woman alive to have all this to look forward to."

"When Payne installs an elevator, it will be more livable for me."

"If we leave for Switzerland right away, it's possible you'll never have to use another elevator again."

"It's not going to happen, Payne. But since you brought the subject up, now would be the time to say what's on my mind."

Diane's gaze swerved to Rainey who wondered what was coming next. She stopped chewing.

"I know why he hired you."

Her bold declaration revealed the fire Payne had been referring to when he'd asked Rainey to be his accomplice.

"The problem is, I'm not sure he told *you* why."

Rainey had no choice but to play dumb. "I don't think I understand."

"Those maps of Payne's are sacrosanct. No one in the hierarchy of his company is allowed inside Crag's Head to see them. He trusts no one to touch them. They're his brainchild, the key to his success.

"Then suddenly he decides to let a portrait artist who paints covers for Red Rose Romance move into his fortress and assist him on drawings that are so complicated no one but Payne himself can understand them?" She left out a brittle laugh.

"I don't think so. I may not be able to walk, but credit me with more brains than that, Rainey. We both know he's installed you here to force my hand because he wants me to go to Switzerland for an operation."

The strength it took to hold the other woman's gaze without flinching called on every nerve and muscle in Rainey's body.

"I've told him I'm not going. Of course he doesn't understand the meaning of the word no. What he's done is pull one of his shrewd business ploys to get me to capitulate by bringing a beautiful woman into his home on the pretext of working for him.

"He knows this will cause our families and friends to talk. What better way to get me to change my mind than threaten to humiliate me."

Rainey's heart sank like a stone. Though Diane's delivery had been unemotional, she had to be dying inside.

"What he refuses to accept is that there's no miracle cure waiting for me at the end of the road. I guess what I'm saying is, the next move is up to you."

She paused to take a drink of her coffee. When she put the cup down again she said, "If you truly thought he was offering you a legitimate job, and yet you continue to stay under his roof knowing what I've just told you, then it will be clear to everyone who loves him that you two are having an affair.''

A groan almost made it past Rainey's lips.

Diane had just called her fiancé's bluff. The fear that an operation wouldn't change anything was keeping her locked in that wheelchair. Rainey could weep for both of them because that fear was holding him prisoner too.

Somehow Rainey needed to say something in a counter move that would still be the truth, yet not jeopardize an already precarious situation.

''I'm aware of his hopes for you,'' she began quietly. ''It's only natural when he loves you so much, but I'm afraid the blame for the job offer lies with me.''

One of Diane's brows lifted in a patronizing gesture. ''Your attraction to him has made you the proverbial putty in his hands.''

''I *am* attracted to him,'' Rainey came back, fighting fire with fire. ''If you're talking physical attraction, then I'd be a liar if I didn't admit it considering I've done eight paintings of him already. He's an incredibly good-looking man.''

The mockery in Diane's smile started to vanish.

''If you're talking mental attraction, I admit to that too. Let me tell you why.'' Now that Rainey was all wound up, it would be therapeutic to get certain things said.

''You don't know very much about me. How could you? I grew up in a small town. My brother loves it there. From an early age on, he knew he wanted to live there forever and run a sportings goods store. Come fall, that dream is finally going to happen for him.

"I was different. I had this dream to move to a big city and see what it was like.

"The money from teaching art in public school was a means of keeping me alive, but it was my freelance jobs that paid me enough to get here. In all honesty, I came to New York hoping I might stumble on to my life. Do you know what I'm talking about?"

Diane brushed some hair away from her forehead. "People like you flock to New York every day looking for the same thing. The difference is, none of them ended up in a courtroom with my fiancé."

A tremor rocked Rainey's body.

"That's true. When the judge was reprimanding me, he said it best. *Call it destiny or fate, you happened to paint the one man whose phenomenal success in life has made him vulnerable to the ugliest elements in our society.*

"It seems that fate, or destiny, whatever you choose to call it, brought me to this house. While your fiancé was upstairs getting changed before taking me to the Boyce's to meet you, I wandered into his study. That's when something amazing happened.

"I saw his maps spread over the walls of the lighthouse. They were so fantastic, I was spellbound. I remember feeling the same way when I was young and came across Tolkien's map of Middle Earth for the first time.

"When Mr. Sterling came back downstairs ready to leave, he found me babbling with so much excitement, I'm sure he didn't know what to make of it. I practically begged for a chance to work with him."

Diane's brown eyes flared in surprise. Rainey could

be thankful for that much reaction. At least she was listening.

"Yes, I'm guilty of wanting to grab at an opportunity to work with someone like him because fate would never allow it to happen a second time. But if you're talking emotional attraction, that's something else again because he's spoken for. He's asked *you* to marry him.

"If you'd seen your fiancé in court, then you'd know he was only there for one reason. To protect *you*. To make certain nothing would ever hurt you again.

"He was a frightening adversary when he thought I'd been out there stalking the two of you. After court ended I thought how blessed you were to have a fiancé who showed that kind of devotion to you. One who'd do anything for you. He'd give his life to see you walk again!" Rainey's voice throbbed.

Diane unexpectedly averted her eyes.

"I discovered the strength of his devotion when he asked me to meet you and help reassure you that I posed no threat to your safety.

"He's a hero in every sense of the word, Diane. *Your* hero. The kind you could read about in those little romance novels whose covers I paint."

She had one more thing to say. This time she turned to Payne who'd been staring at her through shuttered eyes.

He'd enlisted her help. She'd complied with his request and would carry out her part of the bargain for a while longer. But she had to draw the line somewhere because her very existence depended on it.

"Did you tell Diane I'm only here in New York until my brother sends for me?"

"Uncle Payne?"

"In the dining room, sweetheart," he answered his niece without acknowledging Rainey's question.

"I brought Linda with me. She wants to meet Rainey."

"Hi, Linda," he drawled. "Come and have some breakfast with us."

"Thanks, Mr. Sterling."

Seconds later the two teens breezed in the room wearing shorts and tops. Linda was a tall girl with pretty features and a chestnut braid hanging down the middle of her back.

She walked over to Diane. "Hi, Ms. Wylie! How are you?"

"I'm fine, thank you." But Diane didn't sound fine at all. Her voice held a definite tremor.

"I bet you're getting excited for the wedding."

"Yes," she murmured.

"Rainey?" Catherine headed for her. "I'd like you to meet my best friend, Linda Miles. Linda? This is Rainey Bennett."

"Hello, Linda." The teen moved closer. "What beautiful hair you have."

She and Catherine exchanged smiles. "Thanks. I saw the pictures you did for Catherine. They're so good."

"What she's trying to say is, do you think you could draw one of Linda sometime?"

"I wouldn't expect you to do it for free, that is if you had the time to do it."

"I'll make the time, and I wouldn't take your money," Rainey assured her.

Their host got up to pour himself a cup of coffee. "Why don't you girls grab a plate of food?"

"Thanks. We're starving. Oh—before I forget—where did you put *Manhattan Merger,* Uncle Payne?"

"It's in my study. Left-hand drawer of my desk."

"Can I get it now so I won't forget?"

"Go ahead."

"Do you like romances, Linda?" Diane inquired as Catherine left the dining room.

After their previous conversation, Rainey had to give the other woman credit for hanging in there. Payne had said his fiancée was a competitor at heart. Rainey believed him.

"I love them," Linda said. "They're really fun."

"How do you mean fun?"

Catherine's friend found the food she wanted and sat down. "It's fun to see how two completely different people get together, the problems they have to overcome."

"Don't you know that's one of the big concerns about romances? Our magazine did an in-depth article on them some time ago. It wouldn't hurt you to read it. Those stories only show the exciting parts of a relationship, and never deal with the ever after."

"At least the couples in the romances I've read get married, Ms. Wylie. In real life a lot of them live together first, and statistics show that more of them break up later and then kill each other or something."

"Does your mother approve?"

"She doesn't mind. Mom's sick of all the violence and sex on TV."

"Don't tell me there isn't a lot of that in those books."

"Some are graphic, some aren't. What I like is that the two people are really in love and faithful to each other. There isn't any violence in them. My grandma says every man should read one so he'd know how to treat a woman better.''

Rainey drained the rest of her juice so she wouldn't smile.

''Your grandmother reads them?'' Diane sounded incredulous.

''Yes. When I had my tonsils out last year she came over and read one to me. That got me started.''

Their host chuckled. ''You're never going to win this argument, Diane.''

''Let me see that novel, Catherine,'' she said when Payne's niece came back in the dining room. Just then his glance slid to Rainey's. Something was going on with his fiancée. She refused to leave the subject alone.

Catherine handed it to her before hurrying over to the buffet.

''Who wants to go for a sail after we're through eating?''

''We do!'' the girls said at the same time, thrilled over Payne's suggestion.

''What about you, Diane? It's a calm sea today.''

''I believe I will come with you.''

''That's great!'' Catherine enthused. ''We'll all get a tan together.''

''Give me a few minutes to get ready.'' She pushed her wheelchair away from the table and headed for the hallway.

''That's three out of four. Rainey? Does the idea appeal?''

Under other circumstances she couldn't imagine anything more exciting than going out on the ocean with him, but not now. Not ever.

While Diane was still in earshort she said, "If we're going to work together later, I'd better finish my greeting card project while you're gone. The deadline for the artwork is coming up soon."

Payne's niece turned to her with an interested expression. "What are you working on?"

"Right now, a bon voyage card showing a saucy Siamese cat with diamonds around her neck and red silk gloves up to her shoulders. She's stretched out on top of one of those mansard rooftops in an elegant arrondissement of Paris waving goodbye with her tail to a rascal of a mutt."

"Oh how cute!" Catherine cried.

"He has a hobo's stick over his shoulder. There's a little bag tied to the end with a Provençal print scarf. His beret is set at a jaunty angle." Rainey closed her eyes and shook her head. "They're in love."

The girls burst into laughter. So did Payne.

"Can we see it?" Linda sounded as excited as Catherine.

"Of course. When you get back from sailing, come to my room. Have fun everybody."

Grateful the girls were there to provide a buffer against Payne, Rainey left the dining room without looking at him. She hoped it didn't seem like she was running a marathon to get away from him.

For the next three hours she worked steadily on her sketches, but her body broke out in perspiration more than once anticipating the moment when she had to join Payne in his study.

Those had been hellish moments downstairs with his fiancée. She'd practically accused them outright of having an affair.

Tears filled Rainey's eyes. The poor thing had tried to handle her pain and outrage in a dignified manner. It was an awful experience. Rainey refused to put Diane through that again.

From here on out, Payne would have to deal with his fiancée on his own. Rainey would remain in the background a little while longer to work on his maps before she left for Colorado. That was it.

Eventually she heard footsteps in the hall. Payne had come back with the girls. Rainey invited them inside and let them look at her drawings.

Before they left to ride their bikes to Catherine's house, Rainey told Linda to come over on Tuesday morning after Payne left for Paris. Before she got to work she'd do a sketch of Linda and her dog, Hannibal, playing on the beach.

The three of them went downstairs together. Rainey saw them out. When she came back in the house Betty told her Payne had driven his fiancée home and would be back at one to get busy.

Rainey glanced at her watch. She had one hour. Now would be a good time to make a credit card call home and tell her parents what was going on.

Tomorrow she would buy herself a good cell phone. Then she could call her friends and give them a phone number without them knowing her new address. She would ask the post office to hold her mail.

For security reasons as well as personal ones, no one could know she was living temporarily at Crag's Head.

CHAPTER NINE

"DID you really have a good time out there, or were you putting up a front for the girls?"

The limousine would be pulling up in front of the Wylie estate before long.

Diane shot Payne a piercing glance. "Why do you bother to ask me a question like that when you know I hated it."

Payne rubbed his forehead. "Then why did you come sailing and put yourself through misery?"

"To please you. To spend some time with you."

"I realize we haven't had much time alone together lately, but I promised Phyllis I'd watch out for Catherine while they were away. They'll be home tomorrow night. Once I'm back from Paris next weekend, I'll be free for you. We'll do whatever needs doing to get ready for the wedding."

"How would you feel if I flew to Paris with you?"

To say that Payne was surprised by her question was putting it mildly. His fiancée hadn't wanted to go anywhere since the shooting. Though no one had said it, both his family and hers feared she was turning into a recluse.

There was only one reason for the drastic change in her. One person whose performance earlier today had sent thrills and chills through every centimeter of his body.

"Do you want to go with me to please me, or yourself, Diane?"

"Both," she answered honestly.

"Then there's nothing I'd like more." He meant it. If this was the beginning of a metamorphosis, he was overjoyed. Thank God for Rainey. He pressed a kiss to Diane's temple.

She laid her head against his shoulder. "I know you have business, but do you think you could take some time off to shop with me? I'm not that happy with the wedding dress I've picked out. Since we haven't had any pictures taken yet, maybe I'll see something there I like better."

"We'll do it. Would you like to bring someone to keep you company while I'm busy?"

"No. I want to see how I function on my own."

He squeezed her hand. "Good for you."

His elation was too great. He had to be careful. She hadn't mentioned Rainey. Whatever she was holding back would eventually come out, but he wasn't going to broach the subject right now. Not when they'd just entered new territory.

It was like tunneling underground, a precarious business at best. You never knew when the earth might cave in on you, entombing you in blackness.

When they reached the Wylie estate he helped her into the house. "I'll be at the office tomorrow. At some point I'll phone you and we'll make final plans for our trip. Would you like to see a play at the Comédie Française? I can call ahead and reserve tickets."

"I don't know. Why don't we decide what to do after we get there."

"Whatever you want."

The drive back to Crag's Head took long enough that by the time he walked through the house to find Rainey, some of his elation had worn off.

Today Diane had been provoked, and she'd rallied. The fact that she was willing to go anywhere at all constituted a miracle of sorts.

But Paris wasn't Switzerland.

Was it possible she was toying with him to pay him back for involving Rainey in their personal lives? Could it be Diane was pretending to go so far but no further when it came to the bottom line?

Payne didn't want to think the worst where she was concerned, however anything was possible.

"I guess I don't have to ask you how things went with Diane."

Rainey.

His head jerked to the right. He discovered her standing in front of one of his maps.

Every time he saw her, he felt like it was the first time. Something inside him ignited. The pulse throbbed at the base of his throat. It was an involuntary response, and there wasn't a damn thing he could do about it.

"Your fiancée is too intelligent not to have seen through your plan, Payne."

"Nevertheless she's going to Paris with me on Tuesday."

"Really?" she cried with a haunting smile. "Then why aren't you looking happier about it?"

He rubbed the back of his neck. "I don't know. Something isn't right. I've read articles about babies who never crawl. One day they just get up and start walking. But it's rare.

"That's what Diane did today. From recluse to transatlantic tourist, all in the space of a morning."

She moved toward him. "You hurt her by hiring me. I suppose it's not beyond the possibility that she's playing a game with you. But even if she is, your plan did provoke her to this much of a response. You should be rejoicing."

He had rejoiced. For a period of about ten minutes he'd allowed himself that luxury.

"And what if it's just a blip on the screen?"

"Then you'll try something else because it's the way Payne Sterling is made."

"Rainey," her name came out on a half groan. That adorable mouth of hers was such an enticement, he could barely concentrate. The urge to take her in his arms was so intense, he had to force himself to put distance between them.

"You want to know what my theory is?" she went on talking, oblivious to the powerful tremors that shook his body.

"What's that?" he asked with his back to her, struggling for control.

"The talk about romance novels got to her."

"Diane's never read one."

"Oh yes she has. Maybe not a Red Rose Romance, but her literature degree guarantees she's read the classics.

"The point is, since the shooting she's been in a depression and hasn't allowed herself to escape the reality of her situation. But the court hearing has forced her to listen to Catherine and Linda, even Nyla, go on about their favorite kinds of books.

"I believe their conversation has reminded her of your relationship before she got shot—w-when she felt whole and knew she was all things to you," she stammered.

Lord.

"Remember what Linda said? *It's fun to see how two completely different people get together, the problems they have to overcome.*

"Maybe Diane's not ready for an operation yet, but she's decided to go to Paris with you to prove she's trying to conquer her fear and be that vital woman you fell in love with."

His heart almost failed him. "You're wrong, Rainey."

There was a slight pause. "As I said, it was just a theory," her voice trailed.

He'd hurt her when it was the last thing under heaven he wanted to do.

Payne swung around, aware his breathing was ragged. "Where are you going?"

She paused midstride. Turning her blond head toward him she said, "You're obviously upset. I've only made matters worse."

"You're right. I am upset, but you're not the reason. Please stay. I need to talk to you."

There was a tender expression in her green eyes as she studied him. "Tell me about Diane. How did you two first meet? How long ago? I've wanted to know the answers to those questions since the hearing, but it wasn't any of my business."

Payne inhaled sharply. "Diane grew up on Long Island like I did. Our parents have always been good friends. They've traveled in the same circles, had parties with all their children at least half a dozen times every year for years.''

''That explains so much,'' her voice shook. ''You and Diane were—''

''*Not* childhood sweethearts,'' he cut her off. Payne couldn't let the lie continue any longer.

''I'm not in love with Diane. I was never in love with her. She only thinks she's in love with me.''

Rainey's shock rendered her speechless. That was good. He had more to say.

''For the last ten years I've been so involved building my company, I can probably count on one hand the times I've even seen Diane in passing.

''During the last Christmas holiday her family invited mine for brunch. My parents asked them back for dinner. It's a tradition with them. I'd forgotten all about it because I stopped going to those functions by the time I went away to college.

''On the night Diane was shot, I was working at my office alone when I got a phone call from mother. She said Diane Wylie was on her way to my office. Apparently she'd been shopping and had lost track of the time. Would I let her in and bring her to the house for the annual party when I flew home?

''I didn't even know mother was having a party. It was the last thing I wanted to do, but if Diane was already downstairs in the foyer waiting for me to let her come up, I didn't see how I could get out of it. So I agreed.''

Rainey looked shell-shocked. The way she was holding on to the back of one of the chairs, he had the strongest suspicion she needed the support.

"During the flight to Crag's Head we caught up on each other's news the way you do with an old acquaintance. She'd just come back from San Francisco where she'd been interviewed for an editor's job with a magazine there. But she'd decided not to take it.

"In a teasing way I made the comment that she'd probably met a man here and didn't want to leave him. She teased back that I could be right.

"At that point the helicopter landed. Mac had a flu bug and looked like death. I told him to go to bed. He argued with me, but I reminded him we were in the family compound which was secure. Nothing was going to happen."

The more Payne explained, the more he could see Rainey's complexion losing color.

"I decided to drive my own car for a change. We left straight for my parents' home a short distance away. I helped Diane out. We'd just reached the stairs of the house when someone called my name.

"When I spun around, I discovered a strange woman standing near the bushes brandishing a gun. I'd been stalked at least six times since college, but none of the women had ever been in possession of a weapon before.

"It was one of those surreal moments, Rainey. You know it's happening to you, but your brain is slow to react. I pushed Diane out of the way, then lunged for the woman. A shot rang out a split second before I tackled her to the ground. In the background I could hear Diane screaming that she'd been hit.

"Suddenly the whole world converged on us. Family, friends, security, police, paramedics.

"That shot shattered her world and mine."

"Oh, Payne—" Rainey moaned as if she'd been the one wounded.

"Diane didn't want anyone to touch her but me. It was a fight to get her to relent enough to let the paramedics take over. Of course she was in shock.

"She clung to me like a frightened child, begging me to ride in the ambulance with her. I would have thought she'd want her parents, but I did what she asked because I was in shock myself and frantic for her."

"Of course. What a hideous moment for all of you."

"That's the word, Rainey. On the way to the hospital she kept saying that she was afraid she was going to die. Suddenly this whole confession came out that she'd always loved me and hoped to marry me one day."

Rainey bowed her head.

"Diane admitted that she'd gone to the city on purpose to see me. She used my mother by calling her up and pretending that she needed a ride home. Could my mother arrange for her to hook up with me?

"Her ruse worked," he ground out. "She accomplished her objective, but ended up paying a price no one should have to pay."

"No."

"That bullet was meant for me, Rainey. If I hadn't given Mac the night off, he would have dealt with the situation so fast that stalker wouldn't have known what hit her. That's what I pay him for.

"Out of all the nights to give him a break, it had to be that one."

"Stop crucifying yourself!"

"I don't know how. You'd think I would have learned from the other stalking experiences in my life that I'd always be a target and could never let down my guard.

"If you recall, God didn't say 'blessed are the rich and the famous.' That's because He knew those tags carried a terrible price."

"Payne—"

"It's true. When all is said and done, I'm the reason Diane can't walk. The first two months were pure hell for her and for me. Every day I did a balancing act between my office and her hospital room. Each time I entered it, I prayed to hear she'd made a little progress.

"One evening while her doctor was doing rounds, he pulled me aside and told me there wasn't anything else they could do for her. But because she still had some feeling in her legs, he suggested she go to a clinic in Zurich which was renowned for a new kind of operation that was getting results.

"That was the news I'd been waiting for. When I asked the doctor if he'd told Diane about it, he said yes, but she was fighting the idea.

"I couldn't understand it, not if there was any possibility at all that she could walk again.

"Diane and I argued about it until she cried herself to sleep. When I went home I racked my brain trying to figure out how I could get her to change her mind and go."

"So you asked her to marry you," Rainey murmured.

Their eyes met for a long unsmiling moment.

"Yes. I thought my proposal would bring about the

required miracle. I told her I'd take a month off. We'd combine her hospital stay with a honeymoon.

"Since our engagement she's said yes to the idea and then reneged a hundred times. We were still battling over it the day Catherine and Diane came flying into my brother-in-law's study to show me the cover on *Manhattan Merger*."

"That was *my* fault," Rainey cried in anguish. "I should never have taken the risk of painting your face or anyone else's from memory!"

"Who's crucifying themselves now?"

"Touché," she whispered. "Payne—I—I have an idea."

"That's good, because I'm running out of them."

"In a few minutes I'm going to pack my bags and leave for good."

Rainey, Rainey.

"You think I didn't know you were going to say it before you did?"

"Please listen."

She was being all serious and noble. He folded his arms so he wouldn't be tempted to reach for her and never let her go.

"Behold your captive audience."

Like a nervous doe in the forest sensing danger, she backed away from him. "As soon as I've left in the helicopter, drive over to Diane's and surprise her.

"Tell her she was right, that you hired me to make her angry, and now you and I both realize the ploy failed miserably. Let her know I've gone back to Colorado, which is exactly where I'm going after I leave here.

"Then ask her to go away to Paris with you tomorrow

instead of Tuesday. Tell her nothing's more important than her happiness, and that you'll never mention Switzerland again. I honestly believe if you do that, she'll find the strength to go to this clinic.

"I've seen evidence of that Wylie pride you were talking about. It means that deep down the *last* thing she wants is the Sterling name and your protection because she ended up in a wheelchair and you felt guilty about it.

"Like any real woman she wants your love, given freely.

"She knows the only way she can win that love is to fight for it *after* she's done everything in her power to stand on her own two feet first. That's why I'm convinced she'll end up doing what's best for her and you.

"And now I'm going to leave here because it's best for me." She started out of the study. "Will you tell your pilot I'll be ready for takeoff in ten minutes?"

Payne let her go. He had to. His commitment was to Diane. Rainey respected that commitment. She was an honorable woman. In fact she was so many wonderful things, he didn't dare start listing them or he'd never stop.

In less than ten minutes she was back downstairs again with her bags. They walked out of the house together without saying anything. When he'd put her belongings in the helicopter, he turned to help her inside. Her sunny smile would have fooled anyone except Payne.

"You don't ever need to worry about stumbling on to your life, Rainey Bennett. It lives inside you and infects everyone you meet."

Her eyes filmed over. "That's the nicest compliment

anyone's ever paid me. For what it's worth, I meant what I said to Diane. You're a hero in every sense of the word. The next time I read a Red Rose Romance, I'll think of you, but I promise to control the urge to paint you.''

The rotors whipped the air. It was time.

''Be happy,'' she whispered. Her kiss felt like the brush of a butterfly's wing against his jaw.

He closed the door and stepped away from the chopper. The noise it made rising in the air covered the groan coming from the deepest recesses of his soul.

When it was out of sight he broke into a run and headed for the beach. After a half hour's workout he went back to the house to shower and pack a bag.

Downstairs he found his housekeeper in the kitchen.

''Betty? There's been a change in plans. Rainey has decided to go home to Colorado. I'm leaving now and won't be back from Paris with Diane until next Saturday. Call me if there are any problems.''

He phoned Andy to bring the limo around. Soon John and Mac had joined them for the ride to Payne's sister's house. He wanted to say goodbye to his niece in person.

Nyla happened to meet him in the hall and told him Catherine had gone over to the grandparents for Sunday dinner.

''Can I give her a message?''

''That's all right. I'll phone her over there. While I'm here, will you get me those paintings of Rainey's?''

''You bet. Just a minute.''

While Payne waited, he called Catherine's cell phone.

''Hi, Uncle Payne!''

''Hi, sweetheart. I'm glad I caught you.''

''Me too. I guess I left that romance at your house,

but when I called Betty, she said she hadn't seen it. Do you have any idea where it might be?"

He frowned. "I remember Diane asking you to hand it to her. Maybe she still has it. If she does, I'll make sure it gets back to you."

"Thanks. How's everything going?" she whispered.

He swallowed hard. "Better than expected."

"Really?"

"Yes. I'm taking Diane to Paris with me in the morning."

"She's actually going to go on your jet with you?"

"That's right."

"Maybe this means—"

"Whatever it means, it's progress," he broke in. "Because of it, Rainey has decided not to work for me after all. She left to go back to Colorado a couple of hours ago."

A long silence ensued. "She was going to draw Linda's portrait on Tuesday."

Payne didn't know about that. "Tell Linda that Rainey would have done it if she could have."

"I will," she said in a quiet voice. "Uncle Payne? Are you all right?"

Don't ask me that, sweetheart. "I couldn't be better. If Diane can take this step, who knows where it will lead?"

"I'll keep my fingers crossed. I love you. Thanks for taking such good care of me."

Thank God for his niece. "I love you too. What do you want from Paris?"

"For you to be happy."

Someone else he loved had told him the same thing two hours ago.

"Ditto, sweetheart. Give everyone my love. Tell mom and dad I'll be by to see them next weekend."

"I will."

"Here you go," Nyla said as he put his phone back in his pocket.

Payne took the paintings from her. "Thanks for everything. My sister's lucky to have you." He gave her a hug before leaving the house with a precious treasure.

After he got to the office he would leave a note for his secretary to mail them to Rainey. They were her creation. She had the only right to them. If she decided to get rid of them, he didn't want to know about it.

"Andy? Take me to the Wylies'."

Payne intended to follow Rainey's advice to the letter. He'd lost faith in his own instincts, but he believed in hers. She was the one gifted with second sight. Maybe she knew something he didn't.

Two days later he wrapped up a conference early with some of his engineers and returned to his apartment near the Place Vendôme. Thanks to the time Rainey had spent with him on the Paris map, he'd been able to give the men enough work to put them ahead of schedule.

"Diane? I'm back and ready to take you shopping for your wedding dress."

"I'd rather stay in so we can talk."

Payne frowned. Since Sunday when he'd surprised her, she'd been in better spirits than he'd seen her since the shooting. He didn't think he could handle it if she told him she wanted to go home. It would mean she'd slipped back into that immobilizing depression he dreaded.

He put down his briefcase. "You don't sound like you're feeling well."

When he walked in her bedroom, he found her seated in her wheelchair wearing a new two-toned pink suit.

"I like your outfit. You look very attractive."

"I believe you actually meant that. Thank you."

"I've never lied to you about your appearance," he said as he sat down in one of the chairs next to her. "You were a pretty teenager who turned into a beautiful woman."

She eyed him directly. "I realize you've never lied to me. I'm afraid *I'm* the one who takes the honors in that department."

Her comment shocked him.

"When I told you I wanted to come to Paris with you, it was motivated by the lie I told myself about wanting to show an interest in your work. I've told myself a lot of lies, but that's all over."

"What's going on, Diane?"

"This." She held up *Manhattan Merger*.

Surprised he said, "Catherine was looking for it. She asked me if I would find out if you'd seen it."

"I put it in my purse when she wasn't looking because I wanted to read it."

Amazing. "Were you able to get through it?"

"Don't make a joke of this, Payne." Tears welled up in her eyes.

He reached for her hand. "I'm not. It's just that I know you prefer more meaty types of reading material."

"I do, but my curiosity was piqued. Little did I know

the contents of this book would force me to see myself as I really am. It was a horrifying experience,'' she said in a tortured whisper. "Can you ever forgive me?''

"For what?'' Payne was dumbfounded.

"For saying yes to your proposal. I placed you in an impossible situation. Ever since I read the last page of this book I've been waiting for you to come back to the apartment so I could do this.''

She took off the diamond ring he'd given her and folded it in his palm. "I've robbed you of six months of your life. What's worse, you're such a good man, you were willing to sacrifice the rest of your life for a woman you've never loved and never could love. Not the way *I* want to be loved.

"The whole time I was reading this novel, I kept confusing the story line with our lives, Payne. Yours and mine and Rainey's.''

He lowered his head.

"The look in your eyes when you introduced her to me… And then Sunday morning when the love for you came pouring out of hers…

"I could see both of you in the story, wanting each other, yet denying each other because Logan Townsend had a fiancée, and he was an honorable man.

"The only difference between that story and our lives is that I came to my senses first, and could release you from a commitment I should never have let you make. I know why you did it. The sin is on my head for lying to myself that it would all work out in the end.''

"Diane—''

"Before you say anything, you need to know I've called my parents and told them the wedding is off. I shouldn't have been surprised to hear mother say she was relieved. They're going to fly to Paris tomorrow and take me to that clinic in Zurich.

"This book has made me realize that whether I ever walk again or not, I want a man to fall in love with me the way you fell in love with Rainey. The way Logan Townsend fell in love with the doctor who saved his life.

"If I hadn't tried to force something from you that wasn't there, I would never have been shot.

"My obsession over you was sick and wrong. In the end it cost us both unnecessary grief. It's humiliating to have to admit it, but you deserve to know that I recognize what I've done.

"Rainey knew a hero when she saw one in that group photo. She said the judge called it destiny. I *know* that's what it was.

"What if she hadn't painted you, Payne? It started a sequence of events that has freed you and me to live the lives we're supposed to live. Tell her I'm so glad she did it!"

For the first time since the shooting, Payne wrapped his arms around her because he wanted to. "I know you're going to walk again, Diane."

"I have to believe that too. I won't believe anything else." She hugged him hard, then pushed him away.

"What are you standing there for?" She smiled. "Pack your bags. I'm kicking you out of your own apartment because I happen to know there's a woman in Colorado who's dying with love for you. Go to her quickly. And please, please be happy."

CHAPTER TEN

"RAINEY?"

"Yes?"

She heard the zip open on her two man tent. "Are you asleep?"

"Not now," she muttered as Craig crawled inside.

"Liar. I heard you crying."

"Then I guess everybody else did too," she lamented.

"Don't worry about it."

He closed the zip, then sat down cross-legged on the floor in the semidarkness next to her sleeping bag. Now that the sun had gone down, it was cooling off fast. With the screened windows left open, it would be cold inside by morning.

"People are still being flown in. The ones already here are too excited for tomorrow's run to go to bed yet. Besides, I purposely placed your tent away from the others to give you some privacy. Are you ready to talk about Mr. Megabucks yet?"

"Please don't call him that."

"It was a term of endearment," he teased.

"He's anything but that kind of person."

"Tell me about him."

"Right now he's in Paris with his fiancée. They're getting married August first. H-he admitted he isn't in love with her." Suddenly it all came out in a torrent of words. Everything.

Craig let out a low whistle.

He put a hand on her arm. "That's tough."

She wiped the moisture off her cheeks. "After the hearing *you* were the person who told me that one day I'd look back on my big adventure and laugh about it. That counsel is the only thing holding me together."

"But it doesn't do anything for your pain right now. Still it's nice to hear I'm good for something."

"You're good for a lot of things." She sniffed. "Why else do you think I'm here? I'm just afraid you're going to be sorry I joined you on your last river trip."

"Are you kidding? I'm anxious to run some new ideas past you for the store. Tell you what? I can hear the helicopter coming now with the last bunch of tourists. If you're still awake after they're settled, we'll talk."

"Don't worry. I don't think I'm ever going to sleep again."

"Sure you will. After a day on the river tomorrow, you'll sleep like a baby."

"I hope you're right."

"Would I lie to you?"

"You never have before."

"There you go then. You want me to light your lantern?"

"That's all right. I have my flashlight if I need it."

"Okay."

When he left the tent, she lay down again. In this protected area of the canyon, the sound of the helicopter rotors reverberated more loudly than normal against the rocks.

She'd never hear one again without thinking of Payne. The sight of him growing smaller as his pilot whisked her away from Crag's Head filled her with such desolation, Rainey thought she couldn't bear it.

On a sob, she buried her face in the pillow.

The convulsions that shook her body were worse than ever. Her soul was inconsolable.

While she lay there racked in torment she heard the helicopter take off for Las Vegas. It wouldn't be long before her brother came back. She was glad because she knew she needed help to get through the night.

Finally she heard him undo the zip of her tent again.

"Craig?" she called out automatically as he crept inside.

"No. It's Payne."

"That's not funny, Craig."

"I agree," came a deep, familiar male voice.

Convinced she was hallucinating, Rainey grabbed her flashlight and turned it on.

When she saw Payne hunkered down next to her looking so handsome and alive, she let out a cry.

"Shh, darling." He brushed his mouth against hers before turning off the light.

She couldn't believe this was happening.

"I'll explain everything later. All you need to know is that I'm free. Diane has given us her blessing. Now come here to me and let me hold you, feel you."

Her heart thudded feverishly as he unzipped her sleeping bag and pulled her into his arms.

"Rainey—" he said her name on a ragged breath, kissing her in every conceivable place on her face and neck. "I've been living for this."

"I've been dying for it," she confessed against his lips.

Then she gave up her mouth to him and was lost in the fierce hunger of his kiss. They were both starving for each other.

She let out little moans of ecstasy. With each sound he drank more deeply until they were one throbbing entity of need.

Rainey clung to his rock-hard body, arms and legs entwined. Her lips roved over the unforgettable face she'd memorized in her dreams. Now she had the real thing to explore to her heart's desire.

"I love you," she whispered feverishly. "I love you with an ache that's never going to go away."

He cradled the back of her head, kissing her with refined savagery. Then he crushed her against him.

"I'm so in love with you, I don't know if there are words to describe how I feel."

"Those are the words I've been waiting to hear. I don't need any others."

She heard his sharp intake of breath. "Marry me, Rainey. I can't live without you."

"I wouldn't let you."

Once again they were devouring each other.

"You made a mistake crawling in here tonight. I'm already addicted to the taste and feel of you," she confessed when he allowed her to breathe again. "It's possible you'll never get out alive."

He buried his face in her neck. "You smell so good, Rainey. You feel so good. I love to look at you. Everything about you is a miracle."

In a lightning move he rolled her over so he was looking down at her. The full moon gave off enough light for them to see each other.

"Right now I can't see the color of your eyes. All I can tell is that they're dark. At this moment you resemble my *Prince of Dreams*."

His white smile dazzled her. She'd never seen him look like that before.

That's when her breath caught.

The smile faded. "What's wrong, darling?"

"Nothing. It's just something I remembered when I'd finished painting the cover for *Manhattan Merger*."

He kissed the end of her nose. "What was that?"

"You were the embodiment of my dreams come to life on a piece of canvas.

"You had rich dark brown hair that looked vibrant to the touch.

"Your Nordic blue eyes seemed to envision things no one else could even imagine.

"Those rugged facial features denoted a life of hard work, sacrifice and triumphs.

"You had the build and stance of a conquerer beneath your business suit. Someone who dared to explore new frontiers.

"But you were a man who hadn't yet been transformed by a woman's love...

"When you smiled at me just now, I realized that was the ingredient that had been missing. It was missing when you were with Diane, but I refused to acknowledge it. If I were to paint you now, you would look different."

"That's because I am different," his voice shook. "You've transformed me until I don't know myself anymore."

His head descended. Once again they were kissing with a passion that was spiraling out of control.

"Rainey—" he cried. "I don't want to go down the river tomorrow."

"Neither do I."

"I want to meet your family as soon as possible."

"We'll go home in the morning and I'll introduce you. Mother's already a big fan of yours. Dad will be thrilled to learn that the great love of my life really is going to be the great love of my life."

Payne embraced her again. "He'll think this has gone way too far too fast," he murmured into her shimmery hair.

"So will your parents." She kissed his lips quiet. "But no man knows our history except you and me. After the tragedy that befell Diane in a split second's time, I don't want to waste any more of the moments destiny has allotted to us. Life is too precious."

"Amen to that."

He drew her to him in a possessive move that thrilled her to the tips of her toes. "You've never been with a man before have you."

"No. I've been waiting for the right one to come along."

"Oh, Rainey—" He rocked her back and forth for a minute. "Since I don't know how I can wait much longer to make you mine, we need to get married as soon as possible. Out of respect for Diane and her family's feelings, I want to keep it low profile."

"So do I. I've always planned to be married in our family's church. The timing is perfect. Craig will be through here the day after tomorrow."

"That will give my family time to fly out. Catherine will be overjoyed."

"She adores you, Payne, but then who doesn't." Emotion made her throat swell. "Payne? Tell me about Diane."

She heard the deep sigh that came out of him before he turned so they were lying side by side and he could look at her. He traced the arch of her brow with his finger.

"Would you believe she took *Manhattan Merger* with her? When I got back to the apartment on Tuesday afternoon, she'd read it and was waiting for me."

"Oh, darling." Hot tears trickled out of the corners of her eyes. "I was afraid if she ever broke down to find out what was inside, she could be hurt by it."

"Hurt isn't quite the word. She was shaken with guilt."

For the next little while Rainey lay there in wonder while he told her how Diane had given him his freedom and asked for forgiveness.

She kissed his lips. "I'll pray she can walk again."

"We both will."

"I owe Diane my life. She let you go so we could have one," Rainey cried before breaking down in tears.

He held her tight against his heart. "She said the same thing about you. Your paintings put certain forces to work with the result that she wants to walk again and fall in love."

"One day I'll have to call Bonnie Wrigley and tell her everything. She'll be so thrilled to think one of her stories had such a life-changing effect on Diane."

"It changed all our lives, Rainey. I'll never underestimate the power of a romance novel again. Who knows? By the time you've become Mrs. Sterling, my sister Phyllis might be the next highbrow to crack."

Rainey flashed him a mysterious smile. "If she does, can I tell Grace Carlow?"

He gave her a passionate kiss. "Why is that so important?"

"Do you remember the question she asked right at the

end of the hearing about how you found out your picture was on the cover in the first place?''

''I remember everything. That was the day Rainey Bennett entered my life.''

She nestled closer to him, still unable to believe the man of her dreams held her in his arms.

''After court was over, Grace told Bonnie and me it would make Mr. Finauer's day to know Senator Sterling-Boyce's daughter and maid read Red Rose Romances.''

Payne chuckled. ''You're welcome to tell Ms. Carlow whatever you like.''

''That reminds me I better get up and let Craig know we're not leaving with him in the morning.''

''He already knows.''

''How?''

''I had a little powwow with him before I climbed in your tent. He's already welcomed me to the family.''

''I'm so happy I think I'm going to burst.''

''Don't do that,'' he growled against her neck playfully. ''I've got plans for us in the morning. The pilot's going to pick us up at eight. When we reach Las Vegas, we'll take the plane to Grand Junction. I've been anxious to meet my rival.''

She frowned. ''What do you mean? There's no other man in my life.''

''Oh, yes, there is. According to your mother, you and this guy have been inseparable since you flew home from New York. I understand he sleeps in your bed.''

''Winston?'' she half-squealed in delight.

''Who else?'' He chuckled. ''If he's going to live with us at Crag's Head, I want to start making friends with him now. If we can reach the point where he tolerates me, then we'll be doing well.''

"Tolerates you—"

Rainey wrapped her arms around him. "He'll love you. He won't be able to help himself anymore than I can. Diane spoke the truth. I'm the proverbial putty in your hands."

"Such heavenly putty." The kiss he gave her set her on fire. When he finally tore his lips from hers, she wasn't ready to let him go.

"Come on." His breathing had grown shallow. "I don't trust myself in here with you any longer. Let's take a walk to the river and make plans while we wait for the sun to come up."

It already has, darling. Don't you know the whole universe filled with light the moment you set foot in my tent?

The continuous clank of the buoy which marked the channel beyond Phantom Point brought Payne back to a cognizance of his surroundings.

He reached blindly for his bride of twenty-four hours, needing her like he needed air to breathe.

Instead of her warm luscious body gravitating to his, as it had done so many times throughout the night, he found a cool sheet. In place of the avid mouth he yearned to plunder all over again his lips met the pillows redolent of her fragrance.

Coming fully awake, he jackknifed to a sitting position. The semi-dark room below deck revealed he was alone. Maybe she was in the main salon off the galley.

"Rainey?"

No answer.

Though his thirty-five foot sloop was anchored in the bay, it still listed. The swells were bigger than usual.

Payne leaped to his feet and threw on a robe.

He called to her again. Still no response.

That sent him racing for the stairs. By the time he'd reached the deck, his heart was thudding at a sickening rate.

With whitecaps surrounding him, and no sign of his wife in the aft cockpit, a blackness started to engulf him as real as if he'd just been knocked overboard by the boom.

He dashed toward the foredeck on a run. *"Rainey?"* he shouted at the top of his lungs.

"I'm right here, darling!"

Her answering voice had to be the sweetest sound he'd ever heard in his life.

They met midship and fell into each other's arms. He crushed her to him, lifejacket, backpack and all.

"Dear God, I thought I'd lost you—" He was trembling so hard from fear he could hardly stand up. "Don't ever do that to me again."

"I won't— I promise—" Her voice shook. "I'm so sorry I frightened you, Payne. Forgive me."

He couldn't stop kissing her face and hair. "If anything had happened to you—"

She burrowed closer. "I swear I'll never knowingly do anything to alarm you like that again." She lifted wet green eyes to his. "After last night you *know* I love you more than life itself."

Last night…

He hadn't known what living was all about until last night. Her loving had made him feel reborn.

"You *are* my life, Rainey. When I reached for you a few minutes ago, and you weren't there—"

"It's because I love you so much. I wanted you to

catch up on some sleep. While I waited for you to wake up I reached for my sketchbook. All these images were running through my head, but I needed more light so I came up on deck.

"The wind turned fierce a few minutes ago, so I put my things away and planned to bring you lunch in bed. I was just coming back when I heard your frantic voice. I thought maybe something horrible had happened to you and I couldn't get to you fast enough."

He felt the tremor that rocked her body and clung to her. "Something horrible *did* happen. You weren't there when I wanted you."

"That's exactly how I felt when the helicopter flew me away from Crag's Head and I knew I'd never see you again." Tears ran down her cheeks already wet from salt spray.

"That's all in the past," he whispered, kissing her with a hunger even greater than before. "You're my wife now, and I love your plan for lunch in bed. But the next time you feel an irresistible urge to sketch, tell me first. My heart won't be able to withstand this kind of punishment a second time."

"Neither will mine. I adore you, Payne. I couldn't live without you now."

"Then we understand each other," he whispered against her lips. "Come on. Let's get out of this wind and take a nice warm shower."

Her cheeks filled with color. "If we do that first, you're going to be starving later."

He drew in a deep breath. "I'm starving now. For *you.*"

Obeying a need that had grown out of control, he picked her up and carried her back down to their bedroom.

It wasn't until mid-afternoon that they surfaced to fix a meal together and take it back to bed. Once they'd eaten, his gorgeous wife curled up against him with her adorable blond head nestled between his neck and shoulder. He heard a sigh of contentment. Before he knew it, she'd fallen into a sound sleep.

And no wonder.

After their ten-thirty a.m. ceremony at Rainey's family church, followed by a meal at her parents' home, the pilot of his company jet had flown them and his family and bodyguards back to New York.

At that point he and Rainey had taken the helicopter to Crag's Head, where they'd immediately boarded the sloop so their honeymoon could begin.

Once out on the ocean, to give Rainey a view of their home from the water, he weighed anchor in the bay so he could give his bride his full attention.

Until the last few hours there'd been no sleep for either of them. Worried that he might have worn her out with his insatiable appetite for her, it thrilled him to realize her desire for him was every bit as boundless.

He'd married a talented, generous, deeply emotional woman whose passion for life thrilled him to his very soul. Marrying Rainey had set him on the adventure of a lifetime.

She wanted his baby right away. Secretly he'd wanted that too, but he'd told her he didn't want her to feel rushed. That's when she'd asked him to close his eyes while she handed him her sketchbook.

When she gave him permission to look, he looked. She'd entitled the drawing *Our First Little Engineer*. She'd drawn a six-month-old boy wearing boots and a hard hat. He was riding on top of Payne's shoulders. The likeness of father to son was unmistakable. It touched a place in his heart he hadn't known was there.

Rainey's green eyes blazed with light. "I did this the first night you stayed at my parents' house. Since I couldn't creep into bed with you, I did the next best thing to feel close to you."

He'd already been given proof his wife had second sight. Like pure revelation he knew that baby boy was destined to make an appearance at some point.

Putting the sketchbook aside, he'd reached for her. "No more 'next best thing'. I plan to give you so much closeness you'll cry for mercy."

"I'm afraid it's going to be the other way around," she admitted in a tremulous whisper.

"Then we're the luckiest man and woman alive."

"We are." Her voice caught before rapture consumed them for the rest of the night.

Payne drew her sleeping body close against him one more time. Then he laid her down and moved off the bed, compelled to see what she'd been drawing.

He found her backpack and pulled out the sketch pad. After studying the little engineer one more time, he turned to the next drawing and came face to face with himself.

It was the picture on the cover of *Manhattan Merger*. But there was a different woman in Payne's arms, a different look in his eyes. This time he held his adoring wife in his embrace. They both wore their wedding clothes. The gold band she'd given him was on his finger.

She wore his diamond ring and wedding band. The

picture on his office wall had been changed to depict
Crag's Head and the sailboat. There was another little
picture propped on the desk next to Winston. It was
Bruno.

The eager, tremulous look of joy on their faces
brought tears to his eyes. She'd dated and titled it, *The
Look of Love.*

Emotion made his throat close up.

"I wanted to capture our wedding night so we'd have
it forever." Rainey had come up behind him and slid
her arms around his chest. She pressed her cheek against
his back. "I love you so much I never want to do anything to take that look away."

He put the sketchbook on the end of the bed. Turning
in her arms, he cupped her precious face in his hands.
"We'll hang this in our bedroom. It'll be our guiding
star as we navigate through life together."

"Yes—" she cried as her eyes filled.

Payne lowered his head to taste those salty tears before he swept them away to the place destiny had reserved for them.

EPILOGUE

"RAINEY?"

"Yes, Betty?"

"There's someone here to see you."

Rainey was expecting her husband home any minute now. "Who is it?"

"They want it to be a surprise."

Because of security, no one dropped by Crag's Head unless they were family. Unless— Could it be Drew Wallace? He and his wife had been on vacation in Canada. Maybe he'd decided to pay her husband a personal visit now that he'd returned. The poor man was facing a mountain of work.

When Rainey reminded her husband he shouldn't be so gleeful about it, he reminded her that a mountain of work meant his company was still in business, for which they should be grateful. Coming from a soon-to-be trillionaire, that was quite a statement.

"I'll be right down, Betty."

At this point Rainey was eight months pregnant and didn't move nearly as fast as she once had. Sometimes she paused on the stairs to get rid of a leg cramp before taking another step. The calcium tablets were supposed to help, but she still had her moments.

Winston was so cute. He'd stop on the step with her and wait. She could tell Payne found it all very amusing. His blue eyes danced whenever he watched her struggle in an attempt to appear graceful.

He could hardly wait to be a father. They were going to have a boy. Catherine and Linda had already volunteered to baby-sit. Both sets of parents were ecstatic. Rainey's mother and father would fly out the minute she went into labor. Craig would come for the christening. Everything was ready for the big event.

Still wearing her artist's smock, which worked as a perfect maternity outfit, she put down her paintbrush and left the nursery to see who'd dropped by. With the addition of an owl peeking out of a large knothole in the tree, her mural of the forest creatures would be complete.

Winston stayed right with her. When she reached the bottom step and heard her name called, she turned in the direction of the living room. A beautiful long-legged brunette in a periwinkle suit started walking toward her.

"Diane—" she gasped incredulously. *"Look at you!"*

The other woman's smile was radiant. "I was going to say the same thing to *you*."

She stopped in front of Rainey. They eyed each other for a long moment while unspoken messages flowed between them. Then they embraced each other. By the time they let go, they were both laughing and crying.

Rainey wiped her eyes. "You don't know—you just don't know what this is going to mean to Payne."

"Yes, I do." Diane insisted. "And seeing this will take away any residual pain." She lifted her left hand, where Rainey spied a gold band on her ring finger.

"I'm Mrs. Unte now. My husband, Karl, is one of the doctors I met at the clinic in Switzerland. We're expecting a baby too, but I'm only six weeks along."

Three miracles.

"We live in Zurich, but we're home for our first visit. If you can, I'd like you and Payne to come to my parents' house for dinner this evening. I know it's late notice, but we barely arrived and I couldn't wait to see you.''

"I wouldn't have wanted you to wait!" Rainey's heart hammered with excitement. "I can hear the helicopter coming. Why don't you run out and issue your invitation in person?"

"You think it will be all right?"

"How can you even ask me that question?"

Diane smiled, then headed for the entrance hall. Rainey followed at a slower pace, marveling at the other woman's mobility after all she'd suffered.

This was a private moment for two people who'd been through a horrendous experience together. Rainey stood in the doorway to watch from a distance.

Payne couldn't help but see Diane now. The helicopter had landed. She ran toward it, waving her hands.

When Rainey saw her husband jump down and crush Diane in his arms, she could hardly breathe. Two or three minutes passed while the two of them conversed. Suddenly Payne swung her around. Their happy laughter filled the air.

Two people had been let out of prison.

Their joy was full. So was Rainey's.

She rested against the doorjamb, waiting for the most wonderful man alive to tell her all about it. She didn't have to wait long. The second Diane drove off, Payne came running.

As he drew closer she saw the one ingredient that had been missing in their marriage. The look of peace. The one priceless gift needed to make their love complete.

She knew that was what he was trying to tell her as he pulled her into his arms and wept.

MILLS & BOON
Romance

On sale 6th July 2007

Get ready for some summer romance from gorgeous Greece to the crystal clear waters of Cape Cod, the swirling mists of Irish Valentia and the silent majesty of the Outback...

THE FORBIDDEN BROTHER *by Barbara McMahon*

Laura is in a dilemma when she falls in love with her ex-fiancé's twin brother! Is it him she loves, or the mirror-image of a man she was once engaged to?

THE LAZARIDIS MARRIAGE *by Rebecca Winters*

This award-winning author brings you a brooding Greek billionaire you won't forget in a hurry as he battles with his attraction to international it-girl Tracey.

BRIDE OF THE EMERALD ISLE *by Trish Wylie*

Meet cynical Garrett who's about to encounter the woman who will open his heart again...and give him hope for the future.

HER OUTBACK KNIGHT *by Melissa James*

Take an Outback road trip with Danni and Jim as they begin a quest for the truth which might just turn this journey into one of the heart...

MILLS & BOON

Romance

On sale 6th July 2007

Get ready for some summer romance from gorgeous Greece to the crystal clear waters of Cape Cod, the swirling mists of Irish Valentia and the silent majesty of the Outback...

THE FORBIDDEN BROTHER *by Barbara McMahon*

Laura is in a dilemma when she falls in love with her ex-fiancé's twin brother! Is it him she loves, or the mirror-image of a man she was once engaged to?

THE LAZARIDIS MARRIAGE *by Rebecca Winters*

This award-winning author brings you a brooding Greek billionaire you won't forget in a hurry as he battles with his attraction to international it-girl Tracey.

BRIDE OF THE EMERALD ISLE *by Trish Wylie*

Meet cynical Garrett who's about to encounter the woman who will open his heart again...and give him hope for the future.

HER OUTBACK KNIGHT *by Melissa James*

Take an Outback road trip with Danni and Jim as they begin a quest for the truth which might just turn this journey into one of the heart...

Subscribe to
prima
for just 99p

For your first 3 issues*

In Prima there is something for everyone – advice on how to look and feel your best, time- and money-saving solutions, quick-and-easy food, beautiful homes and gardens and, above all, everything you need to get the most out of life.

Subscribe and enjoy

- SAVE over 85% on your first 3 issues
- PAY JUST £5.50 by quarterly Direct Debit – still saving 20% off the cover price
- EXCLUSIVE subscriber offers from Prima Subs Club
- FREE Prima dressmaking pattern every month
- FREE home delivery

Call our hotline and quote ref: MA21

0870 124 1050

Lines are open weekdays 8am-9.30pm, Saturdays 8am-4pm. BT landline calls to 0870 numbers wil cost no more than 10p per minute; calls made from mobiles may cost more.

Or order securely online, visit

www.qualitymagazines.co.uk/MA21